TWO FOR THREE FARTHINGS

MARY JANE STAPLES

TWO FOR THREE FARTHINGS

BANTAM PRESS

LONDON · NEW YORK · TORONTO · SYDNEY · AUCKLAND

TRANSWORLD PUBLISHERS LTD
61-63 Uxbridge Road, London W5 5SA

TRANSWORLD PUBLISHERS (AUSTRALIA) PTY LTD
15-23 Helles Avenue, Moorebank, NSW 2170

TRANSWORLD PUBLISHERS (NZ) LTD
Cnr Moselle and Waipareira Aves,
Henderson, Auckland

Published 1990 by Bantam Press
a division of Transworld Publishers Ltd
Copyright © Jane Staples 1990

Reprinted 1991

The right of Mary Jane Staples to be identified
as the author of this work has been asserted in accordance
with sections 77 and 78 of the Copyright Designs and Patents
Act 1988

British Library Cataloguing in Publication Data
Staples, Mary Jane
Two For Three Farthings.
I. Title
823'.914 [F]

ISBN 0-593-02087-1

Printed and bound in Great Britain by
Biddles Ltd, Guildford and King's Lynn

CHAPTER ONE

The little house in Deacon Street, Walworth, had been enduring sombre days, and today was the most sombre of all. But at least the funeral itself was over, the deceased couple laid to rest. Back from the cemetery, Aunt Glad had done what she could to comfort the two orphaned children, speaking gently to them in their kitchen before tactfully leaving them to themselves for a few minutes while she went to join the grown-ups and her husband, Uncle Perce, in the parlour. There, the talk was solemn and sympathetic, although everyone was relieved to cast aside the subdued and awkward whispering that had prevailed in the mournful church and at the even more mournful cemetery. Still, at least it had been a good Christian burial. There'd been just enough money from the insurance man to pay for the hearse, four black horses and two coffins. Life was hard for people these days, and not too good to them even when they were dead.

The dreadful flu epidemic, having arrived, had swept Mr and Mrs Withers away as if they had never existed. They had taken to their bed on a Thursday and passed away on the Sunday. Miraculously, their two children, a boy and a girl, had been spared. But how much of a miracle was it, a neighbour asked of Uncle Perce, when it left them orphaned in times as hard as they were now? It was rainy April, 1921. The country was still suffering the impoverishment brought about by the Great War, and unemployed ex-servicemen were still tramping the streets of London looking for jobs, any jobs.

It was best to leave the children in the kitchen for the moment. Pitying talk couldn't take place in front of them, especially as it was needful to discuss what was to happen to them. Aunt Glad, with the help of a kind neighbour of the deceased, had supplied a funeral breakfast of sandwiches, biscuits and tea.

Ten-year-old Horace and his sister Ethel, just seven, sat at the kitchen table eyeing the food without much appetite. They called each other Orrice and Effel, as did everyone else, except their schoolteachers. Effel wore an old blue frock dyed black for the funeral day, and given to her by a neighbour. She also wore grey socks and black boots, the boots shiningly polished for her by Orrice out of respect for their mum and dad. An old boater with a black band sat on her dark brown hair, which hung down her back. Her little face was tear-stained. She had taken just a single bite out of a paste sandwich, and had hardly been able to swallow that small mouthful.

Orrice, a huge old dark blue cloth cap with a soft peak on his head, wore a navy blue jersey and black serge trousers, the latter also gifted by a sympathetic neighbour. It hadn't seemed right, expecting

6

the boy to go to his parents' funeral in his patched grey shorts.

He put an arm around his woebegone sister.

'Don't cry no more, Effel,' he said.

'We ain't got no-one now, no-one,' said Effel, a dry sob shuddering through her slender body. She couldn't understand it, she couldn't believe her solid, beefy mum and sturdy dad had gone, that she'd never see them any more. And she and Orrice had no grandparents. All four had passed away years ago.

'We got each other,' said Orrice. 'I'll look after yer, Effel, don't worry.' He felt like a good cry himself, but he couldn't, not in front of his unhappy sister. New tears welled in her hazel eyes and rolled down her smudged cheeks. 'Don't cry, sis, we got to be brave.'

They had been good parents, his mum and dad. They'd never had much, but there'd always been something to eat, and Dad had regularly brought fruit home from his job in the Covent Garden market. And there'd always been a fire in the kitchen in winter. And if he and Effel had seldom had new clothes, their mum always got them good second-hand stuff. Orrice wasn't quite sure where any kind of clothes were to come from now. He felt very sad about the day and troubled by what lay ahead.

'We just ain't got nobody,' said Effel bleakly.

'Well, we 'ave really,' said Orrice, 'we got Uncle Perce and Aunt Glad.'

'Ain't goin' to live wiv their kids,' said Effel. 'Don't like 'em.'

7

'Effel, it ain't no good not likin' them,' said Orrice, who could only see help coming from his aunt and uncle. Aunt Glad was their mum's sister. The only other relative they knew was their dad's brother, but he had gone to Australia years ago. 'We got to put up with some fings, sis.'

'Ain't puttin' up wiv that soppy Nellie, nor wiv that Alfie and 'is runny nose,' said Effel, referring to two of Aunt Glad's five children.

'Alfie's just got ad'noids, that's all,' said Orrice. 'Well, I fink that's what 'e's got. Effel, we got to 'ave a home.'

'We got this one,' said Effel, 'we just ain't got a mum and dad no more, that's all.' Her eyes brimmed.

'Effel, where we goin' to get money to pay the rent?'

'We can 'ide when the rent man comes,' said Effel in mournful hope.

'Not all the time, we can't,' said Orrice. He put down a half-eaten sandwich. 'Come on, let's go an' see what they're saying. We got to see, we got to talk to Aunt Glad.'

Reluctantly, Effel went with him. They stopped before they reached the open door of the parlour. They stopped because of what they heard.

'Orphanage? I wouldn't let no kids of mine be put in any orphanage.'

'I s'pose Dr Barnado's? D'you s'pose Dr Barnado's, Mrs Figg?'

'That's a sort of orphanage too, ain't it?'

'Let's talk sense.' That was Uncle Perce's voice.

'I was only sayin' to Mrs Davis—'

'No, you was to me, Mrs Figg.'

'Don't let's talk like this.' That was Aunt Glad. 'It's all up to me and me 'usband, anyway.'

Orrice and Effel went back to the kitchen. They sat down at the table in silence. Effel began to cry again.

'I ain't goin' to no orphanage,' she sobbed.

'Course you ain't, sis,' said Orrice. 'Nor me. Mum an' Dad wouldn't want us in no orphanage, I betcher. Don't you worry.'

Effel wiped her eyes with the sleeve of her frock.

'Or Dr Banano's?' she said with a gulp.

'Nor 'im, neither,' said Orrice stoutly.

Uncle Perce came in. He was a street cleaner who kept bitter company with muck, litter and horse manure, but if he disliked what he had to tidy up daily, it hadn't affected his inherent tendency to be philosophical about what life could throw at people. He was like most cockneys, resilient. He gave Orrice a pat on his shoulder, and he gave Effel a little smile.

'We'll sort things out for yer, Effel, an' you, Orrice. We'll take yer 'ome with us in a bit—'

'Ain't goin',' muttered Effel.

'What's that, Effel?'

'It's all right, Uncle Perce,' said Orrice, 'except Effel don't feel too good just yet.' Manfully, he blinked away a traitorous tear. 'Nor me,' he admitted.

'Well, course yer don't, Orrice,' said Uncle

Perce. 'Well, none of us is too 'appy, yer know, yer mum an' dad were friends of mine, good friends. Your Aunt Glad an' me, we'll fix things for yer some'ow. 'Ere she is.'

Aunt Glad entered the kitchen. A bosomy woman of thirty-seven, with a hard-working husband and five children to look after, she had much to endure and not a little to complain about. She directed her complaints mostly at Uncle Perce, off whom they bounced as if they had never been spoken, which made her tell him he was getting very aggravating. On the other hand, she wouldn't hear a word against him, which was entirely typical of a cockney housewife.

'There you are, poor loves,' she said. 'Perce, what you been sayin' to them?'

'Just tellin' em—'

'Don't you go upsettin' them, they been upset enough. Orrice, yer kind neighbours is goin' now, an' soon as me and Uncle Perce 'ave tidied up, you can come 'ome with us.'

'Won't,' muttered Effel.

'Now, Effel love—'

'Stayin' 'ere,' said Effel.

'Ain't she a pickle?' said Uncle Perce.

'Now, don't say things like that,' said Aunt Glad, respectfully dressed in black, including her straw hat, 'that won't do Effel no good. Effel love, you got to come 'ome with us, don't yer see? And while you're with us, me and Uncle Perce will see what's to be done for you and Orrice.'

'Yes, don't fret now, little 'un,' said Uncle Perce.

10

Effel, head bent, closed her eyes and squeezed back tears. Aunt Glad sighed, and Uncle Perce grimaced. It was so difficult. They had five children of their own, the youngest being four and the eldest thirteen. Their little house in Kennington, rented, felt crowded out at times. Uncle Perce's wage just kept them going and no more. Two extra children to house and to feed would be a daily strain. But for a while, at least, until a solution was found, they had to take Orrice and Effel in, they had to give their orphaned niece and nephew a roof and a place to sleep, and they had to feed them as best they could.

'Effel, we got to go with Aunt Glad,' said Orrice.

'Ain't,' muttered Effel.

'She'll come, Aunt Glad,' said Orrice. 'Soon as I go out the door with you, she'll foller me. I can't go nowhere without she don't foller me.'

'Well, I've 'eard that's true,' said Uncle Perce. 'Now, if there's stuff you want to bring with yer, Orrice, you can collect it up. Me an' yer Aunt Glad won't be goin' for another fifteen minutes or so.'

'Yes, all right, Uncle Perce,' said Orrice, but he didn't really feel like taking anything with him except his sister. He had to look after his sister, his mum and dad would expect him to.

At the home of her uncle and aunt, Effel gritted her teeth when she found she was going to have to sleep in a bed with her three cousins, Nellie, Edie and Cissie. She hated the idea, she'd always had her own bed. And Orrice was going to have to share a bed

11

with Alfie and Johnny. Orrice already felt sort of squeezed in this little house in which there were seven people living as well as him and Effel. Meanwhile, in the evening, with their cousins sent out of the way, Aunt Glad and Uncle Perce gave them some cocoa and biscuits, and talked to them in the kitchen.

'We're goin' to see you don't 'ave to go to an orphanage,' said Aunt Glad, and Orrice wished she hadn't said that. It made him feel it was a way of saying an orphanage might have to be thought about.

'I should say not,' declared Uncle Perce, raking embers from the stove fire. 'An orphanage? Not bleedin' likely.'

'You mind your tongue,' said Aunt Glad.

'I been mindin' it pretty good these last fifteen years,' said Uncle Perce. 'Listen, kids, I know we're a bit crowded, but don't get worried, yer can stay till we work something out.'

'Oh, that reminds me,' said Aunt Glad, 'one of your neighbours, that nice Mrs Davis, is thinkin' about offering you a 'ome, Orrice, she said she thinks she an' Mr Davis might be able—'

'Orrice ain't goin' there,' said Effel in a little burst of alarm, ''e ain't goin' nowhere wivout me.'

'Yes, we got to be together, Aunt Glad,' said Orrice, who was never going to let any grown-ups separate him from his sister.

'Yes, course you 'ave, Orrice,' said Uncle Perce.

'That's what I thought,' said Aunt Glad, 'it's what I told Mrs Davis, I told 'er you and Effel like to be together. I just wish your Uncle Perce an' me had a bigger house, and a bit more comin' in. It don't seem right 'aving to look around for somewhere else where you can go.'

'It's all right, Aunt Glad,' said Orrice, 'me and Effel knows yer up against it.' He didn't feel keen, in any case, about him and Effel being surrounded by Aunt Glad's three girls and two boys. There'd be fights and ructions, especially as he'd had to punch eleven-year-old Johnny on the nose only a month ago. Johnny was blinking obstreperous, that's what he was.

Uncle Perce suddenly perked up.

''Ere, I just 'ad a thought,' he said. 'Orrice, there's yer dad's brother, yer Uncle Ernie, out in Orstralia, with yer Aunt Amy. They don't 'ave no kids, yer know. Would yer like me and yer Aunt Glad to write to 'em about you? Would yer like to go to Orstralia, if they'd 'ave you? Yer Aunt Glad an' me don't want to push yer off, yer mustn't think that, only—' He stopped. It did sound like an attempt to get rid of them.

'Orstralia?' said Orrice uncertainly.

'Orstralia?' said Effel in tearful horror. 'I ain't goin' there, it's upside-down, me teacher said so at school.' Her mouth quivered. 'I want me mum an' dad.'

'We like Walworth best, Uncle Perce,' said Orrice. Walworth and its homeliness, its fogs, markets and cheerful cockney spirit came a good first with Orrice.

'Well, we could think about it,' said Aunt Glad,

13

who thought Uncle Perce had come up with a bit of sense for once. A new life for two children in Australia might not be such a bad thing. She looked at her husband. 'Australia's not upside-down, is it?' she said worriedly.

'No, course not, it's just that England's on top and Orstralia's under. That's why they call it Down Under.' Uncle Perce was reassuring. 'But we ain't goin' to send Orrice and Effel if they don't want to go. Wouldn't be right.'

'Still, lovey,' said Aunt Glad to Effel, 'at least you can believe yer Uncle Perce about it not bein' upside-down.'

'Ain't goin' there,' said Effel. 'Nor no orphanage.'

'We wouldn't send you and Orrice to no orphanage, Effel,' said Uncle Perce, hiding his worry. He knew he couldn't expect his wife to take on the extra burden of their niece and nephew, she had more than enough to do as it was with their brood of five. 'We'll think of something. There's always a silver linin' 'anging somewhere, yer know.'

Effel cried herself silently to sleep in the crowded bed that night. Orrice didn't have too good a time sharing Alfie and Johnny's bed. Seven and eleven respectively, Alfie and Johnny quickly collared most of the bedclothes. Orrice would normally have fought pugnaciously for his share, but he wasn't in the mood. He made do with the little he could get. Still, Johnny woke up, disturbed by there being three in the bed, thought about things, sat up and

14

said, "'Ere, you Alfie, give Orrice a bit of them bedclothes or I'll kick yer out. That's it, come on. 'Ere y'ar, Orrice.'

'Ta,' said Orrice.

'Sorry about yer mum an' dad,' said Johnny.

Orrice managed some doleful sleep then.

In the morning, Aunt Glad let the orphaned pair stay in bed for a bit while she got four of her offspring off to school. She said she thought Orrice and Effel needn't go to school themselves, not when the funeral had only been yesterday.

When they were up and eating breakfast porridge, Orrice asked if he and Effel could go home and collect some of their belongings. They hadn't brought much with them yesterday. Aunt Glad was pleased to let them go. It was best for them to be out and doing something. Orrice said he and Effel would spend the day at home and come back in the evening. Aunt Glad said all right, be back by six and she'd have a meal ready for them. She made them sandwiches that they could eat at midday.

On their way home, Orrice said to his forlorn sister, 'We got to do some finkin', sis. Well, yer see, I betcher it's goin' to be Orstralia or an orphanage. Aunt Glad and Uncle Perce ain't goin' to be able to 'ave us for long. Mind, it ain't their fault, it's just that they're 'ard-up, an' poor as well, yer see.'

'Ain't goin' to sleep in that bed no more,' said Effel. 'Want me own bed.'

'We'll 'ave to run away,' said Orrice, 'it's the best fing, Effel. We'll find somewhere. I'll do errands

15

for people, an' I bet I could 'elp stall'olders down the market. I bet Mum an' Dad 'ud like it better if we run away an' did fings for ourselves, I bet they'd like it better than if we went to Orstralia or in an orphanage. If we was in an orphanage an' Dad was alive, 'e'd come round an' break the door down.'

''E ain't alive no more,' said Effel, and tears welled.

'Don't cry, sis,' said Orrice, putting an arm around her, 'we'll run away, that's best, don't yer fink?'

'A' right,' said Effel.

When they reached their house, they entered by pulling on the latchcord. The emptiness of the house was a melancholy thing to them. Without their brawny, outgoing mum, it was never going to be a home again.

'We best take some of Mum an' Dad's nice fings,' said Orrice. 'I mean, I betcher they're ours, I betcher that's what the law says.'

'What's the law?' asked Effel, as they stood in the kitchen.

'I dunno exactly, not exactly,' said Orrice, 'except it's what the King says. An' I betcher the King says Mum an' Dad's fings are ours. We'll run away this afternoon, sis, and we'll take the nicest fings wiv us. I'll get a sack. We'll take the alarm clock, Dad's razor for when I grow up, Mum's brooch for you, if it ain't in pawn, the knives an' forks wiv bone 'andles—'

'Knives an' forks?' said Effel, her interest mournful.

16

'Course knives an' forks,' said Orrice. 'When we find somewhere, we got to eat, we got to cut some fings up, like bread. Yer got to fink about it, Effel, and about what yer want to put in the sack, and I best get another one for our clothes.'

'Ain't got no clothes,' said Effel.

'Course you 'ave, soppy.'

'Ain't got nuffink much good,' said Effel.

'Effel, anyfink you got is some good, you can't walk about gettin' all worn an' ragged.'

'A' right,' said Effel. A little dry sob coughed itself into a sigh. 'Orrice, is Mum an' Dad up in 'eaven?'

'You bet,' said Orrice loyally.

'Is Jesus lookin' after them?'

'Course 'E is, that's what 'E's up there for.'

'I wish I was wiv 'em,' said Effel.

'Don't cry, sis,' said Orrice, and put an arm around her again. His little sister could be a terror sometimes, but she was all he had now. And he was all she had. 'Tell yer what, let's eat Aunt Glad's sandwiches.'

'It's only eleven o'clock,' said Effel.

'Well, I fink there's a tin of sardines we could 'ave a bit later,' said Orrice, 'an' some bread as well. I fink I'm a bit 'ungry now.'

They ate the paste sandwiches.

They wandered about the house afterwards, looking at everything. There wasn't really very much they could take, not without burdening themselves with heavily laden sacks. And it didn't do their spirits much good, going round a house that wasn't really a home any more.

Just after noon there was a knock on the front door. Effel quivered.

'Orrice, is it someone come to take us to Dr Banano's?' she whispered.

'Well, I shouldn't fink so, Effel.'

'Don't let's answer in case,' begged Effel.

'We best see,' said Orrice, and faced up to whatever challenge awaited them on the doorstep. It was a policeman. They recognized him as a local bobby. He fingered his chinstrap and smiled at them.

'Morning, Effel. Morning, Orrice.' He was briskly kind. 'You all right?'

'Yes, mister, fanks,' said Orrice, and Effel put herself behind him, as she always did whenever she was a little shy or fearful.

'That's good.' Constable Brownlaw's expression was sympathetic, his manner fatherly. Go round and see those kids, his sergeant had said, it's your beat, you know them best. 'It's been—' He checked. He did not want to say anything that would make Effel cry. 'Well, it's good you're both up and about. But you're not at school, I see. Thought you might not be. Tomorrow maybe, eh? Thought I'd just come round and see if you're both all right. You sure you are? D'you want any help with anything?'

'No, we're all right, mister, honest,' said Orrice, and Effel quivered nervously behind him.

'Gone into long trousers, Orrice, have you?' asked the policeman.

18

'Mrs Lucas give 'em to me for the funeral,' said Orrice.

'Who's going to take care of you?'

'We got our Aunt Glad and Uncle Perce in Kennington,' said Orrice.

'That's the ticket,' said Constable Brownlaw. 'You're going to live with them?'

'Well, for a bit,' said Orrice, 'but they don't 'ave room for us for always. I expect we'll 'ave to go in an orphanage later.'

Constable Brownlaw sighed inwardly. He knew these kids, he knew Effel for her little tantrums and her little shynesses, and he knew Orrice for his boyish pranks and sturdy character. And everybody knew them as an indivisible pair, for wherever Orrice went, Effel was sure to go. They were lovable kids in their attachment to each other. Fate had dealt a scurvy blow in making orphans of them.

'Well, you'll be together,' he said, although he knew that in most orphanages boys and girls were kept strictly segregated for the most part. 'You sure you don't need any help? Are you managing to pack what you want to take with you to your aunt and uncle's?'

'Yes, fanks, mister,' said Orrice, then added bravely, 'we're goin' to take some of our mum an' dad's nice fings, like Mum's brooch an' Dad's pocket watch. And 'is razor for when I get older.' He thought that if the policeman said it was all right to, then it was.

And the policeman said, 'Good, so you should,

Orrice, it's something to remember them by. Take everything you most like.'

'Course, we ain't takin' no furniture,' said Orrice, 'just small fings.'

'Very sensible, Orrice. Be a job, wouldn't it, taking tables and chairs.' Constable Brownlaw smiled again. 'Look, round at the station – well, there's this.' He slipped a hand into his tunic pocket and extracted a stiff brown envelope. Orrice and Effel looked at it, Effel from behind her brother. 'It's a little collection we made at the station, just to give you a bit of cheer. If your aunt and uncle do take you to an orphanage – you sure they would?'

'Well, yer see, mister, they're 'ard-up and they already got two boys an' three girls, and only a little 'ouse. An orphanage ain't what they want, only they ain't got room for me and Effel as well as their own kids, like. It ain't their fault—'

'I see, Orrice. Well, if you do land up in an orphanage, they'll ask you what money you've got, and they'll want to look after it for you, and maybe give you a penny each from it now and again. But if you want to spend some of it before you get there, say on a little treat for yourselves, you go ahead. Here.' He handed the envelope to Orrice, who took it in wide-eyed astonishment. He could feel it was heavy with coins.

'Mister—' He had a lump in his throat. 'Mister, did yer like our mum an' dad?'

'Bless yer, Orrice, salt of the earth your mum and dad were. That's from the station, from all of us. It's rough luck that's come your way, young 'un,

20

but you're good kids, and you'll grow up fine, you and Effel, and don't let anyone discourage you. You keep your chins up all the way. Good luck, kids.' Constable Brownlaw gave them both a pat and a smile, and departed.

Orrice called his thanks, then closed the door and went into the kitchen with Effel. He opened the envelope. Out came the money, pennies, three-penny bits, and even tanners. They counted it. It came to nineteen shillings and sevenpence.

'Cor lummy,' breathed Orrice, 'we're nearly rich, Effel.'

'Can we buy the 'ouse?' asked Effel.

'Well, I dunno about that,' said Orrice cautiously, 'I should fink the 'ouse might cost a bit more than nineteen bob. No, we best keep it for buyin' food. Effel, we got twenty-five bob an' sevenpence in all, would yer believe.' They had found three shillings and eightpence in their mum's purse, and two and fourpence on the chest of drawers in their parents' bedroom, which was where their dad had always put his money at night. 'Well, we best 'ave our dinner now, and run away afterwards.'

As well as the tin of sardines and half a loaf, they also found some Quaker Oats. To stop Effel just sitting and pining, Orrice let her make some porridge. It turned out a bit lumpy, but they put milk and sugar in it and stirred it in their bowls. The resultant concoction was white, glutinous and irregular, and not too much like the porridge their mum put on the breakfast table each morning.

21

'We best 'ave a good wash before we go,' said Orrice, 'we got lots of time.'

''Ad me wash,' said Effel, which meant a lick and a promise at Aunt Glad's. She spooned the porridge into her mouth. She grimaced and cast a covert look at her brother. Orrice was getting on manfully with his lumpy helping. 'Is it a' right?' she asked.

'You betcher,' said Orrice gallantly. 'Yer goin' to be a nice cook, Effel, when yer growed up a bit. Listen, we best have a proper good wash, in case, like. Yes, we best do that.' He was thinking of an empty house that would give them shelter but might have the water turned off. He was a clean boy, and his face, cheerful and earnest by turn normally, always had a fresh look. Effel, however, never minded a smudged face. She was far from the stage of worrying about what she looked like. Her favourite book, which her dad had often read to her, was called *Ragamuffin Jack*. Ragamuffin Jack was her idea of fun. He was always falling into things like duckponds or coal-holes. 'Effel, you listening?' asked Orrice.

'Don't want to,' said Effel.

'You got to 'ave a good wash before we leave.'

'Ain't,' said Effel.

'Yes, you 'ave,' said Orrice sternly, 'we ain't goin' to go out lookin' like orphans. We'll 'ave old ladies comin' up and saying you poor dirty orphans, you best come to a police station. I'll wash yer, if yer like.'

'You ain't combed yer 'air,' said Effel by way of a riposte. If Orrice always had a clean-looking face,

22

his hair, dark brown like hers, always had a tousled look. He hid it under his cap.

'All right,' he said, 'I'll comb it before we leave. Eat yer porridge up, Effel.'

'Don't want it,' said Effel, 'it's—' She made a face, not wanting to admit it was lumpy. 'I ain't 'ungry.'

'No, I s'pose not,' said Orrice. They both had aching hearts, and food didn't have its usual appeal. But Orrice thought he ought to do something to cheer his sister up a bit. He didn't think they ought to go out into the world feeling too miserable. 'I'll eat yourn up for you, if yer like, sis.'

'Me porridge?' said Effel disbelievingly.

'Well, we don't want to waste it, it's nice,' said Orrice, and he tucked into her helping as if it was the best porridge ever made. Effel brightened up. Courageously, Orrice ate it all.

Then they had the sardines, with some bread and margarine. Effel ate dolefully, her spirits low again. The thought of leaving home for ever wasn't something she could easily take in.

'I ain't goin',' she said suddenly.

'Course you are, we got to,' said Orrice, 'we don't want to be a trouble to Aunt Glad and Uncle Perce. I'll look after yer, sis. I betcher we'll meet some nice 'elpful people.'

Effel, again brightening up, said, 'D'you want me last sardine?'

'No, you eat it up, sardines is good for yer,' said Orrice.

'Don't want it. You 'ave it.'

Courageous again, Orrice ate it for her.

They were putting things in sacks. Effel couldn't hold back her tears when they went into their parents' bedroom to look for nice things to take. It seemed a sort of awfully sad room now, all quiet and lifeless. Orrice suffered another lump in his throat. Effel went out, leaving him to look through the room. When they met again on the tiny landing, Orrice's sack a quarter full, Effel had a pile of old dog-eared story books in her arms.

'Effel, yer can't take all them.'

'Goin' to,' said Effel.

'Effel, yer can't, they're too 'eavy.'

'No, they ain't,' said Effel, wanly obstinate.

'Course they are.' Orrice knew he had to be firm. 'Look at 'em, they're nearly makin' yer fall over frontwards. Come on, I'll take 'em back in yer room for yer.'

'I'll kick yer,' said Effel.

'Effel, you know it ain't nice talkin' about kickin',' said Orrice in reproach, 'not now it ain't.'

Effel compromised. She settled for two volumes of Ragamuffin Jack. She also agreed to let Orrice give her a good wash, which he did, her legs and knees as well, although she was quaintly offended at being made to lift her frock and petticoat up. Her petticoat, which had seen its best days, made Orrice think.

'Effel, you got clean ones on?'

'Ain't sayin'.'

'Effel—'

'Mind yer business,' said Effel.

They were finally ready to leave at a quarter to three. Orrice said Effel had best take her coat for when winter came, and that she could wear it to save carrying it in the clothes sack. Effel had charge of this sack. It contained the best of their clobber. Her old brown coat, a rescued cast-off, reached to her boots, covering her dyed mourning frock, and on her head she wore the ancient boater with a black band. Orrice wore his cap, jersey, trousers and boots. His sack bulged at the bottom with the things he'd decided to take, including the old tin alarm clock, his dad's razor, his mum's brooch, a brush and comb, knives, forks and spoons, two enamel mugs, two enamel plates, two wrapped pieces of crest china from Southend, a little sepia photograph of his parents taken on Southend Pier and framed in cheap metal, Effel's rag doll, her two Ragamuffin Jack books, and his dad's battered but still working gun-metal pocket watch.

He took a look from the front door to see if any neighbours were about, then called to his sister.

'All clear, Effel, come on.'

There were new tears in Effel's eyes as she left the only home she had known, the home of her mum and dad. Before Orrice closed the door, she said, 'We ain't never comin' back again?'

'D'yer fink we ought to say goodbye to 'em, sis?'

They stepped back into the little passage.

'Goodbye, Mum, goodbye, Dad.'

Orrice felt he had to close the door very quietly then, and did so.

They walked up the street in the direction of Walworth Road, Orrice carrying his sack over his shoulder, Effel clasping hers to her chest, the tears running down her cheeks. Orrice put his arm around her and they walked on.

He had left a note for Aunt Glad and Uncle Perce, telling them that he and Effel hoped to go to Southend and get a boat to Australia. He thought that would stop them worrying.

CHAPTER TWO

They turned south when they reached Walworth Road. They were both quiet, both thinking of the home they had left and the parents who had gone for ever. Nor was it a great consolation to know they were having to run away, although Effel was sure Orrice would know what to do about everything.

As they passed under the railway bridge, he said, ''Ere, sis, I just thought, we could go an' see that nice lady in the town 'all, the one that 'elped Mum an' Dad when our drains got blocked up. Do yer remember 'er? We took 'er some fruit that Dad brought 'ome from the market.'

Effel brightened as she remembered how she and Orrice had gone to the town hall just before Christmas to take the fruit, and how kind the lady had been.

'Will she look after us, Orrice?'

'Well, I don't s'pose she could do that, not actu'lly look after us,' said Orrice, 'but I betcher she'd 'elp us to find somewhere so that we didn't have to go to no orphanage. I betcher, Effel.'

'A' right,' said Effel.

'Come on, it ain't far.'

They walked bravely on.

*   *   *

Mr Simmonds, in charge of the enquiries in the Sanitary Inspector's department at Southwark Town Hall, looked up as a knock on the door was followed by the entry of a young boy in a huge cap, and a small girl in a battered boater. They each carried a sack. He recognized them, the children of a Mr and Mrs Withers, who had had problems with their drains. His assistant, an efficient-looking young woman, made to rise.

'I'll see to them,' he said, and got up from his desk and went to the high counter, which often served as a protection against irate residents with bitter complaints about council shortcomings. The large cap lifted, and he looked down into the brown eyes of fresh-faced Orrice. Nervously, Effel hid herself behind her brother. Mr Simmonds smiled, and looked owlishly benign in his spectacles. 'Good afternoon, Master Orrice,' he said, 'what can we do for you?'

'Is the nice lady 'ere?' asked Orrice.

'Well, Miss Morris is here,' said Mr Simmonds. He turned to his assistant. 'Are you nice, Miss Morris?'

Miss Morris gave him the kind of look that plainly told him she thought the question puerile.

Orrice, coming up on tiptoe, said, 'It ain't 'er we want, is it, Effel?'

'Can't see,' gulped Effel, 'ain't saying.'

'It's the other lady,' said Orrice, 'the one that was nice.'

'I think you mean Mrs Emily Adams,' said Mr Simmonds kindly.

'I dunno I remember 'er name,' said Orrice, and looked around in hope.

'I'm afraid she's left,' said Mr Simmonds. Orrice's face dropped. 'Can I help?'

'It's all right,' said Orrice, who wasn't going to tell everyone that he and Effel were in need. 'It don't matter, mister.'

'Sure?' Mr Simmonds caught Effel's peeping eye and smiled again. She ducked her head and whispered to her brother.

''E's lookin' at me.'

'We best be goin', mister,' said Orrice. 'Come on, Effel.'

Effel rushed in relief to the door, dragging her sack with her. The puzzled Mr Simmonds watched them go, the boy in his huge cap, the girl in a long, old brown coat that almost swept the floor. He thought there was something pathetic about them. He wondered why they weren't at school.

Orrice decided they'd run as far as the East Street market, where he might be able to start earning money by running errands or carrying boxes for stallholders. Effel could mind the sacks. He had the sense to realize that although they were nearly rich at the moment, they wouldn't be like that for too long. He ought to start earning coppers right away, then when the market packed up for the day, he and Effel could begin looking for somewhere to spend the night, perhaps in an empty house. They could take some food there, say a loaf of new bread for fourpence, and some marge and some slices of corned beef. Or some cheese. Effel liked cheese.

It seemed a long way to Effel, from Deacon Street to the town hall and then to East Street. When they eventually reached the entrance to the market, she found it necessary to tell Orrice she wanted to go somewhere.

'Oh, that's good, that is,' said Orrice, 'why didn't yer go before we came out, yer date?'

'Didn't want to.'

'Couldn't yer wait?' asked Orrice hopefully.

'Course I couldn't,' said Effel.

'Oh, cripes,' said Orrice, 'now we got to look for a public lav.'

'Costs a penny, that does,' said Effel.

'What?' asked Orrice, horrified. A ladies' public convenience was as much a mystery to him as darkest Africa. 'An 'ole penny just to wee. You can buy two cracked eggs for a penny. Effel, can't yer wait till it's dark?'

'Ain't goin' to,' said Effel.

'You got to.'

'Can't,' said Effel.

'Oh, blimey,' muttered Orrice. 'All right, come on.' With his sack over his shoulder, he took his sister's hand and pulled her along the pavement behind the stalls, her clothes sack dragging. He took her to a woman standing at an open door at the side of a market shop. 'Missus?' he said. The woman looked down at him. Orrice turned up his earnest face. 'Missus, could yer do me sister a favour?'

'Not if I don't like the sound of it,' said the

30

woman, a shawl around her shoulders on this breezy April day. Kids could get up to every trick.

'Could she use yer lav, please?' The earnest brown eyes beguiled the woman.

'Eh?' She peered suspiciously at the little girl swamped by a long coat. Effel's teeth were gritted.

'Could yer let 'er, please?' begged Orrice from under his cap.

The woman gave in to understanding and sympathy.

'Come on, then, ducks,' she said, 'come up to me flat.'

Effel disappeared with her, leaving Orrice with both sacks. He sat on the doorstep and waited, interesting himself in the market activities. He liked the hustle and bustle of markets. A man came up, a man in the waistcoat, tieless shirt, knotted scarf, corded trousers and flat cap of a costermonger.

'What yer doing, kid?' he asked.

'I'm just sittin',' said Orrice.

'I thought yer was. I said to meself, I said, that kid's just sittin'. Well, I 'opes yer won't take umbrage if I tell yer yer sittin' in me way. Yer can oblige me by 'opping orf.'

Orrice scrambled up.

'I ain't takin' no umbrage, mister. D'yer want any errands run?'

'Yus, it so 'appens I does,' said the costermonger, 'I wants me old woman to run all the bleedin' way down to the old clothes stall by Brandon Street, but you ain't 'er, are yer, sonny?'

'I'll go for yer, mister, I can run,' said Orrice.

31

'Oh, yer can, can yer?' The costermonger looked impressed. 'All right, orf yer go, then.'

'What's the errand, mister?'

'Don't know, do yer?' A grin flickered.

'No, mister,' said Orrice.

'So it ain't no good yer running, then, is it?'

'Mister, that ain't fair,' said Orrice stoutly.

'It's learnin' yer, sonny, it's learnin' yer.'

'It still ain't fair,' said Orrice.

'Well, 'ow about a clip round the ear'ole?'

'That ain't fair, neither,' said Orrice.

The costermonger grinned again, hugely.

'Well, I likes yer, sonny,' he said. He entered the passage. He turned. His hand came out of his pocket. 'This fair?' he said, and flipped a penny at Orrice, who neatly caught it.

'Mister, yer a sport,' he said.

Effel reappeared. She came down the stairs and eeled her way past the costermonger. He stared at her.

'Where'd she come from?' he asked.

'She's me sister,' said Orrice.

'Beats me, kids all over the place and in me own 'ome. Bessie?' He went up the stairs.

'Effel, you all right now?' asked Orrice.

'Ain't saying.'

'I only asked, that's all, I only asked.'

'Ain't nice, askin',' said Effel.

'Why ain't it?'

'Ain't telling,' said Effel.

Orrice grinned. Funny little thing, his skin and blister was.

'Come on,' he said, and they picked up their sacks and began to wander through the market, its lively atmosphere easing their heartache a little. 'Effel, I told yer we'd meet some nice people. I just been given a penny from that bloke. He give it to me just for talkin' with him.'

''E didn't give me one,' said Effel, her sack again clasped to her chest.

'Well, yer didn't talk to 'im,' said Orrice, looking at what the stalls had on offer.

'Ain't talkin' to no-one,' said Effel. The laden fruit stalls began to make her mouth water. 'Orrice, can we buy an orange each?'

'No, we got to spend our money on fings more—' Orrice thought about a suitable word. He picked one from his dad's repertoire. 'More nourishing, like.'

'I'm 'ungry,' said Effel.

'Oh, that's good, that is,' said Orrice, as he and his sister edged their way through roaming, stopping, starting and dawdling people. 'Should've ate up yer breakfast and them sardines an' bread.'

'Ugh,' said Effel. 'Orrice, I'm 'ungry.'

Orrice stopped to look at a stall selling oranges and dates, the dates freshly arrived from the Middle East. An open crate, three sides down, revealed a luscious square mound of the sticky fruit, the top broken into, the large knife stuck in. They were tuppence a pound. Orrice had a feeling dates were a lot more nourishing than oranges.

'Would yer like some dates, sis?' he asked.

Effel regarded the mound. Her mouth watered again.

'I got to eat somefink,' she said. Her empty stomach gave voice and sent a begging message. It gurgled and rumbled. Orrice heard it.

'Effel, is that you?' he asked.

'Don't know what yer mean,' said Effel, faintly rosy. 'Orrice, let's 'ave some dates, can't we?'

'Course we can, they'll fill yer up better than oranges,' said Orrice. He approached the stallholder, Effel behind him as usual. She was always inclined to use him as a shield in the presence of strangers or when she wasn't sure of things. Orrice asked for a pound of dates. The stallholder cut out a large lump of the compressed fruit. He weighed up a pound in a brown paper bag. He received tuppence from Orrice, also, 'Fank yer, mister. Mister?'

'Well, me young cock sparrer?' said the stallholder.

'Mister, 'ave yer got any bad oranges yer don't want? Only we ain't got the money for good ones, and me sister's 'ad 'ooping cough, and the doctor said oranges was best for girls 'er age.'

''Ere, yer comin' it a bit with 'ooping cough and doctors and oranges, ain't yer, me saucebox?' said the stallholder.

'Mister, you can look at 'er,' said Orrice earnestly. 'That's 'er. Effel, stand still.' Effel ducked her head. 'Can yer see 'er, mister, can yer see she ain't stopped being poorly yet?' Effel dragged up a racking cough.

The stallholder looked solemn.

'And the doctor said she needs bad oranges?'

'No, 'e didn't say bad ones, mister, but it won't matter about ones that's gone off a bit. I could cut out them bits, I don't mind doin' that for 'er. Only being 'ard-up, we can only afford the dates.' Orrice thought. 'I fink the doctor said dates was nourishing.'

'Gawd blimey,' said the stallholder, 'I've 'eard some kids in me time, but I ain't 'eard many like you, young feller. All right, 'elp yerself from under me stall, and next time yer come round don't make me laugh meself to death. Me lovin' trouble and strife ain't keen on being widdered just yet.'

'Ta, mister, yer a sport,' said Orrice. ''Ere, Effel, mind me sack a minute. Now what yer standin' on one leg for? She's always doing that, standin' on one leg,' he confided to the stallholder.

'No, I ain't,' said Effel, and stood on both legs, minding the sacks and holding the bag of dates while Orrice dived under the stall. A woman customer arrived. Orrice saw a dozen or so discarded oranges in a crate. He also saw an empty cardboard box. 'Mister, can I use this cardboard box to put 'em in?' His voice came in garbled fashion from under the stall.

''Elp,' said the woman customer, 'you got a talkin' parrot under there, Charlie 'Awkins?'

'No good askin' me,' said the stallholder. 'Dunno what 'e is, 'cept 'e's been tyin' me up in sailors' knots.' He called down to Orrice. 'Listen, sunshine, why don't yer just take me 'ole perishing stall an' me livelihood?'

'I only want the cardboard box, mister, honest,' said Orrice.

'I'm grateful,' said the stallholder, handing his customer a bag of required dates.

'That's a talkin' parrot all right, or me old man's a cart'orse,' said the woman, and took a look. She met the earnest brown eyes of Orrice, who was on his knees sorting oranges.

'D'yer want one, missus?' he asked.

The woman smiled.

'I'd like one like you, love,' she said, and straightened up. 'Some kids,' she said, paying for her dates.

Effel, who had been waxing indignant, made herself heard.

''E ain't a talkin' parrot, 'e's me bruvver,' she said.

'Well, 'ang on to 'im, ducks,' said the woman, and departed smiling.

The stallholder regarded Effel and her battered boater.

'Oh, yer 'ooping cough's better, is it?' he said.

'I've 'ad measles too,' said Effel.

'Gawd 'elp us, you ain't come to give it to me dates, 'ave yer?'

'Ain't saying,' said Effel.

Orrice emerged, the best of the discarded oranges in the box. He put the bag of dates in too.

'Yer a good sport, mister,' he said, 'fanks a lot. 'Ere, why don't yer sing a song for the man, Effel? Effel can sing a bit, yer know,' he said to the stallholder.

'Ain't goin' to,' said Effel.

'Oh, come on, sis,' urged Orrice, ''e's let us 'ave

36

all these decent bad oranges, so why don't yer sing "Oranges an' Lemons" for 'im?'

'I ain't desp'rate,' said the stallholder, 'but go on then, girlie, give it a go.'

'A' right,' said Effel, and sang, '"Oranges an' lemons, the bells of St Clements,"', then came to a full stop.

'That don't seem much of a singsong,' said the stallholder.

'Don't know any more,' said Effel.

'Course yer do,' said Orrice.

'A' right,' said Effel grudgingly, and sang, '"I owe you five farvings, said the bells of St Martins". Don't know any more.'

'Tell yer what,' said the stallholder. 'How would yer like to sit on me stall next to me dates and I'll see if I can sell the pair of yer for three farthings? Nearly a bargain, you'd be, for three farthings.'

''Ere, we ain't goin' to be sold off no stall,' said Orrice indignantly.

'All right, off yer go, then,' grinned the stallholder, 'before someone comes up an' makes me an offer for both of yer.'

'I'll do errands any time yer want, mister,' said Orrice, shouldering his sack, and taking up the box in his free hand.

'I bet yer would.' The stallholder's smile broke through. 'I bet you're yer mum's one an' only perisher.' At which Effel burst into tears. ''Ere, what's brought that on, girlie?'

Another customer for dates came up, and Orrice took Effel away.

37

'Don't cry, sis, 'e didn't know about our mum.'

Effel, clothes sack in her arms, stifled her sobs.

'It ain't right,' she gulped, 'it ain't right we don't 'ave Mum an' Dad no more.'

'Well, no, it ain't too right, Effel,' said Orrice, 'we just got to make do with each other. We'll be all right, you'll see. We'll find somewhere near the market to live, we can always get fings from under the stalls. There's kind people 'ere, we won't starve.'

Effel sighed. Orrice stiffened slightly.

'Now what?' asked Effel wanly.

'Effel, there's a bobby,' whispered Orrice, ''e'll ask us why we ain't at school. We best duck, sis.'

They ducked to their knees, a stall a barrier between them and the strolling market bobby, who passed by without seeing them. They rose up and went on.

'I'm 'ungry,' said Effel.

'All right,' said Orrice. They found a doorstep. They put their sacks down and sat on the step, Orrice with the cardboard box on his knees. He took out the bag of dates and they began to consume them. No one took a great deal of notice. Two kids eating dates on a doorstep were not an unusual sight. Dates or toffee apples, liquorice bootlaces or fig toffee, kids did eat these things sitting on doorsteps. Effel ate with relish. If her heart was still aching, dates were far easier to get down than bread and marge and sardines. She and Orrice littered the ground around their feet with the stones.

'I like dates,' she said.

'Nourishing,' said Orrice, proud to have found the word.

'Don't like nourishing,' said Effel.

'You got to, nourishing's good for yer.'

'Like dates better.'

'We'll buy that nice new loaf and some marge and cheese for our supper,' said Orrice, 'and 'ave some oranges for afters. I got ten of 'em. Listen, sis, we can go and eat it in Browning Park, it ain't far, it stays open till dark. Then we can go an' look for an empty 'ouse.'

'Ain't lookin', not in the dark,' said Effel.

'No, I s'pose not,' said Orrice. 'You come up with sense there, Effel. Girls don't 'ave much sense, it's nice you got a bit. We best look before we go to the park. We'll do that now. Crikey, all them dates you've ate, there's 'ardly none left. Still, they done us good, I betcher. Come on.'

They shouldered their sacks, and Orrice cradled the box under his arm. They made their way towards King and Queen Street.

'I'm firsty,' said Effel.

'I ain't listening,' said Orrice.

'I'll scream,' said Effel.

'All right,' said Orrice. The dates had made him thirsty himself.

'I'll die, I will,' said Effel.

'Effel, I said all right, didn't I? And yer shouldn't talk like that, not after – well, yer shouldn't.' Orrice stopped. 'Let's see, where's the nearest 'orse trough?'

'Ain't drinkin' out of no 'orse's trough,' said Effel.

39

'Course not. I mean one that's got a drinkin' fountain and a cup on a chain,' said Orrice.

'Don't want water,' said Effel.

''Ere, would yer like a cup of tea, sis, would yer?' asked Orrice. Effel had inherited her mother's love of what came hot, steaming and golden out of a teapot. She liked it better than fizzy lemonade.

'Oh, could we 'ave tea, Orrice?' she begged. 'I won't die then, honest.'

'There's a refreshment place just round the corner in the Walworth Road,' said Orrice, 'only we got to go back the way we come. Is yer legs all right?'

'Course they are,' said Effel, a little girl of boundless energy normally. Since the age of four she had spent countless days walking, trotting or running at the heels of her brother, a boy who was always out and about. She actually adored Orrice, although she never gave the slightest sign of it.

They retraced their steps, going back along the pavement on the left-hand side of the market. With their sacks they looked like a couple of street kids fairly bundled up with goods. They dodged round a fat woman, Orrice leading the way. A figure in blue loomed up. Orrice stopped in dismay, shock and guilt.

A copper, a copper who was plodding unhurriedly towards them, eyes on their sacks.

Oh, crikey, thought Orrice, we've been and done it in, it's the orphanage for sure.

CHAPTER THREE

Orrice felt sick.

Effel quivered.

A woman stallholder yelled.

'Oh, yer thievin' bleeder! Come back 'ere with that! Stop 'im, mister!'

The looming figure of the awesome bobby vanished from the eyes of Effel and Orrice as he darted at speed between stalls to take up chase of the thief. Few sinners operated in the market. The many stallholders were a close-knit fraternity and much more of a collective threat to a sly lifter of goods than he was to them. But occasionally a bolder one surfaced.

Orrice sighed with relief amid shouts, cries and minor pandemonium. The thief, caught by a burly stallholder, was dealt a crafty wallop before being handed over to the bobby. The people and the stallholders of Walworth had no sympathy to spare for men who robbed their own kind.

'Come on, Effel, let's scarper,' said Orrice.

They scarpered up to Walworth Road and turned left at the corner. Toni's Refreshments, as the place was called, was only a little way along. They peered in through the glass-panelled door. Orrice hefted his sack, clutched the box of oranges, squared his shoulders and bravely entered, Effel as close behind him as she could get, her sack dragging again.

The refreshment room was fairly full, mostly of market characters. Two housewives in need of a sit-down and a nice hot mug of Toni's tea were also present. Toni, an immigrant Italian, ran the place with his wife Maria. Toni was excitable, Maria plump and philosophical. From the marble-topped counter, with its glass food containers, Toni looked down at a large soft cap. It lifted. A boyish face showed itself.

'Two penny cups of tea, if yer please, mister,' said Orrice.

Toni stared as a little girl hid herself against the counter.

'What-a you say?' he asked Orrice. 'Penny cups of tea? What-a you think, eh? I lose my shop selling tea for a penny?'

''Ow much, then?' asked Orrice, eyes cour-ageously challenging.

'One fine mug of Toni's tea, twopence, see? One fine china cup of Toni's tea in a saucer, also twopence, see? Two mugs or two cups, four pennies, what-a you think? Isn't it?'

The market characters grinned.

''Ere, we ain't paying tuppence for no cup of tea,' said Orrice. 'Are we, Effel?'

'I ain't 'ere,' gasped Effel muffledly, face burning with shyness.

'You ain't-a paying, you ain't-a getting, see?' said Toni, dark with five o'clock shadow.

'We don't mind paying a penny, but we ain't

42

paying tuppence,' said Orrice. 'Crikey, yer can buy a pound of tea for tenpence.'

Toni clutched his black, oily hair, then smacked his forehead. He appealed to his wife Maria.

'You listen, eh? You hear that? *Mama mia*, I got to stand here and let-a this kid talk me crazy?'

'Ah, crazy, eh?' said Maria. 'You crazy ten times a day.'

'Tea I sell for a penny?'

'We ain't paying tuppence,' said Orrice doggedly. 'Except for two cups. Are we, Effel?'

'Ain't talkin',' gasped Effel.

'Eh?' said Toni.

'Now see what yer done,' said Orrice, 'yer frightened me sister. An' she ain't strong, yer know.'

'I should cry my eyes out and give-a you two mugs of tea for a penny each?' Toni knew the smallest concession to a Walworth kid would bring all his friends round to ask for ice cream at half-price. 'I should break my heart, eh?'

A broad-shouldered young man got up from a table and came to the counter.

'Give 'em a mug each, Toni,' he said, putting down fourpence.

'Mister Adams,' said Toni, 'it don't-a pay to give kids for nothing.'

'Some kids, no,' said Tommy Adams, who ran a glass and china stall in the market. 'Some kids, yes.' He gave Orrice's cap a pat. 'Good on yer, son.'

'Mister, yer a sport,' said Orrice. 'Effel, speak yer fanks to the kind gent.'

'Fank yer, mister,' gasped Effel.

'Mister, if yer want anything done so's I can pay yer back for yer treat, you just say,' said Orrice. He picked up two of the pennies. 'Look, we got our own tuppence for the tea, so yer could take these back. It's only fair, like.'

Tommy Adams, liking the spirit in which the offer was made, took the two pennies. He felt that was what the boy honestly wanted.

'Enjoy yer tea, son,' he said, and left.

Orrice produced two pennies from his own pocket.

'Mugs is larger than cups, Effel,' he said. 'Two mugs,' he said to Toni, 'if yer please, mister.'

'Kids,' said Toni, but a moment later two steaming mugs of hot tea appeared on the counter. Maria had poured.

'Fank yer,' said Orrice.

'You want-a some sugar?' asked Toni, reaching for the bowl.

'Me sister likes two spoonfuls,' said Orrice. 'I likes one.'

Toni sugared the teas accordingly.

'For free,' he said.

'No, it ain't,' protested Orrice, 'not when yer charged us fourpence.'

Customers roared with laughter.

'Got yer there, Toni!' yelled a man.

'Crazy kids,' said Toni, and shook his head as Effel showed her face. She blushed crimson.

'Nice crazy kids,' said Maria, and cut two slices of custard tart, put them on plates and placed them

44

on the counter in front of Orrice, who was holding the mugs of tea.

'What-a you doing?' cried Toni. 'You give-a them that for free?'

'Shush, shush,' said Maria.

Orrice took the mugs to a table, came back for his sack and the box of oranges, and then returned for the custard tart slices. Effel was still hiding herself and her sack against the counter.

'Me sister and me's fanking yer kindly, missus,' he said to Maria.

'Me, I go barmy,' said Toni.

'Come on, Effel,' said Orrice. 'Look, we got tea an' custard tart. Come on.'

Effel rushed herself and her sack to the table, sat down and ducked her head until the brim of her boater shaded her mug of tea.

'Funny, eh, them kids?' said Toni to Maria. Maria smiled.

Effel recovered after gulping some mouthfuls of the hot sweet tea. She and Orrice ate their custard tart in huge enjoyment. Then Orrice brought the box of oranges up on the table. He took the fruit out. Toni, serving a customer, saw ten oranges appear. Market men were grinning. Orrice slipped from his chair and dived into his sack. He groped around, found a knife and brought it out. Sitting down again, he began to cut out deteriorating skin and flesh, putting the pieces on his plate, now devoid of custard tart.

'Hey, you kids, now what-a you think you're doing, eh?' called Toni.

'Orrice, what's 'e keep shoutin' for?' whispered Effel.

'I dunno, I'm sure,' said Orrice.

'Now what-a you see?' said Toni to Maria. 'Look, oranges. I don't-a believe it.'

'Listen, Effel,' whispered Orrice, 'shall we give 'im one?'

'Will 'e stop shoutin' an' lookin', then?' asked Effel.

'Well, 'e ought to if 'e likes oranges. Give 'im this one, Effel, I've only 'ad to cut a small bit off it.'

'A' right,' said Effel, the hot tea having given her Dutch courage. She took the orange to the counter, her long coat scurfing around her boots. She looked up at Toni, who wasn't sure if it wasn't all a dream. 'Mister,' she said shyly, ''ere's an orange for yer. It didn't 'ardly 'ave no bad bit.' She placed the fruit on the counter, going on tiptoe to do so. The customers watched in huge amusement.

'I'm crazy for oranges now?' said Toni, and Effel's lashes dropped over her hazel eyes.

'Would yer lady like one?' called Orrice, never as shy as Effel.

'For me, yes?' said Maria, smiling in delight. Children like these two appealed to her warm Italian heart.

Effel went and took another trimmed orange from Orrice, carrying it to Maria.

'Me bruvver's done it up nice wiv 'is knife,' she said, and sighed because the plump lady looked so kind and motherly. Maria, no more in need of any kind of an orange than Toni was, beamed at the

46

little girl. A market runabout boy came in and asked for two mugs of tea.

'Ah, you want-a for free, maybe?' said Toni in heavy sarcasm.

'Eh?' said the boy. 'You ain't givin' 'em away, are yer, Toni?'

'How do I know, eh? Kids come in, send-a me crazy, how do I know what-a I'm doing? All right, all right, two mugs of tea. Fourpence I want, you got that, eh?'

'I ain't deaf,' said the market lad. 'What's that orange for?'

'Me,' said Toni, and put it under the counter instead of throwing it into his waste bin. Maria noted the gesture and smiled. Effel went back to finish her tea, leaving every customer highly tickled. Orrice, having reduced the oranges to an eatable condition, put them back in the box. His plate and Effel's plate were heaped with sections of cut-out fruit.

'Best go now, sis,' he said, and they took up the sacks again, and the box, and made for the door.

'Hey, you kids,' called Toni, 'you come back again and I go barmy again.' He took a look at the table and saw the heaped plates. He hit himself on the head. '*Mama mia*, you see that, Maria? You kids—'

But Orrice and Effel had escaped.

Maria laughed. Toni grinned.

'We just got to find somewhere,' said Orrice an hour later. It was gone five, and the breezy April

47

day was now cloudy and cool. They had walked and walked, carrying their possesions and the box of oranges. They'd eaten one each, while traversing streets all around the market. They had looked and searched and investigated, but hadn't seen an empty house anywhere.

'I fink I'm all wore out,' said Effel. She was actually more dispirited than fatigued. Lack of success in finding a place to shelter had brought back forlorn thoughts of their home in Deacon Street, and what it had meant to them with their mum and dad there. 'Orrice, couldn't we go back 'ome?'

'We best not, sis, unless yer don't mind goin' to an orphanage,' said Orrice. 'Uncle Perce and Aunt Glad'll be lookin' in to take us. 'Ere, let's go to Browning Park. You can sit there and I'll do more lookin', and come back with the bread an' cheese. That's best, Effel, you 'aving a sit-down and mindin' the sacks.'

'A' right,' said Effel.

The place they called Browning Park was actually Browning Gardens, a little oasis of flowering shrubs and bushes, including mulberry bushes. There were a few bench seats, and old people liked to sit there in the summertime. Two were there at the moment, an elderly couple gazing raptly at shrubs beginning to bud. Orrice saw to it that Effel had a bench all to herself, with the sacks and box placed underneath it.

'I won't be long, sis.'

'I'll scream if you are,' said Effel.

48

'Now yer shouldn't do fings like screamin',' said Orrice, 'yer gettin' a big girl these days.'

'No, I ain't.'

'Yes, you are.'

'I ain't. I'm a little girl, I am. And I'll scream.'

'I'll only buy the bread an' cheese, and do some more lookin' on me way,' said Orrice.

'A' right,' said Effel trustingly.

When Orrice returned half an hour later, carrying a crusty loaf, with some margarine and cheese, Effel was in trouble. The little park was empty of grown-ups, and two boys were worrying the sacks like terriers. The sacks were on the path, and Effel was on the sacks. She was hugging them fiercely. She looked as if she had thrown herself down on top of them to prevent the boys running off with them. Their hands were pulling, jerking and tugging. Effel's teeth were clenched, her own hands gripping the sacks. Orrice broke into a run. He dropped the loaf, marge and cheese on the bench, and he went for the boys, both a year older than himself.

''Ere, 'old orf,' said one boy, and delivered a swipe that knocked Orrice's cap off. Orrice straightaway punched him in his breadbasket, and the boy, staggered, expelled a noisy gust of breath. The second boy leapt at Orrice's back, wound wiry arms around him and wrestled him to the ground. Effel sprang up like a fury. With the ferocity of a sister who had no-one else but her brother, she delivered a succession of rageful kicks. The boy yelled with pain, letting go of Orrice as the first boy re-entered the fray. Orrice was up on his feet in a flash. His dad had taught him the very effective value of a straight right arm. Orrice stuck his out rigidly straight. The first boy ran into the balled fist. It split his lip and dropped him on his bottom.

'Oh, yer bleedin' 'ooligan!' he bawled, as his blood ran.

'Like it, did yer?' said Orrice. 'Yer'll get two more for luck if yer don't 'oppit. Effel, leave off kickin'.'

Effel was still applying the toe of her right boot to the grounded boy, who was suffering the indignity of having been put out of action. A kick from Effel had wounded his stomach. Orrice pulled his tiger-ish sister away.

'Lemme go!' she yelled. Her blood was up. Orrice calmed her down. Both boys sat up, one with a sore stomach, the other with a split lip.

'Oh, yer bleedin' terror,' said sore stomach to Effel, 'yer been an' near kicked me to death.'

'Serve yer right,' said Orrice.

'An' look what yer done to Alfie, 'e's all over blood.'

'I'm bleedin' as well,' groaned split lip.

'Well, yer shouldn't hit girls,' said Orrice, 'specially not me sister.'

'Some sister.' Sore stomach rubbed his bruised middle. 'She's a flaming walloper, more like.'

'Lemme go,' hissed Effel, 'I want to kick 'im some more.'

'Now, sis, you already done 'im in,' said Orrice.

'And you done Alfie in,' said sore stomach.

50

Alfie had a hand to his mouth. Blood was smearing his chin. Effel, relenting, dug into her coat pocket and produced a grubby handkerchief.

''Ere y'ar,' she said to Alfie, 'you can use me 'ankie to wipe it wiv, I don't mind.'

'I'm honoured, I am, I don't think,' said Alfie, but he took the hankie and wiped blood away. 'Oh, me gawd, me mum's goin' to knock me 'ead off when she sees me like this.'

'All right, 'ave an orange,' said Orrice. The box was still under the bench. He pulled it out and gave an orange to each boy. A scrap was a scrap in Walworth, and afterwards, in most cases, you shook hands.

'It ain't all there,' said Alfie. 'Is yourn all there, Eddie?'

'Mine's got a lump out,' said Eddie.

'I 'ad to cut bad bits off, that's all,' said Orrice.

'A' right, I got yer,' said Eddie, and dug his teeth into his fruit. Alfie ate his gingerly, the juice making his split lip smart.

'Listen,' said Orrice, 'wha'd'yer 'it my sister for?'

'Never touched 'er,' said Alfie, 'just wanted a look in them sacks.'

'You was goin' to pinch 'em,' accused Effel.

'Only goin' to look,' said Eddie. 'They ain't swag, is they? You doin' liftin'?'

'Cheek!' cried Effel, knowing what lifting meant.

'Me dad done some liftin' once,' said Eddie, 'up by Norwood, in some posh 'ouse. Only when 'e got the swag 'ome me mum went for 'im with our frying-pan. Laid 'im out, she did. Then she took

51

the swag round to the police station. In a sack it was, just like yourn, an' she dumped it outside the police station door when no-one was lookin'. Me dad wasn't hisself for a week. 'E didn't 'ave no broken bones, but 'e 'ad everything else. Frying-pans don't 'alf cop yer. It don't do no good to do any liftin' in our fam'ly. Is Alfie's lip goin' puffy?'

'Not much,' said Orrice. 'Well, a bit.'

'A' right, I ain't splittin' on yer,' said Alfie generously, 'I'll tell me mum a door come up and 'it me.' He and Eddie finished their oranges, peel and all. 'Well, time we pushed orf. Where'd yer live, anyways, you two?'

'Oh, round 'ere,' said Orrice.

'A' right, see yer, then,' said Eddie. 'No 'ard feelings, eh?'

'D'yer know any empty 'ouses?' asked Orrice cautiously.

'Empty 'ouses? Round 'ere?' Eddie looked puzzled. Walworth had a teeming population. 'Ain't seen none. There's some down Bermondsey. You got swag, after all? You lookin' for a place to stow it?'

'Cheek!' cried Effel again. ''It 'im, Orrice.'

'A' right, a' right,' said Eddie, 'didn't mean it. Just askin', that's all. Come on, Alfie.'

Alfie, Effel's hankie to his sore lip, said, 'Well, so long.'

'You still got me 'ankie,' said Effel.

'Ta for the loan,' said Alfie, and gave it back to her. It was a mess now, but Effel didn't take offence, she stuffed it back into her coat pocket. 'So long,' he said again, and he and Eddie left on a cordial note.

'Crikey,' said Orrice, 'they told us Bermondsey for empty 'ouses. All that way, sis.'

'Ain't goin',' said Effel.

'Nor me. We don't want to run away as far as Bermondsey. Oh, well, s'pose we 'ave supper now, eh? It's a nice new loaf, an' cheese. I only bought two ounces of marge, we don't want to cart any leftover about, it'll get mucky.'

'No, a' right,' said Effel.

The little park was not too warm in the grey light of the cloudy evening, but brother and sister had it all to themselves. Orrice felt they hadn't done too badly with food. They'd had nourishing dates, custard tart and an orange each. Now they sat on the bench and scoffed bread and marge and cheese. The bread was new and crusty, the cheese a golden yellow. They had another orange each afterwards, then finished up the few dates that were left.

'Well, now we got some bread over for breakfast, and two oranges,' said Orrice.

'But we ain't got nowhere to go,' said Effel. 'Orrice, where we goin' to be tonight?'

Orrice was getting a little worried about that. His optimism had taken a knock. But he said, 'Don't you worry, Effel, I didn't do much lookin' when I went for the bread an' cheese, so we still got plenty of streets for proper lookin'. We'll find somewhere, I betcher.'

Darkness had arrived an hour ago, and all their

proper looking had proved fruitless. Orrice thought it a real sell that there wasn't a single empty house. It wasn't very obliging of people not to leave at least one empty house. The darkness was depressing and discouraging, and Effel's feet were dragging. So was her sack. And she was silent. He tried, but he couldn't cheer her up or get her to say anything. They kept walking, Orrice with his eyes open on the lookout for coppers on their beat. They sat on doorsteps now and again to rest. Orrice hung on as best as he could to some optimism as they walked and walked. They both felt that everyone who passed them was certain to be going home to a warm kitchen fireside.

They dodged a copper in Brandon Street when they were thinking of entering Peabody's Buildings and huddling up together on a landing. Their elusive tactics took them into Larcom Street and to St John's Church.

''Ere, we could go in there, Effel,' whispered Orrice.

Effel spoke for the first time in an hour. It was gone ten o'clock.

'It don't 'ave no beds,' she said.

'Well, it's a church, yer date.'

'I know that, I ain't daft,' said Effel.

'We could sleep on a pew,' said Orrice.

'A'right,' said Effel tiredly.

They went in. The darkness of the church seemed to make it like a vast cavern of mystery, black with night. Effel clutched her brother's hand. Orrice made a decision.

54

'Let's go 'ome, sis. There won't be no-one there now. We got the alarm clock, we can 'ave it go off at six and creep out before anyone sees us. Come on.'

Effel accompanied him gladly. She forced her weary legs to make the journey along the Walworth Road. Late trams ran by, and there were some lights in addition to street lamps. They both watched out for coppers, Orrice keeping to himself the worry that Aunt Glad might have locked the front door of the house. Much to his relief she hadn't. The latchcord was in place, and the door opened when he pulled it. They went in. Their home seemed cold and lifeless, as if no-one belonged to it any more. But their beds were rapturous to them. Orrice first found matches and a candle so that he could set the old alarm clock. Then he looked in on Effel by the light of the candle. She was fast asleep in her bed. She'd taken her boots off, and that was all. She'd slipped into bed with everything else on. Orrice went to his own bed and fell asleep as soon as his head touched the pillow.

He was up the moment the alarm went off. He couldn't get Effel up. He woke her, but he couldn't get her to move. The warmth of the bed and its familiarity were something she was reluctant to give up. He went downstairs and put the kettle on. The gas ran out after a minute, and he put a penny in the meter. Then he made a pot of tea, and took a cup up to his sister. There was still a little milk and sugar in the larder. He woke Effel up again, and she greeted the hot tea with instant bliss. He managed to get her out of bed after that and made her wash at the scullery sink, using hot water from the kettle in a bowl, and he had a good wash himself.

They crept out of the house just before seven, after they'd eaten some of their bread. The morning light was growing, and they hastened up the street to the Walworth Road before anyone saw them.

They spent the day in and around East Street market. The market offered them scenes and sounds that were comforting and familiar, and it also offered them crowds in which to hide from bobbies. Orrice said they'd best start looking for an empty house in the streets on the other side of the Walworth Road when they'd had some hot Bovril and toast. Effel liked toast. The day was overcast, with a threat of rain and a slightly chilly breeze, and Effel was in need of something hot. Orrice took her to Toni's Refreshment Rooms at ten o'clock. Toni's dark eyebrows lifted ferociously when he saw them. Maria cast a smile.

'You kids, what-a you want this time, eh?' asked Toni.

''Ow much is two 'ot Bovrils and two slices of toast?' asked Orrice.

'Bovril? Bovril? What-a you think, I run a hospital? And what-a you two kids doing? You don't-a go to school?'

'Effel's 'ad measles,' said Orrice, which she had, a year or so ago. 'I've 'ad mumps.' Which he had, two years ago. 'Effel's still poorly, mister. 'Ow much is the Bovril an' toast?'

'Crazy kids, go away,' said Toni.

'Shush, shush,' said Maria, and went through a door at the back of the counter. Orrice and Effel waited hopefully, Toni prowled about, served a customer, and prowled about again. Maria reappeared with a tray, on which stood two mugs of steaming Bovril and two slices of buttered toast, the toast created under the grill of her gas oven in the upstairs kitchen. Toni smacked himself on the forehead at his wife's weakness.

'What-a you up to, eh? We don't-a serve Bovril or toast. You crazy too?'

'Shush, shush,' said Maria again, placing the tray on the counter.

'Cor, you ain't 'alf a sport, missus,' said Orrice. ''Ow much, if yer please?'

'Penny each Bovril,' said Maria, 'penny for two toasts. You like?'

'You betcher,' said Orrice, fishing for three pennies.

Toni tore his hair.

'I give up, I retire, I don't-a like going broke.'

Orrice paid Maria, and he and Effel carried the Bovril and the toast to a table. Orrice returned for the sacks. Toni watched out of dark, fiery eyes. Maria smiled and patted his arm. Toni grinned. New customers came in. Orrice and Effel devoured the toast and drank the Bovril. They lingered over it, savouring its heat and flavour.

When they were ready to go, Effel scuttled out with her sack and it was left to Orrice to smile and say thanks.

'All right, all right,' said Toni, 'but don't-a you come back again.'

'Nice kids,' smiled Maria. 'Come back when you like, eh?'

'Women, what-a you think of women, eh?' growled Toni. 'Barmy, eh?'

'Nice, she is,' said Orrice, 'like our mum.'

Maria's smile beamed.

Orrice and Effel went to the stallholder selling dates and oranges. His mound of dates was smaller, his mound of oranges glowed. He put on a straight face for the boy and girl. Orrice asked for half a pound of dates.

'Yer sure that's all yer want, me young cock sparrer? Yer sure you don't want me stall and the shirt off me back?'

'No fanks, mister, just a penn'orth of dates. The uvvers done Effel good yesterday, she's better today, ain't yer, sis?'

'Ain't,' said Effel.

'Gawd 'elp us,' said the stallholder, 'you've come to cough 'ooping cough all over me dates, 'ave yer?' He bagged the fruit, weighed it, and handed it to Orrice. 'You tell yer sister she's goin' to get me nicked for selling dates with 'ooping cough. Right, let's see yer copper coin, sunshine.'

''Ere y'ar, mister.' Orrice paid his penny. 'Mister, we gotter go callin', could we leave our sacks under the stall till we come back?' Orrice had realized that carrying the sacks around all day was a bit daft.

'I knew you'd come for more'n dates,' said the stallholder. 'What's in the sacks? Bombs?'

'Course not, we ain't Bolshies,' said Orrice. 'It's just fings we've collected.'

'All right, shove 'em under.'

It was a relief to unburden themselves and to go freely in search of a roof for the forthcoming night. They covered streets on the other side of the Walworth Road. Orrice showed revived optimism, but Effel soon became morose. They did see one place, but its windows were boarded up and so was the door. After two hours they went back to the market, where they ate hot faggots and pease pudding in a shop that specialized in providing this favouite cockney repast. The succulent meal cost Orrice and Effel sixpence. Orrice said living was expensive when you were running away, they'd best just have bread and marge for their tea later on. He thought he ought to look for a job. Wearing long trousers, people might think he was fourteen. Effel didn't think it was much good getting a job when they hadn't got nowhere to live yet. Orrice said they'd do some more looking, and if they still couldn't find nowhere they could sleep at the house again, they could creep back in when it was dark.

It rained for a while during the afternoon. That brought Effel's spirits low. Orrice tried to cheer her up, but secretly he was feeling discouraged, not only because they hadn't got a roof, but also because there was nothing to do except walk about. Normally he liked walking about, he liked shops and markets and lots of people, but it wasn't the same when he didn't have a mum and dad to go home to. And he hadn't been able to find anyone who wanted him to run errands.

The rain finally stopped, they retrieved their sacks before the market closed down, and went to Browning Gardens to eat bread and marge. They sat on a bench and Orrice cut slices from what was left of yesterday's loaf.

'Yer cut it all fick,' complained Effel.

'But we got to eat well, sis. Fin slices ain't goin' to do us much good. There y'ar, look, I put lots of marge on that slice. An' we can have some dates after.'

'A' right,' said Effel.

Later, when it was dark, they entered their old street again. Much to Orrice's bitter disappointment, this time the door was locked. Effel gave a muffled wail of anguish. Orrice supposed Aunt Glad had been round again to look for them and had removed the latchcord when she left.

They decided to go to St John's Church again. Effel was worn out, Orrice carrying on in determined fashion. They'd be all right in the church. It might be a bit awesome, but it would provide shelter. And they'd be out of the way of grown-ups. Grown-ups would ask questions. So would bobbies.

It began to rain again on their way. They hurried. A glimpse of a bobby in Larcom Street sent them scurrying on to Browning Street, Orrice carrying both sacks at this stage, and Effel nearly falling over in her weariness.

At midnight it was raining hard, and the rain was

chill. They were huddled together in the doorway of a house in Morecambe Street. With the rain was an April wind, and the wind blew the rain into their faces. They were wet, cold and very tired, and every so often a sob shook Effel. Orrice cuddled her and she put her cold face in his shoulder. Orrice was uncomfortably sure he'd let his sister down by not providing her with a roof.

They thought, of course, of their home and their mum and dad. They thought of the warmth of the kitchen fire, and the blissful comfort of their beds. They thought of the sounds of their dad getting up at five in the morning to go to his work in Covent Garden, and of snuggling rapturously down knowing they could go back to sleep and not get up themselves till eight, when their mum would have hot porridge ready for them. Orrice thought of his dad's hearty, manly strength, and Effel thought of her mum's warm, capacious bosom whenever she needed a comforting cuddle.

Orrice knew they couldn't stay where they were. The rain kept gusting at them inside the shelter of the shallow doorway. The street was silent, every house in darkness. Rain skittered over the street surface in the light of a lamp-post.

'Orrice.' Effel gulped back a sob. 'We got to go somewhere.'

'Yes, we best go to the church, even if we do get wetter on the way,' whispered Orrice, 'we could—' He stopped as they heard slow and deliberate footsteps. Effel, shivering, clung tightly to her brother. Orrice watched. In the light of the lamp he saw a figure on the other side of the street, a figure in a cape and helmet, and the cape was wet and shiny with rain. The local bobby was on his midnight beat, making measured progress, his police lamp in his hand. Because of the street lamp, Orrice was sure he and Effel would be seen, even from the other side. But the bobby passed by. Orrice waited before whispering again. 'Effel, let's go to the church, we could get dry and put uvver clothes on.'

Effel, at the mention of the church, said with all the pathos of a mourning heart, 'Oh, I wish I was in 'eaven wiv our mum and dad.'

'Sis, yer shouldn't say that, Mum an' Dad wouldn't want yer to, they wouldn't want yer to die yet, and you 'ave to die before you can go to 'eaven. Come on, let's go now. It ain't far, it's—' He stopped again, hearing other footsteps, different in their rhythm. They were the quick footsteps of someone hurrying to get out of the rain.

It was a man. He came out of the gusting rain, and he caught them before they could move as he turned in at the doorway.

'Good God, what's this? Who are you, and what're you doing here?'

Their hearts sank.

CHAPTER FOUR

The man was tall. He loomed above them, rain running from an old Army trenchcoat and dripping from the brim of his trilby hat. Jim Cooper, ex-serviceman, thirty years old and minus his left arm, stared down at the huddled figures of a boy and girl. He was just home from a late evening stint at the United Kingdom Club near Blackfriars, where he worked in the kitchens. There he did every kind of odd job required of him, including washing-up, at which his one hand did the work of two in the way of a man determined to surmount his handicap.

The boy spoke.

'Please, mister, we're only sittin', we ain't doin' anyfink except just sittin'.'

'But where's your home, why aren't you there? D'you know what the time is?'

Orrice drew a breath. Some instinct told him to confess.

'Please, mister, we're orphans,' he said, and Effel pushed her face deeper into his shoulder.

'Oh, my God,' said Jim. That was a blow to the heart. He had been an orphan boy himself. Worse, an illegitimate orphan. He had never known his father, and he could not remember his mother, for she had been knocked down and killed by a tram when he was only three years old. He had grown up in an orphanage, knowing no family, no relatives. But one day, when he was five, a woman had come to see him, a woman called Lily Downes, in service as a lady's maid. She had been his mother's closest friend, and only recently had she discovered he was in this orphanage. She brought him comfort and friendship. She visited him four times a year, out of affection for his dead mother.

From Lily Jim learned about his mother, a country girl called Betsy Miller who had come to London to go into service. She was pretty, bubbly and laughing. Lily became her best friend. After a year in service with a family in South Norwood, Betsy began to talk about a lovely soldier she had met on one of her days off. She was an affectionate young lady, but not fast, no, no-one could ever say she was fast. It was not long before she showed the signs of being very much in love, but these were followed by little moments when she was obviously unhappy. She confessed to Lily that her soldier had gone overseas with his regiment. But since he had given her an engagement ring before he left, Lily did not think she ought to be quite as unhappy as she was.

The shock came when she gave birth to a son in the early spring of 1891. The family she and Lily worked for were outraged, and Betsy was dismissed. She departed with her child in a desperate search for another post. She had not said who the father was. Only Lily knew it was the soldier, and that Betsy had not heard from him for months. Lily said to Jim after he had left the orphanage, 'I don't think he ever knowed about you, Jim. He went off to the African wars with Kitchener before you was born, and probably before your mother knowed you was on the way even. He was probably killed dead by them Fuzzy-Wuzzies. So don't think too hard of him, and never think hard of your mother. She was a sweet woman, she suffered having to tell her parents about you, they was strict church people. I went to the village in Hampshire where your mother come from, I went while you were still in the orphanage, I wanted to tell her parents where you was, but their son wouldn't let me in. You've got to know, Jim, that your mother loved you, she did, and she loved your father. She wouldn't of given herself to any man she didn't love. It's not every child that's born of love, like you was. Your father wrote to her from Africa, then his letters stopped coming, which was when he was probably killed, only the Army never got in touch with her about it, well, I suppose because she wasn't what they call a next-of-kin. Not his wife, you see.'

'Mister?' said Orrice tentatively, for the man was so silent, just standing there and looking down at them, the wind sweeping him with rain.

Jim came to.

'You're wet through, the pair of you,' he said quietly. 'I think you'd better come up with me to my room and wring yourselves out.' He rented just one room, with a gas ring, a coal fire, a bed and some neat and tidy sticks of furniture. He was under notice to quit at the moment, not because he and his landlady, Mrs Palmer, had fallen out, but because she wanted the room for her elderly brother, recently bereaved by the loss of his wife. Jim quite understood. He had a fortnight to find new lodgings. That was no problem. There were always families in Walworth looking for lodgers to help out with the rent. 'We'll be quiet, kids, we don't want to wake sleeping people, do we?'

'Mister?' said Orrice, a little overcome.

'Oh, Orrice, could we go up wiv 'im?' begged Effel, emotionally overcome herself at the thought of a cosy room with four walls, a ceiling and perhaps some warmth. She lifted her head. Jim saw a pale little face and wet eyes. He also saw childish entreaty.

'Come on,' he said, and used his key to open the door. Getting to their feet and picking up their sacks, Effel and Orrice followed him into the dark passage. Jim struck a match and lighted a candle that stood in its holder on the hallstand. Picking it up, he led the way up the stairs, the boy and girl creeping up after him. One stair faintly creaked, but that was the only noise, and Jim warmed to the pair in the way they were taking such care to be quiet. He opened the door of his room, put the candle down on a little table, and struck another match. He lit the gas mantle. Orrice and Effel ventured in, and he closed the door. They saw then that the left sleeve of his trenchcoat was empty, its end tucked into the coat pocket. Effel, wet and shivering, stared at it. Orrice winced in boyish sympathy.

66

In a corner of the room was the gas ring. Jim lit that too, his manipulation of match and matchbox dexterous. The fire was laid. He thought for a moment, then applied another match to that. The paper took instant hold. It flared, and a moment later the chopped sticks of firewood began to spark and crackle. Effel regarded the leaping flames in bliss.

'Oh, mister, ain't that nice?' she said.

'And a hot drink, that would be nice too?' said Jim, taking his hat off.

They looked up at him. He was dark, his hair blue-black, his cheekbones sparse of flesh, his face long. His appearance might have been saturnine had he not owned a wide, good-looking mouth and the little lights of a friendly man in his grey eyes. People who had known his mother might have said he had inherited some of her warmth, some of her willingness always to believe the best of people. Jim had left the orphanage at sixteen when he secured a job with a small building firm and lodgings with a family in Millwall. He went to evening classes to better himself, and he devoured books.

There was, however, the ever-present inquisitiveness of people and friends about his background, his family, and his admission of illegitimacy made some feel sorry for him. It also made parents steer their daughters away from him. If he did not like either reaction, he at least eschewed bitterness or self-pity. He felt himself to be as good as other men, and he took most setbacks philosophically. However, when war was declared in 1914, he turned his back on the awkward moments of his social life by joining up.

He lost an arm in 1917. That took him out of the war, but not back into his old job. A one-armed man was not too useful to builders. He picked up temporary work from time to time. Not until five months ago did he click for a permanent job when, after working on a temporary basis in the UK Club, the manager took him on as a fully-fledged member of the kitchen staff. It was not the kind of job he had hoped for at the beginning of his working career, but a job was a job these days, and this one at least kept him physically active. With his small pension and his wage, he was content for the time being. Like many other men, he was waiting for the country's economy to improve. He even had a little money saved. He also had his father's name, Cooper, given him by his mother.

'Oh, can yer make us 'ot cocoa?' asked Effel, the crackling fire a joy to her. 'But yer only got one—' She stopped and blushed. She couldn't think how anyone could make cocoa with only one hand. 'Orrice could do it for yer, mister,' she said shyly.

'Orrice?' said Jim, removing his coat. They saw the pinned-up left sleeve of his jacket. Effel gulped. Orrice looked awkward. 'Who's Orrice?' asked Jim, smiling.

'Please, 'e's Orrice and I'm Effel. 'E's me bruvver and I'm 'is sister.'

'Is that a fact?' asked Jim gravely, hanging his hat and coat on the door peg. 'Horace and Ethel?'

'Orrice and Effel Wivvers,' said Orrice.

'I see.' Jim accepted what everyone else did. 'Well, I'll see to the cocoa, Orrice, while you and Effel get your wet things off. Here's something for you, Effel.' He opened the door of a cupboard and took an old woollen dressing-gown off its hook. Effel received it shyly, hid herself on the blind side of the bed in her modesty, and began to undress. He filled a kettle from a pitcher and put it on the gas ring. In front of the fire, its coal beginning to glow, Orrice took his clothes off, standing to let the warmth caress his naked young body. Jim gave him a towel and he rubbed himself briskly down with it.

Effel, peeping, whispered, 'Mister, could yer give me a towel too, could yer, please?'

Jim got a fresh one from the cupboard. He took his weekly wash to the laundry in Walworth Road, round the corner from Browning Street.

'Coming, Effel,' he said, and threw the towel. It sailed over the bed and landed on her. Effel was warmer. There was a fire burning and a kettle on the gas ring. And there was a nice man looking after them. So Effel almost giggled as the towel arrived on her head. She used it to take the damp from her body, then wrapped herself in the dressing-gown. It enveloped her, and it spread itself on the floor around her feet. Jim, putting cocoa into enamel mugs, saw her emerge from her hiding-place, a little girl in an old woollen tent, arms full of her clothes. Orrice had his short woollen pants back on, that was all.

'Orrice, oh, yer naughty boy, standin' like that not dressed,' she said. 'Yer got to excuse 'im, mister, we been walkin' two days, we been every-where, lookin' an' walkin', an' all down the market too where a man on a stall let Orrice 'ave some oranges what 'e 'ad to make good. I 'spect 'e's tired, so yer got to excuse 'im lookin' rude.'

'Crikey, she's talkin',' said Orrice to the fire.

'That's good for all of us, talking,' said Jim, 'but not too loud, of course.'

'Oh, no,' breathed Effel, blanching at the thought of going back into the cold wet night because of loud talking.

Jim made the cocoa and put in a little milk from the can.

'Effel, lay your clothes over the fender,' he said, 'then you can both drink your cocoa. And while you're drinking it, tell me all about yourselves. I know you must both be very tired, it's well after midnight, but I think I'd like to know a little about you before we get you tucked down.'

'Yes, mister,' said Orrice. He and Effel received the hot cocoa gratefully, and they sat on the rug in front of the fire to drink it. He looked again at Jim's empty sleeve.

'Our dad was in the war,' he said.

'And I look as if I was too, do I?' asked Jim.

'Was yer?' asked Orrice.

'We all were, weren't we, in our different ways?' said Jim.

Orrice, relishing the hot cocoa, said, 'I dunno about that, mister. I mean about what everyone did in the war, except—' He thought about what to say. 'Except most people still got both their arms.'

'Oh, there are thousands worse off than me,' said Jim. He sat down. 'And it's you two I want to hear about. So tell me.'

They told him their story. Jim did not need to own great perception to sense the heartbreak. It was not only in the loss of both parents, it was also in their realization that their only relatives, Uncle Perce and Aunt Glad, could not permanently house them. But many aunts and uncles had children of their own, problems of their own, and a depressing lack of money. Jim could not condemn Uncle Perce and Aunt Glad. Nevertheless, he could understand why the heartbreak of the boy and girl was the more acute. He himself had been spared that kind of anguish, for at the age of three he would probably have suffered more from bewilderment than anything else. It was not until he was several years older that the sad moments had come, and with them a longing to have known his mother and father.

Lily Downes had filled in many blanks for him. When he left the orphanage he was given his birth certificate. That told him what Lily told him. Mother, Betsy Margaret Miller, spinster. Father, John James Cooper, bachelor. He often thought that one day he would go to his mother's birthplace, the village of Elderfield in Hampshire, and see if he had any relatives there. Something must have happened to the few personal possessions she had at the time of her death. Letters and so on. He had nothing of hers, not even a photograph.

He fully understood why Orrice and Effel did not want to go to an orphanage. Every kid sensed that

71

life at an orphanage was of a regimented kind. And there was no institution that could give this brother and sister what their parents had given them. He suspected they might have been a rough and ready couple, but affectionate for all that. Cockneys were typically of that kind, large-hearted and with great family loyalties.

What to do with these kids, what to do about them? Jim knew what officialdom would expect him to do, but he took all officialdom with a pinch of salt. He had little time for rules and regulations that were supposed to be for the good of people, but in the main made things easier for those who administered them from the offices of town halls, county halls, government departments and institutions.

'Well, tomorrow we'll have to see about things,' he said.

'Mister, you been swell,' said Orrice, 'and me an' Effel don't want to be no trouble. Yer real swell, takin' us in for tonight, and we don't want yer to go to no more trouble than that. Yer won't tell no-one we're running away, will yer?'

'No, I won't tell, Orrice, cross my heart,' said Jim, but that was a promise that might be difficult to keep.

Effel whispered in her brother's ear.

'Mister,' said Orrice, 'Effel wants to know are yer really goin' to let us sleep in a bed tonight?'

'Yes, in this one,' said Jim, 'and I think it's time you kipped down now.'

A minute later they were in the bed, Effel

wearing the old dressing-gown, Orrice his woollen pants. They fell asleep almost at once. Jim settled for the fireside rug, with a chair cushion for a pillow. After his years in the Army he could sleep anywhere. A fireside rug and a cushion represented relative luxury. All the same, he lay awake for a while, thinking about what alternatives there were to an orphanage. Effel and Orrice slept in bliss, Effel dreaming she was sailing through warm billowing clouds of fleecy white, and Orrice dreaming of squashy oranges.

CHAPTER FIVE

Orrice and Effel were still asleep at half-past eight the next morning. Jim, drinking his breakfast cup of tea, sat at the little table, regarding an empty shell, all that was left of his soft-boiled egg. He was not a man of ifs and buts. He gave necessary thought to a problem and came uncompromisingly to a decision. If it did not turn out to be the right one, he was always prepared to take the consequences. He had made an instant decision once, to turn right instead of left in a captured German trench on the Passchendaele Ridge. He had had to accept the consequences of that, an amputated left arm.

Now he came to a decision about Orrice and Effel. For the time being he must take care of them. His landlady, Mrs Palmer, would have to know about them, and he had to give her a story that would stand up. He could not bring himself to send these pathetic kids back to the streets to wander about in hope, dodging coppers, avoiding school, scraping pennies together for their sustenance, sleeping in doorways and looking for a miracle to happen. There were no miracles. Jesus had used them all up in Galilee. There were all sorts of kids in Walworth, rascals, ragamuffins and truants among

74

them. Orrice and Effel, somehow, were not quite like most of them. Their attachment to each other was obvious and touching. He had to take care of them until a better alternative offered itself. But they had to attend school. Education, however elementary, was the most important thing in a child's life, although few children realized it. Most would happily give it a miss, not knowing how bitterly they might regret it later on.

These two could stay away from school again today, perhaps. But they must go tomorrow. He must speak to Mrs Palmer, and he must go out to look for new lodgings, lodgings for Orrice and Effel as well as himself. What was his weekly income? Together his modest pension and his modest wage amounted to thirty-four shillings a week. He would need two bedrooms, one for Effel and one for Orrice and himself, plus a room for living in and with cooking facilities. He might accordingly have to find as much as ten bob for rent, leaving twenty-four shillings to keep the three of them.

He caught the smell of dates. He got up, looked in a crumpled paper bag and saw a small sticky mess of them. He put them on the fire. They fizzed and sizzled. He looked at the sleeping pair. Orrice's tousled head was visible. Effel's tangled hair spilled over the pillow. Their breathing was even. He went down to speak to Mrs Palmer, a woman of fifty-five, her husband a plumber. He advised her that his niece and nephew had come to stay with him for a while. Mrs Palmer knew nothing of the fact that he had no relatives, that he was illegitimate. She had never asked pointed questions or nosy ones, being a woman who took people as she found them.

'They've come 'ere?' she asked.

'Unexpectedly, I'll admit,' said Jim easily. 'Trouble in the family, I'm afraid. Not the sort of things friends or relatives want to talk about. You know how it is.'

'That I do. But 'ere, Mr Cooper?'

'I couldn't say no. They were waiting for me when I got back from work last night. On the doorstep. Too shy to knock.'

'They knew you had late workin' hours?' said Mrs Palmer, grey-haired and stout.

'It gets around families,' said Jim. 'All that time in the rain, poor little devils. I told them you'd have made them welcome, that they could have waited in my room, but like most children they're shy with strangers. They'll be here only until I get new lodgings, which I will just as soon as I can.'

'Well, you're being downright kind to them, I must say,' said Mrs Palmer, 'but you do know me brother Wally's comin' tomorrow week, like I said? Now his wife's gone, poor woman, he can't manage 'is house by hisself, specially as he's still working, and he fancies just a quiet little room on his own with us, and he gets on well with me husband. I'm sorry I've had to ask you to leave according, you've been a welcome lodger, but you see how it is, and you'll need more space, anyways, if your niece and nephew are goin' to be with you for a while.'

'I can't argue with that, Mrs Palmer. Don't worry now, I'll have moved out before your brother

76

arrives. But you don't mind them being in my room for the time being?'

'But can you manage? A boy and girl and yourself?' Mrs Palmer obviously wondered how old the girl was.

'They're only young,' said Jim. 'Ethel's seven and Horace is ten.'

'Oh, you can put the girl on me parlour sofa at night till you go,' offered Mrs Palmer out of consideration for what she thought proper. Many people in Walworth set great store by being proper, never mind the difficulties posed by poverty.

'That's very kind of you,' said Jim, 'I'll tell her.'

'And I'll be pleased to keep my eye on them for you when you go off to your work this afternoon.'

'That's even kinder,' said Jim. His hours were from four in the afternoon until midnight, but he was always free to leave in advance if his work was finished. He did not mind the awkward hours. He had no real social commitments. He was wary about women. The closer a relationship with a woman became, the closer the inevitable problems came. He sometimes felt he was simply waiting, that somewhere, sometime, a woman would appear, a woman who did not mind in the least about a man being illegitimate, providing he did not wear devil's horns. Meanwhile, the local lending library was open to him during the day, and he spent enjoyable hours there. He was also an avid book borrower. He thought public lending libraries constituted one of the finest privileges a civilized country could bestow on its citizens.

'I'll give 'em tea this evening, if you like,' said Mrs Palmer, motherly generosity prompted by her lodger's Christian outlook towards his troubled relatives. She could never think why some nice woman hadn't taken him on as a husband. No nice women minded about a kind man only having one arm. 'I'll be pleased to make them tea.'

'Bless you, Mrs Palmer,' said Jim, who had an easy way of talking to people.

'My pleasure, I'm sure,' she said, pleased that Mr Cooper hadn't made any fuss about accepting notice to quit.

He went back to his room. He made two mugs of hot Bovril, then woke Orrice and Effel. Effel, opening her eyes, gazed up at him in sleepy incomprehension. Orrice came to at once and sat up.

'Rise and shine, my hearties,' said Jim briskly, 'it's nine o'clock. There's hot Bovril. That'll make your noses shine. Then you can wash and dress, and I'll give you a breakfast of boiled eggs. Effel, kindly state your preference, soft-boiled or hard-boiled?'

Effel pulled the sheet up over her face in a rush of shyness.

'We both like soft-boiled,' said Orrice. 'Crikey, I dunno we ever met anyone more swell, mister.' He slipped with boyish suppleness from the bed. Jim smiled at the hidden Effel, turned the sheet down and ruffled her hair. Effel blushed. 'Come on, lazybones,' he said.

The little clouds of sadness came back to darken her eyes. She and Orrice still didn't have anyone,

78

just this kind man for a little while. He was going to give them breakfast, and then they would have to start running away all over again, looking for somewhere that would keep the rain off them at night. Effel felt that to get out of the warm bed would bring comfort to an end all too soon. But she got out, the old dressing-gown still wrapped around her slim body. Orrice was gulping his Bovril. She sipped hers with her eyes darting little glances at Jim. The Bovril was flavoursome, the room warm from the fire.

'Now, my beauties, kindly listen,' said Jim. 'Ears to the front, both of you. Stand to attention, Orrice. And you, Effel. That's it, chests out.' Effel winced. She didn't like playing games when she felt sad. 'Now, until things are properly sorted out, I'm going to look after you. That means—'

'Eh?' said Orrice in astonishment. 'Wha'd'yer mean, mister?'

'I mean you and Effel can't be left to wander about,' said Jim, a figure of adult authority in his trousers, shirt, tie and braces. 'Can't be allowed. Not good for you or your futures. Someone's got to take charge of you. To start with, I'll take charge. Hands up all those with objections.'

Neither put a hand up, but Effel whispered, 'Orrice, what's objections?'

'It's like arguin',' said Orrice. 'Mister, yer really goin' to look after us?'

'Can't have you wandering off into nowhere. And it's back to school tomorrow. You're excused today, Effel's got a bone in her leg from too much

79

wandering about yesterday. Now, kids, I want good behaviour, kindness to dogs and cats, no fighting with other kids, and washing behind your ears. Manor Place Public Baths on Fridays, and polished boots and clean hankies every day. No wiping noses on sleeves. Haircut for you sometime, Orrice. Tangles out of your hair today, Effel. Combs and brushes will be used daily. Got all that?'

'Oh, lummy,' said Orrice, 'yer kiddin' us, mister.'

'No, I'm not,' said Jim. 'Anything wrong with your Bovril, Effel?'

Effel, her mouth open, mug clasped in her hands, was staring up at him with a mixture of awe and disbelief. He was a grown-up of a kind new to her, his soldierly speech commanding, his eyes very direct. She saw the left sleeve of his shirt pinned up. She gulped.

'Effel don't always go in for talkin', mister,' said Orrice, 'except when she does yer can't 'ardly stop her and it don't 'alf hurt yer ears. Don't mind 'er now, mister, she likes 'er Bovril all right, don't yer, Effel?'

'Ain't talkin',' gulped Effel, and hid her face by ducking her head and drinking her Bovril.

'See, I told yer, mister,' said Orrice. 'Mister, are yer really goin' to look after us?' He could not help asking the question again. He was fascinated but cautious. A boy of sense, he knew it was his responsibility to protect his little sister. His mum had liked to settle down with the *News of the World* on Sunday afternoons, and would say things like,

80

'Well, yer'll never believe this,' to his dad. Sometimes what she couldn't believe seemed to Orrice to have something to do with girls disappearing and ending up in a Turkish slave market where sultans bought them. Orrice didn't want Effel being bought by any sultan.

Jim noted the boy's serious expression.

'Yes, I really am going to look after the pair of you, Orrice. Can't have you spending your nights on rainy doorsteps. Can't have you taken off to an orphanage unless there's no alternative. I think you're asking if you can trust me.' Jim smiled. 'Good question, Orrice. Well, cross my heart, if I can trust you and Effel to keep your boots polished, your hair combed and your ears washed, you can trust me to look after you. Hold on, we'd better have your opinions. How d'you feel, the two of you, about living with me until your ship comes home? You're entitled to your say.'

Orrice looked at Effel. Effel darted an upward glance at Jim. She edged up on Orrice and nodded vigorously.

'She likes yer, mister,' said Orrice. In his straightforward way, he added, 'I likes yer too.'

'Good,' said Jim briskly. 'Right, then, that's settled. I'll be obliged if you'll be a credit to your mum and dad.' Effel gulped again. 'That hurts a little, Effel? But you'll want to talk about them sometime soon, when it doesn't hurt so much, and you can always talk to me. Now, between us and other people, I'm your uncle and you're my niece and nephew. That's going to save people asking

81

questions. My landlady knows you're here. I've told her you're staying with me for a while. Understand?'

'Yes, mister,' said Orrice, quick on the uptake.

'Not mister, Orrice. Uncle. Uncle Jim. Right? Right, Effel?'

Effel looked at the dressing-gown heaped around her feet and whispered, 'Yes.'

'I'll boil your eggs now, and you can wash and dress afterwards.' Jim lit the gas ring, poured water into a little tin saucepan and put it on. 'You can take your time, and don't forget to comb and brush your hair. I'll be going out. I have to call on your Aunt Gladys and let her know what's happening.'

'Oh, cripes,' said Orrice, 'she'll want to take us to the orphanage.'

'Well, she'll have found you and Effel are missing, but I don't think she'll have gone to the police yet. I think she'll call at your home again sometime today before she does that. She'll feel it's her duty to go to the police eventually. I shall have to comb and brush my own hair, put my best suit on and be nice to her. Wait a moment, you'll both have to come with me, of course.'

'Ain't goin',' breathed Effel.

'Who said that?' asked Jim, popping the eggs gently in.

'Effel said it,' answered up Orrice. 'Effel, we got to do what 'e says.'

'Ain't goin',' said Effel.

'Well, when she's washed and dressed, Orrice, put her in one of those sacks and we'll carry her,' said Jim.

'All right,' said Orrice.

'No, I ain't goin' in that,' said Effel, 'I'll be squeezed to me death, I will. Ain't right, puttin' little girls in sacks.'

'I fink we got a problem with Effel, Uncle Jim,' said Orrice solemnly.

'Ain't goin' in no sacks,' said Effel.

'More comfortable on two legs,' said Jim, timing the eggs.

'A' right,' said Effel.

That settled, Jim served them a breakfast of soft-boiled eggs with slices of bread and margarine. Effel and Orrice sat down at the little table and ate with the healthy appetites of a girl and boy relieved of the worst consequences of their bereavement. After-wards, Jim left them to wash at the handbasin that Mr Palmer, a plumber, had installed in the upstairs lavatory, while he went out to do a little shopping.

'Effel, yer got to.'

'Ain't got to,' said Effel. 'Won't.'

'I'll punch yer,' said Orrice.

'I'll kick yer,' said Effel.

''E won't be yer uncle if yer don't get yer 'air combed.'

'Yes, 'e will, 'e said so.'

'Only if yer got them tangles out.'

'Won't,' said Effel, 'it 'urts.'

'Well, mine 'urt, but I still combed it.'

'You got a boy's 'ead,' said Effel.

'What's the difference, yer soppy date?' asked Orrice.

'Made of wood, that's what,' said Effel. 'Wood don't 'urt like a girl's 'ead does.'

'Effel, yer playing up,' said Orrice, 'I betcher 'e ain't goin' to like it.'

'Oh, a' right,' said Effel, 'you do it for me.'

'Me? Comb yer 'air?'

'Do it,' said Effel, and sat down on a chair.

'Women,' said Orrice disgustedly, but he picked up the comb and went to work. Effel gave tight little yells. The comb tugged and pulled. 'Crikey, what yer got on yer 'ead, anyway?' asked Orrice. 'Barbed wire? I'll do me 'and an injury, I will.'

'Yer pulling me 'ead off,' gasped Effel.

'Yer won't miss it,' said Orrice, 'it ain't been no good to yer. Girl's don't need to 'ave 'eads really. There's nuffink in 'em.'

'Hate yer,' said Effel. 'Want me mum, I do.'

'Don't say fings like that, sis.' Orrice dragged the comb through a tangled strand. 'It don't do no good.'

'No, a' right,' said Effel, and sighed. The comb wrestled with the strand. She gritted her teeth, then said, 'Orrice, where's 'e got to? Ain't 'e comin' back?'

'Our new uncle?'

'Yes, 'im. Oh, yer pullin' me 'air out—' Effel stopped as the door opened and Jim came in, a brown paper carrier bag in his hand.

'A little food for meals,' he said. He looked at Effel. She blushed and dropped her head, the comb standing stiffly in her thick hair. Jim thought that in her dyed black frock, with her hair disordered, she looked a quaint little thing. 'Orrice, what's happened to Effel's hair?'

'I been trying to comb it,' said Orrice.

'Looks like a haystack,' said Jim.

'There y'ar, told yer, Effel,' said Orrice.

'Didn't,' said Effel, eyeing Jim uncertainly.

'We'll see to it,' said Jim. 'First, let's tidy up. Orrice, fill the water jug from the tap in the lav. Effel, put all the breakfast things in that bowl next to the gas ring.'

Effel, about to say she wasn't going to, said instead, 'Me?'

'There's a good girl,' said Jim. 'I'll make the bed. What's that?' He pointed to a shapeless heap on the floor.

'It's Effel's coat,' said Orrice, on his way out with the pitcher.

'Effel?' said Jim, turning the pillows and shaking them.

'Fell orf the chair,' said Effel.

'It's that kind of coat, is it? Pick it up and hand it to me.' Effel picked the coat up and held it out. He took it from her and addressed it. 'Pay attention, coat. Whenever Effel hangs you up or folds you over a chair, kindly don't fall off and look untidy, or you'll be shot at dawn.'

Effel looked at him, trying to make him out, trying to understand how he could be an uncle to her and Orrice, and if he would be a bit grumpy with them. She watched him hang the coat up, then in a slightly reluctant way she began to collect the breakfast things for washing-up. Her mum and dad

85

had never asked her to do things like that. Orrice came back with the pitcher, filled the kettle and put it on the gas ring.

'I'll do the washin'-up, if yer like, Uncle Jim,' he said.

'Good,' said Jim, the bed made. 'Right,' he said, 'morning inspection. Let's have a look at the two of you.' He inspected their faces. 'Good.' He inspected their ears. 'Fairly good. Now for Effel's haystack.' He contemplated the problem of her hair. He was totally a beginner at this sort of thing, and he had no real idea of what Effel and Orrice wanted of him in the way of guardianship. Kindness, naturally. What else? He knew that as a young boy he himself had often longed for simple fun. Simple fun didn't happen too often at orphanages. He knew what he wanted from Effel and Orrice. Cleanliness, a reasonable amount of obedience, and a commendable amount of self-respect. He couldn't let them run wild, however engaging they might be. 'Right, you do the washing-up, Orrice, and I'll mount an attack on Effel's haystack.'

Effel gritted her teeth as he began work with the comb. He drew it through the ends of tangled strands, and the tangles gave way. The comb moved further up. Effel bore it mutinously but bravely. Her hair began to feel soft to the comb, to run through the teeth with faint whispers. The strands eventually hung tidily over her neck. Jim thought about the necessity of new lodgings. He had made two calls while he was out, but neither had opened up the possibility of three rooms. It was not going to be as easy as renting one room or two. Not many households had three rooms to offer. Three rooms meant the whole of the upstairs in most cases. He had better get a move on.

Effel's hair shone. It ran freely and took the comb freely. Its natural little waves rippled. It was, however, in need of a wash. So, probably, was Orrice's. It was difficult for any kids to keep clean in Walworth, and the sooty atmosphere was no respecter of hair. But there were advantages in living in the area. There were a large number of streets in which the compact terraced houses, built while Queen Victoria was still alive, offered homely accommodation to people able to afford the very reasonable rents. Also, living was cheap, the East Street market a boon. A seasonal glut of vegetables or fruit could mean giveaway prices. Lastly, the people, with few exceptions, had hearts of gold. So one put up with the dust of summer and the soot of winter.

Orrice, washing-up done, took a look at his sister's hair.

'Crikey,' he said, 'yer got proper hair, Effel, yer look like a girl.'

'I'll kick you,' muttered Effel.

'No kicking,' said Jim, 'it's a punishable offence.'

'Cor, a wallopin', I bet,' said Orrice.

'I ain't goin' to be walloped,' said Effel.

'Probably no sugar in your tea,' said Jim.

Effel, looking down at her feet, said, 'What's me 'air like?'

Jim moved behind her, placed his hands on her

ribs and lifted her until she could see herself in the mirror above the mantelpiece. He was aware of her young body stiffening in his hold. He set her down.

'How's that?' he asked lightly.

'It's a' right,' said Effel. The look of her hair had actually been a surprise to her, but she was guarded this morning in her attitude towards him. He took some new yellow ribbon from the carrier bag, cut a length with scissors and tied it round her hair, Orrice in wonder that he did it with only one hand, even making a bow.

'Right,' said Jim, 'now we're going out to call on your Aunt Gladys, and then invite prospective landladies to see what my niece and nephew look like with clean faces, clean ears and combed hair. Hats on. No coats. It's a nice day. Good grief, that's a hat, Effel?' He regarded the battered boater with a smile. In the morning light it was his first real look at it. It sat a little tiredly on Effel's head. 'Yes, very nice, Effel, but what's that on your mop, Orrice?' Orrice looked all huge cap and no eyes.

'It's me cap,' he said, 'me dad give it me last year, 'e didn't want it no more.'

'I see, off we go, then,' said Jim. He led the way out, Orrice closing the door behind them. They went down the stairs. Mrs Palmer appeared in the little passage.

'Morning, Mr Cooper, these children's your niece and nephew?' she enquired.

'This is Ethel, and that's Horace,' said Jim.

'My, I never seen cleaner faces,' smiled Mrs Palmer. But she thought their parents must be very poor, because their clothes were pitifully shabby. Still, clean faces could count for more than clothes. 'They look sweet, Mr Cooper.'

Orrice turned pink under his cap. Fancy being called sweet. And when he was a growing boy and all.

'Fairly tolerable handfuls, Mrs Palmer,' said Jim, 'and I'm taking them out to help me search for new lodgings.'

'Oh, yes, and I got some names and addresses for you,' she said. 'They're people that's got rooms to let.' She pulled a piece of paper from her apron pocket and gave it to Jim.

'Much obliged,' he said. 'Thanks. Come on, kids.'

They left the house, with Orrice muttering, 'I'm a boy, I am. I 'ope she don't go tellin' everyone I'm sweet, 'cos I ain't. And I dunno you could say Effel is.'

'Oh, Effel will pass with a push,' said Jim. He offered the little girl his hand as they were about to cross Walworth Road. Effel made instinctively to take it, then drew back. She still wasn't sure of things, nor of him. He wasn't her dad, nor like her dad.

He took them to Kennington, Orrice directing him to Aunt Glad's house. Brother and sister walked down the street a little way and awaited the outcome of the interview.

Aunt Glad, just about to make another trip to Deacon Street in the hope of finding the missing orphans there, answered a knock on her door. A

89

gentleman of kindness smiled at her and lifted his hat. She noted his lost arm.

'Good morning,' said Jim, 'are you Mrs Williams, Mrs Gladys Williams?'

'Yes, that's me,' said Aunt Glad, taken with his politeness. 'To what do I owe the pleasure, Mr—?'

'Cooper, Jim Cooper. I've come about your niece and nephew, Ethel and Horace Withers.'

'Oh, lor' – oh, they're all right, ain't they?' Aunt Glad's worry over them leapt into apprenhension. She associated Jim's civility with authority. Something had happened to Orrice and Effel. 'They've not 'ad an accident, 'ave they?'

'No, nothing like that, Mrs Williams, nothing at all to worry about.' Jim was reassuring.

'But I am worried, I been thinkin' about goin' to the police, you've got to tell me if they're all right.'

'They are. Could I talk to you? Have you got time? The children spoke well of you.'

'Oh, come in, come in,' said Aunt Glad. She took him into her parlour, traditionally crowded with furniture, and the windows hung with old lace curtains. 'I was just goin' to Deacon Street to look for them. Me and me 'ubby went the other night when they didn't come back 'ere for the supper I 'ad ready for them. We couldn't 'ardly believe the note Orrice left, sayin' they were goin' to Southend and 'oping to get a boat to Australia. Oh, them poor loves, thinkin' Uncle Perce an' me only wanted to get rid of them.'

'No, they didn't think that, Mrs Williams,' said Jim, 'they simply didn't want to be a trouble to you.'

'Do sit down, I'm sure,' said Aunt Glad, uncertain about him, but liking his open and friendly look. Authority didn't usually look friendly, nor have a missing arm. 'How did you know about them, 'ave you got them at a police station somewhere?'

Jim, seated, carefully explained the position, and gave her details of what had befallen her niece and nephew.

'They're fine now, Mrs Williams.'

Astonished, Aunt Glad said, 'You took them in, Mr Cooper?'

'It seemed the best thing to do,' said Jim. 'Orrice thought, of course, that his little note to you would relieve you of worry. Kids think in simple terms, I suppose. He thought running away would be a very simple solution. Mrs Williams, I'll come to the point. I've no family myself, I'm a bachelor relying on kind landladies to put me up, and as I'll soon be moving to new lodgings, with room for the children, I'm quite willing to look after them until such time as things might be better for you and your husband, when you might want to look after them yourselves.'

'Well, bless me soul,' said Aunt Glad in new astonishment, and eyed him searchingly. She couldn't see anything about his looks or his appearance that made her feel he was a dubious piece of work. And she was sensible enough to realize that if he had anything shifty or underhand in mind, then he wouldn't have come to see her. 'Well, I don't know as I could rightly say, Mr

Cooper, I can't think at the moment what to say at all.' She gave him another look. 'You been in the war, Mr Cooper?'

'In the infantry,' said Jim.

'It cost you yer arm,' said Aunt Glad.

'It wouldn't have been any good to me the way it was at the time.'

Out of a mixture of worry, relief and uncertainty, came a little smile from Aunt Glad. Perce had a bit of a sense of humour himself, he didn't let things get him down any more than this man with the nice kind eyes did.

''Ave you got a decent job?' she asked.

'With the United Kingdom Club,' said Jim, although he didn't know if she would think kitchen work decent for a man.

'I don't know if it would be all right, a man by hisself lookin' after a boy an' girl, I just don't know. I just know me and me 'usband couldn't be sure we could bring them up proper 'ere, we got five of our own. If we 'ad more room and a bit more money comin' in – well, I don't want anyone to think we don't care for Orrice and Effel—'

'It's impossible for you, Mrs Williams,' said Jim, 'but it's not for me. I'd like to give it a go.' He wondered if he wasn't being daft. Perhaps he was. But it wasn't such a bad thing, living for a couple of kids instead of just for himself. 'I'll leave it to you and your husband, I'll understand whatever decision you make.'

'Yes, I'll 'ave to talk to 'im,' said Aunt Glad. 'Mr Cooper, it'll be 'ard for you, won't it, tryin' to

92

manage two children, an' you sore disabled?'

'Oh, I'm luckier than some,' said Jim, 'and I think I could manage. Besides, it's not good for any of us to live too long on our own. You get set in your ways, and selfish. I'll be a crochety old hermit by the time I'm forty, unless I change my ways. Looking after Ethel and Horace would be a great help.' His smile made him look as if he was mildly laughing at himself. He had, in fact, escaped the gloom and misery of becoming a soured man. His inherent equability enabled him to dwell more on the good things of life than the bad.

'Well, I got to say that though I've only just met you, I'm sure you won't ever get crochety, Mr Cooper,' said Aunt Glad with a surprisingly nice smile. 'You've got to be a good man to offer a home to Orrice and Effel, and if it turned out all right, me an' me 'usband would 'ave cause to be thankful to yer. Yes, I'll speak to 'im, but I'd 'ave to know a bit more about you first.'

'You're entitled to know,' said Jim. 'My parents are dead, unfortunately, but I've grandparents still alive down in Hampshire.' That was pure wishful thinking, of course, born of the thought of a hopeful journey to his mother's birthplace one day. 'My job at the United Kingdom Club is steady—'

'Oh, I'm sure,' said Aunt Glad.

'It makes for steady living,' said Jim. 'And I'm lodging with Mr and Mrs Palmer at sixteen Morecambe Street in Walworth. Until I move, that is. I'll let you know my new address. I'd make sure, of course, that the children get their schooling and behave themselves.'

'Oh, I'm sure,' said Aunt Glad again. She liked him, and she liked the possibility that Orrice and Effel would have someone who'd care for them and be kind to them. 'Effel's a bit funny at times, when she won't talk to no-one except 'er brother. She follers 'im about like 'is own shadow.'

'Engaging,' smiled Jim.

'Mind, as well as 'aving to speak to me 'usband, I'd best 'ave a talk with Orrice and Effel too. Are they at your lodgings, Mr Cooper?' Impressed though she was by his looks and manner, Aunt Glad knew the matter could go no further unless Orrice and Effel were both in favour. And Effel was quite likely to want a mother, not a father.

'They're only down the road, Mrs Williams,' said Jim. 'They're waiting. I thought it best for you and me to have this little chat before bringing them to your door.' He did not need to put on an act. He was a friendly man of naturally friendly conversation. He spoke easily to the children's aunt, and naturally. 'I'll call them.' He got up and went to the front door, opened it and stepped outside. There they were, waiting a little way down the street. He signalled to them. Orrice began to run. Effel yelled in a tantrum and stayed where she was. Orrice stopped, turned and went back to her. She aimed a kick at him. Orrice, quite used to that, dodged it, took her by the hand and brought her.

'Effel's playing up,' he said.

'You run orf wivout me,' said Effel.

'Come on,' said Jim, 'your aunt's waiting to find out if you want to live with me.'

Aunt Glad very much wanted to find that out. Orrice made no bones about being affirmative, and accepted his aunt's reproach for running away and giving her and Uncle Perce more worry. Effel stood on one leg, plucked at her frock, stood on two legs, darted uncertain glances and finally said, 'Ain't saying.'

'Effel?' said Aunt Glad.

'Effel, you got to say,' complained Orrice.

'No, I ain't,' said Effel, looking at her feet.

'Well, this don't look very 'appy, Mr Cooper,' sighed Aunt Glad. She knew she simply couldn't let Orrice and Effel live with a man who was really a stranger unless they were both happy about it.

'Oh, come on, Effel, yer daft date,' said Orrice fretfully.

'Effel, you only need to say yes or no, love,' said Aunt Glad kindly, 'yer Uncle Perce an' me will understand.'

'Want to go wiv Orrice,' muttered Effel.

'I'm goin' wiv Mr Cooper,' said Orrice determinedly.

'A' right,' said Effel, still looking at her feet.

'Effel, d'you mean you'd like to 'ave Mr Cooper look after you?' asked Aunt Glad.

'A' right,' said Effel.

'Are you sure?' asked Jim gently.

'Yes, a' right,' said Effel, and in shyness stood on one leg again.

'Well, Mr Cooper, I best speak to me 'usband,

and I expect he'll come round an' see you this evening,' said Aunt Glad.

'D'you think he'd call at the United Kingdom Club?' asked Jim. 'I'll be at work there this evening. My landlady will be keeping an eye on the children.'

'Me 'usband won't mind seein' you there,' said Aunt Glad. A smile flickered. She looked at Orrice and Effel. 'There, lovies, p'raps it's goin' to turn out all right for you. We'll see what yer Uncle Perce says.'

'Fanks ever so much, Aunt Glad,' said Orrice. He thought. 'We likes Mr Cooper. Don't we, sis?'

'Ain't saying,' said Effel.

'Aunt Glad, I'm goin' to 'ave to belt Effel if she don't stop playing up,' said Orrice.

'No belting, Orrice,' said Jim.

Aunt Glad smiled.

After they had gone, she put on her hat and coat, and went to call on Mrs Palmer of sixteen Morecambe Street, Walworth. What she was told by Mrs Palmer about Mr Cooper put her mind completely at rest, and she fully understood why he had referred to the children as his niece and nephew. She felt she could be recommendable when speaking to her husband.

Uncle Perce received the news with interest and optimism. Still, he'd better go and see the bloke. Aunt Glad said Mr Cooper wasn't a bloke, he was a gent and a soldier of the war who'd lost his left arm. Don't you go throwing your weight about when you see him, all you got to do is talk to him sensible, and man to man, and see if you think we'd be right to let him have Orrice and Effel. Have you got that, Percy Williams? Uncle Perce said he'd got it all right, in his earhole. Aunt Glad said I'll give you earhole. Her eldest boy Johnny cut in to say his dad was a barmy comic. Aunt Glad, rounding on her son, said don't you talk about your father like that or I'll box your ears.

Acceptable family ructions prevailed.

CHAPTER SIX

Jim had some hopeful prospects for lodgings, at the addresses given to him by Mrs Palmer. He was committed to guardianship now. Not by law, by promise. When he reached Walworth Road, he did not offer to take Effel's hand. Effel, he knew, was going to make up her own mind about what kind of relationship she wanted with him. But as he crossed the busy road with her and Orrice, he placed his hand lightly on her shoulder.

Reaching Browning Street, he said, 'Anyone tired?'

'Not me,' said Orrice, thinking his mum and dad would be pleased for him and Effel because they'd found a new uncle. 'You tired, sis?'

'Course not,' said Effel, who had followed her brother on foot all the way to Ruskin Park more than once.

'Right,' said Jim, 'on we go then, footsloggers, to Rodney Road.'

Orrice went happily, Effel with her old boater bobbing. Today was a different day for them. Yesterday had been mournful, offset only by desperate little hopes. Today they had someone who was going to keep them out of an orphanage, someone who had a funny way of talking to them

and a smile in his eyes. Orrice was responsive, Effel
still shy and cautious. The images of their mum and
dad were still with them, trapped in their grieving
minds, but hopes for a life acceptable without their
parents were no longer desperate. They did not have
to be nervous of people looking nor of policemen
stopping them and asking them questions. They
could leave everything to the man who had only one
arm and called himself their Uncle Jim.

'Does it 'urt, please?' It was a sudden impulsive
question from Effel as they walked towards Brandon Street, where Samuel Peabody, American
philanthropist, had erected a block of flats for poor
people.

'Does what hurt?' asked Jim. 'Looking for
lodgings?'

'I fink she means yer arm, Uncle Jim,' said
Orrice.

'Oh, that.' Jim smiled. 'It hurt at the time, it
doesn't hurt now.'

'Why?' asked Effel.

'Well, because it's better than it was,' said Jim.

'Is it nice being better?' asked Effel.

'Course it is, yer daft lump,' said Orrice. 'I
dunno, the questions she asks. We're best off,
Uncle, when she ain't talkin'.'

'Why?' asked Effel.

'Why d'yer keep askin' why?' asked Orrice.

''Cos I do, that's why,' said Effel.

They crossed Brandon Street into Stead Street.
This was the poorer quarter of Walworth, where
people were hard put to rise above the breadline.

Parish relief was an indispensable part of existence for many families here. Lucky was any family that had a steady and stalwart breadwinner. And such families moved as soon as they could to the neater, better-looking streets, such as those near the town hall like Wansey Street, Ethel Street and Larcom Street. Jim knew, however, that the cockneys never wholly lost their earthy humour or their spirit of defiance. There were exceptions, of course, there were those who descended to drinking cheap methylated spirits. That took them fast to delirium and the grave.

Reaching Rodney Road, with its mixture of dwellings, some good in stolid Victorian fashion and some indifferent, Jim continued on with his foundlings. He thought of them as his foundlings, having discovered them when they were newly orphaned.

'Head up, Effel. Step smartly there, Orrice. Eyes open for number twenty-one, in which resides Mrs Tompkins, according to Mrs Palmer.'

'Yer comical, Uncle Jim,' said Orrice.

'Hope not,' said Jim. 'Won't do for your guardian to be comical.'

'Why?' asked Effel.

'Oh, lor', she's off,' said Orrice.

'I likes comical,' said Effel.

'All right, I'll do comical faces for you at Christmas,' said Jim. 'Here we are, number twenty-one. Face still clean, Effel? Good. Cap on straight, Orrice? Good. But where's your face?'

'Under me cap,' said Orrice.

'Thought you'd lost it,' said Jim. Effel actually giggled. 'Knock, Orrice,' said Jim.

Orrice reached for the knocker and thumped it. The door opened almost at once. A long-limbed, gawky-looking woman, calico apron over her black skirt and grey blouse, regarded Orrice severely.

'Young man, you after bashin' me door down?' she asked, and Effel hid herself behind Jim.

'I only knocked, missus, honest,' said Orrice, 'but yer get some knockers that's a bit 'ard on a door. Course, yer don't always know, if it's yer first time of knockin'.'

'Don't give me no lip,' said the woman. 'Like a roll of thunder, it was, and near shook the roof orf me 'ouse.' She eyed Jim in curiosity.

'Mrs Tompkins?' he said.

'I'm her.'

'I understand you've got rooms to let.'

'So I have. Who might you be enquiring on account of, may I ask?'

'Self and the children,' said Jim.

'No children,' said Mrs Tompkins, 'got enough of me own. There's two rooms for a single gent. No children, specially not the kind that go bashin' doors in.'

'Well, sorry you've been troubled,' said Jim.

'It's no trouble, mister, it's just how it is.'

'Good morning,' said Jim.

'Pity you're not a single gent,' said the woman. 'You got nice looks.'

'You're not bad yourself,' said Jim. 'Come on, kids.' He led them away.

Effel said, 'Is Orrice a basher?'

'Well, he was to Mrs Tompkins.'

''E better not bash me,' said Effel, 'I'll kick 'im if 'e does.'

'No bashing or kicking,' said Jim, and consulted Mrs Palmer's little list. 'Right, Chatham Street next. That's where a few Billingsgate porters hang out. Orrice, if you've got some cotton wool on you, fill Effel's ears with it.'

'What's cotton wool?' asked Effel.

'Wadding, yer date,' said Orrice.

'I ain't got earache,' said Effel.

'You might have, if any of the porters are home from their work,' said Jim. 'We'll chance it.'

They walked the short distance to Chatham Street, the day crisply bright. Some women were gossiping at open doors. A man was sitting on a doorstep smoking a clay pipe. He watched Jim's approach.

'I got one like that, mate,' he said, pointing his pipe at Jim's empty sleeve.

'If you want a pair, you can have mine,' said Jim, 'I never use it.'

The sitting man, one-armed, bellowed with laughter and roared a few boisterous words after Jim and the kids. Orrice whistled in amazement.

'Cor, I ain't 'eard many like that,' he said.

Two gossiping women eyed the trio. Jim was in search of number fifteen.

''Ello, ducks,' said one, 'yer got kids, I see, so what yer lookin' for down 'ere, yer fairy godmother? Yer can 'ave me, if yer like, I got 'alf an hour to spare.' Her companion shrieked raucously.

'I'm a bit busy at the moment,' said Jim, passing them by, 'I'll drop in later.'

Effel gasped. 'Oh, you ain't goin' to leave us, are yer, mister?'

'It was just a joke, Effel,' said Jim.

'Don't like it 'ere,' said Effel.

'Good point, Effel. We'll give it a miss. Let's see.' He stopped to look at the list again, at the last address. The two women called, loudly encouraging him to make up his mind. 'Right, off we go again, Effel. Dawes Street, Orrice. Other side of East Street. Wait.' He checked the time by his pocket watch. 'Gone twelve, d'you know that? Shall we feed our faces first. What d'you say?'

'I'm 'ungry, please,' said Effel.

'Uncle Jim, I got to tell yer, I'm near faint,' said Orrice.

'We'd better cure that,' said Jim, and walked on with them.

'Effel 'ad stomach rumbles yesterday,' said Orrice.

'Didn't,' protested Effel.

'Yes, yer did, and in the market too. Sounded like a train was comin'.'

'Didn't,' said Effel.

'Yes, it did,' said Orrice, 'and through a tunnel too. Still, she ain't bad for a girl, Uncle.'

'No, you're not at all bad, are you, Effel?' said Jim.

Effel, thinking about that, said, 'I'm 'ungry.'

'How about eggs and bacon?' asked Jim.

'Oh, crikey, not 'alf,' said Orrice. 'Effel likes eggs an' bacon, don't yer, sis?'

'Want a piggy-back,' said Effel.

'Oh, all right,' said Orrice. They stopped. 'Come on up, then.'

Effel, suddenly springy, leapt on to her brother's back. Orrice hoisted her, wound his arms around her legs, and carried her.

'On to eggs and bacon, then,' said Jim.

'Uncle Jim, we got money of our own, like I told yer,' said Orrice.

'We'll save that,' said Jim, 'for birthdays and Christmas.'

'An' rainy days, like me dad used to say,' said Effel, jigging on her brother's back.

'Crikey, she's talkin',' said Orrice.

Toni's Refreshments beckoned the hungry. It was half-full at the moment. It would be quite full by one, customers dining on eggs and bacon and a variety of sandwiches, the latter all made with new, crusty bread. Maria was busy slicing a loaf, Toni busy cooking on gas rings. He dished up bacon with two fried eggs, plus bread and butter, to a stallholder. Following which, his expressive eyes popped as they beheld a young boy and a small girl entering in company with Jim Cooper. Jim took them to a table, then came to the counter.

'Kids,' said Toni, 'I don't-a believe it, not again. What-a you doing with them, Jim?'

'They're mine,' said Jim.

'No, no,' said Toni, 'not them kids. Look at that, would you believe?'

Orrice was waving to Maria. Maria smiled and waved back.

'Orphans,' said Jim. 'My niece and nephew.'

'*Mama mia*,' said Toni, 'them kids?'

'They're all right,' said Jim. 'Eggs and bacon three times, Toni, with bread and butter.'

'Crazy country,' said Toni, putting rashers into the pan. 'Just-a like Italy. Always kids. Good luck, eh?'

'We all need a bit,' said Jim.

When the plates were set in front of Orrice and Effel, they stared at the food in delight. There was also a glass of fizzy lemonade each.

'Fank yer,' said Orrice from his heart. Effel mumbled her gratitude. Jim returned to the counter.

'Orrice,' whispered Effel, picking up her knife and fork, 'd'you fink 'e might get grumpy wiv us sometimes?'

'Well, he ain't got grumpy yet,' said Orrice, 'and I like 'im.'

Jim came back with his own meal.

'Right,' he said, 'for what we are about to receive—?'

'May the Lord make us truly fankful,' said Orrice.

'You already started,' whispered Effel.

'Everyone start,' said Jim.

Effel ate a mouthful of bread and butter and

bacon, then took a rapturous swallow of the fizzy lemonade. Her stomach gurgled and a little burp arrived. She went fiery red.

'Train's comin' through the tunnel again,' said Orrice. Effel's stomach gave another gurgle. 'It's got stuck in the tunnel. That's what,' said Orrice.

'It ain't, it ain't,' said Effel, and cast an embarrassed glance at Jim. He winked.

Effel ducked her head.

The homely-looking woman at the door of her house in Dawes Street said apologetically, 'I'm that sorry, but it's only one room. It's got a gas ring and a fireplace, but it's just the one room, and we had a single gentleman in mind.'

'Can't be helped,' said Jim, Orrice beside him, and Effel behind Orrice. Out of curiosity, he asked, 'Don't you sometimes have single ladies in mind?' There were thousands of single ladies, robbed by the huge casualties of the war.

'Oh, single gents don't get as fussy as single ladies.'

'I see,' said Jim. 'Well, thank you. Come on, kids.'

'Oh, just a minute, mister,' said the homely woman. 'I just remembered, I heard tell from a friend of mine that an acquaintance of hers has got rooms goin' in Wansey Street. That's up by the town hall. You could try there. It's number nineteen, name of Pilgrim.'

'Pilgrim?'

'That's right. Good luck.'

'Thanks,' said Jim, and because the matter of

suitable lodgings was important and pressing, he set off with Effel and Orrice for one more call. 'Anyone tired yet?'

'I ain't,' said Orrice.

'I'm a bit,' said Effel.

'All right,' said Jim, 'we'll go back home and Effel can have forty winks. You can keep an eye on her, Orrice, while I go to Wansey Street.'

'I s'pose that's best,' said Orrice, who would have preferred to keep going the rounds.

'Ain't goin',' muttered Effel.

'Ain't goin' where?' asked Orrice.

'Ain't goin' where 'e said,' muttered Effel.

'Oh, dearie me, oh, bless me soul,' said Orrice pityingly, 'where are yer goin', then?'

'Wansey Street,' said Effel.

'I dunno we're ever goin' to make anyfing of Effel, Uncle Jim,' said Orrice, as they crossed the market into Orb Street. 'First she says she ain't goin', then she says she is. Women, I dunno.'

'Changed me mind,' mumbled Effel.

'Women,' said Jim, and laughed. He had a purpose in all this walking. It kept these two active, it kept them from sitting and grieving. He knew their sadness was still present. It showed in Effel's little moments of quietness, and in Orrice sometimes saying, 'Me dad—' and then stopping. Being out and about was, thought Jim, the best thing for them at the moment.

Wansey Street, next to the town hall, had a distinctly superior look, the terraced houses well-kept, stone window sills a clean light brown, polished windows dancing with light in the April sunshine.

'Well, I dunno, Uncle, do you?' said Orrice. 'I dunno it ain't a bit too respectable.'

'You're respectable, Orrice. So is Effel.' Jim smiled. 'Neither of you have been nicked for pinching or disturbing the peace, have you?'

'What, me and Effel?' said Orrice.

'You haven't. Good,' said Jim. 'And you've both been kind to old ladies, I'm sure.'

'What old ladies?' asked Orrice, looking at a middle-aged lady crossing the street. Her respectability was very evident. She was carrying a rolled umbrella, and had a crisp feather in her hat. Crikey, he thought, if they came to live here, would Effel have to wear a feather in her boater? It wouldn't last long, she'd tease cats with it.

'I think we'll all pass with a push,' said Jim. Number nineteen had iron railings and two steps. He knocked. There was no answer. He knocked again. Still no answer. He tried a third knock in hope. There was no response.

'They're out, that's what,' said Orrice.

'Why?' asked Effel, who thought they ought to be in.

'Now 'ow do I know?' said Orrice. 'They got to be out or they'd come and answer.'

'We'll call again,' said Jim. 'But back home now. I have to leave at half-past three for my work. Mrs Palmer's going to treat you to tea later, and then I want you early to bed, my beauties. Have you got toothbrushes?'

'We don't 'ave none of them,' said Orrice, 'we got socks and uvver fings, we ain't got no toothbrushes.'

'That's got to be put right,' said Jim, walking them home, 'or all Effel's teeth will drop out before she's ten. So will yours, before you're twelve.'

'All of 'em?' said Orrice.

'Every one,' said Jim.

'Crikey, Effel,' said Orrice, 'yer'll be a toothless 'ag like old Ma Ricket when yer ten.'

'Course I won't,' said Effel. 'Will I?' she asked Jim.

'We'll save you from that, Effel. Which school do you two go to?'

'Sayer Street,' said Orrice.

'Ain't goin' there no more,' said Effel.

'Who said that?' asked Jim, walking between them along Walworth Road.

'Effel did,' said Orrice.

'Didn't,' said Effel.

'Well, it wasn't old Mother Riley,' said Orrice.

'Ain't goin',' said Effel.

'Don't either of you like Sayer Street School?' asked Jim.

'Not much,' said Orrice.

Jim thought. St John's Church School in Larcom Street would be a good option. Nobody knew them there. Nobody would ask them too many questions. And if they could get lodgings in Wansey Street, St John's School would be only a stone's throw away.

'All right,' he said, 'we'll call in at St John's now

109

and see the headmistress. We've got time.'

Mrs Wainwright, headmistress at St John's, looked the two children up and down. Effel exhibited nervous fidgets. Orrice, cap off, was respectful but not overawed. Jim was quite equal to the atmosphere in the study.

'Their guardian, Mr Cooper?' enquired Mrs Wainwright politely, a slender lady of fifty.

'With the agreement of their next-of-kin, their aunt and uncle, Mr and Mrs Williams of thirty-one Penton Place, Kennington,' said Jim, with all the easy conviction of a man who believed that what made sense was preferable to what was fiddlingly exact. Besides, it was as good as true, never mind that his role hadn't been legalized. Further, he had taken to the kids, and he knew it. They represented a challenge to his set ways as a bachelor. 'I did myself the compliment of telling myself it would work out better for them than life in an orphanage. I'm a close friend, of course.' He did not say to whom he was close.

'Dear me, such responsibility for a man,' said the headmistress.

'For a woman too, I should think,' said Jim.

'A woman is a more natural guardian.' The headmistress, slightly severe of manner, nevertheless offered that comment with a smile. Jim responded with a nod of agreement. 'I have to admire your gesture, Mr Cooper, it's very Christian. But is it necessary to take the children away from their present school?'

'Not necessary, no, but St John's will be nearer, and I prefer church schools. Also, Ethel and Horace favour the change.'

'Well.' Mrs Wainwright did some thoughtful musing. 'How old did you say they were?'

'Ethel's seven, Horace is ten.'

'Your birthday, Ethel?' enquired the head-mistress kindly.

Effel looked for a moment as if she was going to say she wasn't telling. Jim's hand fell lightly on her shoulder, and she said, 'Feb'ry fourf.'

'Fourth,' said Mrs Wainwright who, with her teachers, spent many hours trying to get cockney children to sound their aitches and distinguish between 'f' and 'th'. 'And yours, Horace?'

'Jan'ry ten, missus,' said Orrice.

'Ma'am,' said Mrs Wainwright.

'Yes'm,' said Orrice, and she looked at him. His fresh face was almost angelic, hiding the pugnacity of his spirit. She made a note on her desk pad, then said, 'Long trousers when he's only ten, Mr Cooper?'

Knowing Orrice liked his long trousers, Jim said, 'Well, shorts and brittle knees don't go too well together.'

'Horace has brittle knees?'

'Long trousers do give them some protection,' said Jim.

'He may get laughed at,' said the headmistress. Few boys went into long trousers before the age of fourteen.

'He'll speak up for himself,' said Jim.

111

'Yes'm, I got a tongue,' said Orrice. 'Me dad always said—' He stopped.

'It's all right, Horace,' said Mrs Wainwright, a kind heart beneath her starched white blouse. 'Very well, Mr Cooper, they may begin on Monday.'

'Not tomorrow?'

'Give them until Monday,' said Mrs Wainwright understandingly. Children bereaved needed a little time to face up to school.

'I'm very obliged,' said Jim.

Surprisingly, Effel spoke up.

'Fank you, miss,' she said.

'*Thank* you,' said the headmistress with a slightly pained smile. 'Thank you, ma'am.'

'Yes, fank you,' said Effel.

'Oh, dear,' said Mrs Wainwright.

'It'll come right in the end,' said Jim, and his warm and cheerful goodbye left her feeling pleased to have obliged him.

'Right,' said Jim at twenty-five past three, 'I'm off in five minutes. That leaves you in charge, Orrice.'

'I gotcher, Uncle Jim,' said Orrice. They had just had a nice cup of tea, and a currant bun each, bought from the baker's by Jim first thing this morning.

''Oo you in charge of?' whispered Effel.

'You,' said Orrice.

'Crumbs,' said Effel, feeling that made her valuable.

'Stand guard over Effel, and all our worldly goods, Orrice,' said Jim, 'and make sure you're

112

both in bed by nine o'clock. At five, Mrs Palmer will call you down and treat you to a rattling good tea. Best behaviour, don't forget, and clean hands. Tomorrow morning we'll see about buying clothes and toothbrushes for you.'

'We got clothes, we brought some,' said Orrice.

'Yes, I've seen them,' said Jim. 'Very nice. But you'll both need more, especially for school. After that, we'll call again at that house in Wansey Street. Well, that's all for now. So long. Be good now.'

When he had gone, Effel said uncertainly, ''E's comin' back, Orrice, ain't 'e?'

'Course 'e is, sis, 'e lives 'ere. If 'e didn't come back, 'e wouldn't 'ave nowhere to live.'

'I just asked,' said Effel, 'that's all. I just asked.'

'All right,' said Orrice.

'Orrice, d'you like 'im?'

'Course I do, soppy, don't you?'

'Ain't saying,' said Effel.

When Jim reached the club, the manager intercepted him.

'A word, Jim. We're losing Bob Edwards, he's going to Australia with his family next month. Look here, you're too good for kitchen work. How would you like to take Edwards's place and help us keep the books?'

Jim had never done book-keeping in his life, but he gave the offer instantly favourable thought.

'Well,' he said, brain ticking over.

'It pays thirty bob a week, you know.'

'I'm a bit rusty,' said Jim.

113

'You've got three weeks to brush it up.'

'Fine,' said Jim, making a mental note to borrow relevant reference books from the library. The extra shillings a week would be a great help. Especially now. 'I'm grateful for the opportunity.'

'Better than kitchen work for a man like you, Jim. Better hours too, eight-thirty to five-thirty.'

That, thought Jim, was a clincher. He decided something of a very pleasant kind was happening to his life.

Library, here I come. Lodgings, show yourselves.

Later that evening, Uncle Perce called at the club. The manager gave Jim fifteen minutes to talk to his visitor. It didn't take Uncle Perce more than ten minutes to sum up this man. Aunt Glad had been right. He was a bit of a real gent, and an old soldier, and what's more, a bloke you could talk to and listen to.

'Good on yer, mate,' said Uncle Perce in the end. 'I tell yer, I'm grateful the kids bumped into you. I got trust in you. Put it there.' He shook hands heartily with Jim. 'They're good kids.'

'Yes, I like them,' said Jim.

'Good on yer,' said Uncle Perce again, and it was settled.

Back in the house a little after midnight, he found Effel and Orrice deep in slumber. By the light of the candle he looked down at them. Effel lay with all her childish woes in limbo. In her modesty, she was wearing the old dressing-gown again, the collar tucked up around her neck. She was lying on her side, her open mouth touching the pillow. Little burbles of sound travelled muffledly over the pillow. Orrice lay on his stomach, face quite buried, his breathing deep and relaxed.

With healthy sleep claiming them, they were out of their forlorn little world for the moment. They had endured bravely. They had not walked the streets weeping. They were lovely kids.

CHAPTER SEVEN

There was a neatly penned notice on a postcard in the window of the newsagents in Walworth Road. It read very well.

'*A Suite of Rooms to let for two Respectable Single Ladies at 19 Wansey Street.*'

It had been put in the window that morning at a cost of tuppence a week.

Inside the house, Miss Rebecca Pilgrim was polishing the stairs banister when the front door knocker sounded. She descended the stairs, placed the cloth and tin of polish in the drawer of the hallstand, and opened the door. On the step stood a middle-aged woman heavily stout, and a young woman perceptibly thin.

'Morning, you the one that's got rooms to let?' enquired the former from under a loud purple hat.

Miss Pilgrim regarded the callers frostily.

'They're for two single ladies,' she said.

'We're single,' said the stout woman. 'Well, I'm widdered and Amelia ain't married yet. D'yer mind showing us the rooms and telling us 'ow much the rent is?'

'There are three rooms,' said Miss Pilgrim, and paused. 'The rent is a pound a week.' She had actually decided on twelve shillings.

116

'A pound?' The stout woman quivered. ''Oo yer kiddin'? Yer don't think a body can pay that, do yer?'

'I'm sorry, then. Good morning.' Miss Pilgrim closed the door. The knocker was rapped immediately. She reopened the door. 'Yes?'

'All right,' said the stout woman, 'we'll offer ten bob. Can't say fairer than that, no-one could. Yer got to be kiddin' when yer say a pound.'

'Good morning,' repeated Miss Pilgrim stiffly, and closed the door again. The letter-box flap was pushed open and the stout woman shouted through it.

'Yer 'eartless haybag, I'll 'ave yer up for extortin', you wait!'

Miss Pilgrim took out the cloth and polish, and went back to the work of making the shining banister shinier. One could accept the eccentricities of many of the poor people of Walworth. One did not have to accept the loud and blowsy, however sensitive were one's Christian instincts. To have a woman like that in the house was unthinkable. Miss Pilgrim asked for forgiveness on account of the little lie she had told, and went on polishing.

The knocker summoned her again fifteen minutes later. This time a pleasant-looking woman was there.

'Good morning, I've just seen the notice in the newsagents. Is this the house?' The woman smiled. 'I'm Mrs Purvis.'

'The rooms are for two single ladies,' said Miss Pilgrim.

'Oh, I'm enquiring for my niece, who's coming down from Northampton.'

'It's a suite of three rooms for two single ladies.'

'Yes, I do see,' said Mrs Purvis, 'but if my niece paid the full rent, I'm sure that would be all right, wouldn't it? What is the full rent?'

'Twelve shillings,' said Miss Pilgrim.

'Twelve? But that's nearly as much as some young ladies earn.'

'That is why I have suggested it is suitable for two ladies.'

'I don't think you'll get anyone paying twelve shillings, not in Walworth, not for lodgings. You can rent a house for twelve or fourteen.'

'Not a house like this,' said Miss Pilgrim. 'The suite is two bedrooms and a living-room with some kitchen facilities. And own amenities.'

'All the same,' said Mrs Purvis, and shook her head. 'No, I don't think my niece can afford twelve shillings a week. I suppose I could ask around to see if another young lady would share with her.'

'Please do that,' said Miss Pilgrim. 'Good morning.'

She spent the next ten minutes frowning. She was quite unused to this sort of thing. But she needed the money. It was bitter to have to admit it, but she did. Her mother had left her an income of ten shillings a week, inherited from her father. She could not afford to touch the capital, which lay invested in government securities. She supplemented this by doing fine needlework at home, the finished articles being bought by a firm that sold them for four times the price they paid her. These earnings just about paid the rent of the house, fifteen shillings. All other expenditure had to be found from her weekly investment income of ten shillings. She was, she realized, as poor as a church mouse, and would remain so unless she elected to go into lodgings. She disliked intensely the prospect of an existence in an upstairs back room and a poky bedroom. She was not by nature cut out for that. The alternative was to let her three rooms upstairs and live downstairs. She could reconcile herself to that. She would retain her privacy, and twelve shillings rent from her lodgers would constitute a weekly windfall and allow her to live fairly comfortably.

Other applicants arrived to interrupt her reflections. They were two female persons. She could not, in all conscience, call them other than that. They had bright avaricious eyes, powdered faces, painted lips and wore beady-eyed fox furs around their necks. They exuded an aroma of cheap scent and addressed her as 'Ducky'. She froze at what she suspected them to be, told them the rooms were taken and closed the door on them.

'Here we are again, kids,' said Jim at five minutes to eleven. 'You keep your fingers crossed and I'll summon our good fairy.' He knocked. 'Well, I hope it's our good fairy.'

The door opened. Jim saw a woman clad in a black velvet dress that reached to her ankles. It was a well-preserved garment, the waist and bodice still trim, but the best of its nap had long since gone. Age had worn away its original glossiness and given it a matt finish. It accordingly gave her a stiff look. Her abundant black hair was brushed back from her forehead, parted down the middle, and dressed in a large bun at the back. Her face was handsome but a little severe, her untouched mouth as firm as a man's. Her eyes were startlingly blue and framed by long stiff black lashes. Her expression was discouraging.

She regarded Jim and the boy and girl forbiddingly. She saw the pinned-up sleeve of the man's jacket. Her look slightly softened, and she perused him more acutely. One could often distinguish men who had been in the trenches, whether or not they had lost limbs. They had a different look.

'Good morning, madam,' said Jim. Silently, she examined the children, a girl in a blue frock and a boater with a blue band, and a boy in a brown jersey and dark brown trousers. On his head was a ridiculously large cap with a soft peak. Jim had been to a second-hand clothes shop in the market to fit out Effel and Orrice as economically as possible for the time being. But he had not been able to persuade Orrice to give up his huge cap for a smaller one. The cap had belonged to Orrice's dad, and Orrice was proud of it. Because of the woman's silence, Jim again said, 'Good morning, madam.'

'Yes?' said Miss Pilgrim, who did not think the morning had been at all good. Nor did it look as if an improvement had arrived.

'I understand you've rooms to let.'

'You can read, I hope?' said Miss Pilgrim.

'Yes, of course—'

'It's a disgrace if you can't read at your age.'

'I read quite a lot, in fact,' said Jim equably. Certain now that lodgings for himself and the kids weren't going to be easy to come by, he was prepared to put up with the eccentricities already obvious in this stiffly dressed woman with an equally stiff look. One could never tell, in any case, what lay beneath the most forbidding front. 'Reading's a hobby of mine.'

'Good reading is an education, I should hope,' said Miss Pilgrim, and raised a dark eyebrow as she saw the little girl move to hide herself behind the boy. 'Did you not see that the suite of rooms are available to single ladies only?'

'Well, I'm glad for the single ladies,' said Jim with a smile, 'they seem to be getting a rough deal elsewhere. But no, I wasn't aware of your preference. Were the rooms advertised, then?'

'In Mr Smith's window.' Mr Smith ran the newsagents.

'We missed that, didn't we, youngsters?' said Jim.

'Oh, lor',' said Orrice. Effel, almost out of sight behind him, said nothing.

'We were recommended by a lady in Dawes Street, who knew a friend of yours,' said Jim. 'I suppose you wouldn't consider letting the rooms to us?'

'Certainly not,' said Miss Pilgrim. 'I should hope you could provide your wife and children with a

121

decent rented house instead of a lodging of three rooms. Not that there's anything wrong with my house, or with the rooms, but three for a family of four are quite out of the question.'

'I'm not married,' said Jim, 'I'm the guardian of these children. They've just lost both their parents in the flu epidemic.'

Miss Pilgrim frowned, as if she would have rather not been told.

'I'm sorry, sincerely sorry,' she said, 'but I find it difficult to believe that as their guardian you apparently do not have a suitable home to offer them.'

'We're very squeezed in my present lodgings, that's a fact,' said Jim, 'which is why I'm looking for better and roomier accommodation.'

'Yes. Yes.' Miss Pilgrim, strict Christian and daughter of a missionary, was vexed to find herself becoming uncomfortable. 'But I wish to let the suite to two single ladies. It is not suitable accommodation for a man who has two children in his charge.'

'It sounds happily suitable to me,' said Jim, 'but I understand your feelings. Well, we'll look elsewhere. Thank you, anyway, for talking to us.' He gave her a wry smile. Her look became stiffer, her discomfort increasing.

'I am sorry,' she said, 'but I have been opening my door all morning to unsuitable applicants.' At which, Orrice gave her a sorrowful look. He did not think himself unsuitable, or Effel, or their new uncle. Miss Pilgrim, catching his look, experienced further vexation. 'Good morning,' she said, and closed the door.

Jim sighed. He liked both the look of the house and the look of the street.

'Well, it wasn't our good fairy, after all,' he said. 'Never mind, let's go round to Mr Smith, the newsagent, and see if he can help us.'

The door opened again as they descended the steps. They turned.

'One moment,' said Miss Pilgrim, and fixed Orrice with eyes bluely frosty. She had felt most offended by his look. 'Are these children baptized?'

'Of course,' said Jim, surprised at the question, and taking for granted that Mr and Mrs Withers, in the tradition of most cockney parents, had certainly had Effel and Orrice baptized.

'They go regularly to church?'

'May I ask, madam—'

'I am Miss Pilgrim.'

'The children's parents took them regularly to church,' said Jim, plunging into the unknown.

'Your name, please?'

'Cooper, Jim Cooper.'

'Yes. Very well. I shall think things over, Mr Cooper. You may call again this afternoon. I cannot say whether or not I may let the rooms to you, only that I'll think it over. Good morning again.' Miss Pilgrim closed the door decisively.

As they walked away, Orrice said, 'Crikey, what a funny woman, I betcher she's starchy all over, I betcher she's even got starchy drawers, I betcher she can't even bend over. That's a sorrowing fing,

Uncle Jim, not being able to even bend over. She couldn't even pick up anyfing she dropped.'

'Yer naughty, saying that word,' complained Effel.

'What word?' asked Orrice.

'Ain't telling,' said Effel.

'Stiff petticoats don't always mean no heart,' said Jim. 'She's going to think it over. And Orrice, as she might think in favour of us, kindly watch your language when your sister's present.'

'That's good, that is,' said Orrice, stepping out in springy fashion, 'I dunno when Effel ain't present, I dunno when she ain't treadin' on me 'eels or gettin' in me way or jumpin' on me back, I dunno I ever 'ad a time when I was by meself. Uncle Jim, we goin' to come back an' see that lady again?'

'Yes, we are, Orrice. It's a nice house and a nice street, close to your new school and the church.'

'Ain't goin' to no church,' muttered Effel.

'Uncle Jim, we don't go to no church,' said Orrice, as they entered the familiar ground of Walworth Road. 'Mum and Dad always let us go down the market Sunday mornings.'

'That's going to alter, Orrice.'

'Oh, cripes,' said Orrice.

'Ain't goin',' said Effel.

'Black mark, Effel,' said Jim.

'What's a black mark mean?' asked Orrice.

'It means watch out,' said Jim. 'Two black marks mean dry bread and water.'

'Cor, Effel won't like that.'

'Don't care,' said Effel.

'Yer new frock looks nice, sis.'

'Ain't talkin',' said Effel.

'Best thing, that, sometimes, not talking,' observed Jim. 'Silence is often golden. Well, let's hope the lady with starched petticoats will take us in.' He had faint hopes himself. 'Now, suppose we buy a loaf of bread and some tasty ham, make sandwiches at home and then take a tram ride to Ruskin Park and have a picnic on a bench? With a bottle of lemonade? The sun's out, Effel's looking pretty and Orrice a proper little gent. How about it, kids?'

'Oh, yes,' said Effel, and came out of her no-talking mood. She did a little skip. 'I like the park, it's got grass.'

'Yer can't walk on it,' said Orrice. 'Well, yer can if the park-keepers ain't got their mince pies on yer, and even if they do see yer, yer all right as long as yer can run fast. Can we go, then, Uncle Jim?'

'We'll do that,' said Jim, 'and when we come back we'll call again on Miss Pilgrim.'

Effel said, 'Can I hide behind yer when we get there, mister?'

'If you want to,' said Jim.

'You got to excuse 'er,' said Orrice, 'she's only little and she don't like being looked at.'

'Well, tell her from me that pretty little girls are bound to be looked at,' said Jim, 'and that when she's older she might even get boxes of chocolates as well as looks.'

'She'll still want to 'ide behind yer, Uncle, she's shy, yer see,' said Orrice. 'Ain't yer, sis?'

'Mind yer business,' said Effel, who felt an instinctive need for the protection of a grown-up, but still wasn't sure about a man who wasn't her dad.

CHAPTER EIGHT

'You may enter,' said Miss Pilgrim.

'Thank you,' said Jim.

Miss Pilgrim had given considerable thought to the matter, more especially after other people had knocked on her door without in the least impressing her. It had seemed to her, once she had reconciled herself to taking in lodgers, that the process of selecting the most suitable would be quite straightforward. After all, her advertisement had clearly stated applicants were to be respectable. She had envisaged two young ladies of Christian virtue willing to share a living-room with basic kitchen facilities, and out at work all day. She had not envisaged having to interview applicants who were clearly not respectable. One young woman had declared she would rent one bedroom for five shillings, but didn't wish to share any part of her existence with some female she didn't know. Miss Pilgrim had told her she did not consider that at all Christianlike, and had thereupon been accused of being a stupid old – well, the word was not one she would repeat, even to herself.

Uncomfortable though it was to admit it, the most presentable person had been the man with two wards, a boy and a girl. He had been pleasantly well-mannered and polite, and the children did not seem like noisy nuisances, although the boy had been precocious in giving her a look of reproach. She wrestled at length with her Christian self and with what was right and what was suitable. Her Christian self told her she could not dismiss the need of a man who had taken on the guardianship of two recently bereaved children. Her reserved self told her that she would not feel right with a man in her house, that it would not be either suitable or proper. Worse, a man's close presence would arouse unwelcome memories.

Her Christian self prevailed.

She took them into her parlour, where the lace curtains, lace table overlay, delicate ornaments and tasteful, well-preserved furniture gave the room a predominantly feminine look, even a pretty look. She walked to an armchair. Her clothes rustled and crackled. Jim saw a little grin slide over Orrice's face. Miss Pilgrim removed a cushion from the armchair.

'You may sit here, child,' she said to Effel. Effel gulped, sat down on the very edge of the armchair and pulled the brim of her new boater down until it shielded her from being looked at. Miss Pilgrim did not ask Jim or Orrice to seat themselves. At this initial stage she elected to preserve a cautious and formal front, to avoid encouraging anything in the way of the smallest familiarity. She faced Jim, her clasped hands on her firm stomach. 'I have given your application serious thought, Mr Cooper.'

'That's kind of you, Miss Pilgrim,' said Jim, hat

in his hand. Orrice had his cap off. Miss Pilgrim noted the boy's need of a haircut.

'It doesn't do a Christian woman credit to turn away a man with two children to look after, unless there are more unfortunate persons on her doorstep,' she said. 'The rooms I have to offer are not to be bettered in the matter of cleanliness, which is something I insist on in my house. While there are no frills or fripperies, the rent of twelve shillings a week includes use of all bed linen, the sheets and pillow-cases going into my Monday wash, and spare ones put in their place. The children must go to bed clean, and I must ask if they have any weak habits.'

Jim knew she meant did Orrice or Effel wet the bed. They had not wet his bed.

'No ailments of that kind, Miss Pilgrim,' he said.

'Their behaviour?' she enquired, with Orrice gazing at her as if she had come from a world unknown to him.

'Oh, they behave like a boy and girl,' said Jim, 'but I prohibit rowdyism.'

'I should hope so, Mr Cooper,' she said, and Jim felt he was being addressed by a schoolmarm. She had obviously not yet entered the twentieth century. All the same, she was handing out hope. 'Do you drink?'

'Drink?'

'Me and Effel do, missus,' said Orrice, 'we—'

'Boy?' said Miss Pilgrim freezingly.

'Well, lemonade an' cocoa an' tea, like,' said Orrice humbly, 'except Effel likes tea most—'

129

'Young man, I am speaking to your guardian. Also, I am not Mrs.'

'Yes'm. No'm.'

Miss Pilgrim, handsomely imposing, resumed her catechism of Jim.

'Do you drink, Mr Cooper?'

'Well,' said Jim, 'I—'

'I hope you are not addicted, Mr Cooper. Drink weakens a man's Christian faith and his sense of responsibility. A man who takes to drink is a poor creature. I cannot permit the introduction of beer and spirits into this house. If you are addicted, please say so.'

'I'm not addicted, Miss Pilgrim, but I admit to enjoying a small glass of beer in a pub now and again.'

'H'm,' she said. But she noted his lost arm again, and his look of a man who had endured, which to her was a sign that he had fought in the trenches. One could not be wholly critical. 'I should hope no more than that,' she said.

'I do all things in moderation,' said Jim, almost lost for words at the formidable Victorianism of this incorruptible female. He wondered how old she was. His own age? Younger? No. Older? Perhaps. Was it important? Not really.

'Do you indulge in tobacco?'

'Moderately.'

'Well, that is not a sin,' said Miss Pilgrim in Christian tolerance, 'merely a bad habit. Should we come to terms over these rooms, please do me the courtesy of not smoking in my house. It will set a bad example to the boy. I assume that as you have accepted the serious responsibility of becoming guardian to these children, you are not an unworthy man, that you do not blaspheme or conduct yourself in indifferent fashion. I practise strict Christian principles that include self-denial and self-discipline, my father having been a missionary in China until I was twenty, when he and my mother and I returned to London for him to take up his work at the Bermondsey mission. This he did for eight years until he died of a heart attack, having worn himself out in the service of God. I then considered it my duty to look after my mother, who suffered from malaria and herself died six months ago. We chose, after the death of my father, to remain in this house, having lived here since our return to London from China. And I chose, after the death of my mother, to remain here, for the house bears the imprint of both my God-fearing parents. It need not concern you, the reason why I am willing to rent out the upper floor. Where are you employed, Mr Cooper?'

Jim, experiencing for the first time since he had come to manhood the bemusing effects of a Christian female's missionary zeal, said in a slightly helpless way, 'Where? Oh, where, yes. At the United Kingdom Club near Blackfriars.'

'That is a club run for the benefit of servicemen?'

'It is.'

'One could not call it an unworthy establishment, I imagine. But is drink sold there?'

'In moderation,' said Jim, 'but the staff aren't permitted to indulge.'

'I'm pleased to hear it. I have known the sad and undignified effects of inebriation.'

Jim looked astonished, then sympathetic.

'I'm sorry,' he said, 'I'd never have thought it.'

Miss Pilgrim stared at him with freezing blue eyes.

'Mr Cooper, are you imputing to me, in front of these children, a weakness I have never suffered? Neither I nor my father, and certainly not my mother, ever touched the smallest drop of alcohol.'

'I'm sorry, my word I am,' said Jim, 'I should have known at once I was drawing the wrong inference.'

'Oh, lor',' breathed Orrice, and Effel's boater tipped lower.

'Miss Pilgrim,' said Jim, facing up to the frosty blue eyes, 'I realize, of course, that you meant you had seen the effects of drink on other people. I do apologize.' He wanted that suite of rooms. They were self-contained, they were just right, and in them he and the kids could keep out of the dragon's way. 'Stupid of me.'

'Very well, I shall accept your apology,' said Miss Pilgrim. She cast a reproving look at Effel, who was fidgeting. Effel, catching the look, crammed her boater down over her face. 'What is wrong with that child?'

'Please'm, she's shy,' said Orrice.

'That's true,' said Jim.

'Well, one cannot object to that,' said Miss Pilgrim, 'it is a sign of sensitivity, and sensitivity is a sign of humility before God, which is a Christian virtue. Child, put your hat where it belongs, on your head.'

'Oh,' gulped Effel, and her boater fell to the floor. Miss Pilgrim stooped, rustled, and picked it up. Jim thought it an instinctive gesture to keep the floor looking tidy. She placed the boater firmly back on Effel's well-combed hair. Effel blushed crimson.

'Hats on young ladies are for keeping on,' said Miss Pilgrim. 'What is your name, child?'

Effel ducked her head again.

'Effel,' she said.

'Effel?' said Miss Pilgrim.

'Ethel,' said Jim.

'I see.' Miss Pilgrim might have voiced disparagement of Effel's pronunciation had she not lived among cockneys for eleven years. 'How old is she?'

'Seven,' said Jim.

'What is your name, boy?' asked Miss Pilgrim of Orrice.

'Orrice,' he said.

Miss Pilgrim looked down her nose.

'I think you mean Horace,' she said.

'Yes'm, Orrice.'

'How old are you?'

'Ten,' said Orrice proudly. When you reached double figures you counted for something.

'Mr Cooper,' said Miss Pilgrim, 'are you agreeable to the rent of twelve shillings a week?'

'I am,' said Jim, 'and must say it's generous of you to include laundering of the bed linen.'

'Who is to do your other laundry? You cannot,

surely.' It was her first reference to his handicap.

'Oh, I'll take all our weekly stuff to Ashford's Laundry,' said Jim.

'I see.' Miss Pilgrim looked as if that entailed profligate expenditure of money. 'Perhaps you would now like to inspect the rooms and decide if they suit you?'

'Thanks,' said Jim, 'I'd very much like to take a look.'

'Then please follow me.'

They all followed her, Effel scrambling from the armchair to get as close to Jim as she could. Miss Pilgrim sailed handsomely from the parlour and crossed the little hall to the stairs. She hitched her skirts and ascended. She rustled and whispered, and Orrice rolled his eyes, a little grin appearing again. Jim glimpsed shapely ankles in brown stockings. Her long-legged body ascended regally. She turned on the landing and led the way to the front bedroom. It was of a comfortable size, its two windows overlooking the neat street. As she had said, there were no frills or fripperies, except that the lace curtains matched the prettiness of those in the parlour. The mahogany furniture was plain, simple and practical. There was a large wardrobe, a washstand with a bowl and pitcher, a chest of drawers, a dressing-table, one upright chair, a double bed and a small bedside table on which stood a candle in its holder. The single gas mantle was covered by a pearl glass globe. The bed was covered by a patchwork overlay. The linoleum was spotless, and there were floor rugs, one on each side of the bed. A framed picture of a Highland stag hung on one wall.

'This, of course, is the larger bedroom,' said Miss Pilgrim.

'It's excellent,' said Jim, who felt there was a missionary's practical imprint on the room.

'Excellent? You are sure? I do not mind people being frank. Frankness is the child of truth.'

'And tact is the child of kindness?' smiled Jim. The smile seemed slightly to affront Miss Pilgrim. 'No, I'm not using tact now,' he said, 'the room is excellent. You did say the rooms couldn't be bettered. I believe you.'

Miss Pilgrim felt she could not fault his manners. She led the way to the second bedroom. While smaller, its square size was adequate. The furniture was a little less plain, being of walnut, and the single bed was covered by a blue quilt. The dressing-table had a glass top and three connecting oval mirrors. The window overlooked a small garden, a brick wall separating it from its neighbours. There was actually a small rectangular lawn and a flower bed. Jim was impressed with such an outlook. He turned to scan a framed tapestry hanging above the bed. He read the biblical quotation.

'*The Lord is my Shepherd.*'

This had been her bedroom, of course. It had a neat crispness to it. Yes, that was her. Crisp.

'Well, Mr Cooper?' she said.

'I'm impressed,' he said.

'This room, of course, would do for the girl,' she

135

said, making it clear that whatever arrangements obtained in their present lodgings, this was what would obtain here.

'Lovaduck,' said Orrice, emerging from instinctive restraint, 'I betcher you'll like this, Effel.'

'Won't,' breathed Effel, but Miss Pilgrim caught the word and looked down at her from what seemed to Effel an awesome height. She dodged behind Jim.

'What was that you said, child?'

'Nuffink,' gasped Effel.

'Mr Cooper, these children need speech improvement,' said Miss Pilgrim.

'They'll get it at school,' said Jim, 'but they're natural cockneys, of course.'

'That is no excuse for allowing their speech to remain slipshod,' said Miss Pilgrim. 'In any environment, Mr Cooper, some respect should be paid to the King's English.'

'Well, certainly, we don't want them to upset the King,' said Jim.

'Is that an attempt at levity, Mr Cooper?'

'A little passing comment, Miss Pilgrim.'

The striking blue eyes gazed suspiciously at him. Jim tried a smile.

'Now the living-room,' she said abruptly, as if a man's smile was untrustworthy. Rustling along the landing, she rapped her knuckles on a closed door. 'That is the small room.'

Orrice, thinking that might mean a little room to play games in, impulsively opened the door. He saw a toilet, a handbasin and a water tap.

'Oh, just a lav,' he said.

'I do not subscribe to the belief that boys should be seen and not heard, Mr Cooper, but I do not like forwardness in any of them,' said Miss Pilgrim.

'It's best discouraged,' agreed Jim.

Orrice said, 'I only looked to see – well, I was 'oping that if I got a clockwork train set one day, there'd be room—' He stopped. 'I dunno what I was 'oping,' he said.

'Hoping,' said Miss Pilgrim.

'Yes'm,' said Orrice.

She led them into the living-room, the same size as the front bedroom. There was a sofa in brown leather upholstery, a matching armchair, a dwarf bookcase, and, in the bay window, a small table with three upright chairs. A polished wooden coal scuttle stood to one side in the hearth, and there was a brass companion set on the other side. The empty fireplace shone with blacklead. Above the fireplace hung a picture, a framed watercolour of a mission house in China. On an iron stand on the top of a four-feet-high cupboard was a framed trio of gas rings.

'There is crockery in the cupboard,' said Miss Pilgrim, 'also a kettle, teapot and a small saucepan. The books in the case are part of a collection.'

'They won't be touched, Miss Pilgrim,' said Jim with feeling, 'I've too much respect for books, especially other people's, to be careless with them.'

'It has never occurred to me to leave books untouched and unread, Mr Cooper. Respect for books and how they have come about is an excellent thing, of course, but not to the extent of locking them up. That bookcase is not locked, and you may read any of the volumes you care to, while not allowing the children to introduce jam or marmalade to them. That is, if you decide the rooms will suit you at the rent mentioned. You need not decide now—' For once, she hesitated. She wanted to remove that notice from the newsagent's window as soon as she could, or more unsavoury persons would come knocking on her door. 'But I should appreciate a quick decision.'

'We'll take the rooms, Miss Pilgrim,' said Jim.

Miss Pilgrim gave him her first look of approval. She favoured people who did not scratch their heads and procrastinate.

'Very well, Mr Cooper. I shan't object to any natural high spirits in the children, but shall expect you to see their behaviour is never unreasonable. Shall we go down to the parlour and settle the final details?'

They followed her down. She rustled with every step, and Jim was sure she actually did wear a starched petticoat. He also felt the pretty look of the parlour possibly reflected her mother's tastes, and that she had refrained, out of respect, from placing a practical look on it.

'You've a very attractive parlour,' he said, noting a glass-fronted bookcase whose every shelf was full.

'It is how my mother liked it,' she said. Bull's-eye, thought Jim. 'If you and the children would care to sit down for a moment, I will get you to sign the tenancy agreement.' Jim and Effel seated themselves on a small chesterfield, and Orrice sat in an armchair, cap over one knee. 'I have drawn up the agreement myself, being adequately versed in the writing of documents for my father.' Miss Pilgrim opened the drawer of a small sideboard and extracted a sheet of paper. 'You will please read it.' She handed it to him. He scanned it. It was well-worded and he could not fault it, although in Walworth a written agreement was a rare thing. A landlady simply provided a rent book and made an entry each week on payment. If a lodger defaulted or proved too troublesome, out he went.

'I'll sign,' said Jim.

'Very well. When do you wish to move in?'

'Tuesday?' he suggested, knowing he had to move by Wednesday, when Mrs Palmer's brother was moving in.

'I am agreeable to that,' she said. She could now walk round to the newsagents and get that card removed from the window. 'Your week, then, is from Tuesday to Tuesday, your tenancy beginning next Tuesday.' She was crisply businesslike. Orrice did a little leg stretch and his cap fell from his knee to the floor. 'Master Horace,' she said, 'my floor is not the place for hats or caps.'

'No'm,' said Orrice, and picked his cap up. 'It just fell off me knee, like. I s'pose it ain't used to being on me knee, it's mostly on me head nearly always. Me dad give it to me, Miss Pilgrim, and it was nearly always on 'is 'ead too. Before 'e give it me, I mean. You can ask Effel.'

'I don't think I need to do that,' said Miss

139

Pilgrim, and inserted the date of the tenancy commencement. Jim signed it. She produced a copy that she had also made. She signed it.

'I see we need witnesses,' said Jim.

'I am seeing the vicar later today. He and his wife will witness the copy I've signed.'

'I'll get my landlady and her husband to witness the other,' said Jim.

'You saw that a week's notice can be given by either party?'

'Yes, I saw that.'

'Very well,' she said, 'I'll expect you and the children on Tuesday. At precisely what time?'

'I'll move in at ten in the morning. The children will come after they've finished school in the afternoon. They're at St John's.'

'The church school?' Miss Pilgrim again showed approval. 'That is an excellent educational establishment, with a good grounding in the Scriptures and reading aloud for speech improvement. Did you say ten o'clock? But what of your work?'

'For the next couple of weeks or so, I'm working from four in the afternoons until midnight. Then I take over a permanent day duty from eight-thirty to half-past five.'

'I am relieved to hear it,' said Miss Pilgrim firmly. 'It would not do for a guardian's wards to be left alone every evening.'

Jim, refusing to be ruffled, smiled and said, 'I've sorted that out with my new hours.' He had also borrowed a book-keeping manual from the library. 'Well, thank you for everything, Miss Pilgrim, you've been very kind and helpful. We'll all do our best to be model tenants.' He and the children came to their feet. 'Say goodbye to Miss Pilgrim, Ethel.'

'G'bye,' gasped Effel.

'Goodbye, child.'

'Goodbye, Miss Pilgrim,' said Orrice.

'Goodbye,' said Miss Pilgrim, and saw them out. She noted that the children's energy released itself, the boy taking a flying leap from the top steps, and the girl executing hops and skips over the pavement. She noted the long-limbed stride of Mr Cooper, who was minus his left arm. If she could find no fault with his speech, that of the boy and girl was cockney at its most grating. She closed the door and stood in the little hall for a moment, wondering if her Christian gesture meant she was taking upon herself a cross of burdensome weight and complexities.

Her mouth compressed to a firm line. What the Lord had brought to her she would endure. She had, after all, endured far worse when she was a naive and carefree young woman of twenty. For all her strong will, she shuddered at the memory of what had happened at the mission station in China. Then her mouth compressed even more firmly, and she shut the memory out.

CHAPTER NINE

'Well, kids?' said Jim, pouring tea.

'I dunno she ain't too posh for us,' said Orrice.

'She?'

''Er,' said Orrice.

'Her?'

'Miss Pilgrim,' said Orrice, stirring his tea.

'That's better,' said Jim.

Effel, sipping tea in bliss, spoke up.

'I likes 'er,' she said.

'Eh?' asked Orrice.

'Well, I finks I likes 'er,' said Effel cautiously. She darted one of her quick glances at Jim. 'She crackles. I likes crackles.'

'Told yer, didn't I?' said Orrice gleefully. 'I betcher she's starched all over.'

'Well, we're lucky,' said Jim. 'We've – Effel, sit up.' Effel glowered and muttered and sat up. 'Listen, we've probably clicked for the best lodgings in Walworth, and for a landlady of Christian goodness. Never mind her starch. You heard, didn't you, that she's going to wash our bed linen for us?'

'It's goin' to be a bit bovversome, though,' said Orrice, 'Effel an' me ain't never 'ad to put up with Christian goodness, and me dad always said it don't 'alf cramp yer style, yer can't do nuffink without first askin' permission in case what yer goin' to do upsets them Ten Commandments.'

'You'll learn, Orrice,' said Jim.

'Oh, lor',' said Orrice, 'you ain't goin' to 'eap Christian goodness on our 'eads as well, are yer, Uncle Jim?'

'I'm going to peel and boil some potatoes for you,' said Jim, 'and leave you to warm them up for your supper with some slices of new corned beef and some tomatoes. And some military pickle. And there's a cake from the baker's. I can trust you to bring the potatoes back to the boil without scalding yourself, Orrice?'

'Course yer can, Uncle, I boiled a ton of spuds in me time, ain't I, sis?'

'Don't remember,' said Effel, 'but I likes corned beef an' pickle.'

'After supper,' said Jim, 'you can read the Bible to Effel, Orrice.'

'Eh?' gasped Orrice.

'There's a Bible in the cupboard. Something from the New Testament.'

'Cripes,' breathed Orrice, 'yer ganging up with Miss Pilgrim, Uncle Jim.'

'Doing my best to co-operate,' said Jim. 'And I think it'll do for you two to still call me Uncle Jim.' So far, Effel hadn't called him anything, except mister once or twice. 'That was for the benefit of Mrs Palmer, but you understand I'm simply your guardian as far as our new life is concerned. Do you understand?'

'Yes, course we do,' said Orrice, 'don't we, sis?'

'A' right,' said Effel.

'Good,' said Jim. 'Don't forget the Bible reading, Orrice.' He was thinking of their relationship with Miss Pilgrim. 'Read Effel the first chapter of St Luke.'

'Ain't goin' to listen to *that*,' glowered Effel.

'Yes, you are,' said Orrice, 'if I'm blooming well goin' to read it you can blooming well listen, or I'll drown yer.'

'No drowning,' said Jim, 'just a little Bible reading.'

'Blooming daisies, what a life,' said Orrice, 'I ain't never read from the Bible before.'

'This evening will be a good time to start,' said Jim.

On Friday morning, following Orrice's report that Effel hadn't played up, that she'd listened like he was reading from a Ragamuffin Jack book, Jim took stock of his finances. He had thirty-nine pounds and twelve shillings in the Savings Bank, nineteen shillings and sevenpence in his pocket, his weekly wage of twenty-five shillings due tonight and his monthly pension due on Monday.

'Kids,' he said, 'we're well off at the moment.' From Tuesday, when he was to pay Miss Pilgrim twelve shillings rent in advance each week, he would be relying on a pound or so to keep the kids and himself in clothes and to pay for all those extra things that always cropped up in life. That would be augmented next month by the additional five

144

shillings he would earn for helping to keep the books. He thought he could manage. 'Yes, at the moment, we're prosperous.'

'I ain't 'alf glad for yer, Uncle Jim,' said Orrice. 'Real prosp'rous?'

'Up to a point,' said Jim, who was as fairly casual about money as he was about ups and downs. Life at the orphanage had taught him to be grateful for the little things, and life outside the orphanage had taught him that most people's lives were about little things. Big things and miracles happened to only a few. One was up sometimes, one was down sometimes. You could aim for the moon if the notion took you, but if you fell it was from a great height. Most people in Walworth managed to survive, managed to smile. They too made the most of little pleasures, little strokes of luck. A little stroke of luck could offset a year's setbacks.

As long as one kept a certain amount of money for a rainy day, if one could keep it, the rest of it was for spending. The maxim in Walworth was, 'Yer 'ere today, mate, yer could be gorn tomorrer.' Which meant if your old woman hadn't got a shilling to take twenty-eight pounds of washing to the Bagwash Laundry, you left it until next week. A week's more dirt wasn't considered anti-social in Walworth.

Jim felt nineteen Wansey Street represented a stroke of great luck. There couldn't be better lodgings for him and the kids. What a remarkable woman Miss Pilgrim was. Victorian, puritanical, stiff, unbending, starched, precise and willing to give them excellent lodgings and more for twelve shillings a week. He supposed she had worked it out to her satisfaction. Yes, she would have done that. What had she got under the bodice of that ancient black dress of hers? A handsome bosom, certainly. A warm heart in addition, despite her strict religious ethics and her severity? Well, nothing must be done to offend her. Although their bed linen would go into her own wash each week, it was still a very human gesture, and generous. Nowhere were he and the kids likely to get better terms. Her strict Christian beliefs and her eccentricities must be heeded and accepted.

'Effel, Uncle Jim's gorn all quiet,' whispered Orrice.

Effel, worried, whispered, ''E ain't goin' to leave us, is 'e?'

'I was thinking we'd better go out and get both of you properly fitted up. You've got your second-hand clobber for knocking about in.' Jim suddenly wondered if Miss Pilgrim had decided to make her offer because she felt a man with one arm could not properly manage to do all the things he needed to do for two children. She had made no direct comment at all about his infirmity. 'Yes, I think we'd better buy you both something for school and for Sundays. We don't want our good fairy, Miss Pilgrim, giving us looks.'

'Uncle, I got to say it,' said Orrice, 'she doesn't seem like no good fairy to me.'

'She looked at me,' said Effel. Looking wasn't as likeable as crackles.

146

'Well, we'll put you in a nice Sunday frock, Effel,' said Jim, 'then she'll enjoy looking at you. Right, hats on. Effel, where's your hair ribbon?'

'Dunno,' said Effel.

'Can't have that.'

'It's 'ere,' said Orrice

'Oh, a' right,' said Effel. 'You do it,' she said to Jim.

'Pardon?' said Jim.

'Please would yer?' asked Effel, and Jim, one hand deft and manipulative, tied the ribbon around her hair and finished with a bow.

'Where's your boater?' he asked.

'Can't find it,' she said.

'Look under the bed.'

Effel looked under the bed. She pulled out her boater.

'That Orrice,' she said, 'where 'e puts fings.'

'Me?' said Orrice. 'Me? That's good, that is, I don't fink. I'll plonk yer one.'

'No plonking,' said Jim. 'March.'

They all went out on another excursion. Jim kept them so active that it was only in the evenings, when he was at work, that they thought about not having their mum and dad any more. Orrice revelled in every excursion. To him, it was really lively being out with their new uncle, their guardian. Effel went along with each outing in the way of a little girl still not quite sure exactly what her new life was all about, or exactly what their guardian meant to her.

Jim called in at the post office to draw five

pounds from his savings, and he helped Orrice open an account with the money the boy still had. Orrice deposited a pound of it. The woman at the counter, giving him the book, said, 'Could I see what you look like under your cap, Master Withers?'

'What for?' asked Orrice cautiously.

'I'm curious to see if there is anyone,' smiled the woman. Orrice, not given to being as retiring as Effel, lifted his cap. 'My,' said the woman, beaming, 'aren't you a pretty boy?'

Orrice nearly fell over in his horror.

'Me?' he gasped in outrage.

Effel giggled.

''Oo's a pretty boy, then?' she said.

'I'll kill yer,' bawled Orrice, much to the amusement of other people.

'No killing,' said Jim, 'especially not in public.'

Orrice slammed his cap back on, pulled it down to his nose, marched to the door in high blind dudgeon and cannoned into an entering woman.

'Oh, hexcuse me, I'm sure,' she said.

'He's a little off colour at the moment,' said Jim.

'Can't tell if 'e's on or orf under that cap,' said the bumped woman.

''E's pretty, yer know,' said Effel, and Orrice, with a strangled yell of rage, hurled himself through the door into the street. He fell over the feet of an elderly man. It wasn't the best few minutes of Orrice's life. He marched along with Jim and Effel, with strange noises issuing from under his cap.

Jim bought two black skirts, two white bouses and two pinafore dresses for Effel to wear to school.

148

And a yellow frock for Sundays, plus vests, knickers, shoes and socks. Effel was open-mouthed. She'd never seen so many actually new clothes, and she'd never worn shoes, only boots. She consented to try the frock on. Jim thought she looked delicious.

'Yes, very nice, Effel,' he said, at which Effel rushed back into the changing-room.

'That's a shy one,' said the assistant.

'She wasn't in the post office,' growled Orrice.

In the boys' department of a men's outfitters, Jim bought Orrice two good quality woollen jerseys, one dark blue, the other dark grey, and two pairs of trousers. He also bought him underwear, socks and shoes, and a Sunday suit for fifteen shillings. Orrice wasn't sure about a Sunday suit, he'd never had any kind of suit, and he didn't want other boys catcalling him. But Jim prevailed, and Orrice tried the suit on.

'Oh, don't 'e look more pretty?' cried Effel.

'That's done it, that 'as,' said Orrice, 'I ain't 'aving no suit.'

'Wrap it up when he's taken it off,' said Jim to the assistant.

'Might as well be dead, I might,' muttered Orrice. When they were outside with their many parcels, he said between grinding teeth, 'I dunno I'm goin' to let me sister live for more'n a few more days.'

'I don't care,' said Effel.

'I betcher yer would,' said Orrice, 'I betcher you'd holler when I'm cuttin' yer bonce orf.'

'Wouldn't,' said Effel. 'Would it 'urt?' she asked Jim.

'Only at the time,' said Jim. 'But no cutting off of bonces, Orrice.'

'Only Effel's,' said Orrice, 'that's all I'm beggin' yer, Uncle Jim, just Effel's.'

'Forbidden,' said Jim. 'Now, who fancies fried eggs and bacon again at Toni's?' He guessed, correctly, that eggs and bacon were a treat to the kids.

Effel and Orrice were totally in favour, although Orrice said he wasn't going to take his cap off. Jim said caps would be removed at all meal times. Orrice growled that Effel would say things out loud about his looks.

'Effel, no talking out loud in Toni's,' said Jim.

'Don't want to,' said Effel.

'Afterwards,' said Jim, 'we'll buy toothbrushes and toothpowder for both of you.'

Toni looked up at the entrance of Jim and the kids.

'Ah, good-a morning, sir,' he said to Orrice. 'Good-a morning, signorina,' he said to Effel, who at once planted herself rigidly behind Orrice. Toni grinned.

'It ain't funny, mister,' said Orrice.

'Eggs, bacon and bread and butter for three, Toni,' said Jim, 'and lemonade for sir and signorina.'

'You got kids, I got eggs-a bacon coming up pretty quick, Jim,' said Toni, and put his pan to work. He watched them seat themselves at a table.

150

He saw Orrice take his cap off. 'Hey, what you think, Jim,' he called, 'first time I see that kid. Hey, you kid.' Orrice turned his head. 'Hey, what-a you wear that cap for, kid? You're a fine-looking boy, eh?'

Orrice turned slightly red. Effel simpered with mischief.

'Oh, well,' said Orrice, 'I s'pose that ain't as bad as being called pretty. You 'eard that, Effel?'

''Oo's a pretty boy, then?' said Effel, but not out loud, only in a murmur.

Orrice ground his teeth.

'I ain't got the strength to 'old meself back, Uncle Jim,' he said. 'I just got to shut Effel up, I just got to spread 'er all over the pavement when we get outside.'

'Well, just this once,' said Jim.

'There, you 'eard that, sis, didn't yer?' said Orrice.

'Ain't saying nuffink out loud,' said Effel.

Jim took them to their new school on Monday morning, Effel in new white blouse, sensible black skirt and her better boater. With the class of seven-year-olds seated, Effel stood beside the teacher's desk.

'Children,' said the teacher, Miss Forster, 'say hello to our new pupil, Ethel Withers.'

'Hello!' bawled the class of boys and girls.

'Hello, Ethel, if you don't mind,' said Miss Forster.

''Lo, Effel!'

'Go and sit down, Ethel,' said Miss Forster, 'there's a place in the front row, next to Daisy Rogers.'

'Don't like 'er,' muttered Effel under her breath.

'Pardon?'

'Nuffink,' said Effel.

Miss Forster took the girl's hand and led her to the desk. Daisy Rogers made room. Effel sat down, mutinously.

'There's pencils there, look,' said Daisy, lifting the desk lid.

'Oh, a' right,' said Effel, yellow ribbon around her hair, white blouse so neat-looking to herself that it almost worried her.

Miss Forster set them to work after the Scripture lesson, the pupils using coloured crayons. She walked round the desks, encouraging and cajoling. Crayon drawing was very popular, and the pupils became absorbed in their fanciful creations. Miss Forster stopped to look at Effel's drawing-book. The page showed round dots of different colours, each conglomerate of dots forming a rough circle, and the whole forming a large circle.

'What's that, Ethel?' asked the teacher.

'A wreaf,' said Effel, who knew from her experiences at her other school that it was no good telling teachers she wasn't talking. If you did that they made you stand in front of the class with everyone looking at you. You felt silly. 'A wreaf like at funerals, miss.'

Having received certain information from the headmistress about both new pupils, Miss Forster said gently, 'Yes, I see. Well, do you know, Ethel, it's very good. Why, it's impressionist.'

'What's imp – what's that?'

'It's a method some famous painters use. See, you've made an impression of a wreath of different flowers. The little circles are all heads of flowers, aren't they, close together?'

'It's for our mum an' dad,' said Effel. Her head dropped and her eyes were suddenly wet. But she wasn't going to cry, not in front of a classful of other children. Miss Forster lightly patted her shoulder.

'It's very good, Ethel,' she said, and moved on.

'Don't you like it 'ere?' whispered Daisy. 'I'll look after you. See, I'm drawing a cat.'

'We 'ad a cat,' said Effel, and wondered what had happened to it.

Orrice too had stood by a teacher's desk to be introduced. The teacher was Mr Hill, known as Whiskers behind his back because he had a large grey moustache. The class was for nine-year-old and ten-year-old boys and girls. Orrice's eyes flickered about, ready to alight on anyone making faces at him because he was new here.

''Ere, sir,' called a boy from the back, 'he's got his farver's trousers on.'

Girls giggled. Orrice took a note of the boy.

'Stand up, Higgs,' said Mr Hill.

'Yessir,' said Higgs, a slim boy, and stood up.

'Did you say farver's trousers?'

'Yessir.'

'Father's, Higgs, father's.'

153

'Yessir.'

'Kindly say it.'

'Yessir. Farver's, sir.'

'I'm onto you, my lad,' said Mr Hill. 'Ten minutes reading aloud for you in a moment. And kindly note that Horace Withers's trousers fit him. So they can't be his father's. Withers, find a place at a desk.'

Orrice walked straight up a gangway between desks, found a spare place next to a girl, and eyed Higgs across the gangway. Higgs met the challenge with a bold grin. The girl whispered, 'Is that really your name – Horace?'

'What's yourn, then?' asked Orrice.

'Alice French. Fancy long trousers.'

'Fancy a frock with egg on it,' said Orrice.

'Oh, it isn't,' protested Alice.

'All right, only jokin',' said Orrice, and gave her a smile. It wasn't fateful to give girls a smile, it just showed them you were willing to put up with them being girls.

Nine-year-old Alice looked into joking brown eyes and at a fresh, healthy face. Her lashes fluttered.

'You're ever so nice,' she said.

'Oh, gawd,' said Orrice. That was the trouble with girls. You couldn't have a sensible conversation with them.

'Attention, class,' said Mr Hill. 'Scripture books out.' He tapped his desk with a ruler, and his pupils came to order. 'Higgs will read out loud from the top of page ten, where Jesus is comforting His disciples.'

154

'Oh, blooming blimey,' muttered Higgs to himself. He thought that what Jesus said to His disciples ought to remain private. But he began. '"Let not yer 'eart be troubled yer believe in God believe also in me in me—"'

'Punctuation, Higgs.'

'Yessir. "In me Farver's 'ouse are many mansions—"'

'In me Farver's 'ouse?' said Mr Hill.

'Yessir.'

Mr Hill shook his head.

'You can do better than that. Look at the spelling. You've turned my into me, Father into Farver, and house into 'ouse.'

'Yessir. Sorry, sir.' Higgs continued. '"If it were not so I would 'ave told yer and if I go—"'

'Cheeky,' said Mr Hill. 'You're dodging the column. Go back to "In my Father's house."'

'Yessir.' Higgs groaned. Painfully he said, '"In my Father's 'ouse – house – there are many mansions."'

'Better,' said Mr Hill. 'Not exactly perfect, but better.' He persevered with the boy. The class listened. Finally, the teacher said, 'All right, improvement noted, Higgs. Now, would you like to say something cordial and in fairly good English to our new pupil, Master Withers?'

'Yessir. Like you said, 'Orace Wivvers ain't wearing 'is farver's trousers.'

Mr Hill sighed. The class couldn't think why. Higgs's speech sounded all right to them. It was teachers who talked funny.

Orrice experienced a reasonable morning. Arithmetic was no problem to him. He helped Alice with hers. She surreptitiously slipped him a boiled sweet. He popped it into his mouth.

'No, it's not for now,' she whispered, 'you'll catch it sucking sweets in class.'

'I'm suckin' it now to show yer I appreciate it,' murmured Orrice, dividing 27 into 405 with ease.

'Oh, could we sit next to each other every day?' asked Alice.

Orrice almost swallowed his boiled sweet in his alarm. He had all the problems he wanted with Effel, always at his heels and getting in his way. He didn't want another girl doing it.

'I'll let yer meet me sister at dinnertime,' he said. Effel would see Alice off.

At dinnertime, half the children went home for a meal. The rest stayed to eat what they had brought with them. Some had sandwiches, some just two slices of bread and marge, some an apple and a piece of cake. Jim arrived with fresh sandwiches for Effel and Orrice, who received them from him at the gate to the playground.

'Brawn sandwiches with pickle,' he said.

'Yer a sport, Uncle,' said Orrice.

'Don't like brawn,' said Effel, unwrapping hers with a lack of interest.

'Course yer do, I seen yer eat tons of brawn,' said Orrice.

'That's wiv 'ot potatoes,' said Effel, 'not between bread.'

'Try it,' said Jim, and she took an obedient bite. She chewed and swallowed. 'Awful?' said Jim.

'I likes the pickle,' said Effel. It was Hayward's famous Military Pickle.

'How did the morning go?' asked Jim, watching kids running about the playground.

'We done drawing,' said Effel, and took another bite. With her mouth full, she mumbled, 'I done a wreaf for our mum an' dad.'

'A wreath?' said Jim.

'I drawed it,' said Effel mournfully.

'Well, that was a nice thought, Effel,' said Jim. 'Ethel,' he mused correctively. 'I'll be leaving you cold meat and boiled potatoes again for your suppers. A bit boring, but it's only for this evening. Tomorrow you'll go from school to Miss Pilgrim's. I'll prepare a nice supper for you.'

'Ain't goin',' said Effel.

'You're goin',' said Jim, 'or Orrice will drown you.'

'You went an' said no drowning,' protested Effel.

'That was yesterday, or the day before,' said Jim. 'So long now, be good. You too, Orrice.'

'So long, Uncle,' said Orrice.

Jim, going on his way, stopped and turned.

'Give Effel another Bible reading this evening,' he said.

'Crikey, Uncle Jim, yer givin' me an 'ard life, you are,' said Orrice. Jim smiled and went on his way. Orrice and Effel went back into the playground. Alice came up, bright-eyed and fair-haired in a pinafore dress.

''Lo, Horace,' she said.

''Oo's she?' asked Effel aggressively.

'She's Alice,' said Orrice, 'she'd like to meet yer.'

'You look nice,' said Alice to Effel, 'what's your name?'

'Ain't got no name,' said Effel.

'But you have to have a name,' said Alice, one of the pupils, a minority, who didn't massacre the King's English.

'Ain't telling you,' said Effel, who regarded Orrice as her exclusive property and all other girls as interlopers.

'She's Effel,' said Orrice.

''Lo, Ethel,' said Alice.

'G'bye,' said Effel.

'Oh, I'm not going anywhere,' said Alice, 'except can you come and do skipping with me, Horace?'

Effel muttered a hiss of rage, and Orrice tottered.

'Skippin'?' he said, horrified. 'Skippin'?'

'I've got a new skipping-rope,' said Alice, 'with pink handles. It's over there.'

Over there was where girls were skipping and eating sandwiches in between.

'I don't do skippin',' said Orrice, slighly hoarse.

'Oh, I'll show you,' said Alice, as eager as a girl already in love, 'I'll show you how we can skip together.'

Orrice, aware of boys playing leapfrog and other manly games, said, 'I don't feel well.' And he didn't.

Effel hissed, ''E ain't goin'. 'E's my bruvver, not yourn.'

'But he's ever so nice,' said Alice.

Effel jumped up and down in her jealous rage.

'Go away, or I'll kick yer!' she said.

'Now, Effel, that ain't nice,' said Orrice.

'Don't care,' said Effel, 'I'll kick all 'er teef out, I will!'

'No, yer won't,' said Orrice.

Fiendishly, Effel said, 'I'll make 'er go away, I'll tell 'er you're pretty, that's what I'll do.' Orrice tottered again.

'Oh, yes, he's the nicest-looking boy ever,' enthused Alice.

'That's done it,' said Orrice, 'I'm goin' to shoot meself, I am. I don't 'ave anyfing to live for now. I dunno, I betcher I done more good turns in me life than I've 'ad 'ot dinners, and where's it got me, go on, Effel, tell me that. 'Ere, excuse me, I'm sure, but what do you want?'

Higgs had arrived, with two other boys.

'Oh, I just wanted to show me mates yer wearing yer dad's trousers,' said Higgs.

Orrice, not liking any mention of his dad, showed a firm, balled fist. 'See that?' he said. 'No, yer can't see it, can yer? It ain't close enough. Now d'yer see it?' The hard young fist stopped inches from Higgs's nose.

'I've seen bigger,' said Higgs.

'Bigger or smaller don't count,' said Orrice, 'it's how 'ard it feels when it cops yer sniffer. Which it is goin' to if yer don't take yer face away.'

'Some other time, Wivvers,' said Higgs, and sauntered jauntily off with his pals.

'Oh, you did talk to him heroic, Horace, and he's ever such a show-off,' said Alice. 'Do come and skip, and I'll ask my mum if you can come to tea.'

Effel uttered a suppressed scream of fury.

'Yes, well, if yer don't mind, Alice, I've got me sandwiches to eat, and I've got to go to the cloakroom as well,' said Orrice and left at the double. Effel ran after him. Alice sighed.

But there she was, sitting next to him in the afternoon class. And there was Orrice, appalled at the prospect of being followed about not only by his sister, but by a girl with a skipping-rope that had pink handles. Pink. Even his big-shouldered dad would have wept for him.

CHAPTER TEN

When classes were over for the day at four o'clock, Orrice noticed Alice lingering just outside the school doors. He dodged back into the boys' cloakroom. He took two or three cautious looks, but she was still there. He heard her ask a boy, 'Have you seen Horace?'

'Never 'eard of him,' said the boy.

She disappeared a few minutes later, and Orrice made for the gates and for Effel, who'd be waiting there. Alice popped up, but there was no Effel.

'Where's Effel?' he asked.

'She's gone after you,' said Alice.

'Now how could she 'ave?' said Orrice. 'I haven't gone, you can see I'm still 'ere.'

'Oh, I think she thought you'd gone, and she started running to catch you up,' said Alice.

'Crikey, what a carry-on,' said Orrice, and made tracks for Turquand Street, which would take him to Browning Street and up to Morecambe Street, where they were living with their guardian.

Effel ran about, looking. She didn't know where she was. She was always with Orrice, and recently with both him and their guardian. She always left everything to Orrice, including the geography of new ground. Her knowledge of this area's back streets, different from those around Deacon Street, was hazy. She was furious with her brother for going back to their lodgings without her, and she ran in a temper to catch him up, except that when she got to Browning Street she wasn't sure where to go from there. She ran and darted all ways without seeing him, and she didn't even know the name of the street in which they were living. She saw a policeman coming towards her. She turned and scampered round a corner, and she scampered on.

A little later she asked a lady where Walworth Road was. She knew Walworth Road. She felt she could find familiar signs there. She was directed to it. Reaching it, she stood looking, this way and that. She was a little agitated now. The trams were something of a comfort to her, for they were very familiar. Perhaps Orrice was in this road, looking at shops. He liked wandering about. She walked, her feet hurrying her, towards the town hall. She reached Browning Street, very familiar. She and Orrice and their guardian had been in Browning Street lots. There was a turning they had taken lots. She hurried down Browning Street, came to King and Queen Street, hesitated, then turned into it. Had she gone on only a fairly short way, she would have reached Morecambe Street and recognized it. But she went running along King and Queen Street. She came to East Street, the market. That panicked her a little. She'd already been in the market twice during her running search. She again missed Morecambe Street by turning right instead of left.

She reached Walworth Road again. She ran in and out of pavement crowds. Tired and very agitated, she sat down in a shop doorway, tears of distress beginning to spill. People passed by. A man stopped. He stopped in front of her, peering at her.

''Ere, what's the trouble, girlie, what's them tears for?'

He had a large mouth, a large nose, and bushy black eyebrows. Effel did not see the genuine sympathy in his eyes. Cockneys had very warm hearts for little girls. Effel only saw the large nose and the bushy black eyebrows. She jumped to her feet and rushed away, and he lost sight of her among the pedestrians.

Effel just ran and ran.

Darkness had fallen over London when a hall porter put his head around the door of the main kitchen, sighted Jim and called to him.

'Better come a minute, if you can, Jim, there's a boy askin' urgent for you. Say's his name's Horace.'

Jim dried his hand, took his apron off, received a nod from the chef, and went to discover what had brought Orrice to the club. Orrice was in the hall, by the door, cap in his hand, fingers twisting it.

'Orrice?'

'Effel's run off,' said Orrice. He looked worried and weary. He had been searching for hours, walking and running, asking and looking. Mrs Palmer, the landlady, and her husband were out on the steets of Walworth now, conducting a search, and Mr Palmer had talked about riding up to King's

163

College Hospital to see if Effel had had an accident and been taken there. Orrice poured out his worries.

'You haven't seen her since the end of classes?' said Jim.

'Well, no.' Orrice was kicking himself for hanging back on account of Alice. 'One of the girls said she'd gone off after me. Effel thought I'd gone when I 'adn't, and I wouldn't 'ave gone without 'er, honest. She ought to 'ave known that. I'm real worried, Uncle Jim.'

'Well, I'd say she hasn't run off, Orrice,' said Jim gently, 'I'd say she simply got herslf lost. It's a maze of streets, our part of Walworth, and she probably still can't pinpoint our lodgings. She's a very young girl, and it's a new walk for both of you, from the school to Morecambe Street.'

'But it's an easy one,' said Orrice, a bit desperate.

'To you perhaps.'

'But could yer come, could yer 'elp me look for her?'

'Of course. Hold on a moment.' Jim went to see the chef. He was back in less than a couple of minutes. 'Come on, Orrice, let's cut through and get a tram in Blackfriars Road.'

His calm approach reassured Orrice a little, but on the tram the boy was still restless. Jim knew that brother and sister were inseparable. They argued with each other, quarrelled with each other, and made fun of each other. But they were still a united pair. More so since the death of their parents. Jim wondered if a policeman had picked up a wandering

164

Effel, or if Effel herself had gone to a police station. He doubted she had, she was still at the stage of associating policemen with orphanages. In her way she was a determined little girl, but still wholly reliant on Orrice. Almost certainly she'd got herself lost, even though the school wasn't all that far from Morecambe Street.

Once off the tram, they hurried to Morecambe Street, to their lodgings, in hope. The Palmers were out, obviously still looking, proving themselves friends in a crisis. And there was no sign of Effel.

Jim did not want to go to the police for help, not yet at least. His relationship with the children was a tenuous one. There was always the possibility that authority would not approve him as a guardian.

Orrice said, 'We got to find 'er, we got to.'

'Yes, we have,' said Jim.

'I just thought.' Hope brightened Orrice. 'D'you fink she might've gone to me Aunt Glad's? She knows where Aunt Glad lives all right. If she got lost but found Walworth Road, she'd know 'ow to get to Aunt Glad's from there.'

Something occurred to Jim. Effel had confessed she had drawn a wreath for her mum and dad. If lost, if unable to find Morecambe Street and her brother, to what would her lonely and frightened mind point her? The home of her mum and dad?

'Orrice, does she know how to reach Deacon Street?'

'She would from Walworth Road,' said Orrice.

'And she could get into your parents' house?'

'She'd just pull the latchcord, except last time we went it wasn't 'anging.'

'Orrice, let's go there.'

'I think you've got sense, Uncle Jim.'

Very odd, thought Jim. Orrice had said think instead of fink. They hurried to Deacon Street. The latchcord was hanging. Uncle Perce had been picking up things.

There she was, upstairs, curled up on her parents' bed, worn out and crying quietly in the darkness. Jim struck a match and lit the gas mantle. Orrice rushed to the bed.

'Effel, oh, yer monkey,' he said, 'yer nearly been me death. Wha'd'yer go an' get lost for?'

Effel uncurled herself, came to her knees on the bed, and flung her arms around her brother's neck. She sobbed wetly into his shoulder.

'All over, Effel,' said Jim, 'don't worry now.'

'Orrice run orf, 'e left me,' wept Effel.

'No, I didn't,' protested the highly relieved Orrice, 'you went off wivout waitin' for me. Now yer don't need to cry any more, sis. Come on.'

Effel unwound herself and got off the bed. Her nose was wet and pink. Jim took his handkerchief out. He put it to her nose.

'Blow, Effel,' he said, and Effel blew. He gave her little nose a good wipe. 'Better?' he said.

'Want to go 'ome,' said Effel, nose dry but eyes wet.

Touched, Jim said, 'Come on, then.' He reached. Effel held her arms out and he took her up. She held on to him. Orrice retrieved her boater from the

166

foot of the bed. Jim carried Effel down the stairs. Orrice put the gas out and followed. The front door was still open. A figure appeared, a policeman's lantern switched on, and its light illuminated the man and the child.

'What's all this, then?' asked Constable Brownlaw, who had seen a light in the bedroom of a house still awaiting new tenants.

'So that's it,' said Jim a little later. He was in the parlour with Orrice and Effel, and the constable.

'Well, I don't know,' said Constable Brownlaw. 'By rights, you should all come to the station. By rights you should. But it's late for the kids, and Effel's had a bit of a long day. You all right now, Effel?'

'Yes please,' whispered Effel.

'You all right, Orrice?'

'You bet,' said Orrice. 'You ain't goin' to take us to no orphanage, are you, mister?'

'You like living with Mr Cooper?'

'We like it lots, don't we, Effel?'

'Want to go 'ome,' said Effel.

'Home?' said Constable Brownlaw.

'Wiv me bruvver,' said Effel. 'And 'im,' she said, with a look at Jim.

'Well, Mr Cooper, I'll just have a word tomorrow with their aunt and uncle. See what they say, y'know, before I think about a report. But I'd like your address first.' Jim gave him the Wansey Street address. 'Ah, that's where you said you're moving tomorrow. Very good, sir. Well, you'd best get

167

Effel back to your present lodgings now, and give her a nice mug of hot cocoa.'

'I couldn't see Soupy,' said Effel.

'Oh, the cat,' said Orrice.

'Ah, a neighbour's taken your cat in,' said Constable Brownlaw. 'All right, off you go, then, Mr Cooper, I'll turn the gas lamp out.'

'Thanks very much,' said Jim, 'thanks for everything.'

'Good night, sir. Good night, kids.'

He watched them go down the lamplit street, the one-armed man carrying the tired little girl. Well, he thought, there's some men with two arms who couldn't do a better carrying job than that.

The door of nineteen Wansey Street opened. Miss Rebecca Pilgrim presented herself in a crisp white plain blouse and long black skirt. She wore no jewellery of any kind, not even a brooch, but she did have a black armband around the left sleeve of her blouse. Jim supposed she was still in mourning for her dead parents. Miss Pilgrim could have told him she was mostly in mourning for her withered illusions.

'Good morning, Miss Pilgrim.'

'Good morning, Mr Cooper.' Her handsomeness wore its severe look. 'It is nearly fifteen minutes past ten.'

'Yes, I said ten, didn't I?'

'Ten o'clock was when I expected you.'

'It was a little difficult to detach myself from Mrs Palmer, my landlady, and I also couldn't find my

168

collar studs. So sorry.' Jim smiled. Miss Pilgrim's eyebrow went up, as if a smile and an apology had no right to be offered together. 'I left them in the end. My collar studs. But I do have the one I'm wearing. Men and their collar studs, is that what you're thinking?' Jim could not help being easy and communicative with people, but Miss Pilgrim seemed to believe that informal dialogue should not take place until an acceptable acquaintance had been established, for her startlingly blue eyes stared coolly at him from between the long stiff lashes.

'I have never concerned myself with men's collar studs, Mr Cooper. My father was perfectly capable of looking after his and knowing where they were. Please come in.'

Jim hefted his luggage case and entered. The case contained his and the children's clothes, and a few other things. He had not had to worry about furniture, and his possessions were few. He was not a collector of things, except books, for he had never been able to afford anything of real value. He had to go back to Morecambe Street for the books and other items, such as toilet articles.

'It's a lovely morning,' he said in the little hall.

'Yes.' Miss Pilgrim was not given to discussing the weather. She thought such discussions trivial and useless. Nowhere in the New Testament was it on record that Jesus had discussed the weather with his disciples. 'I will lead the way, Mr Cooper.'

'Thanks,' said Jim. The luggage case was heavy, but his one arm had developed extra strength and muscularity. He followed her up the stairs. The hem of her hitched skirt swayed, and the starched lace of a long white petticoat crisply peeped. The garment rustled in Victorian fashion. She led the way to the front bedroom.

'For you and the boy, of course,' she said, 'although I cannot yet afford to replace the double bed with singles. You would prefer singles, perhaps?'

'Oh, Horace and I will manage with the double,' said Jim, placing the case on the bed. 'I need to unpack right away, I've to take the case back for other things, including my books.'

'I approve of books, serious books,' she said, hands crossed over her stomach rather in the manner of a stern workhouse matron.

'I like all kinds myself,' said Jim, opening up the case. 'Any book improves one's knowledge, even if only a little, don't you think so?'

'It does not necessarily improve one's mind,' said Miss Pilgrim.

'That's a point,' said Jim, removing clothes and placing them on the bed, 'but not one that's ever occurred to me.'

Miss Pilgrim, watching his one hand at work, said, 'I should hope, as the children's guardian, you would endeavour to improve their minds by selecting their reading.'

'Treat me lightly,' said Jim with another smile, 'I've only just taken the job on.'

Again she seemed to find his light approach out of place.

'You must take your responsibilities seriously,' she said. 'By the way, there are hangers in the wardrobes, Mr Cooper. If you will give me the girl's things, I will take them to her room and hang them for you.'

'You're a paragon, Miss Pilgrim, do you know that?'

Miss Pilgrim looked startled, even shocked.

'I am a weak creature before God, Mr Cooper, as most of us are.'

'Most of us certainly are,' said Jim, 'but you are certainly not. You're very exceptional. My word, a forest of hangers,' he said, as he opened the wardrobe. 'Would you like to take Ethel's clothes and shoes, then? I'd be much obliged.'

'Very well.' Miss Pilgrim lifted a heap of folded clothes and underwear from the bottom of the case. Jim placed Effel's spare pair of new shoes on top of the heap, and offered a grateful smile. Her stiff lashes remained stiff. 'Do not make the beds on Mondays,' she said. 'That is when the bed linen will be changed. And please make sure all rubbish is placed in the dustbin outside the back door.'

'I've got you,' said Jim.

'Pardon?'

'We'll do that. I really appreciate having you take care of our bed linen.'

'My bed linen, I think, Mr Cooper,' she said.

'Yes, of course,' said Jim, pleasant and agreeable of manner. 'We'll all do our best not to make too much work for you.'

'I consider housework a small but worthwhile occupation, Mr Cooper,' said Miss Pilgrim, the armful of clothes resting against her bosom. 'We cannot all be great painters or great musicians. God in His infinite wisdom bestows a variety of talents, and even those of us with only small talents have the gift of a pair of hands.'

'It all comes down to that at times, perhaps, a pair of hands,' smiled Jim.

'Which we possibly take for granted until we lose one,' said Miss Pilgrim. 'I am sorry about your loss.'

'Don't mention it,' said Jim, 'I'm used to it now. Oh, Ethel's socks.' He picked up two pairs from the bottom of the case and placed them on top of the shoes. Miss Pilgrim received the small extra burden without fuss, and she carried the heap to the smaller bedroom. Jim hung clothes in the wardrobe and placed other items in the chest of drawers. Miss Pilgrim made short work of putting Effel's clothes away. She returned.

'When do you commence civilized day duties?' she asked.

'Monday fortnight,' said Jim.

'Monday fortnight? That is almost three weeks. I was under the impression it was two weeks.'

'I must have been too approximate,' said Jim. 'So sorry. Which reminds me, here's the first week's rent.' He handed her twelve shillings. She at once went downstairs to enter the payment in a rent book. She returned and gave him the book.

'It is not a good thing for a boy and girl to be left alone in the evenings,' she said.

'They've been very good up to now,' said Jim. 'Orrice—'

172

'Who?'

'Horace. He's a sensible boy. I don't think they'll break your furniture up.'

Her frosty look arrived.

'Is that a joke, Mr Cooper?'

'More of a reassurance, I hope,' said Jim. 'I'll go and get my books and other things now.'

'That is not very sensible, two journeys with a heavy case,' she said. 'A boy with a small handcart would have been more practical.'

'The small handcarts are sitting in back yards,' said Jim, 'and boys are all at school.'

'I see. Yes, very well.' She looked, however, as if she did not think he had made a sound point.

When he turned up again, the case was obviously even heavier. From her opened door, she frowned at him.

'It's no problem,' said Jim, 'and exercise is good for me.'

A passing neighbour stopped to look.

'Good morning, Miss Pilgrim,' she said.

'Good morning, Mrs Hardiman,' said Miss Pilgrim, and Mrs Hardiman looked at Jim and his large luggage case.

'He's not selling things, is he?' she asked. 'I 'ad someone call last week, selling combs and 'air-clips and suchlike, would you believe. Gypsy, I thought.'

'No, Mr Cooper is not selling things, Mrs Hardiman,' said Miss Pilgrim politely. 'I am letting my upstairs suite to the gentleman and two young wards of his.'

'Oh, my, yes, I 'eard you was renting out, Miss

Pilgrim,' said Mrs Hardiman, avid with interest under her granny bonnet. 'That's the gentleman? Mr Cooper, you said? Good morning to you, Mr Cooper, I'm Mrs 'Ardiman, I lives farther down. Well, I'm sure they'll make nice lodgers for you, Miss Pilgrim, and all for the best, as they say.'

'Yes, good morning, Mrs Hardiman,' said Miss Pilgrim, and closed the door. 'Here is your door-key, Mr Cooper.' She picked a key up from the top of the hallstand drawer. Jim put his case down and took it. 'I hope, apart from your present hours of work, you won't keep late hours.'

'I can't afford to,' said Jim.

'Many of us shoulder the cross of poverty,' she said, 'but we are all enriched by nature's wonders. I do not wish to interfere, it is not my place to, but I should like to know if the children are expected to get tea or supper for themselves while you are at work.'

'Firstly, I'll take sandwiches to the school for them at midday,' said Jim, 'and prepare supper for them before I leave in the afternoons.'

'A cold supper? Sandwiches at midday, and a cold supper?' Miss Pilgrim was plainly disapproving. 'Really, Mr Cooper.'

'Well, Horace will heat up potatoes—'

'I should not like a young boy using lighted gas rings, Mr Cooper.'

'He's very capable,' said Jim.

'I should still not like it, and am surprised that you have no qualms. Do you not know that most domestic accidents involve children?'

174

'Is that a fact, Miss Pilgrim?' Jim looked thoughtful.

'It is, Mr Cooper.'

'I'll need to think.'

'Please do,' said Miss Pilgrim, 'please think about active children and boiling water. I am sure you would not forgive yourself if there were an accident while you were at work.'

'No, I wouldn't,' said Jim. 'I think I may have been too casual, and I think I'm going to value any advice you care to give. It's been my experience that the soundest advice always comes from women. I've a feeling you and I will get along fine, Miss Pilgrim, you're a quite splendid person.'

A little frown marked her smooth brow.

'Mr Cooper, I am not used to being addressed in that way.'

'You're not used to being called splendid?' said Jim.

'We are still comparative strangers, Mr Cooper.'

'You've still been splendid to me and the kids.'

'Kids?' Miss Pilgrim's crisp blouse quivered. For all that she had lived eleven years in Walworth, she did not like common words to be tossed at her by an adult.

'Horace and Ethel.' Jim sensed her preference for refined conversation, if it was at all possible. 'I'm not a City gentleman, as you'll have noticed, I'm pretty ordinary and inclined to sometimes sing a tune when I open my mouth.'

'Sing a tune?' Miss Pilgrim looked as if she had let a whistling barrow-boy into her house.

'In a manner of speaking,' said Jim. 'So if you do us a kindness – no, if you do us more kindnesses, I'll probably come up with a cockney eureka, and certainly call you splendid or priceless or even saintly.'

'Really, Mr Cooper, what nonsense,' she said firmly. 'I have mixed with all kinds and lived among the people here for eleven years. I've heard many things I would rather not have heard, but I haven't heard such nonsense as that. You must excuse me now, I have work to do.' Miss Pilgrim turned and sailed past the staircase into her kitchen, all canvas rustling.

Jim went smiling up the stairs, carrying his heavy case.

About to leave the house at ten to twelve, with sandwiches for the kids, he was detained by Miss Pilgrim.

'Mr Cooper, I hope you won't think I am interfering, but until you take up your day duties, I am willing to cook a hot midday meal for you and the children. That will leave them only needing an evening tea.'

Jim, touched by the gesture, said, 'That's true Christian generosity, Miss Pilgrim, but I couldn't put you to such trouble.'

'It is no trouble,' said Miss Pilgrim, 'I am accomplished in all the domestic arts, and I cook for myself at midday. Naturally, I must charge you for the food. It will only be until you have finished working a late shift, but until then I do not like to think the children will not have one hot meal a day.'

'What can I say except that I think you—'

'Kindly do not call me saintly. Have the children come home for a hot midday meal from tomorrow. You must let me know if there is any food they dislike.' And Miss Pilgrim returned to her kitchen.

Orrice and Effel were at the school gates. Alice, munching an apple, was hovering, and Effel was in a temper about it. So far, however, all little tantrums had had no effect on Alice, whose sweet nature could absorb all stings and arrows.

'Here we are, kids,' said Jim, and handed a packet of sandwiches to each. 'Ham and tomato for you, Orrice, ham and pickle for Effel.'

'Ham?' said Orrice, cap in the boys' cloakroom, hair tousled. 'Crikey, me and Effel don't 'alf like ham, Uncle Jim.'

'Ugh,' said Effel.

'Did I hear something, Effel?' asked Jim.

'Don't like 'am,' said Effel.

'You sure?' said Jim.

'Well, a' right,' said Effel.

'Horace?' called Alice, and Jim looked at the hovering girl in a pretty pinafore dress.

'My word, there's a young beauty,' he said. 'Have you clicked, Orrice?'

''E ain't talkin',' muttered Effel, unwrapping her sandwiches.

'Course I am,' said Orrice. 'I got to tell yer, Uncle.' He gloomed over his own sandwiches, but took a bite at one, all the same. 'I got to tell yer that I dunno if me life's worth livin'.'

'Horace?' Alice was moving slowly up on him.

'You've got problems, Orrice?' asked Jim gravely.

'Well, I got Effel goin' on at me about running orf and leavin' 'er yesterday, which I didn't but which she keeps saying I did, and I got Alice after me to skip with 'er and go and 'ave tea with 'er at 'er mum's. I dunno what 'arm I ever done anyone to get me life all messed up like this.'

'Poor old chap,' said Jim. It was new to him, and it was enlivening, having Orrice and Effel to talk to and to listen to. 'Your brother's sorely tried, Effel.'

'No, 'e ain't,' said Effel, through bread, ham and pickle, ''e's lettin' 'er sit wiv 'im in class, 'e is. 'E better not do any kissin' wiv 'er, that's all, 'e better not, I'll scratch 'im all over if 'e does. She ain't 'is sister, I am. She ain't lost 'er mum an' dad, I 'ave, an' she's got a toffee-apple face, an' I bet she's all sticky. Ugh. I'm goin' to pull all 'er 'air out, you see if I don't, you Orrice.'

'Lovaduck,' said Orrice, 'don't she go on when she's talking? Didn't I tell yer, Uncle, it's best when she ain't talkin'?'

'I can't deny it, Orrice, you did tell me that,' said Jim.

'Horace, can you come and skip?' Alice was close.

Effel hissed. Orrice turned his head.

'I'm a bit busy, Alice,' he said, 'I'm talkin' to me Uncle Jim, an' besides, me legs don't feel very well.'

Alice laughed and came right up. Jim looked down at her. He saw engaging prettiness.

'Are you Horace's uncle?' she asked. 'Isn't he a nice boy, he helps me with my sums in class – ouch!' Effel had trodden on her foot. 'Ethel, do mind.'

'Ethel?' said Jim.

'Wasn't me,' said Effel, and ate some sandwich.

'Ethel?' said Jim again.

'Oh, she didn't mean it,' said Alice.

'Ethel?' said Jim yet again.

'Oh, a' right, sorry,' said Effel, but looked fiendish. A boy called to Alice, a favourite with many of the young males. 'Someone wants yer,' said Effel.

'Oh, I'd rather be with you and Horace,' said Alice, and looked up at Jim. She smiled. 'I told my mum what a lovely boy Horace is.'

Orrice went pale. Effel shrieked with fiendish laughter.

''Oo's a loverly boy, then?' she shouted. Orrice went for her. She dodged around Alice and then ran. Orrice bounded after her, roaring at her.

'Oh, I'd better go and help poor Ethel,' said Alice, eager to join the fray and to get herself chased by Orrice.

'Yes, off you go, Alice, and give him one in the eye,' said Jim. He stood at the gates, watching, remembering his years at the orphanage and the discipline that kept high spirits repressed. He saw Alice running with the untrammelled joy of the young. He saw Effel scampering, twisting and

179

dodging, one uneaten sandwich in her left hand, a half-eaten one in her right. He saw Orrice in chase of her, darting around playing boys and girls, and he saw Alice catch him up and get between him and his sister. She danced about in challenge. Orrice halted and clutched his forehead.

Jim left then, a smile on his face. Orrice had problems.

CHAPTER ELEVEN

The school bell, ringing, signalled the end of classes. At a few minutes after four, Higgs and his two friends were waiting at the gates. Effel and Orrice came up, and Alice was not far behind.

''Ere, you, Wivvers,' said Higgs.

'Now what?' said Orrice, cap on, shoulders squared.

''Ands orf Alice, that's what,' said Higgs. 'And take yer farver's togs orf when yer get 'ome. Yer got that, Wivvers?'

'No, I ain't got it,' said Orrice, 'I wasn't listening.'

'Oh, yer wasn't, wasn't yer?'

''Oppit, faceache,' said Orrice.

'Yer got a way of upsettin' me, Wivvers,' said Higgs, he and his two friends forming a barrier.

'Don't you 'it my bruvver,' said Effel.

'Now, Effel, you ain't goin' to get worried about 'im, are yer?' said Orrice. ''E couldn't even damage a bag of monkey nuts.'

'Oh, yer gettin' me real upset,' said Higgs. 'Alice, come 'ere.'

'Shan't,' said Alice.

'Come 'ere,' said Higgs, and grabbed her arm and pulled her. He fell over then. Orrice had landed a right to his jaw.

Mr Hill came running up a minute later. He separated the contestants, Orrice having become embroiled with Higgs and both his friends. Effel was also embroiled, delivering kicks. So was Alice.

Miss Pilgrim, answering a knock on her front door, opened it. On the step stood Orrice and Effel. Effel had her head bent, and Orrice was hidden by his cap.

'We've come, Miss Pilgrim,' said Orrice, 'can we go up?'

'Boy, lift your head,' said Miss Pilgrim, having remarked a tear in his trousers and dust on his jersey. Orrice lifted his head. Beneath the peak of his cap he revealed, reluctantly, a puffy left cheek, a discoloured left eye and a cut on his chin. 'Disgraceful,' said Miss Pilgrim. Effel gulped. 'Do you hear me, boy?'

'Yes'm,' said Orrice.

'You've been fighting.'

'Yes'm,' said Orrice. He thought. 'But not much.'

'On your first day here and only your second day at St John's, you've been fighting?'

'Only a little bit,' said Orrice.

'Disgraceful,' said Miss Pilgrim.

'Please, it—' Effel's voice collapsed under the stern look of their new landlady.

'You had better come in. Wipe your feet first.' Miss Pilgrim had placed a rope mat on her front step, to ensure soles were reasonably clean when they encountered the hall mat. Carefully, Effel and Orrice wiped their feet, and under the eye of Miss

Pilgrim wiped them again on the hall mat. 'Take your cap off, young man.'

'Yes'm,' said Orrice, and took it off. His hair was dusty and awry, his discoloured eye very perceptible.

'Go into my kitchen,' said Miss Pilgrim, closing the front door.

'Please'm—'

'At once. You too, Ethel.'

The kitchen was bright because its window looked out on to the little green garden and not the brick wall of a back yard. Light travelled to the window without interference. Pinewood furniture of a simple and practical design looked so freshly scrubbed that it was awesomely clean to Orrice and Effel. The linoleum shone. The range was alight, its fire damped down for the moment. An iron kettle stood on the hob. China cups, hanging on the dresser's hooks, gleamed. Beyond the kitchen was the scullery with its sink and tap, and its door to the garden. Orrice saw the green of grass and the golden heads of daffodils. Crikey, he thought, it's like the country.

'Miss Pilgrim, I only—'

'Disgraceful,' said Miss Pilgrim for a third time. She put a firm hand under his chin and lifted his face. She examined his bruised eye and his puffy cheek. Effel stood nervously on one leg. 'Sit down, boy,' said Miss Pilgrim, and drew out a chair from the table.

'Yes'm,' said Orrice, and sat down.

'What is wrong with your leg, child?' asked Miss Pilgrim of Effel. 'Is it hurt?'

Hastily, Effel put her left foot to the floor.

'Oh, she's always doing that, Miss Pilgrim,' said Orrice. 'She's always standin' on one leg. It don't mean anyfing. She just does it.'

'H'm,' said Miss Pilgrim. She took up a basin from the dresser, went out to the sink and turned the tap on. She came back with water in the basin, and a clean flannel. 'Sit straight, boy,' she said. Orrice straightened his back. Miss Pilgrim dipped the flannel and applied it wet and cold to his bruised eye and his puffy cheek. She repeated the process several times. Orrice found the cold wet flannel soothing. 'Does it hurt?' she asked.

'No'm. Well, not much.'

She cleaned up the cut on his chin, dabbed it dry with cotton wool and applied a little iodine, Effel watching with her mouth slightly open and her lashes flickering nervously.

'Just bruises,' said Miss Pilgrim. 'There will be no more fighting, young man, not while you are living in my house.'

'No'm,' said Orrice.

'Who were you fighting with?' she asked sternly.

'I dunno,' said Orrice. You didn't give names to grown-ups. No-one would speak to you if you did that.

'You don't know?'

'I never 'ardly ever seen 'em before,' said Orrice.

'Them?'

'Yes'm.'

'Disgraceful behaviour,' said Miss Pilgrim. 'It is not to happen again. Look at your trousers.'

Orrice regarded the torn knee of his trousers.

'It's just a tear, Miss Pilgrim.'

'Go upstairs, take your trousers off and get your sister to bring them down to me. That tear must be sewn.'

'Well, I—'

'At once.'

'Yes'm,' said Orrice, and left the kitchen with Effel. Upstairs, in their new lodgings, he said, 'Crikey, Effel, I betcher she ain't 'alf goin' to make us jump around. Well, yer better do what she says.' Orrice pulled his jersey up, unbelted his trousers and took them off.

'Ain't goin',' said Effel.

'Now, Effel, you got to. You said you liked 'er.'

'Didn't.'

'Yes, yer did.'

'Oh, a' right,' said Effel. She took the trousers down, knocked nervously on the kitchen door and waited.

'Come in, child.'

Effel rushed in, placed the trousers on the chair and rushed out again. Fifteen minutes later, Miss Pilgrim called to them from the foot of the stairs. There was silence for a few moments, then Orrice's head appeared over the landing banister.

'Yes'm?' he said.

'Your trousers, boy.'

Orrice came down the stairs, wearing other trousers. Miss Pilgrim gave him the repaired garment.

'Yer a sport, Miss Pilgrim, honest,' he said, and

she looked into brown eyes earnest with gratitude, albeit the right one was slightly swollen.

'I hope this incident will not repeat itself, young man. You and your sister are to come down to my kitchen at six o'clock, when I will give you your supper. I have discussed matters with your guardian, Mr Cooper. He has left me food to cook for your supper, and from tomorrow you will come here for a hot midday meal and return to school afterwards. This is until your guardian changes his hours of work. Is that quite clear?'

'You're goin' to give us an 'ot meal at school break times, Miss Pilgrim?' said Orrice, gaping.

'One hot meal a day is very necessary for boys and girls.'

'And we're to come down for an 'ot supper at six this evening?' said Orrice.

'That is what I said, boy.'

'Crikey, yer a real sport, Miss Pilgrim.'

'Kindly do not address me as a real sport, young man. Be down promptly at six.'

They were down promptly at six, having in the meantime thoroughly explored their new lodgings. Miss Pilgrim sent them straight back upstairs to wash their hands. When they came down again, she placed their supper before them. Jim had provided Miss Pilgrim with sausages, potatoes, tomatoes and onions, such being a reflection of his masculine tastes and his preference for simple bachelor cooking. Orrice gazed with joy at the fried onion rings and the creamy-looking mashed potatoes. Effel blinked. Miss Pilgrim, seated at the table with them, a pot of tea and bread and butter constituting her own meal, eyed Orrice as he picked up his knife and fork.

'We will say grace first,' she said.

'Yes'm,' said Orrice.

'We thank thee, Lord, for thy goodness and for bestowing on us that which is our sustenance this day.'

'Amen,' said Orrice.

'Amen,' gasped Effel, in awe at the savoury food and the stern, handsome lady who had cooked it.

'Kindly use the napkins,' said Miss Pilgrim.

'Beggin' yer pardon'm?' said Orrice faintly. He related napkins only to smelly babies.

'Here, child,' said Miss Pilgrim to Effel, and picked up the folded napkin beside the girl's plate, shook it out and tucked it into the neck of Effel's blouse. Oh, a bib, thought Orrice, they're for babies, too, what a funny woman. All the same, he unfolded his own napkin and tucked it into the neck of his jersey. Then he and Effel set to, he hungrily, Effel with the nervous cautiousness of a little girl continuing to be dubious about what was happening to her life. She had woken up last night, thought unhappily of her mum and dad, and cried a little before going to sleep again.

Miss Pilgrim ate bread and butter, drank tea and kept an eye on the table manners of these cockney children. The boy had rough edges, but to her relief he did not eat noisily. And the girl was almost dainty. That was because of her nervousness, which

187

Miss Pilgrim assumed was shyness. It had been no hardship to cook for them. She enjoyed many of the domestic arts, including cooking. If her first lodgers proved to be a little more troublesome than two respectable single ladies might have been, she must bear with that. They at least meant she did not have to go out and find a job, something which she viewed with distaste. She did not mind voluntary work for charity, she did not like the thought of working in a shop or office for a wage.

'Apart from the regrettable fight,' she said, 'how did you both get on at your new school today?'

'Ain't telling,' muttered Effel automatically.

'What was that, child?' asked Miss Pilgrim sternly, and Effel blushed crimson.

'Please, nuffink,' she said, and filled her mouth with sausage, which put her out of conversational action for the moment.

Orrice said, 'School's all right'm, but there's that Alice French, yer know.'

'Alice French?' said Miss Pilgrim. 'Yes, I do know her, and her family. Alice is a sweet child.' Effel choked on the sausage. 'What is wrong, Ethel?' Effel swallowed, the sausage went down, and she cast a fierce little look at her brother. It was all his fault. Fancy hitting that boy just because of that Alice. 'Have you lost your tongue, miss?' asked Miss Pilgrim crisply.

'Please'm,' said Orrice, 'Effel don't go in for talkin' sometimes.'

'Nonsense,' said Miss Pilgrim. Effel filled her mouth with mashed potato and onion rings, putting

188

her tongue out of action again. 'I should not like to think that is an absurd way of defining sulks. Sulks are not becoming, Ethel. And lift your head, child, your nose is almost in your supper.'

Effel reluctantly lifted her head. She blushed as she caught the direct glance of the striking blue eyes.

'Please'm,' said Orrice, having made a young trencherman's inroads into his supper, 'Effel don't 'ave sulks, it's just sometimes she don't talk.'

'You have no problem, boy,' said Miss Pilgrim.

'Well'm, I ain't shy like Effel—'

'Ethel,' said Miss Pilgrim with corrective reproof.

'Yes'm,' said Orrice. 'Still, you should've 'eard 'er dinnertime at the school gates, goin' on at our Uncle Jim about me and that Alice. That Alice, Miss Pilgrim, I dunno what I done to deserve 'er and 'er skippin'-rope. I ain't saying she ain't a nice girl—' An unsuppressible hiss escaped Effel. 'But boys don't do skippin', Miss Pilgrim, it makes yer look like a poof.'

The blue eyes gathered familiar frost.

'Boy,' said Miss Pilgrim, 'there are expressions I do not like to hear in my house, particularly from children.'

'I was only saying, like, I was only saying,' said Orrice. 'I can't get it into that Alice's 'ead that I don't do skippin'.'

'You are very fortunate, young man, that a girl as sweet as Alice is willing to be friends with you.'

'Yes'm,' said Orrice, and thought. 'Well,' he

said, 'I dunno it's friendly follering me about with a skippin'-rope that's got pink 'andles. Pink, Miss Pilgrim, would yer believe. It don't 'ardly bear finking about.'

Miss Pilgrim gave him a critical look. She saw a boy who needed a haircut, whose face was marked from brawling, who had a fresh, healthy complexion unusual in a Walworth urchin, and whose brown eyes were asking the whole world to look at what was happening to his social life.

'Nevertheless, Master Horace,' she said, 'I am sure your guardian, Mr Cooper, would like it if you got into no more fights and responded to Alice's gesture of friendship.'

'Yes'm,' said Orrice, and thought more as he polished off his supper. He looked up, eyeing their stiffly handsome landlady in alarm. 'Beg pardon, Miss Pilgrim, but yer don't mean do skippin' with 'er, do yer?'

'If that is her wish, why not, boy?'

'I'll fall down dead,' gasped Orrice.

'Nonsense.'

Effel uttered a strangled cry.

'Effel's feeling sick,' said Orrice. 'So am I,' he added, but only in a growling, barely audible mutter.

'Child, there is something wrong with you,' said Miss Pilgrim to Effel. 'What is it?'

Effel, in her fury, came out with it.

'Orrice ain't skippin', not wiv 'er, 'e don't even do it wiv me, and I'm 'is sister. She ain't nobody.'

Shocked, Miss Pilgrim said, 'Child, you are not

190

to speak like that, not at this table. Do you hear?'

'Want me mum,' said Effel, and a tear rolled. Miss Pilgrim sighed.

'There, finish up your food,' she said, 'and I will forget your little naughtiness. There is hot jam tart to follow. Do you like that?'

'Crikey, jam tart's scrumptious,' said Orrice. 'Miss Pilgrim's a real sport, ain't she, Effel?'

'Don't want none,' said Effel.

'Very well,' said Miss Pilgrim. She got up, removed their plates, took the jam tart out of the oven, cut Orrice a large slice and served it to him. She cut a small slice for herself. Orrice tucked in. Effel eyed the tart forlornly, then cast a glance at Miss Pilgrim. She gulped.

'Please, miss—' She gulped again.

'Well?' said Miss Pilgrim.

'I likes jam tart,' whispered Effel.

Silently, Miss Pilgrim served her.

'Say fank you, Effel,' said Orrice.

'Fank yer, miss,' said Effel, and bent her head and tucked in.

When they had finished, Miss Pilgrim gave them each a glass of water. Orrice asked if he and Effel should do the washing-up. Miss Pilgrim said it was pleasing to hear children offer, but preferred to do it herself. Her china was valuable to her.

'We're goin' out now,' said Orrice.

'Out?'

'We like goin' out.'

Miss Pilgrim, who had needlework to do, said, 'Very well. There is no need for me to tell you your guardian expects good behaviour from you. You are not, of course, to play ball games in the street—'

'We ain't got no ball'm,' said Orrice.

'I had not finished speaking, boy. You are not to play ball games in the street, or mark out the pavements for hopscotch or to kick tin cans about. My neighbours are used to relative quiet, and I should not want to be indirectly responsible for bringing rowdiness to the street. Be in at eight o'clock – you will hear the church clock chime. That is to be Ethel's bedtime here according to your guardian. Very well, off you go now.'

'Yes'm,' said Orrice. 'Miss Pilgrim, Effel and me want to fank you for the best supper ever.'

'I am satisfied to have helped to put a hot meal into you,' said Miss Pilgrim.

They escaped into the street, where Effel said, 'She don't like us.'

'Well, she don't ackcherly unlike us,' said Orrice, 'or she wouldn't 'ave cooked us that supper, or that jam tart.'

'Ain't goin' to no bed at eight o'clock,' said Effel.

'Yes, you are.'

'Ain't.'

'Yes, you are, or I'll wallop yer,' said Orrice. 'We got to do what Uncle Jim says.'

'Oh, a' right,' said Effel grumpily.

CHAPTER TWELVE

Jim, arriving at his work, stopped in the entrance hall of the club to say hello to Molly Keating, daughter of the manager. She was just coming out of her father's office. A brunette of infectious vivacity, she looked flawless in a lace-necked cream blouse and a well-fitting brown skirt. She worked part-time for her father.

''Lo, Jim old thing,' she said.

'Hello to you too,' said Jim.

'I'm tickled pink you're coming out of the kitchens into the book-keeping,' said Molly. 'Kitchen work, blow that for a lark, it's not what you should be doing. Port in a storm, that's all. I've just told Dad, as it happens, that you'll change my image of book-keepers. I've always thought them owlish. Good on you, Jim.'

Jim had a suspicion then that he owed his promotion to the manager's daughter. It did not deflate him or injure his pride. He simply thought, if it were true, that it was a typical gesture of help from a girl with a cheerful and generous nature.

'I'm keeping my fingers crossed that my ignorance won't show,' he said, 'and I'm doing what I can about that by studying this book-keeping manual.'

'That's what you're carrying, is it?'

'To get my nose into at break times. It doesn't seem too mysterious.'

'You've never done any book-keeping at all?' asked Molly.

'Keep it dark, Molly, or I'll be out on my ears before I've started.'

'No problem, lovey,' said Molly, 'I'll give you a hand as soon as you start.'

'You're a good friend,' said Jim.

'Hope so,' said Molly, 'it might mean being asked out one time.'

'And that,' said Jim, 'might mean I'll get thumped by your steady.' He had always kept his distance with Molly. He had had too many setbacks not to be wary in his relationships with women. These days he avoided getting himself into a situation where disclosure of his illegitimacy was inevitable.

'I don't have a steady,' said Molly.

'Well, you should,' smiled Jim, 'not all the young men around here can be that blind.'

'What young men?' asked Molly. She had a point. It was 1921 and the war had only been over two and a half years. The conflict had taken the lives of a million young men. Young women like Molly had to put up with a dearth of suitors.

'There'll always be one for a girl like you,' said Jim.

'Good-oh,' said Molly, 'send him along when you spot him, will you?'

'Pleasure,' said Jim, and went to the kitchen.

★ ★ ★

The following morning, having served up hot breakfast porridge, Jim sat down at the table in the bay window of the living-room. The kids spooned sugar over their porridge and stirred it in.

'So, young Horace, you got into a fight, did you?' said Jim.

'Yes, but like I just told you, Uncle, I didn't 'ardly know nuffink about it,' said Orrice.

'I don't think that's true,' said Jim.

'Well, yer can't split,' said Orrice.

'I suppose a black eye's honourable, and splitting isn't. But they're not going to like it at St John's.'

'No, well, we got to report to the 'eadmistress first thing,' said Orrice.

'Who's we exactly?'

'Oh, them and us,' said Orrice casually.

'Who's us?'

'Orrice ain't telling,' mumbled Effel through porridge.

'He can tell me,' said Jim.

'Well,' said Orrice cautiously, 'it's me first, then—'

'Stop telling,' breathed Effel.

'We got to tell our uncle, sis.'

'No, we ain't.' Effel grumbled over her porridge. ''E ain't our uncle.'

'I'll wallop you,' said Orrice.

'No walloping,' said Jim. 'You were saying?'

'Yes, Uncle, it's me and Effel and that Alice. And some boys.'

'Ethel,' said Jim, 'you and Alice were in the fight?'

'Wasn't,' said Effel, head bent.

'Is that a fib, Ethel?'

'Ain't telling,' said Effel.

'Well, you'll all have to take your medicine,' said Jim, 'and I'll have to talk to Miss Pilgrim after you've left for school. And remember you're coming here for your midday meal.'

Effel whispered, 'Is 'e grumpy wiv us, Orrice?'

'Are yer, Uncle Jim?' asked Orrice.

Jim regarded the boy's black eye and slightly swollen cheek.

'I don't think it meets with our kind landlady's approval,' he said, 'nor your headmistress's, but what's the enemy look like?'

Effel giggled then.

They stood before the headmistress, six of them. Orrice, Effel, Alice, Higgs, Stubbs and Cattermole. Orrice had his scars, Effel and Alice were unmarked, Higgs had a lumpy jaw and a black eye, Stubbs a bruised forehead and Cattermole a bruised cheek. Orrice had given a very good account of himself.

Mrs Wainwright, the headmistress, looked sorrowful. Mr Hill, also present, looked resigned. Boys were always boys. That was an unchangeable fact.

'Explain yourselves,' said the headmistress, looking at Higgs.

'Me?' said Higgs plaintively.

'You to begin with, yes.'

'I just fell over, mum—'

196

'Ma'am, if you don't mind.'

'I just fell over, ma'am,' said Higgs.

'I fell on top of 'im,' said Orrice.

'I went an' tripped,' said Cattermole.

'I dunno for sure what I did, ma'am,' said Stubbs, 'I think I must've gone an' tripped too.'

'Dear me,' said Mrs Wainwright, 'what have we here, Mr Hill? Four boys all clumsy enough to fall over at the same time?'

'It's food for thought,' said Mr Hill.

'And two girls, what did they do? Alice? Ethel? Kicking? Actually kicking? Is this true?'

'Well, you see, ma'am,' burst Alice, 'Horace was only—' She stopped as Orrice nudged her. The headmistress saw the nudge.

'Continue, Alice,' she said.

But Alice knew what the nudge had meant. She wasn't to tell tales. So she said, 'Please, ma'am, I don't know, I only remember Ethel being awf'lly upset when they all fell over.'

'Wasn't,' breathed Effel, scowling at her feet.

'What was that, Ethel?' asked Mrs Wainwright. Effel went deaf. 'Alice, is that all you remember?'

'Yes, ma'am,' said Alice, crossing her fingers behind her back.

'Dear me. Well, you two girls will never disgrace yourselves again. Never, do you understand?'

'Yes, ma'am,' said Alice.

'Do you understand, Ethel?'

Effel went deafer.

'She understands,' said Mr Hill, who thought Orrice's sister owned a lethal right foot.

'You may go, you girls,' said Mrs Wainwright.

The two girls left. In the corridor, Alice whispered, 'Oh, poor Horace, he'll get the cane.'

'I'll pull yer 'air out if 'e does,' breathed Effel.

Mrs Wainwright addressed the four boys.

'I will not have fighting or brawling at the school gates or anywhere else in the school. You will each receive a stroke of the cane.' She produced the cane from the cupboard. Mr Hill hid a smile. That was always as much as the headmistress could bring herself to apply, a single stroke. 'Do you understand your punishment and the reason for it? Do you also accept it?'

'Yes'm,' said Orrice.

'Yes, a' right, ma'am,' said Higgs, and Stubbs and Cattermole nodded.

'Horace Withers, put out your right hand,' commanded the headmistress, and Orrice complied, turning his palm flatly upwards. The cane swished. It smote his hand, stinging it. Orrice grimaced. She liked his stoicism. She dealt similarly with the other boys, then she said to Orrice, 'You haven't made a very good start at this school, Master Withers.'

'No, ma'am, sorry.'

Mr Hill said, 'You've all had the minimum, you young terrors. Justice has been tempered with mercy. Thank your lucky stars.'

'Yes, ta very much, sir,' said Cattermole. They had all taken their medicine without fuss.

'Go to your classes,' said the headmistress, and they left. She gave Mr Hill a rueful look. 'I do dislike this kind of thing.'

198

'Sometimes you're left with no option,' said Mr Hill. 'What a collection of muscle. Long time since I've seen a scrap like that. It looked to me as if Withers was taking them all on, with a little help from his sister and Alice. And what an excuse, they all fell over together. Let's hope you've made them think twice about a return bout, mmm? Brave performance, headmistress.'

Just before entering the classroom, Higgs said to Orrice, 'I'll get yer somewhere else some time, Wivvers.'

'I'll enjoy that,' said Orrice, 'but I don't fink you will.'

Later, in class, Alice whispered, 'Is it hurting?'

'Is what hurting?' asked Orrice.

'The cane.'

'Not much,' said Orrice, 'but I won't be able to hold any skippin'-rope.'

'Never mind,' whispered Alice, 'I brought apples for us playtime.' When playtime came, she gave Effel one too. Effel took it, jumped on it and ground it to pulp. 'Oh, Ethel, look what you've done,' said Alice, 'you can't eat it now.'

'Ain't goin' to, neither,' hissed Effel.

'Never mind,' said Alice forgivingly, 'here's another one.'

Effel screamed in rageful frustration.

Jim knocked on Miss Pilgrim's kitchen door.

'Come in,' she called, and he entered.

'Good morning, Miss Pilgrim.'

'Good morning, Mr Cooper,' she said. She took her apron off and hung it up. In a white blouse crisp with starch, black skirt draping long legs in straight severity, she regarded her lodger a little accusingly.

'Yes, I know,' said Jim, wryly.

'What do you know, Mr Cooper?'

'I know what you're thinking.'

'I doubt that, Mr Cooper.'

'You're not thinking Horace is a young hooligan?'

'I am thinking, Mr Cooper, that as the boy's guardian it was remiss of you not to ensure his good behaviour at his new school.'

'Yes, black mark against me, Miss Pilgrim, but the fact is I'm treading a little gently at the moment. They still feel the loss of their parents, and I can't yet bring myself to apply a heavy hand.'

'Heavy hand?' Miss Pilgrim's blue eyes showed frosty disapproval. 'I hope, Mr Cooper, you are not considering assault and battery in place of simple Christian discipline. A smart rap over the knuckles is as much as I'd permit in this house.'

'Assault and battery?' Jim laughed. The striking blue eyes turned even frostier. 'Good grief, nothing of the kind, Miss Pilgrim. I don't go in for that sort of thing. I suspect, in any case, that Horace was standing up for himself.'

'I am relieved to hear you have a Christian attitude, Mr Cooper, although I have to say it was disgraceful of Horace to get into a fight during his first week at St John's. I hope you'll ensure it doesn't happen again.'

'I rather fancy the headmistress will have turned his ears pink by now,' said Jim. 'I must thank you for attending to his wounds and for giving him and Ethel such a fine supper last night. They were rapturous about it. You really are a splendid person.'

'Nonsense,' said Miss Pilgrim. 'I'm going shopping now, I must buy for the midday dinner. I will charge you for everything at the end of the week.'

'Can't thank you enough,' said Jim, who had book-keeping to study. 'Oh, if it's any help, I've discovered Ethel and Horace are partial to hot faggots and pease pudding from the shop in the market.'

'Faggots and pease pudding?' Miss Pilgrim positively quivered. 'You aren't serious, I trust?'

Jim rubbed his chin and said cautiously, 'Hot faggots and pease pudding are considered a treat by Walworth people, aren't they?'

'They may be, Mr Cooper, but I should want to know what went into the faggots before I served them in this house, or before I carried them home in a basin. I shall bring back wholesome food that doesn't have a question mark to it.'

'Happy to leave it to you, Miss Pilgrim,' said Jim cheerfully.

'The boy needs a haircut,' said Miss Pilgrim.

'Right, he does,' said Jim, 'I'll see he goes to the barber's on Saturday morning.'

Things, thought Jim, went quite well that first week. Over the midday meals, always perfectly

201

cooked and served, Miss Pilgrim's attitude towards the children was firm but not unkind. She did not ask him to correct their little faults, she took it upon herself to do so. Jim liked that. He could not see it as interference, he saw it as typical of her straightforwardness. The other way would have made her sound a complaining woman. She would not permit slouching or slipshod table manners, but she saw to it that they ate well, and she did not suggest at any time that they should be discouraged from making conversation. She dealt coolly with Effel's little mutterings and little sulks, and as an intellectual woman took a keen interest in her progress at school. Effel was not very forthcoming about that, either to Jim or Miss Pilgrim, viewing them both with the mutinous look of a child who wasn't going to believe anyone could think school was interesting. It was Effel's private opinion that schools ought to be for grown-ups only, as grown-ups were the ones who went on about them. Orrice's reactions were different. He found lessons easy, and accordingly school wasn't a trial to him. He answered up brightly in his replies to Miss Pilgrim's enquiries. He had only one complaint, and it was a complaint Effel shared with him. He couldn't get rid of that Alice French, he said.

'Boy,' said Miss Pilgrim sternly, 'must you speak of that sweet girl in such a deplorable way? Get rid of her indeed.'

'But, Miss Pilgrim,' protested Orrice through a lump of hot potato, 'she's 'aunting me.'

Miss Pilgrim eyed him aloofly. Jim coughed.

'You should not speak with your mouth full, Master Horace,' said Miss Pilgrim. 'What do you mean, haunting you?'

'I can't get rid of 'er, honest, m'm. It don't matter where I sit in class, she's always gettin' next to me. And I got two of 'em follering me about in the playground, 'er and Effel. I'm sorely tried, I am, Miss Pilgrim, I ain't got no life of me own. And that Alice, she's goin' to get me to go to Sunday tea even if it kills 'er.'

'Your sister's name is Ethel, boy. Ethel.'

'Yes'm, Effel.'

'You must help these children with their pronunciation, Mr Cooper,' said Miss Pilgrim severely.

'Give you my word,' said Jim who, with one arm missing, ate in the American fashion.

'Master Horace,' she said, 'if Alice has invited you to Sunday tea, you must accept.'

'Eh?' said Orrice, stricken.

'Of course you must.'

''E ain't goin' wivout me,' breathed Effel.

'Sit up, child, and lift your head when you speak,' admonished Miss Pilgrim. 'What was it you just said?'

'Nuffink,' grumbled Effel.

That was one of many similar pieces of dialogue.

Each afternoon before he left for his work, Jim prepared tea for the kids. When they came home from school, all they had to do was take it out of the little cupboard used as a larder. It was to be eaten at six o'clock, but they could help themselves to a slice of bread-and-butter beforehand if they wanted to. And at six o'clock, Miss Pilgrim took them up a pot of tea to have with their meal. This was because she did not like unsupervised children dealing with a kettle of boiling water. She always asked them if their hands were clean. If they weren't, she reminded them that cleanliness was next to godliness, and insisted they washed them immediately. Orrice didn't mind. Effel minded a lot. Her mum had never made her do things like that, nor had her dad. Miss Pilgrim wasn't her mum, and the man who was looking after her and Orrice wasn't her dad. He was in league with Miss Pilgrim, because he made her wash herself everywhere she showed. Her face, her ears, her neck and her knees.

Jim took them both to Manor Place Baths on Saturday morning. He placed Effel in charge of a beefy woman attendant in the women's section, and Effel nearly died when she saw the size of the bath and the huge amount of hot water in it. She yelled.

'I ain't, I won't, I'll get drownded!'

'Come on, me little ducks, let's get yer in,' said the woman, and whipped the small girl's clothes off. Effel screamed as she was lifted and dumped. Hot water swallowed her, swamped her, surged around her and brought sensations of bodily bliss.

'Oh, crikey,' she breathed, 'ain't it good?'

'Like it, do yer?' said the beefy attendant. 'Thought yer would, once you was in. 'Ere y'ar, little lady, 'ere's yer soap.' She handed Effel a large yellow cake of Sunlight. 'An' there's yer back scrubber. Give yer ten minutes. We're busy Saturdays. Soap yerself all over now, make the most of yer sixpenn'orth.'

When Effle emerged from the Victorian building in company with Orrice and Jim, she was pink and shining.

'Nearly drownded, I did,' she complained.

'Course yer didn't,' said Orrice, fresh-faced and newly clean.

'Yes, I did,' said Effel, casting an accusing glance at Jim. 'Well, I nearly did.'

'We all did,' said Jim. 'Well, nearly. What d'you think of Effel's after-bath look, Orrice?'

'Can't 'ardly believe it,' said Orrice. 'Lummy, don't a bath make yer feel good all over, Uncle Jim?'

Effel let go an arrow. ''Oo's a pretty boy all over, then?' she said. With street kids about, Orrice turned pale. Imagine any kids hearing a thing like that.

'Uncle Jim, can I chuck Effel off a bridge?' he asked.

'No chucking off bridges, Orrice,' said Jim, and sent the boy off to the barber's. When the lad arrived back in their lodgings, Effel took a sly look at him and mimicked Alice.

'Oh, you're awf'lly lovely, Orrice.'

Orrice went for her. Effel ran, out of the living-room and down the stairs, shrieking. Orrice caught her at the foot of the stairs, and they both fell to the floor of the little hall. Miss Pilgrim appeared.

'Disgraceful! Get up, both of you.' Effel and

Orrice scrambled to their feet. Jim showed himself at the top of the stairs. Miss Pilgrim looked up at him. 'Mr Cooper, my house is not a boxing ring or a fairground. Kindly inform your wards of that.' She rustled stiffly back to her kitchen.

'Come up here,' said Jim. They went up. He read them a minor riot act and sent them out to the market. When they returned, he despatched them downstairs to make their peace with Miss Pilgrim. Orrice knocked on the kitchen door.

'Come in.'

They went in, Orrice bearing a wrapped sheaf of bright-headed daffodils, bought in the market. Effel hid herself behind him. An aroma of cooking food assailed their noses.

'If yer please'm,' said Orrice, 'we're sorry and would yer kindly accept these daffs, if yer please'm.'

Miss Pilgrim regarded the flowers in surprise. Orrice gazed in hope at her. Her clear searching eyes sought Effel. Effel gulped and hid herself deeper at her brother's back.

'Thank you, Master Horace,' said Miss Pilgrim, and took the sheaf. 'What is the matter with your sister?'

'She don't like showing 'erself when she's got worries, Miss Pilgrim,' said Orrice. 'She finks yer goin' to throw 'er out.'

'Thinks,' said Miss Pilgrim.

'Yes'm.' Orrice untied his tongue. 'Thinks,' he said.

'Good. Ethel, show yourself.'

206

Effel emerged, head hanging.

'Sorry,' she said.

'Well, I'm sure it won't happen again,' said Miss Pilgrim graciously. 'I am quite used to children through my mission work, but not to thumping, bumping and rolling ones. Also, I don't wish either of you to break your legs. I will see you all at midday dinner. Thank you for the flowers, both of you. But such extravagance. However, off you go.'

'Thumping, bumping and rolling,' said Jim, over a stomach-filling meal of steak-and-kidney pie.

'Pardon, Mr Cooper?' said Miss Pilgrim.

'Can't have that,' said Jim. 'Told 'em so. Can't have racketing about, or thumps and bumps.'

The severe blue eyes regarded him suspiciously.

'We agreed, Mr Cooper, on good behaviour.'

'Do you hear that, kids?' said Jim.

'I won't fump Effel indoors again, Miss Pilgrim,' said Orrice, 'only in the street.'

'Incorrigible boy, I hope your guardian will see to it you don't thump your little sister in this house or out of it.'

'Yes,' said Jim, 'and it's thump, young man, not fump.'

'I ain't—'

'Aren't,' said Jim.

Puzzled, Orrice said, 'I aren't sure—'

'I'm not sure,' said Jim.

'Crikey,' said Orrice, 'now I dunno where I am.'

Miss Pilgrim coughed. Jim hid a smile.

'I'll serve the rice pudding,' said Miss Pilgrim.

'Rice puddin'?' said Orrice, eyes glowing. 'Cor, yer a swell, Miss Pilgrim.'

'That is an absurdity, boy. However, the daffodils were not. I think, Mr Cooper, you will be able to turn these children into children of the Lord.'

'Don't want no Lord,' mumbled Effel, 'just me mum an' dad.'

'Oh, dear,' sighed Miss Pilgrim.

CHAPTER THIRTEEN

On Sunday morning Miss Pilgrim departed early for church, but not before she had made it clear she expected her lodger to take his wards to the service. Church and God's Commandments, she said, shaped the minds of children and taught them the difference between self-indulgence and self-discipline.

Effel, discovering she was about to be taken to church, said, 'Ain't goin'.'

'Untrue,' said Jim.

'Ain't,' said Effel.

'Is,' said Jim. 'We're all going. That's why you're wearing your Sunday frock. Now put your boater on.'

'Don't like you,' muttered Effel.

'Well, you're stuck with me at the moment,' said Jim.

'Ain't goin' to no church,' said Effel.

'You're askin' for it, you are, sis,' said Orrice, who wore a new Sunday cap. It was against his will, but Jim had advised him his old cap wasn't a church-going one.

'Well, never mind,' said Jim, 'you and I will go, Orrice. Come on.' He and Orrice left the house. Effel stamped around, ran down the stairs and opened the front door. She saw them walking up the street. By the time they reached St John's Church she was close behind Orrice. Orrice turned and saw her. People were crowding in.

Effel aimed another arrow. Loudly, she said, 'Oh, ain't you pretty in yer Sunday suit, Orrice?'

The fates were against Orrice that morning.

The service opened with a hymn. In a front pew, with some ladies of her acquaintance, Miss Pilgrim stood to sing in a clear, fearless soprano. Effel mouthed inaudibly over the hymn book Jim had placed in her hands. Across the aisle, she saw Alice French with her mother and father. Effel scowled. Alice smiled.

The service got under way. Effel didn't mind the hymns too much, but everything else reminded her of Scripture lessons at school, which were boring. Orrice took it all in his stride. Orrice was adaptable. Effel was cast in a more rigid mould.

Alice sought to catch Orrice's eye.

''Aunting me, that's what she is,' growled Orrice during a hymn, but he put a penny in the collecting plate as a sign that he recognized his mum and dad had gone to a Christian heaven.

The sermon was all about Fight The Good Fight. The vicar, mellow of voice, spoke mostly of the fight against hardship. He was not too concerned about the antics of the devil, implying that his parishioners could recognize that dark gentleman when he knocked on their doors, and could, with a few exceptions, send him packing. Hardship was the greater menace to the people of Walworth.

Effel fidgeted. Jim thought about his dead

mother, and the fact that he didn't even have a photograph of her. She must have had some possessions when she died. Where had they got to?

Orrice kept his eyes off Alice and on the pulpit. But there was no escape. She was waiting for him when he came out of the church, her mum and dad with her. Alice whispered to her mum, a plump lady with a stalwart-looking husband.

'So you're Horace Withers,' said Mrs French.

'Who, me?' said Orrice in alarm. Effel, close by, began to grind her teeth.

'I'm Alice's dad,' said Mr French, 'and Alice 'ud like you to come to tea one Sunday.' Mr French eyed the boy with an amused smile. This was the one Alice had gone potty about. He could see why. There wasn't a healthier-looking boy in Walworth, nor a better-looking one. Kids were fun, especially nine-year-old daughters potty on a boy. 'Any Sunday you like, 'Orace.'

'Me?' gasped Orrice, wondering why life was dealing him blow after blow. Only his new uncle represented a decent bit of luck. 'Me?' he gasped again.

'Do say when, Horace,' begged Alice, stunningly pretty in a yellow frock and little bonnet.

'Take your time, young 'un,' said Mr French with a little grin. He could sympathize with the boy. He caught the eye of a tall one-armed man, who winked at him. Jim and Mr French both understood Orrice's problem.

'I dunno when I can say when,' said Orrice desperately.

211

'Next Sunday?' suggested Alice.

'Next Sunday?' queried Orrice, and received a kick in the back of his right leg from Effel. People, pouring out of the church, stopped to speak to friends or neighbours, and the churchyard, bright with April sunshine, became a hubbub of voices. In the distance could be heard the strains of a marching Salvation Army band. Orrice searched for escape words. 'I'm busy next Sunday.'

'Oh, you're not,' protested Alice.

'I'm busy most Sundays. Well, I will be, like. It's Miss Pilgrim's garden, yer see. She's our landlady. I got to 'elp wiv 'er garden on Sundays.'

'Yes, we heard she'd took in lodgers,' said Mrs French.

'Yes, well,' said Orrice, and stopped. Cool blue eyes were looking straight into his. 'Oh, cripes,' he muttered, 'now I done it.'

'Good morning, Mrs French, good morning, Mr French.' Miss Pilgrim's crisp voice cut in. 'Alice? Good morning. The sermon was encouraging, wasn't it?'

'Something like with our backs to the wall let's advance,' said Mr French, a man of thirty-four who had seen service with the Army in France and who considered himself lucky in stepping straight into a job as a railway ganger after being demobbed.

'We are all in service to God, we are all fighting His battles in our own way,' said Miss Pilgrim. 'Some more so, some less so. Alice, how pretty you look.'

Young Alice blushed a little.

212

'We're just asking Horace to Sunday tea, Miss Pilgrim,' she said.

'That is a kind Christian hand to a newcomer,' said Miss Pilgrim, and caught Jim's eye. Because Orrice was being trapped, Jim gave his handsome landlady a smile and a little wink. Miss Pilgrim stiffened in the way of a woman to whom a wink was more heathen than Christian. She said, 'I don't think Horace will be too busy in my garden, Alice.'

'Oh, thanks ever so,' said Alice, who had a natural way of doing justice to the King's English, her mum coming of a respectable family in Brighton. 'Horace can come next Sunday, then?'

'If his guardian gives permission,' said Miss Pilgrim. It was all over the neighbourhood by now, the fact that two new pupils at St John's School were in the care of a guardian, a Mr Cooper, and that they were lodging with Miss Pilgrim.

'You've my permission, Horace,' said Jim, and Orrice gave him a look of soulful reproach. 'But of course, if you really are busy—?'

'Well, I might—' Another kick arrived in the back of Orrice's leg.

'Come about half-four, Horace,' said Mrs French kindly, 'and we'll have shrimps and winkles.'

Effel, behind Orrice, uttered a suppressed gurgle of rage. Her boater and face suddenly materialized. She was pink with jealous fury. But before she could deliver herself of anything shocking, Jim interposed.

'This is Ethel, by the way. Horace's little sister. Say hello, Ethel.'

213

'Ugh,' said Effel under her breath. Out loud she said, 'Orrice don't go nowhere wivout me.'

'Well, love, you come to tea too,' said Mrs French.

'Oh, yes, d'you want to, Ethel?' asked Alice.

''E can't go wivout me,' said Ethel, hotly jealous. Fiendishly, she added, ''E'll get lost if I don't go wiv 'im.'

'Me?' said Orrice faintly. That was Pelion piled on Ossa. 'Me get lost, me?'

'It's only Crampton Street,' said Mrs French, 'number fourteen. Next Sunday, then, Horace. And Ethel too.'

Orrice felt sick. He knew it would soon get out at school, that he was going to Sunday tea with Alice French. That Higgs, he'd smirk all over his clock.

Mr French caught Jim's eye again. Jim smiled. It struck Mr French that a man with one arm had taken on a packet of problems with these two kids. But he must be a bit out of the ordinary in getting lodgings with Rebecca Pilgrim. Regular particular, Miss Pilgrim was, and an old maid before she was forty. Some said before she'd even come of age. Might have had something to do with a bit of a scandal in China when she was twenty. Her mother, Mrs Pilgrim, a lovely old girl but a bit faded, had told Mrs French during the war that there'd been a man out there in China, that he'd died from the bite of a poisonous snake just before the Pilgrim family left the mission and came back to England. Mr French couldn't see that as a bit of a scandal, or that it could turn a girl of twenty into an old maid. Oh, well, a girl of twenty and a man, said Mrs French. Yes, what about it, asked Mr French. Well, you wouldn't understand, you've never been a girl of twenty, said Mrs French.

Still, there it was. Rebecca Pilgrim was an old maid. The last woman to take a man in as a lodger. And two kids as well, and her as fussy and pernickety as an old hen, demanding upright Christian behaviour of everyone. Everyone said she'd got a mission, which was to turn Walworth into the most upright Christian place in England. Be a job, that would. Bet she'd have a go at turning Jim Cooper into a missionary.

'Well, come on, kids,' said Jim, 'let's walk home with Miss Pilgrim.'

'A' right,' said Effel, but cautiously.

'Goodbye till school tomorrow, Horace dear,' said Alice.

Orrice almost died on the spot. Effel ground her teeth. Jim said goodbye to the French family. Orrice recovered with an effort, but as he began the walk home with Effel, Jim and Miss Pilgrim, he expressed his feelings bitterly.

'I dunno, I been called some names in my time, I 'ave,' he said, 'but I ain't never been called Orrice dear. Nor ain't I ever 'ad to go to Sunday tea wiv a girl. I been done down an' jumped on, I 'ave. I dunno what the blokes at school's goin' to say, I betcher they won't believe it. I dunno I believe it meself. Bleedin' 'ell—'

'Boy!' Miss Pilgrim, shocked, cut him off.

'Steady, Horace,' said Jim pacifically.

'I ain't said nuffink,' said Orrice aggrievedly. 'It's all right for you, Uncle Jim, you ain't been called Orrice dear, nor sorely tried like I been.'

'Nonsense,' said Miss Pilgrim, starch crisply rustling, long legs taking her firmly along. Smoke was rising from chimneys on this bright May day. Sunday dinners were cooking, and not every family was solely using gas ovens. 'I've never heard such a fuss. You've been invited to tea with a very nice family. That is a compliment.'

'Ugh,' said Effel indistinctly.

'What did you say, child?'

'Wasn't me,' said Effel.

'Mr Cooper,' said Miss Pilgrim, 'do your parents know you are now the guardian of these two children?'

Jim grimaced. New people in his life inevitably asked quite natural questions. Mrs Palmer, a woman who minded her own business, was among the few exceptions.

'My parents are dead, Miss Pilgrim. They died when I was young. I was brought up in an orphanage.'

'I'm sorry,' said Miss Pilgrim, 'that is a hard cross for any child to bear.' They turned into Walworth Road. 'However, you seem to have overcome misfortune and disability remarkably well. That is to be admired. It's possible that in accepting guardianship of this boy and girl, you were remembering your time in an orphanage. Ethel, pull your socks up.' Ethel, walking ahead with Orrice, muttered to him.

216

'Ain't goin' to, she ain't our mum.'

'Ethel,' called Jim, 'pull your socks up.'

Effel grumbled, stopped, stooped, and pulled them up. Going on again with Orrice, she let her grumble be known.

'Ragamuffin Jack don't 'ave to pull his socks up.'

'Ragamuffin Jack?' said Jim. 'I've heard of him.' He quoted, with Miss Pilgrim sailing crisply along beside him.

> *'Ragamuffin Jack wore a very ragged hat*
> *And two very old odd socks,*
> *His socks fell down on his way to town*
> *And his dog ran away with a fox.'*

Effel, turning her head, looked at him with new eyes.

'Oh, yer know Ragamuffin Jack, mister?' she said.

'Needs his socks pulling up,' said Jim.

Effel giggled, and Orrice said, 'Yer funny sometimes, Uncle Jim, ain't he, Miss Pilgrim?'

'I could not say,' said Miss Pilgrim, 'I have no sense of humour.'

'Oh, you're young yet,' murmured Jim cheerfully, 'you'll acquire one.'

'I'm afraid, Mr Cooper, you are sometimes given to nonsense of a kind unsuitable to your age.'

'Good morning, Miss Pilgrim.' Elderly Mrs Hardiman appeared as they turned into Wansey Street. 'Out with yer lodgers, I see.'

'I am merely returning from church with them,' said Miss Pilgrim. 'Good morning, Mrs Hardiman.' And she sailed on.

* * *

She was ready to serve dinner at two. Jim made sure he and the kids arrived punctually at her kitchen table. A joint of roast beef appeared. Orrice and Effel gazed at it in mouth-watering awe. Awe was their constant companion at Miss Pilgrim's table. Everything was so posh. To start with there was always a crisp, ironed tablecloth, something their mum had never bothered with much, unless Aunt Glad and Uncle Perce were present. And Miss Pilgrim's cutlery and china shone. A glass water jug, full, sparkled with light. Jim's own impression of their landlady's kitchen in general was that she was such an immaculate champion of cleanliness that the soot and grime of Walworth had long given up laying siege to her house and possessions.

Picking up her carving knife and fork, she glanced at him.

'Do you wish to carve, Mr Cooper?' she asked, and he thought the question carried an implication of her willingness to believe him capable of slicing a joint.

'No, you carry on, Miss Pilgrim,' he said. 'I'm able to, but only on a meat dish with a central holding spike.'

'Very well.' She carved efficiently and quickly, and the slices of beef fell softly, tenderly and lusciously from the joint. She cut Jim's slices into small pieces. She served the meat with batter pudding, light and crisp, rather than thick and solid Yorkshire pudding. The roast potatoes were perfect, the horseradish hot. Effel said she didn't want no cabbage.

'She must have green vegetables, Mr Cooper.'

'Yes, make an effort, Ethel,' said Jim.

'Don't want to,' muttered Ethel. Miss Pilgrim gave her a stern look. Effel gulped. 'A' right,' she said, and received a modest helping.

With everyone served, Miss Pilgrim suggested Jim should say grace.

Jim said, 'For what we are about to receive let us be truly thankful, not only to the Lord but to Miss Pilgrim, whose Christian kindness is a blessing to us.'

'Amen,' said Orrice and Effel, and began to tuck in.

'Amen,' said Miss Pilgrim in reserved fashion, and cast a look at Jim. He smiled. 'Really,' she said. She was not receptive to compliments, and regarded them with suspicion. And from a man, a smile as well as a compliment made her inwardly wince.

The Sunday dinner was consumed with relish by her lodgers. She wondered what she was about in permitting her privacy to be invaded at certain meal times, especially as the children's table manners were little short of atrocious. Mr Cooper spoke to them at intervals, but in far too indulgent a way. The boy needed to be cured of his habit of reaching across the table for salt or pepper, and the girl of wiping her nose either on her sleeve or her napkin.

For afters, there was date pudding and piping hot custard, ambrosia to Orrice and Effel. Orrice remarked that Miss Pilgrim was spiffing.

'Angelic,' said Jim.

'I am not in the least angelic, Mr Cooper,' she

said. 'I am a practical Christian, having discovered a bowl of rice to be of far more value to a starving child than a hundred angelic smiles or well-meaning sermons.'

'Yes, that makes sense,' said Jim affably, 'but this date pudding is still angelic.'

'Could I 'ave some more?' asked Orrice, having scoffed his in quick time.

'More?' said Miss Pilgrim, much as if Oliver Twist had arrived at her table. 'More?'

'If yer please'm,' said Orrice. 'It ain't 'alf good, and it's 'elping me forget the 'orrors of me life.'

'What horrors?'

'I told yer, Miss Pilgrim, you know, that Alice French, callin' me Orrice dear an' makin' me go to—'

'Enough, boy,' said Miss Pilgrim with awesome severity. But she gave him a second helping of the pudding. 'I should hope, Mr Cooper, since you're a well-read man, it won't be beyond you to teach this boy a few social graces. It really is quite painful to have him refer to sweet Alice French and her kindnesses as the horrors.'

'Black mark, Horace,' said Jim. Orrice grimaced, Effel muttered.

'Mr Cooper,' said Miss Pilgrim, 'you said your parents were dead. Do you have grandparents still alive?'

Did he? Maternal or paternal? They'd be old, in their seventies at least.

'My mother's parents live in Hampshire,' he said.

It was wishful thinking, it implied they were still alive.

'You must take your wards to see them one Sunday, I'm sure they would like the train ride. Train rides open up a little of the world to Walworth children.'

Orrice and Effel looked up eagerly, and Jim said he'd take them one day.

'When's one day?' asked Effel.

Making up his mind, Jim said, 'Next Sunday morning. And when we've done the washing-up for Miss Pilgrim, how about a bus ride this afternoon to Hyde Park?'

''Yde Park?' said Orrice. 'Crikey, we'd like that, wouldn't we, Effel?'

Effel said yes, at which Miss Pilgrim informed Jim she did not require anyone to do her washing-up, and that he could take the children out as soon as he liked.

'Can't be done,' said Jim, 'not until we've shown our appreciation of our splendid dinner. We'll do it, Miss Pilgrim, dishes, pots, pans, everything. Leave it to us while you put your feet up.'

'I am not so old, Mr Cooper, that I need to put my feet up,' said Miss Pilgrim with a touch of acidity, 'and nor am I used to having my domestic routine rearranged for me.'

'Oh, rearrangements are sometimes good for all of us,' said Jim, 'especially for women, who are always on the go. You take a rest.'

'Certainly not.'

'We'll vote on it,' said Jim. 'Hands up on our side

221

all those who can't wait to get at the washing-up.' He put his own hand up. Orrice followed suit. Effel sat on both her hands. 'Carried unanimously,' said Jim, 'Ethel's voting with a smile.'

'Ain't,' said Effel mutinously.

'But you meant to,' said Jim, 'so it counts. Off you go to your sitting-room, Miss Pilgrim.'

'Certainly not,' she said again. She had no intention of leaving her precious china at the mercy of two careless children and a man with one arm. But Jim, insistent, had Orrice and Effel organized in no time. He washed every item himself, using his one hand with dexterity. Normally, at the club, he rinsed everything under a hot tap, and everything was placed in racks to dry. Now, Orrice and Effel did the drying, with tea towels, Effel in a slightly petulant way. She mumbled that her mum and dad hadn't ever made her do things.

'Well, I'm different,' said Jim, 'I like kids to give a hand, and I like it that you're volunteering, Ethel.'

'I don't fink I like you,' grumbled Effel.

'Ungracious child,' said Miss Pilgrim, who was bustling about and taking things from Effel and Orrice as soon as they'd been dried. She did not want anything to remain too long in their undisciplined hands. It was a relief to her when the job was finished and she was able to get them out of her kitchen.

In Hyde Park, after an exciting bus ride, Jim walked them around the extensive acreage of

London's most popular playground. The expanses of green grass and the sun-dappled waters of the Serpentine were breathtaking to Orrice and Effel. London was still recovering from the war, but there was nothing depressing or shabby about this green oasis in the centre of the metropolis. Effel stared at well-dressed ladies and girls in bright frocks and hats. Orrice took in the wonders of the park and the adventurous look of boats on the Serpentine. At a refreshment kiosk, Jim bought them an ice-cream wafer each. Orrice was overwhelmed, and felt that he and his sister had a new dad. Effel still wanted her old one back.

CHAPTER FOURTEEN

On Tuesday morning, Jim knocked on Miss Pilgrim's living-room door.

'Come in.'

Entering, he found her immersed in her needlework.

'That looks lovely,' he said.

'I hope so,' she said. 'What is it you want, Mr Cooper?'

'To see you,' he said. Her handsome countenance took on a familiar coolness. He noted the brushed perfection of her thick black hair, but even its shine seemed austere. 'The second week's rent is due, and I also have to settle the food bill. Is it inconvenient just now?'

'Not now you're here,' she said. 'The rent is twelve shillings, and the cost of the food is nine shillings and fourpence.'

'Is that all? Nine shillings and fourpence for the three of us?'

'I shop economically, Mr Cooper. I don't like coming home feeling I've failed to get value for my money.'

'You've given us first-class value,' said Jim. 'Let's see, rent and food. Twelve bob plus nine and fourpence. One pound, one and four.'

'Correct,' said Miss Pilgrim, and Jim placed the money on the table with the rent book.

'Don't worry about the rent book entry at the moment,' he said, 'I can pick it up later.'

'Very well. I am, as it happens, in the middle of some very delicate work. I'll return the book in twenty minutes, when I'm going out to shop for today's midday meal. Thank you, Mr Cooper.' It was a cool dismissal. Jim went back to his book-keeping manual.

She came up to his room twenty minutes later wearing a grey hat and the stiff-looking black dress that reached to her ankles. It was years out of fashion, but it dignified her tall figure. She gave him back the rent book.

'Many thanks,' said Jim. She nodded and left. He heard the rustle of her clothes. She was undoubtedly still in favour of starched Edwardian petticoats.

After she had been gone five minutes there was a knock on the front door. Jim went down to answer it. A slim, good-looking woman in her mid-thirties stood on the step, her spring coat very fetching, her hat crisp and smart. She eyed him in frank curiosity.

'Good heavens,' she said, 'could you possibly be her husband?'

'Ask me another,' smiled Jim, 'I'm not quite with you.'

'Is Rebecca at home?'

'Are you looking for Miss Pilgrim?'

'I am. I'm Mrs Audrey Lockheart. May I ask who you are?'

225

'Well,' said Jim, 'in the first place, I'm nobody's husband, I'm Jim Cooper, a bachelor. I'm afraid Miss Pilgrim's out.'

'Oh, I really don't mind waiting,' said Mrs Lockheart with a smile. 'I'm very much acquainted with Miss Pilgrim. May I come in and wait if she isn't going to be too long?'

'Of course,' said Jim, intrigued. The visitor looked as if she had very little in common with Miss Pilgrim fashion-wise. Not only was there an elegance in the look of her coat, and a stylishness to her hat, there was a newness to both items. 'Yes, do come in, Mrs Lockheart.' He stepped aside and she entered. He closed the door and debated for a moment. Miss Pilgrim was a close guardian of her privacy. He could not be certain she would approve if he gave the freedom of her sitting-room to a caller, even if the caller had declared herself an acquaintance. 'Would you like to wait upstairs?'

'I'll be quite happy to, Mr Cooper. You did say Cooper? Yes, I thought you did. Does Rebecca – Miss Pilgrim – have a sitting-room upstairs?' Mrs Lockheart, personable, was gently enquiring.

'Well, no,' said Jim, 'I live upstairs with my two wards, a boy and a girl. But you're very welcome to wait in our living-room.'

'How kind, thank you so much.' Mrs Lockheart began to ascend the stairs, the post-war length of her coat allowing her to show sleek calves and faultless stocking seams. Jim followed her up and took her into his living-room, where the table was spread with papers covered with book-keeping scribbles. 'Well, this is cosy, isn't it?'

'Please sit down,' said Jim, and she unbuttoned her light coat, hitched the skirt of her grey costume and seated herself, her movements fluent, her manner that of a woman able to communicate easily with people. 'I'm not sure how long Miss Pilgrim will be,' he said. 'Not too long, probably. She's only gone to the shops.'

'I'm in no hurry,' said Mrs Lockheart. 'It's many years since I last saw her, so half an hour, or even an hour, won't test my patience. It's really very kind of you to let me wait in your living-room. I'm sure I've interrupted you in some work or other.'

'It's no bother,' said Jim.

Mrs Lockheart eyed his disability with visible sympathy.

'Is it too personal to ask if you've suffered an unfortunate accident, Mr Cooper?'

'It's not a bit personal,' said Jim, 'and I wouldn't say it was an accident. It was more to do with the fortunes of war. Fortunes sometimes favour you, and sometimes they don't.'

'Ah, the war.' Mrs Lockheart's reaction evinced itself in the wry smile of a woman unable to understand how men could engage in such murderous conflict. 'I don't know you, Mr Cooper, I really don't know you at all,' she said. 'Meeting you isn't knowing you, but I'm still able to say I'm glad you escaped the slaughter, even if it was at the expense of your left arm. One can make judgements from first impressions, don't you think so?'

'Yes, sometimes,' said Jim. 'At other times, first impressions can be very deceptive. I had a platoon officer, a junior officer, whom I thought a first-class snob and a first-class swine, but on the day I took bullets and then a bayonet in my arm, and a bullet in my thigh as well, he was the one who hauled me out of the German trench and got me back to our lines, under fire the whole time. When I thanked him he said, "You're a bit of old England, Cooper, and I hope old England can make good use of what's left of you." I've been careful about first impressions since then.'

'That is one of the better stories of the war,' said Mrs Lockheart. 'Has old England made good use of what the war left of you?'

'It's given me a job,' said Jim, reserving what he thought of the Government's apparent indifference to unemployed ex-servicemen.

'This is really much more pleasant than waiting on my own,' said Mrs Lockheart. 'I'm addicted to conversation, you know.'

Jim thought from her stylish clothes and mode of speech that she was upper-class. An upper-class woman was new to him.

'Good conversation, of course,' he smiled. 'I don't know just how pleasant your wait will be, I can get very boring.'

'Men who are very boring never mention the possibility that they might be.' A light little laugh escaped her. 'It's something that never occurs to them. May I take my coat off, it's really warmly cosy in here, isn't it?' She stood up. Jim, as dexterous as ever with his one hand, helped her off with her coat. She turned, smiled her thanks, hitched her tailored grey skirt again, and sat down again. Her slim, silken-sheathed legs shone, the light rippling over the silk. Jim blinked. Mrs Lockheart smiled softly. He suddenly thought, watch this one. 'Mr Cooper, may I ask what your relationship with Rebecca is?'

'Relationship?' Jim regarded her in curiosity. 'There's no relationship, Mrs Lockheart. Miss Pilgrim is my landlady, and I might say a very kind one.'

'Dear me,' murmured Mrs Lockheart. She crossed her legs. The silk flashed in the light from the window. A delicate, lace-hemmed underskirt was visible for a brief moment. 'Am I to understnd Rebecca Pilgrim has a lodger, Mr Cooper?'

'Three,' said Jim. 'Myself and my two wards.' He smiled. 'Orrice and Effel.'

'Who?'

'Horace and Ethel.' Jim, knowing that book-keeping was out until Miss Pilgrim returned and took Mrs Lockheart off his hands, made innocuous conversation. 'They're orphans, brother and sister, and a great help to me. Well, it is a help to a man like me, since they'll stop me turning into an old stick-in-the-mud. Do you have children, Mrs Lockheart?'

'Regretfully, no,' said Mrs Lockheart. Stylish, attractive, and with an air of affluence, she seemed effortlessly at ease in what Jim supposed were relatively humdrum surroundings. Oddly, she seemed to be regarding him with distinct interest. 'Did you know Rebecca Pilgrim before you became her lodger, Mr Cooper?'

'No. Why d'you ask?'

'Oh, I merely wondered. She was an extraordinarily attractive young woman when I first came to know her.'

'I can believe that,' said Jim, 'she's now a very handsome woman. Did you meet her in China? I understand her father ran a mission there.'

'Indeed, yes, he did.' Mrs Lockheart looked gently reminiscent. 'The Reverend James Pilgrim. Dear me, such a godly gentleman, and Rebecca such a help to him, a girl of sweetness and laughter. Well, that was the impression one had.'

'Pardon?' said Jim.

'Oh, have I said anything amiss? We mentioned impressions before, didn't we?' Mrs Lockheart smiled.

'First impressions,' said Jim.

'Oh, one's first and second impressions of Rebecca were of a young lady quite delightful,' said Mrs Lockheart, 'and sweetly dedicated to the welfare of the Chinese orphans housed at the mission station. There, we've touched on orphans again. Your two wards are orphans, you said. How admirable of you to have become their guardian. I'm in favour of guardians, I'm sure they're less demanding than parents. But what a responsibility for a bachelor.'

'It's more of a challenge than merely living for oneself,' said Jim, wondering what on earth had made her mention Miss Pilgrim in a way that implied her nature and character were suspect.

'One could say it's a privilege merely to be alive, Mr Cooper. Nature has surrounded us with beauty and colour, and we only need to close our minds to the failings and wickedness of some people to appreciate we live in a world of natural wonders.'

'Not everything's perfect,' said Jim. 'We've all got weaknesses, and nature blotted its copybook when it plagued us with rats, mice and mosquitoes. And seasickness.'

'And untimely death,' said Mrs Lockheart. 'But no, one can't blame every untimely death on nature. I must blame the war for the loss of my husband, Major George Lockheart.' She sighed, shook her head, and smiled wryly. 'He was killed during the German offensive in 1918. I haven't enjoyed being a widow. George was such an entertaining man, and so generous. It was like him to leave me well provided for. And earlier, you know, I lost my brother, my only brother. Life can deal hard blows.'

'It was that kind of war,' said Jim, 'it wrecked some families.'

'Oh, my brother Clarence wasn't a war casualty. No, no, not at all. That is another story.' Mrs Lockheart came gracefully to her feet and moved to the window. She regarded the view. It was of the backs of terraced houses. 'Goodness me, who would have imagined Rebecca living in Walworth?' she murmured. 'But is that a little garden below? Rebecca's little garden?'

231

'She fashioned it, I believe, and tends it,' said Jim, beginning to find his visitor somewhat cryptic.

'A remarkable woman,' said Mrs Lockheart.

'Yes, she is, and very kind.'

Mrs Lockheart turned, and Jim thought her smile had a slightly sharp edge to it. She moved back to her chair in an abstracted way. Automatically, her hands plucked at her trim skirt as she reseated herself.

'Rebecca isn't back yet?' she said.

'She went out only five minutes before you arrived,' said Jim.

'And here I am, still waiting, still taking advantage of your kind hospitality and offering you very dull conversation. I'm sure you'd be doing something interesting if I weren't here. I suppose, Mr Cooper, you've never been to China?'

'I've seen France and Flanders,' said Jim, 'and the Isle of Wight. Most people here set their sights on Southend. It's the cockneys' own seaside. No, I've never been to China.'

'It holds an abundance of Chinese.' Again a light laugh escaped her. 'My husband was never enamoured of it, but my brother Clarence found it very invigorating in terms of business.'

'Is that a fact?' Jim could not summon up a great deal of interest in a man he had never known. However. 'He ran a business in China?'

'Clarence was a broker in Shanghai. Shanghai, you know, is full of Europeans addicted to the excitement of making their fortunes. Missionaries, of course, deplore men's devotion to Mammon, and the Chinese call the Europeans foreign devils.'

'Is that because Europeans in China make their fortunes at the expense of the Chinese?' asked Jim.

'I wonder? Perhaps it is.' Mrs Lockheart murmured to herself. 'But there are Chinese opium millionaires by the dozen, Mr Cooper. Such a shame about Clarence, when he was doing so well. I can never think of his death merely as water under the bridge. Some things, yes, like old quarrels or one's youthful mistakes. Clarence had so much to live for and was remarkably popular. Such a shame to have died at his age. But, of course, there are hidden characteristics in many people, aren't there?'

'What does that mean?' asked Jim. 'That your brother wasn't what he seemed? That he didn't deserve his popularity or that he committed suicide?'

Mrs Lockheart, looking shocked, said, 'Mr Cooper, how can you say such a thing?'

'Wasn't it a fair comment? I thought it was.' Jim felt there were slightly odd undertones to the conversation. 'You said your brother had much to live for and was very popular, but that there were hidden characteristics in many people. So I assumed you had your brother in mind.'

'Oh, dear,' said Mrs Lockheart reproachfully, 'that's very unkind on poor Clarence.'

Well, ruddy hard luck on poor old Clarence, thought Jim.

'Sorry if I jumped to the wrong conclusion,' he said. 'What did happen to him, then?'

'Yes, I must ask Rebecca exactly what did happen. Clarence was staying at the mission house at the time. But no, it's nothing that would interest you.' Mrs Lockheart mused on her reflections, and Jim thought yes, it may not interest me, but she's making a strange attempt to whip up my curiosity. 'Do you know Rebecca well, Mr Cooper?'

'Miss Pilgrim? Hardly at all.'

'Really? I'm to believe that when you're living in her house?'

'I've only been living here a week,' said Jim, who had no intention of gossiping about his remarkable landlady.

'But you're an interesting man, I think, with a very nice way of making a stranger feel at home. I like informal men.' Mrs Lockheart smiled. Jim had his bottom informally perched on the edge of the dwarf bookcase. 'Well, after a week of living in Rebecca's house, what does an interesting man think of her?'

'That she's kind,' said Jim, who had a feeling now that Mrs Lockheart was trying to point a finger at Miss Pilgrim. It put him instinctively on his landlady's side. She might be stiff and starchy, the kind of woman to make a man conscious of his shortcomings before she even opened her mouth, but the fact was she had thrown a lifeline to him and the kids, and had done so with generosity. And if Mrs Lockheart, by contrast, was appealingly feminine, the fact was that she had only just met him and accordingly had to be a little out of order in trying to point a finger, if that indeed was what she had in mind. 'I'm still wondering, Mrs Lockheart, what made you mention there were hidden characteristics in many people.'

'Oh, but it's true, isn't it?' she said. 'Some of us are much deeper than our friends and acquaintances would ever suspect, and are capable of surprising things. Why, when one considers it was a serpent that shattered the tranquillity of the Garden of Eden, isn't it the most surprising thing that such a godly man as the Reverend James Pilgrim should become so attached to them?'

'Them?' said Jim.

'Serpents,' said Mrs Lockheart with a gentle shake of her head. 'Clarence thought it most odd. So did I. Rebecca said her father found snakes extremely interesting, and laughed about it. She was very captivating, you know, when she was laughing or smiling, and she had beautiful blue eyes. Everyone thought her a sweet angel.'

'I know very little about Miss Pilgrim,' said Jim a trifle brusquely, 'and nothing at all about her father, except that he was a missionary who spent some years in China. And I'm totally ignorant about snakes. Miss Pilgrim, I hope, will be back any moment—'

'Oh, China isn't known for its snakes,' said Mrs Lockheart, 'it isn't a tropical country, Mr Cooper. It does get very hot in the summer but can be bitterly cold in the winter. Most species of snakes are indigenous to the tropics. They like constant warmth, you know. Of course, there are probably Chinese adders just as there are English adders, but

I've never heard of an English adder being found in someone's bed, have you? Dear me, we're managing to pass the time very equably, aren't we? Interesting conversation can make a passing hour very pleasant. Did I mention Rebecca's father had a snakehouse constructed at the mission, so that he could study his specimens at leisure?'

'No, you didn't mention it,' said Jim. He felt the undertones were uneasy now, and he didn't like that. 'But you did mention water under a bridge, and I think that's what all this is now.'

'But there are still waters too, aren't there, still waters that run deep?' Mrs Lockheart's smile did nothing to change Jim's dislike of the undercurrents.

'There aren't any around here, Mrs Lockheart, just people trying to keep their heads above the usual kind of waters.'

'Yes, Walworth is an area of poverty, isn't it?' she said. 'I imagine Rebecca regards it as a place where she can still do good work, she was always very much her father's daughter. Perhaps good work makes up for other things. I'm sure she was in love with Clarence, although at his death you would not have thought so. I don't believe she shed a single tear. Isn't that surprising?'

'It's nothing to do with me,' said Jim. The woman did not look like a pedlar of mischief or unpleasant insinuations, but he knew he'd be a fool not to recognize there was something definitely unpleasant behind her oblique references to snakes, still waters, hidden characteristics and the death of

236

her brother. 'And it doesn't really concern me.'

'No, of course not, but it's interesting, isn't it? Does Rebecca do good work here?'

'I believe she's an interest in a mission in Bermondsey, which isn't far away.'

'She helps out at a Bermondsey mission?' Mrs Lockheart's smile was all of cryptic. 'Perhaps she sees that as a form of penance.'

'I'm sorry, but I'd rather you didn't continue with remarks that—' Jim stopped as his keen ears picked up the sound of the front door being opened. 'I think Miss Pilgrim's back.'

'Miss Pilgrim? Rebecca?' Mrs Lockheart looked slightly surprised, as if the expected had become the unexpected. 'Oh, yes. Good. I haven't seen her for years, it will be quite a reunion. I've been looking forward to it very much, although I'm not sure how she will feel.' She came to her feet, picked up her coat and placed it over her arm. 'Thank you so much for your company, Mr Cooper, it's been so interesting talking to you. I do hope we'll meet again.' Her smile seemed that of a woman in pleasurable anticipation of a reunion. 'Goodbye for now.'

'Goodbye,' said Jim, his feelings mixed. One should like a woman whose looks and femininity were as appealing as hers, and whose manner was so civilized, but he was not sure that he did. There had been too many veiled remarks, too much wandering from one thing to another. He opened the door for her and she smiled as she left. He heard her descending the stairs, and he closed the door. He had an odd suspicion that Miss Pilgrim was not going to enjoy the reunion. He sat down and resumed his book-keeping studies, but found it difficult to concentrate. He was listening. But the solidly built house did not communicate its sounds at all clearly when doors were closed. He shook his head at himself and applied himself to his studies with determination.

A sound did reach his ears after ten minutes, and with jolting clarity. It came from the neat little hall below.

'Wretched woman!' It was Miss Pilgrim's voice. 'Leave my house, take yourself off, and at once!'

A laugh came, a laugh that Jim thought was mocking.

'How dramatic.' Mrs Lockheart's voice, neither so sharp nor so biting as Miss Pilgrim's, was quite clear all the same. 'False anger will do you no good, Rebecca. I know, you see, I have always known. But what I still don't know is why you did it. Poison of that kind is a venomous thing. Poor Clarence did not deserve that. But now that I've found you, you are done for.'

'Rubbish. I can face my God.' The front door was pulled open. Jim was on his feet now, his own door open a little, his listening compulsive. 'Go!'

'I shall be back, Rebecca Pilgrim.'

The front door was sharply closed. Jim ventured out on to the landing.

'Hello there,' he called lightly. Miss Pilgrim looked up at him from the hall.

'Kindly don't let unwanted visitors into my house again, Mr Cooper,' she said.

'So sorry,' said Jim. 'She said she was an acquaintance of yours, and asked if she could come in and wait until you were back.'

'An impositon.'

'The lady wasn't an old acquaintance?' Jim, out of disturbed curiosity, was probing.

'That is not the point. I'm not a saintly Christian, as I've told you, and my door is closed to certain people. Whenever there's a visitor and I am out, please be so good as to ask them to call again.'

'I'm sorry, Miss Pilgrim, to see you distressed.'

'I'm not in the least distressed, I am merely vexed.'

'Can I help?'

'Help? With what?' From the hall she stared frostily up at him.

'With whatever's vexing you.'

'What nonsense. Allow me to begin preparing the midday meal, or it will be late.' With her familiar starchy rustle, Miss Pilgrim disappeared.

It occurred to Jim that for all the imperturbability of Mrs Lockheart, the woman had a screw loose.

At half-past eleven the same morning, Mrs French called at the school and spoke to the headmistress. The headmistress communicated at once with Mr Hill, and Mr Hill addressed his class, informing the boys and girls that Alice French had mislaid her skipping-rope yesterday. Would the pupil who had found it please say so.

No-one said so. Everyone simply looked blankly at everyone else. Alice blushed slightly. She knew her mum had come to see the headmistress about it, although she had asked her not to.

'Well, let's wait until the dinnertime break,' said Mr Hill tactfully, 'then the rope might come to light. Or someone in the other classes might be handing it in now. We'll see.'

During the break, an eleven-year-old girl approached Mr Hill and told him she'd seen a new girl pick the skipping-rope up from the playground bench and go off with it.

'What new girl?' asked Mr Hill.

'I don't know 'er much, sir, I think she's Ethel Somebody.'

Mr Hill sighed. Ethel Somebody, of course, was the sister of Horace Withers, a bright boy with potential. Mr Hill waited until brother and sister returned to the school after dinner at their lodgings. He took the little girl aside, and he called Alice over.

'Alice, your missing skipping-rope,' he said.

'Oh, yes, blessed thing,' said Alice. 'Well, you see, sir, Mum was cross I didn't come home with it yesterday. I told her I hadn't actually lost it, not actually, I just couldn't remember about it, and she said well, someone's got to remember, that skipping-rope's new and it cost money.'

'Can you remember, Ethel?' asked Mr Hill. Effel, head bent, fidgeted and mumbled. 'I didn't hear that,' said Mr Hill.

'Oh, Ethel wouldn't know anything about it, sir,'

said Alice, 'she's Horace's sister.' Which meant that as far as Alice was concerned no sister of Horace could be accused of pinching.

'Well, do you know, Ethel?' asked Mr Hill.

'Don't know nuffink,' said Ethel, feet itching to bear her away.

'Does that mean you didn't pick the rope up from the bench yesterday and go off with it?'

'Oh, Ethel wouldn't have done that, sir,' said Alice.

Effel muttered.

'Did you take it home just to play a joke?' asked Mr Hill. If that was a lifeline, Effel didn't recognize it.

'Ain't got no 'ome,' she said, 'nor no mum and dad, not like she's got.' The bell rang for afternoon classes, and she scampered off. Alice followed. Mr Hill looked for Orrice. Seeing him, he beckoned. Orrice arrived, and Mr Hill explained the position to him tactfully and kindly.

'Well, Effel might've 'idden it for a joke, sir,' said Orrice, 'but she wouldn't 'ave nicked it. Effel don't go in for nickin'. Nor me. Our dad would've walloped us. Effel's a bit funny sometimes, but she ain't a tea leaf.'

'I'm sure,' said Mr Hill. They were a ragtag and bobtail, many of the Walworth kids, and some did nick little things from each other. But the moment their dads got wind of it, such things quickly reappeared. 'However, she was seen with the rope. Look here, tell you what, you talk to her. If anyone can find out what she did with it, you can. Can't you? Talk to her. I'd like to have the rope returned by the time classes start tomorrow morning.'

'It ain't like Effel to take someone else's fings,' said Orrice.

'No, but you've lost your parents. I'm sorry to mention that, it's been hard on both of you, but it might have something to do with Ethel's actions. It might be affecting her in a different way from you, Horace. So talk to her during this afternoon's break.'

Orrice did so, taking his sister aside in the playground. Alice looked on from afar.

'Effel, did you mess about wiv Alice's skippin'-rope yesterday?'

'Don't know nuffink about it,' said Effel.

'You sure?'

'Serve 'er right,' said Effel, 'now yer can't skip wiv 'er no more.'

'Here, 'ave you hid it?' asked Orrice. 'It's daft. Yer know I don't skip wiv 'er, anyway, I ain't turnin' meself into no cissy. I wouldn't be able to look no-one in the face if I turned cissy, nor if me sister went in for nickin'. Alice won't mind if you took 'er rope for a joke. Did yer hide it or didn't yer?'

'Dunno,' said Effel.

'Course you know, you ain't as daft as that. Look, what's Uncle Jim goin' to say when 'e knows?'

''E ain't nobody,' said Effel.

'Yes, 'e is,' said Orrice, ''e's lookin' after us, 'e can't be nobody. Effel, d'you want me to bash yer?'

'Dunno, don't care,' said Effel, and Orrice could

242

get no more out of her. Reluctantly, he reported failure to Mr Hill. Mr Hill sighed and reported to the headmistress. When classes were over for the day, Orrice and Effel were told to go and see the headmistress. She addressed them kindly, telling them she wanted the matter cleared up by tomorrow morning. If it was, then she would not have to ask their guardian to come and see her.

It worried Mrs Wainwright that she might be doing the little girl an injustice, that she might be innocent. And there was also the unhappy fact that sister and brother had both been recently orphaned. Some allowances must be made for the disturbing effect such a traumatic happening might have had on the girl.

What worried Orrice was the thought that the whole school might soon be calling Effel nasty names.

'Look,' he said on the way home, 'yer don't want everyone saying you nicked Alice's rope. Our mum and dad wouldn't like that, and our Uncle Jim ain't goin' to be too bloomin' joyful.'

''E ain't our dad,' said Effel.

'I know that, don't I? Why'd yer keep telling me what I already know? But 'e saved us from being sent to an orphanage, didn't 'e?'

''E grumbles at me,' said Effel.

'Cor, you fibber, 'e ain't ever grumbled at no-one, it's not grumbling when 'e tells yer to pick up fings you've dropped. Effel, yer can tell me, can't yer, if yer took that skippin'-rope or not?'

'Ain't saying.'

243

'I bet yer know where it is, I just betcher.'

'Ain't talkin'.'

'Right,' said Orrice, 'I'm goin' to wallop yer silly when I get yer 'ome.'

When they arrived at nineteen Wansey Street, Miss Pilgrim, set of face, let them in. They wiped their feet carefully on both mats, and Orrice, under their landlady's strict eye, took his cap off. Miss Pilgrim at once noted there was gloom all over his fresh young countenance. She also noted Effel was scowling. Closing the door, she asked, 'What is wrong with you two?'

'Me bruvver's goin' to 'it me,' said Effel

'Well, I got a good mind to, Miss Pilgrim,' admitted Orrice.

'You will do no such thing,' said Miss Pilgrim. 'In the absence of your guardian, I must take it upon myself to forbid you to even think about it. Brutality will be your lot all the days of your life if you exercise it now, at your age. And, Master Horace, as Shakespeare says, the evil that men do lives after them.'

'Oh, crikey, Miss Pilgrim,' protested Orrice, 'it ain't evil just thinkin' about wallopin' Effel, is it? Not just thinkin' about it.'

'Deeds are the children of thoughts, young man.' Miss Pilgrim studied the boy and girl again. Effel, of course, was hanging her head. Orrice met her gaze in his fearless way. 'What has been happening?' she asked.

'Yes, what's goin' to 'appen, that's what I'd like

244

to know,' said Orrice, deeply gloomy. 'I'm goin' to
'ave to fight all of 'em, I am.'

'You are going to fight no-one, do you hear?'

'Miss Pilgrim, I got to, I got to fight everyone
what calls Effel a tea leaf. Effel ain't a tea leaf, she's
just playing up, which is why I 'ad a good mind to
wallop 'er.'

Miss Pilgrim, who knew tea leaf was cockney
rhyming slang for thief, said, 'Go into the kitchen,
both of you.' They went in, Effel muttering. She
followed them. 'Master Horace, I think you had
better explain.'

Orrice explained in somewhat garbled fashion,
such was his disgust with events. It did not prevent
Miss Pilgrim drawing a correct picture. She gave
Effel's boater a stern look.

'Lift your head, child,' she said, and the boater
came up and Effel's face appeared, her mouth
closed mutinously. 'I believe, miss, you've no liking
for Alice French.'

'Ugh,' said Effel.

'Or her skipping-rope.'

'Ain't saying.'

'Absurd child, you have made yourself unhappy.
Go into the scullery.'

In the scullery, she poured warm water from the
kettle into a bowl in the sink. She washed Effel's
hands with a soapy flannel. She washed them
thoroughly, and then scrubbed them. The palms of
Effel's hands turned pink. Miss Pilgrim examined
them.

'Miss Pilgrim, what yer doing?' asked Orrice.

'You have said, Master Horace, that Alice's skipping-rope had pink handles. Your unhappy sister carries the mark. God has his own way of pointing a finger. Ethel, why did you take the rope?'

Effel, staring at her pink palms, gulped.

'I – I—'

'Yes?' said Miss Pilgrim crisply.

'She wants to take Orrice away from me,' said Effel painfully.

'Child, no-one can do that. Horace is your brother, no-one can—' Miss Pilgrim came to a halt. Her dark lashes flickered and her mouth compressed. Then she went on. 'No-one can take him away from you. What did you do with the skipping-rope?'

'Effel, you ain't nicked it and lost it, 'ave yer?' said Orrice bitterly.

'No, I just put it in the cloakroom, under a lav,' burst Effel. 'I didn't nick it, I didn't. I just put it where she couldn't find it.'

'Oh, yer sorely trying me,' said Orrice.

'Come, come, young man, we've all been guilty of childish naughtiness,' said Miss Pilgrim. 'But we'll have no more of it from either of you. No more pranks from you, Ethel, and no more fighting by your brother at the school gates. Go back to the school, both of you. It will still be open. Retrieve the skipping-rope and take it to Alice at her home in Crampton Street, number fourteen. Ethel, you are to apologize to Alice and to let her know you wish to be friends with her.'

'Me?' said Effel in horror.

'Yes, you, miss. Then there'll be no more foolishness. Off you go now, both of you.'

They went back to the school. The playground was empty and quiet, one or two teachers still in the building. Effel darted into the girls' cloakroom, while Orrice kept watch. From under the S bend of a lavatory system, Effel pulled out the folded skipping-rope. She rejoined Orrice, who sighed with relief at the sight of the rope and its shiny pink handles. They walked to Crampton Street, on the other side of the Walworth Road. Crampton Street was a mixture of dwelling places, a block of flats sitting between houses that varied between the good and the indifferent. Number fourteen was a pleasant-looking terraced house.

Orrice knocked. Alice answered the door. Her surprise quickly turned into a happy smile.

'Horace, it's you,' she said, much as if his arrival was the event of the year.

'Yes, me and Effel's both come,' he said. 'Effel found yer skippin'-rope. She's sorry it got lost, ain't yer, sis?'

Effel looked as if she was going to deny that, but she thought of Miss Pilgrim and God.

'Sorry,' she said.

'It was in the girls' cloakroom,' said Orrice, 'me and Effel went back to the school to look for it.'

'What's going on?' Mrs French put in a plump and enquiring appearance.

'It's Horace and Ethel, Mum,' said Alice happily, 'they found my skipping-rope and brought it back.

247

It was in our cloakroom, I must have left it there. Wasn't it nice of Ethel to find it and bring it? You're awful sweet, Ethel.'

'Yes, a' right,' said Effel.

'Well, I'm glad it's been found,' said Mrs French. Whatever she thought of the way it had reappeared, she was unable, as a mother, not to feel for the orphaned girl and boy. 'We won't fuss about it any more. Nice of you to bring it, Ethel, and you, Horace.'

'Shall I give Horace a kiss, Mum?' asked Alice.

Orrice went faint. There were boys in the street.

'We got to get back to Miss Pilgrim,' he said hoarsely, 'come on, sis.'

'A' right,' said Effel. She thought of Miss Pilgrim again. 'You can kiss me bruvver, if you like,' she said to Alice.

Alice planted an adoring kiss on Orrice's cheek. Mrs French laughed. The boy was blushing. Orrice, thinking his life might as well come to an end here and now, went blindly off with Effel. He managed to find his voice when they reached Walworth Road.

'Now yer been an' really done it, you 'ave,' he said, 'yer went an' told Alice to kiss me wiv all them boys lookin'.'

'You blushed, you did,' said Effel.

'Me? Me?'

'Fancy blushing,' said Effel.

'That's it, make it so me life ain't worf livin' no more,' said Orrice.

Effel giggled.

Answering the door to them when they got back, Miss Pilgrim took them into her kitchen.

'Well?' she said.

'We done it, Miss Pilgrim,' said Orrice, 'we gave Alice 'er skippin'-rope back and Effel said she was sorry.'

'Good. And Ethel made it clear she was willing to be friends?'

'I told 'er she could kiss me bruvver,' said Effel in fiendish glee.

'H'm,' said Miss Pilgrim, noting Orrice's scowl.

'Orrice blushed,' said Effel.

Orrice grabbed his sister.

'Master Horace!' Miss Pilgrim was sharp and commanding.

'Well, I'm done for, I am,' growled Orrice.

'She finks me bruvver's ever such a pretty boy,' said Effel.

Orrice rolled his eyes in despair.

'That's enough, Ethel,' said Miss Pilgrim. 'And kindly remember to confess your naughtiness about the skipping-rope to your guardian when you see him tomorrow morning.'

Effel, however, refused to confess, and Orrice, not given to telling tales about his sister, kept his peace.

CHAPTER FIFTEEN

The Sunday morning train from Waterloo steamed through the Surrey countryside on its way into Hampshire. Jim, Effel and Orrice had a compartment to themselves. The boy and girl, faces close to the windows, stared in excitement at every passing scene. The sun shone over the gentle hills, and gold dappled the fields. Effel could hardly believe the moments when real live cows came into being before her astonished eyes. Standing cows, walking cows, and cows solemnly chewing the cud. Orrice took in the wonder of open spaces where there weren't any houses to be seen, just trees and meadows. He and Effel chattered animatedly to each other. Effel was in her best Sunday frock and boater. She also wore a clean face. Orrice was in his suit and Sunday cap.

Jim sat in deep thought. He really did not know what the day would bring. If any of his mother's relatives were alive, he had no idea what their reactions would be to a visitor claiming to be her illegitimate son. Did they know she had had a son? Had she told them? If so, none of them had ever come to the orphanage to see him. Such thoughts had crossed his mind before, and he had concluded that either his mother had told none of her relatives or, if she had, none were interested in him. But he had always known he would make this train journey one day. It was something he had had to do. One day.

The village, Elderfield, was not far from Petersfield. The train stopped at Petersfield, and they took the local line to Lower Bordean. From there they walked half a mile to Elderfield by way of a country lane, where primroses were flowering along the edges of the ditches and Effel, rapturous, begged to be allowed to pick some. Jim managed to shift her off that idea by pointing out the golden allure of pristine dandelions. Effel swooped on them. Orrice decided it wouldn't actually be cissy to give her a hand, so he picked some too and loaded them on to her, much to her delight. After five minutes in her clutching hands, the golden heads drooped on limp stalks, but Effel still remained rapturous.

Jim, the children beside him, approached the first houses of the village in a tentative mood. The whole village consisted of only a few dwellings, no more than half a dozen houses and a couple of old cottages. To the side of one house was a tiny shop that sold tobacco, confectionery and a small range of groceries. It was open for the morning.

Everything was utterly quiet. Only the murmurous sounds of early summer came to the ear. Effel stared as a huge bumble bee alighted on wisteria growing against a cottage wall.

'Oh, crikey,' she gasped. The bumble bee took wing and flew away. 'Orrice, did yer see that, did yer see it?'

'Bumble bee,' said Orrice, 'I seen some in Ruskin Park.'

Jim surveyed the village street, all part of the country lane. He was here now, with the kids. There was no point in avoiding the issue. He turned and went back to the tiny shop, Orrice and Effel on his heels. He descended a step and pushed open the door. A bell jangled. Effel gazed at a dummy packet of Cadbury's milk chocolate in the shop window. Her mouth watered. She entered the shop behind Jim, Orrice following. A little counter was bare except for a tin of Osborne biscuits. Grocery items stood on shelves. A petite old lady appeared.

'Good morning,' said Jim.

'Eh?' she said, and peered at him. She seemed to find him suspect. She looked at the children. 'Who's they?' she asked.

'That's Effel,' said Jim, 'and that's Orrice.'

'What's they got?'

'Dandelions,' said Jim.

'Been in they danged old war, I see.'

'No, we ain't, missus,' said Orrice.

'Bain't talkin' to you,' said the little old lady, and Effel sidled to hide herself behind Jim. 'What's they want, soldier?'

'Four ounces of bull's-eyes twice, thanks very much,' said Jim.

'Eh?'

'Those,' said Jim, pointing to the large glass jar of bull's-eyes on a shelf behind the counter.

'They's not lemon drops.'

'Bull's-eyes,' said Jim.

252

'I know, I know. Who they for?'

'The children. Four ounces each.'

'Yer a sport, Uncle Jim,' said Orrice, and watched the little old lady weigh the sweets on brass scales. Her bright button-eyes caught his look. She put one extra bull's-eye in a twist of brown paper for luck. She did the same with the second four ounces, humming to herself.

'Sixpence, they is,' she said.

'Each?' said Jim, startled.

'Pound. Same for foreigners as for folks. Thruppence, they be, this lot.'

Jim handed the copper coins over, and gave the packets to Orrice and Effel.

'Yer spiffin', Uncle,' said Orrice.

Effel's thanks were mumbled. Orrice had established a very easy relationship with Jim. Effel's approach was still cautious and guarded.

'They's from up to London?' asked the old lady, face brown and wrinkled.

'So we are,' said Jim. 'I was wondering—'

'Bain't nothing here for London foreigners.'

Jim, accepting an offering from Orrice's twist, said, 'Well, there's your bull's-eyes. They're something. I wonder, are there any people called Miller living here?'

'Eh?'

'Miller,' said Jim, bull's-eye in his mouth.

'Bain't none in my shop, nor my upstairs. Some up to Quarry Lane, though.'

'Where's that?'

'Elderfield.'

'Isn't this Elderfield?'

'Bain't ever been nothing else.'

'You mean there's more houses farther on?'

'They's catched on,' said the little old lady, button-eyes twinkling. 'Two cottages. First be where the Millers live. Got chickens.'

'Are they old people?'

'Eh? Bain't no old people up by here, mister. Just people.'

'Thanks,' said Jim. A grin appeared. The little old lady winked at Orrice. Orrice winked back.

'They's a saucy lad,' she said. 'Girls be kissin' 'ee already, I'll be bound.'

Effel giggled. Orrice crushed a half-sucked bull's-eye between grinding teeth.

They left the shop and went through the tiny village and on for two hundred and fifty yards, when they reached the first of two cottages, old stone dwellings with small windows. The first had a neat front garden, and on the wall beside the door a rambler rose was bursting with shoots and leaf.

Jim, halting, said, 'Look, kids, this is where I have to see some people. Would you mind waiting here a while? I hope it won't bore you.'

'We don't mind, Uncle Jim,' said Orrice.

'No, a' right,' said Effel.

'We'll sit on the grass,' said Orrice.

'That's the ticket,' said Jim, and walked up the path and knocked on the cottage door. It was nearly eleven o'clock. He had arranged to get back to Waterloo a little after three. Orrice and Effel were due for Sunday tea with Alice and her family.

The door opened. Jim found himself looking at a slim, elderly woman with smooth silver hair, wearing a kitchen apron over blouse and skirt. If her hair was silver with age, her face was unlined except for a few little crow's-feet around her grey eyes. Seeing him, a tall man with a resolute look, and a missing left arm, her hospitable smile was a little tentative.

'Excuse me,' said Jim, 'but are you Mrs Miller?'

'That I am,' she said, 'I've been Mrs Jonas Miller these fifty years and more. Could I ask where you've come from, and why?'

'I'm from London, and I've come hoping to talk to you and your husband.'

'Ah?' she said, regarding him in curiosity. 'My husband's at church with my daughter-in-law. My son, he's up mending the chicken wire. I didn't catch your name, Mr—?'

'I'm Jim Cooper.' His name was as much as he thought he should give at this stage. He felt he had to take a little time to lead up to the rest of it.

'Cooper?' Her smooth brow wrinkled, as if the name was making her search her memory.

'Yes. Could I talk to you for a few minutes?'

'I were just starting to prepare dinner, but come in a while, I don't like keepin' a visitor on my doorstep.' She led him into a small parlour, cosy with old leather-upholstered furniture that gave the room a brown mellow look. 'Sit you down, if you wish.'

'It's all right. Look, I heard about you years ago,

255

from a friend of mine, when I was living in an orphanage.' Existing was really the word.

'Orphanage?' The smooth brow wrinkled again, and she gave him a closer inspection. A little tremor touched her mouth. 'You were an orphan?'

'I'm afraid so. Mrs Miller, I haven't come to make myself a worry to you, believe me, but have you ever heard the name Cooper before?'

Mrs Miller, aged but wearing her years finely, stood very still, and he knew he had struck a chord.

'I be worried right now about answering that,' she said quietly.

'Don't be,' said Jim, 'there's too much water under the bridge. My father's name was Cooper. John James Cooper. He served in the Army.'

'Oh, lord,' breathed Mrs Miller.

'Will it upset you to know my mother's name was Betsy Miller?'

Mrs Miller paled in shock and put a hand to her throat. Jim felt he had prepared her a little unfeelingly, that he had been too quick with his submission of the facts, after all. His mother's mother must be seventy and more. Had he been unfair, springing the facts on her when she did not have the support of her husband?

'I—' Mrs Miller's hand tightened on her throat.

'I'm sorry, I shouldn't have come out with it like that,' he said.

'No,' she whispered, 'I thought one day perhaps – one day—' She drew a breath. 'Such a sadness. Poor dear Betsy. It be true, you're her son?'

'Yes, you can believe me.'

'Yes.' She seemed a little vague then. 'But only one arm, more sadness.'

'That was the war.'

'So cruel,' she said, and her eyes wandered. 'We would have come, but Arthur—' She stopped.

'Your husband?'

'Our son.' She looked worried then. 'He were so angry, so ashamed, hating the man who – who—'

'My father?'

'Not married to Betsy, not married.' She looked at the sunlit window through which the neat front garden could be seen, and the high hedge that hid the presence of Effel and Orrice, patiently waiting. Jim saw framed photographs on the mantelpiece. Family photographs, he thought. Was his mother's photograph among them? He could see none of a young woman or a girl. 'Arthur didn't like the shame of it.'

'I'm sorry. I understand. In a village like this, yes, I understand. But I thought – well, I've nothing of my mother's—'

'Oh, you best go,' she breathed, and Jim heard the sound of footsteps on a tiled floor. A moment later a large burly man in shirt and breeches put his head round the door. His eyes alighted on Jim and on Mrs Miller's agitated expression. He came in, his large face red and beefy, his sandy hair slightly tousled, his blue eyes searching.

'Who's this, Ma?' he asked, his voice gravelly.

'He's just going,' said Mrs Miller palely, and Jim felt that here was a man large enough, powerful enough and strong-minded enough to play God to

257

his family and his neighbours. It exuded from him, his belief in himself.

'Where you from?' he asked.

'I was looking for a country cottage where some children could spend a summer holiday,' said Jim.

'Ask at farmhouses, man, not people's cottages. You're a townie, I reckon. Ask at farmhouses, but watch out for shotguns. Good day to you.'

'Well, thank you for trying to be a help,' Jim said to Mrs Miller with an easy smile, and left. Neither of them saw him to the front door. And even before he opened it he heard the gravelly voice at work.

'You weren't thinking of invitin' town kids here, Ma, were you? You can forget that. Should've sent that loon packing.'

Jim stepped out into the sunshine, closed the cottage door and stood on the step. The emotions he had guarded and hidden from the impossible Arthur surfaced so strongly that his teeth clenched. He had found his mother's family home and his grandmother, a simple but kind countrywoman, a woman who could tell him about his mother, and exactly what she was like. He had also found his mother's brother, a boor of a man and the fly in the ointment. But Jim meant to make the journey again, to get to know his silver-haired grandmother and perhaps his grandfather too. His teeth unclenched and he swallowed to get rid of the painful lump in his throat. He took a deep breath, steadied himself, walked up the path, turned right into the lane and found Effel and Orrice sitting on the grass verge counting dandelions. They had picked others, scores of them.

'Here I am, kids,' he said.

Orrice looked up. His boyish grin appeared, and Jim understood why young Alice thought him spiffing. Effel cast her familiarly quick glance, then went on counting dandelions.

'We goin' now, Uncle?' asked Orrice.

'Yes, we'll go back to the station, pick up the picnic bag we left there, and have the picnic on the train home. I don't think we'll ramble about, it'll tire you and Ethel, and you've got Alice's tea party later.'

'Oh, crikey, it ain't going to be a party, is it?' said Orrice. 'Not a girl's tea party, it's only goin' to be Sunday tea, ain't it?'

'I was thinking of Alice in Wonderland,' said Jim.

'I don't want none of them larks,' said Orrice, 'I got enough problems already.'

'I don't mind,' said Effel.

'Come on, troops, on your feet,' said Jim. 'That's it. Right, chest out, Ethel. Cap straight, Horace. Good. Off we go, then.'

They went, Jim thinking about Mrs Miller and the large, domineering man who was obviously her son Arthur. And Arthur, it seemed, had been forceful enough, even as a young man, to coerce his family into rejecting his sister, who had conceived a child out of wedlock. In a tiny village like Elderfield, perhaps, that kind of rejection had always been on the cards. Jim, however, did not feel disposed to leave things stuck in mid-air.

★　★　★

259

There was a newcomer to the congregation in St John's Church at the morning service. She sat in a pew several rows from the front. She smiled from time to time at the people on either side of her. And more than once she picked out the figure of Rebecca Pilgrim in a front pew. At the end of the service she remained in her seat while the bulk of the congregation left. As Miss Pilgrim advanced along the aisle, Mrs Lockheart lifted her head and smiled at her. Miss Pilgrim did not return the smile. She did not acknowledge her in any way. She went on, out of the church and straight home, where she deafened herself in the event of a knock on her door.

Mrs Lockheart, however, did not follow. She lingered outside the church, introducing herself to a group of gossiping women. And having introduced herself, she took the lead in the conversation. The women began to listen, first in puzzlement, then in curiosity, and finally with a mixture of reactions.

Jim, Effel and Orrice picnicked on the train back to Waterloo, again having a compartment to themselves. Effel and Orrice thought everything was more spiffing than a Bank Holiday on Peckham Rye. Orrice remembered that tomorrow was Whitsun Bank Holiday, and he asked Jim if he and Effel could go off to Peckham Rye on a tram.

'I been there,' said Effel, eating her way through a peeled boiled egg.

'But they got a fair on Bank Holidays,' said Orrice.

'Been there,' said Effel.

'What about Hampstead Heath?' asked Jim. 'Have you been there on a Bank Holiday?'

Hampstead Heath on a Bank Holiday was a rousing playground for cockneys.

'Cor, no, we ain't ever been there, Uncle,' said Orrice.

'Well, I'm off all day until seven in the evening,' said Jim, 'so I'll take you both there. I think we can dig into our pockets and find a few pennies for the swings and roundabouts.'

'Yer really a sport, Uncle Jim,' said Orrice, 'an' yer a swell too, ain't 'e, Effel.'

'Yes, a' right,' said Effel grudgingly, and through the last mouthful of boiled egg.

When they arrived back at their lodgings, Jim made the kids wash themselves and freshen up. Then he sent them off to their Sunday tea with the French family in Crampton Street. Orrice went with gloom on his face, Effel with a new approach. Seven years and three months old, she already had a mind of her own and the developing instincts of a female born to outwit the male. Her plan of action was fixed in her mind. Every time Orrice looked as if he was going to be won over to Alice, Effel was going to say what a lovely boy he was, that he was getting ever so pretty. She and her brother were received hospitably by Mr and Mrs French. Alice glowed to see how healthy Orrice looked from his day out in the country. With a ribbon in her hair and a sash around her frock, Alice did the honours as the

261

hostess's daughter by embracing her guest. Orrice's face, brown from sunshine, turned pale.

'It's ever so nice you've come,' said Alice.

'Me bruvver's a lovely boy,' said Effel, and made the Sunday tea purgatory for Orrice from start to finish.

Jim, on his way out to post a letter to a wartime comrade of the trenches, was detained at the door by Miss Pilgrim. He thought her severely handsome in a mid-grey blouse and dark grey skirt.

'Forgive me, Mr Cooper, but I cannot help wishing to know if you enjoyed your visit to your grandparents. It must be a consolation to have grandparents.'

'Yes, my maternal grandparents are all I've got,' said Jim. 'The visit was all I expected, and the kids enjoyed the train ride. The countryside had them in fits.'

'Fits?'

'Of wonder. And joy, I think.'

'I see. Yes. Most children in Walworth are sadly deprived of wonders and joys. I am in approval of the care you are giving Ethel and Horace, Mr Cooper.' Miss Pilgrim's severity became less forbidding. 'I hope to remark a gradual improvement in their speech under your guidance. It is difficult for many cockney children to make the most of their talents, to climb the ladder of life any higher than their parents, simply because they are held back by their slipshod use of the English language. It's a mistake to suppose genius is confined to the well-

262

educated. Unfortunately, in cockney children it can be smothered by their environment and their own people.'

'You have to remember cockneys don't like sounding posh,' said Jim.

'That's exactly what I mean,' said Miss Pilgrim earnestly. 'They address themselves very sarcastically to those who try to improve their speech and better their lot. It's most discouraging. I've a feeling Horace is a bright boy, that he may have something to offer the world when he's older, but he'll find many doors closed to him unless he can express himself acceptably. It doesn't mean he has to sound posh, as you put it.'

'I agree with all you say, Miss Pilgrim,' said Jim, noting her earnestness, 'and I'll bear it in mind. By the way, I'm taking Ethel and Horace to Hampstead Heath tomorrow for the Bank Holiday fair. Why don't you come with us?'

'I beg your pardon?' Miss Pilgrim, taken aback, stared in astonishment.

'Yes, good idea, I think,' said Jim briskly. 'We'll leave at ten. I'll do another picnic. We had one on the train today, we'll have another on Hampstead Heath tomorrow. I don't have to get to work until seven in the evening, it's a short shift on Bank Holidays. Put a couple of hatpins in your hat, or it might blow off when we're riding the roundabout. Well, I'm just going to stroll down to the pillar-box, I've a letter to post—'

'Mr Cooper! Really.' Miss Pilgrim was at her frostiest. 'I am not in the habit of being taken for granted, and certainly not in respect of a Hampstead Heath fairground. It is not the kind of thing that appeals to me in the least.'

'Oh, all the fun of the fair can be exhilarating,' said Jim. 'Don't decide now, Miss Pilgrim, think about it. You deserve an outing, especially on a Bank Holiday. I won't do boiled eggs again—'

'Boiled eggs?' Miss Pilgrim's composure was showing little cracks. 'Boiled eggs?'

'I've some ham—'

'Mr Cooper, go and post your letter,' said Miss Pilgrim, and disappeared into her sitting-room. Jim strolled down to the pillar-box, posted his letter and strolled back. He put his kettle on to make himself some tea. He heard Miss Pilgrim ascending the stairs, and the rustle of her arrival at his door. She knocked. He pulled the door open. She regarded him in her cool way, a few degrees warmer than her frosty air. 'Very well,' she said, 'but I will provide the picnic. Some simple food and a good crisp lettuce. With a vacuum flask of hot tea. Ten o'clock tomorrow morning, I think you said. Yes, very well, Mr Cooper.'

'Good,' said Jim, who had a growing feeling that underneath all her starchiness a woman was trying to get out.

'I frankly feel your wards will be safer if we are both there to keep an eye on them,' she said in serious vein. 'There is a dubious element present in crowded fairgrounds, as well as what you call an exhilarating one.'

Jim, keeping his face straight, supposed she was

264

referring to the gypsy element. As a disciplined Christian, she probably regarded the undisciplined ways of gypsies as a throwback to the paganism of their roving ancestors.

'Well, I'm glad you'll be coming, Miss Pilgrim,' he said. 'Between us, we'll see to it that Horace and Effel don't get carried off.'

Miss Pilgrim gave him a pitying look.

'Really, how absurd, Mr Cooper. I am merely thinking Horace might be robbed of his pocket money. He informs me he has a few shillings in his pocket. However, I—' She was interrupted by a knock on her front door. 'I'll answer it.'

She made her way downstairs. In the little hall, she hesitated, as if suddenly reluctant to answer the knock, after all. Then her mouth set firmly, and she opened the door. Orrice and Effel, back from Sunday tea with Alice and her parents, looked up at their tall, commanding landlady. Orrice did not seem as if he had enjoyed himself, although Effel appeared very pleased with things. She wiped her feet quickly and darted in. She scurried up the stairs. Orrice went rushing revengefully after her, caught his foot on the first stair and fell. He got up, looking disgusted.

'I just got to wallop 'er, Miss Pilgrim,' he said.

'What has your sister done now, young man?' asked Miss Pilgrim.

'It don't bear tellin' no-one,' said Orrice, grinding his teeth. 'Except, well, when we was leavin' she told Mrs French not many sisters 'ad bruvvers prettier than I was.'

The ghost of a smile actually touched Miss Pilgrim's firm lips.

'I think, Master Horace, you had better address your complaints to your guardian,' she said.

Orrice addressed several complaints to Jim, all concerning Effel's behaviour over the Sunday tea. Effel, he said, kept going on about what he looked like in his Sunday suit, and Mr French kept falling about laughing. And that Alice, she kept agreeing with Effel.

'It's no good, Uncle Jim, you just got to let me wallop me sister.'

'No walloping, Horace.'

'But I promised meself I'd bash 'er silly when I got 'er home,' said Orrice.

'Hard luck, old chap, can't be allowed. Still, what've you got to say for yourself, Ethel?'

'Nuffink,' said Effel.

'Nothing, Ethel, nothing.'

'A' right,' said Effel.

CHAPTER SIXTEEN

The day was fine. Miss Pilgrim wore a plain white blouse, flowing dark brown skirt and brown hat. Jim carried the bag containing the picnic she had prepared. They took a tram to the north side of the river, then an omnibus to Hampstead Heath. Miss Pilgrim sat with Ethel, and Jim with Horace. In that way she avoided informal contact with the children's guardian. But she came up against the assumption of the cheerful bus conductor, who clipped four tickets with a flourish and said, 'Well, yer got a couple of bright kids to keep yer 'appy, missus.'

'You are making a mistake,' she said.

'Yer means they're a couple o' perishers? I got two like that meself.'

There was nothing Miss Pilgrim could offer to that piece of typical cockney brashness except a telling silence.

They found Hampstead Heath alive with people. Londoners were flocking to enjoy its funfair. It was a place for family outings on Bank Holidays, where for a few pennies children and grown-ups could sample the excitement of the Big Wheel, the pleasure of merry-go-rounds, the rhythm of the swings and the challenge of the coconut shy. One

267

could guess one's weight before stepping on scales, and receive the penny back if the guess was right, or attempt to ring a bell with a mighty blow of a hammer. That was mainly for dads, of course, although the prizes on offer were mostly for children. And for another penny, one could have three attempts to ring one of the many prizes set out on a round table. All these were only a few of the various excitements and challenges available.

Effel was breathless at a spectacle that was picturesque and full of magic. It was a much bigger funfair than the one on Peckham Rye. Ebullient and extrovert cockneys at play created revelry. Shrieks and squeals mingled with huge shouts of laughter, and the music that blared out from merry-go-rounds was indispensable to any Bank Holiday.

The painted horses of a roundabout, with their flaring nostrils, streaming tails and legs moulded to a gallop, made Effel dance in excitement.

'A roundabout ride first?' suggested Jim.

Effel was all for it. It was not the last word in excitement for Orrice, but he was willing to make it a start. Miss Pilgrim, viewing the scene like a woman wondering what she was doing here, was quite sure she would keep her distance from everything that moved, including merry-go-rounds.

'I don't mind,' said Orrice graciously.

'Right,' said Jim. 'Orrice, you take hold of the picnic bag.'

But Miss Pilgrim resolutely refused to allow him to transfer the bag to anyone but herself. She spoke firmly about that, going on to say she was not willing to permit her carefully prepared picnic to be taken for a ride on any of these fairground whirligigs. And as she did not intend taking any ride herself, she said, she would look after the bag.

Jim marvelled that a woman so strikingly handsome could, without any effort at all, make herself sound like an old maid. He knew she wasn't that old, for she'd said she returned from China with her parents when she was twenty. China. Each time the name of that country entered his mind he thought about the odd and disturbing things Mrs Lockheart had said. He put it out of his mind now.

'It's harmless fun, a ride on a roundabout, Miss Pilgrim.'

'Take the children, then, and leave me here.'

She stood and watched them join a throng of people on the merry-go-round. Effel rode with Jim, and was exuberant. Orrice rode in condescending fashion. Other children and grown-ups went round and round with them, the painted horses moving up and down in stately fashion, and in time to the music, which was loudly rousing, with cymbals clashing. Children ran in and out of the watching crowds. Miss Pilgrim wondered why she had come.

Effel and Orrice, appetites whetted, wanted other rides. Jim took them around the fair, Miss Pilgrim following in stiff, upright style. Orrice prevailed on Jim to take him and Effel on the Big Wheel. Jim invited Miss Pilgrim to change her mind and join them. Miss Pilgrim easily resisted the Big Wheel. Effel, when their carriage reached the top, shrieked at being so far above the ground. Orrice turned not a hair. Jim treated them to rides on other fun machines, including the switchback, which Orrice found truly exciting. Effel, held securely by Jim, grew breathless at the speed and the rush of air. Miss Pilgrim watched this death-defying ride with a frown. Really, that was simply not what Mr Cooper should be doing, nor any one-armed man. Especially not when he had a small girl in his charge.

'That was much too dangerous,' she said when they rejoined her.

'But it wasn't 'alf a cracker,' said Orrice, 'I betcher you'd 'ave liked it, Miss Pilgrim.'

Miss Pilgrim, recalling flying skirts and shrieking girls, said, 'The exhibition was deplorable, young man, the speed reckless, and such infernal machines are not for me. I am relieved you are all alive. Really, Mr Cooper, such recklessness on your part.'

'Well, how about trying the safety of the coconut shy?' suggested Jim. 'We'll make sure Ethel doesn't stand at the wrong end. How about trying to win a coconut for Miss Pilgrim, Horace? How do you feel about coconuts, Miss Pilgrim?'

'I think I could put one to good use in my kitchen,' she said graciously, and they made their way to the coconut shy.

'Roll up, roll up!' bawled the man in charge. 'Three shies a penny, 'alfway for lydies an' little 'uns. Roll up!'

'She's small as well as little,' said Jim, putting his hand on Effel's shoulder. 'Quarter-way for her, what d'you think?'

'Yes, all right, matey,' said the man. Jim paid for

all four of them. Miss Pilgrim said very well, she would participate this once. Orrice collected three balls each from the crate and handed them out.

'Let's shy at that big one, Uncle Jim,' he said, 'there's more of it showing.'

'Right,' said Jim, 'and if any of us hit it keep going until we knock it out and before Curly can straighten it.'

''Oo's Curly?' asked Effel.

'The bloke in charge.'

''E's bald,' said Horace.

'In the Army,' said Jim, 'all bald blokes are called Curly.'

Orrice laughed, Effel giggled. Miss Pilgrim looked unimpressed. Effel wanted first go, and the man in charge let her stand only a few feet from the elevated coconut. Effel threw enthusiastically but hopelessly.

'Oh, the bleedin' thing,' she said.

Miss Pilgrim gazed in disapproval. Jim coughed.

'Never mind, sis,' said Orrice, 'yer didn't do bad. She's only a girl,' he said to Miss Pilgrim.

'Who needs speaking to,' said Miss Pilgrim, 'and I am waiting for your guardian to do so.'

'Black mark, Ethel,' said Jim. Wooden balls flew at other elevated coconuts. 'Mind your language, my girl. You next, Horace. Halfway.'

Orrice launched each ball as if his life depended on it. He struck with his third shy. The coconut rattled and trembled. Jim went into action at once, using his strong and sinewy right arm. He struck with his first throw, missed with his second, and struck again with his third. The coconut took a list. The man in charge, busy collecting pennies from new customers, took a look too late, for Miss Pilgrim, handbag and picnic bag in Jim's care, delivered her first wooden ball like a cricketer aiming at a wicket from cover point. The ball smashed into the listing coconut and it fell to the ground. Bystanders gave her a yell of lusty appreciation.

'Good on yer, missus, good on yer!'

'Well, sod me,' said the man in charge. Miss Pilgrim's frosty stare devoured him. Orrice ran to retrieve the coconut. The man in charge tossed him a replacement. 'Top it up, sonny,' he called, and Orrice put the new coconut in the wooden cup. Miss Pilgrim still had two balls left. Jim eyed her in amazement. She threw as strongly and as effectively as a man. Her first throw sent the wooden ball careering a few inches wide of the target.

'Yer bleedin' scorched it, missus,' yelled another appreciative cockney, 'yer got it smokin'. Nah give it the works.'

Miss Pilgrim's round-arm throw of the last ball delivered it at a cracking pace. It struck the coconut full on, and the coconut, vibrating with shock, jumped from the cup and fell.

'Well, stone the flamin' crows,' said the man in charge.

'You beauty, missus!' yelled yet another ecstatic onlooker.

Orrice ran and grabbed the fallen prize.

'Pardon me, guv,' said the man in charge to Jim,

272

'but yer trouble-an'-strife's costin' me 'ard-earned money. Them coconuts is a bob a time.'

'Well, tell you what,' said Jim, 'pay me fourpence to give to the kids, and I'll take her away.'

'Certainly not,' said Miss Pilgrim, a flush of excitement actually showing on her face. She produced a penny. 'Three more balls, if you please. Also, I am nobody's trouble-and-strife. Come, three more balls.'

Orrice, having deposited the second coconut in the arms of his sister, who clutched both to her chest, picked three more balls from the crate and handed them to Miss Pilgrim amid the uproarious cheers of the onlookers. The man in charge, accepting her penny, said, 'Have a heart, missus, I got a wife and six kids, and I don't grow me own coconuts, yer know.'

'Stand back,' said Miss Pilgrim. She delivered the wooden balls, one after the other, Effel watching with her mouth open, Orrice in admiration, Jim with a smile and the crowd bawling encouragement. All three balls were on target. There were three successive cracks as the coconut was struck. But it stayed in the cup. 'Three more balls,' demanded Miss Pilgrim.

'Eh?' said the man in charge.

'You 'eard, baldy,' roared a large man, 'take 'er copper coin.'

It was taken, and again Orrice supplied her with the balls.

'Your hat's crooked, Miss Pilgrim,' murmured Jim.

'First things first, Mr Cooper,' said Miss Pilgrim. She looked distinctly flushed. She flexed her right arm, fixed her eye on the target and threw. The ball whistled by the new coconut and thudded against the canvas shield. The second smashed it free of the cup and it dropped to the ground. The crowd fell about in joyful hysteria. She did not wait for a replacement, she took aim at the adjacent target. She missed by a whisker. She dusted her gloved hands. 'Enough,' she said. Orrice picked up the third fallen coconut. 'Come along, Mr Cooper. Horace, you and Ethel take charge of the nuts.'

'Cor, you ain't 'alf a caution, Miss Pilgrim,' said Orrice.

'Boy, kindly do not address me in that way,' she said, and led them out of the crowd.

'But, Miss Pilgrim, I betcher there ain't no-one can beat yer at knockin' down coconuts,' protested Orrice, 'I betcher.'

'Yes, where did you learn to throw like that?' asked Jim.

'In China,' replied Miss Pilgrim. 'My father and I found it rewarding to teach outdoor sports to Chinese orphans at the mission station. The Chinese are very adept and will willingly learn anything one cares to teach them. Including cricket. My father was always very good at cricket.'

'I think you are too,' said Jim.

Miss Pilgrim stopped. She adjusted her hat, taking out the two pins, resettling it on her abundant hair and pushing the pins back in. Then she looked around. Effel gazed at her in new awe.

Miss Pilgrim's clear blue eyes alighted on three children in ragged clothes, two boys and a girl. They were sharing an apple, taking a bite each in turn.

'Master Horace,' said Miss Pilgrim, 'present the three coconuts to those children.'

'Eh?' said Orrice.

'Don't say eh, Horace,' said Jim, 'say yes, Miss Pilgrim.'

'But, Miss Pilgrim, yer won't 'ave none left,' said Orrice.

'Their need is greater than ours, young man.'

'I want one,' grumbled Effel, 'I ain't never 'ad no coconut.'

'What was that?' asked Miss Pilgrim.

'Nuffink,' growled Effel.

Orrice carried the coconuts to the three ragged children with the air of a martyr. The kids, presented with the coconuts, gaped in disbelief.

'Whatcher givin' us these for?' asked one boy.

'I ain't givin' 'em to yer,' said Orrice, 'that lady is. Me, I 'urt all over.' The kids, clutching a coconut each, stared at him, then at the figure of Miss Pilgrim. A moment later they were up and away, running and scampering and whooping, and making themselves scarce before there was a change of mind. 'Cor,' said Orrice to himself, 'she's nice really, but she's barmy as well. Fancy wallopin' three coconuts like that, then givin' 'em all away.' But he managed to give her a smile on his return, and Miss Pilgrim looked down into his healthy face and admiring brown eyes.

'Thank you for that little errand, Master Horace,' she said, 'now I will pay for you and Ethel to go on a swing.'

'Ain't goin',' said Effel, rageful at not having a coconut.

'Mind your manners, child.'

'Ain't got no manners,' muttered Effel, 'don't want none, eiver.'

Jim took her by the hand. She pulled away, but he held on and he took her aside. He waited until a family passed by before speaking. Then he said, 'I think enough is enough, young lady. Don't you?'

'Ain't saying.'

'Well, I'm saying.'

'Want me mum an' dad,' said Effel.

Jim stooped to look at her. She stared at the ground.

'Ethel?' he said. She kept her head down. 'Don't you think I know that? Don't you think Miss Pilgrim knows it too? Come on, little lady, come and say sorry to her, and then take a ride on a swing with Horace.'

'A' right,' said Effel. She lifted her head. 'Could yer win a coconut for me, mister?'

'Well, after you've had your swing, we'll go back to the coconut shy, and I'll see what I can do.'

'A' right,' said Effel, and went to make her peace with Miss Pilgrim. 'Please, I'm sorry,' she said, and Orrice looked relieved. Miss Pilgrim, finely tall and upright, regarded the small girl gravely.

'Do you wish to go on the swings with your brother?' she asked.

The noise of the funfair, the sound of its music and the atmosphere born of extrovert cockneys making the most of their Bank Holiday, still had their hold on Effel, and she nodded eagerly.

'All right, I'll take yer, sis,' said Orrice.

'Very well,' said Miss Pilgrim, 'and afterwards we'll find an open space and have the picnic.'

They made their way to the swings, which were in popular demand. Orrice and Effel had to wait before one was available. Cockney girls were laughing and shrieking as they rode high with boys, and Effel jigged about in her eagerness to participate. She and Orrice took their turn. Orrice pulled in muscular and boyish fashion. Effel held on, yelling at him. Orrice pulled harder, and the swing described its graceful arcs, much to Effel's shrieking delight.

'Kids, of course, know how to enjoy themselves,' said Jim, watching.

'Age makes us wiser, perhaps, but we pay for that by acquiring inhibitions,' said Miss Pilgrim, eyes on the uninhibited, on the laughing, roaring boys and the shrieking girls as swings soared.

'You're not speaking as an old lady, are you?' said Jim.

'That is an impertinence, Mr Cooper.'

'Beg to point out you're not an old lady, you're the champion conker of coconuts. Your performance, Miss Pilgrim, rocked Hampstead Heath.'

'Really, Mr Cooper,' she said stiffly, 'I do wish you would not attempt to drag me into absurd conversations. I have no sympathy for the absurd.'

'Shall I take you up on a swing, then?' smiled Jim.

'Thank you, no,' said Miss Pilgrim.

'I thought I should ask you.'

'Very well,' she said.

'Pardon?'

'We must wait until the children come off so that Horace can take care of the picnic bag.'

'You mean you'll take a ride with me?' asked Jim.

'I have not been on a swing since I was a girl. It isn't an impossible venture for me now, I hope.'

'It's usually fun,' said Jim. He had not been serious in asking her, he could not see the unbending Miss Pilgrim finding fun on a fairground swing. She did not fit the part at all. On the other hand, she had been an exhilarating surprise at the coconut shy.

Orrice gaped when he was asked to mind the picnic bag so that Miss Pilgrim and his Uncle Jim could take a ride. Miss Pilgrim also placed her handbag in his care. He and Effel watched her take her seat in a swing. She did so with a kind of stiff formality, sitting upright and wrapping her gloved hands firmly around the tassel of the rope. Jim sat long-legged and at ease, his one hand on the rope. The attendant gave the swing a push, and Effel stared wide-eyed as her guardian and Miss Pilgrim began to swing to and fro. Jim was all smiles. She wore a cool expression. He became vigorous. He liked activity. He had a fund of energy. Miss Pilgrim maintained her fixed, upright posture, pulling modestly on the rope. The swing gathered momentum. Swings on either side of them were soaring, girls squealing.

The hem of Miss Pilgrim's skirt fluttered, disclosing whisking white lace of a starched petticoat. She noted the vigorous strength of Jim's one arm. She frowned a little, her body moving to the increasing momentum.

'There is no need to overdo it, Mr Cooper,' she said.

'Heave-ho, Miss Pilgrim,' said Jim, and pulled with a will. The swing began to soar. Miss Pilgrim's posture suffered a sudden radical change. At the top of a high arc she lost her seat and the stability of her legs, and as the swing plunged downwards her flowing skirt and her lacy petticoat billowed high. For a breathtaking second or so Jim found himself looking at the longest legs he could have imagined on a woman. In sleek black stockings they reached high to a glimpse of magnificent white thighs that disappeared into the most delicate of lacy white undergarments.

'Mr Cooper!' She burst into outraged protest.

'Oh, good grief,' said Jim, and stopped pulling. Miss Pilgrim, face burning, covered herself. She was not unaware of boys hooting with laughter and girls giggling in the other swings.

Watching from the ground, Orrice said, 'Crikey, did yer see that, Effel? All that white starch?'

Effel giggled.

Miss Pilgrim said icily, 'Stop this swing, Mr Cooper.'

Jim let it settle. His quick eyes caught sight of something else then, the dart of a man in a flat cap towards Orrice's back. The picnic bag rested on the ground beside the boy's legs, the strap of Miss Pilgrim's handbag dangling from his fingers. The darting man snatched and was away in a flash. Jim leapt from the swing as Orrice turned and shouted. Jim ran fast, passing Orrice at speed. Orrice followed on. Jim kept his eyes on the flat cap, a blue jersey and black trousers, the thief eeling his way through the wandering crowds. Orrice was shouting.

'Stop, you fief, stop!'

Jim was travelling like a sprinter. Out of the swing, Miss Pilgrim watched as he disappeared amid the Bank Holiday bustle, Orrice following. The thief cast rapid glances over his shoulder. Jim was closing in, people falling aside from his path. Orrice's yells were taken up.

'Stop, thief!'

The working people of London had no time for the pickpockets and thieves who preyed on them at fairgrounds. Ascot or Lords were fair game. Fairgrounds weren't. Orrice collected a posse of punitive-minded men.

The thief ran, darted and twisted, going in and out between stalls and people. Jim kept after him, never losing sight of him, and he closed rapidly as the man raced downhill. When he was right on his heels, Jim took a running kick at the thief's backside. It bowled him over. He dropped the handbag. Jim swooped. A cudgel, wielded by an accomplice, caught him on the back of his head. His cap saved him from serious injury, but the blow still sent him sprawling. He landed on top of the handbag. The thief sprang up, and he and his accomplice rushed down the hill. A dozen men roared in pursuit. Orrice stopped and went down on his knees beside Jim.

'Uncle Jim, what they done to yer?' he asked anxiously.

Jim turned over, looked up into Orrice's concerned eyes and blinked. He sat up, put his hand to the back of his head and winced.

'I think I'll take a minute's rest, old chap,' he said, 'I'm winded.'

'I fought 'e'd laid yer real low, Uncle, yer took an 'orrible clout from a big geezer what run up behind yer. But yer got Miss Pilgrim's 'andbag back. Crikey, fank me lucky stars yer did.'

People crowded round, offering help, if help was required. Jim shook away dizziness and climbed to his feet. His one-armed look made the crowd mutter obscenities about the thief.

Miss Pilgrim arrived, with Effel and the picnic bag. She regarded Jim expressionlessly.

'My handbag, I think,' she said.

'Pleasure,' said Jim, and handed it to her.

'Miss Pilgrim, cor, Uncle Jim didn't 'alf get—'

'Never mind that.' Miss Pilgrim cut Orrice off abruptly. 'Come this way.' And she took herself off from the gawping people, her long legs striding, Effel in her wake. Jim looked at Orrice.

'I fink she's got the rats, Uncle Jim,' said Orrice.

'And I think I've got a headache,' said Jim. He gave the boy a wink. Orrice grinned.

They followed on.

The whole of Hampstead Heath looked a playground on this fine Whitsun Monday. The fair, seen from higher ground, dominated the scene. Around it the Heath was dotted with countless families making inroads into picnics. For some it was bread and cheese and pickled onions, and the cheapest kind of fruit. For others there were boiled eggs as well as cheese, and perhaps a bag of tomatoes. For dads there were bottles of brown ale, for mums of a buxom kind there were bottles of Guinness, for mums of a thin kind there were Iron Jelloids taken with a swig of R. White's lemonade, and for kids there was lemonade or kola water, the latter the forerunner of American cola. Among families a little more affluent than most, large pork pies were divided up, and there was fruit cake or tins of pineapple chunks to follow.

Miss Pilgrim, having found a spot high on the Heath, produced her picnic of finely-cut sandwiches, blushing tomatoes, lettuce and cucumber. A new fruit cake was to follow, together with apples. A flask of tea was also included. Orrice and Effel did full justice to the provisions, and Jim ate with enjoyment. Miss Pilgrim ate with reserve, sitting straight-backed on the grass. Orrice, always voluble, even when tucking in, explained in detail the chase in pursuit of the thief.

'Cor, Miss Pilgrim, when Uncle Jim catched 'im—'

'Caught him, boy.'

'Yerse, well, when 'e did, Miss Pilgrim, 'e bowled the bleedin' nicker over—'

'Language, Horace,' said Jim.

'Horrid boy, must you be so coarse?' asked Miss Pilgrim.

'Me?' Orrice looked mystified. 'But I ain't said nuffink, Miss Pilgrim, you ought to 'ear 'em at Covent Garden where me dad worked.'

'I have heard them, thank you,' said Miss Pilgrim, delicately slicing a tomato. 'The language there is no excuse for a small boy.'

'Me? I ain't small, Miss Pilgrim, I'm growin' like rhubarb. Anyways'm, you should've seen Uncle Jim, 'e lifted the geezer ten feet in the air, 'e did. Kicked him right up the bum while they was both still runnin'.'

Jim choked on lettuce and cucumber. Effel giggled. Miss Pilgrim stared coldly at Horace, then at Jim.

Jim said, 'There are ladies present, Horace.' He leaned to whisper to the boy. 'Don't say bum or bleeding, say bottom and blooming. Don't say nuffink, say nothing. Let's hear you.'

'All right, Uncle Jim,' said Orrice, 'bottom, bloomin' an' nothink.'

'What on earth is that boy saying now?' asked Miss Pilgrim.

'I'm only saying about the geezer what nicked yer

283

'andbag, Miss Pilgrim,' said Orrice earnestly. 'Uncle Jim copped 'im a beauty, honest, only a big geezer went for Uncle Jim then. Conked 'im when 'e wasn't lookin'. Give 'im an 'urtful 'eadache.'

'Well, I'm sorry about that, of course,' said Miss Pilgrim, 'but I think I warned you, Mr Cooper, of the unpleasant types to be found at fairgrounds. Ethel, don't wipe your fingers on your frock. There's a damp cloth there. Use that.'

Lummy, thought Orrice, she's got the rats all right.

But nothing could spoil the picnic for him and Effel. It was a treat, eating in the warm sunshine, with the music of the merry-go-rounds reaching the ears, and kids playing leapfrog on the Heath. Jim thanked Miss Pilgrim for the food on behalf of himself and the children. She merely nodded. Effel mumbled something about a coconut.

'Do speak up, child,' said Miss Pilgrim.

'I think Ethel's reminding me I promised to try to win her a coconut,' said Jim.

'You wish to return to the fairground?'

'We can, can't we?' said Orrice.

'If that is what you want. I shall return home while you spend the afternoon here.'

'Good,' muttered Effel for her own ears alone.

'I don't like you going all the way on your own,' said Jim.

'Nonsense,' said Miss Pilgrim, 'I am very self-sufficient and quite happy in my own company. I do not require any escort.'

Jim looked rueful, Orrice looked puzzled, and

284

Effel looked satisfied. When everything had been cleared and tidied up, Miss Pilgrim departed and Jim took the kids back to the fair, although he failed to win a coconut. But he did win a doll for Effel at the shooting gallery, handling the rifle with one arm and using Orrice's shoulder as a rest. Effel was rapturous.

Miss Pilgrim, far from rapturous, asked Jim to see her when he arrived back with the children. She confronted him in her sitting-room.

'I have decided, Mr Cooper, that you and your wards are not suitable lodgers. I am giving you a week's notice from tomorrow, Tuesday. I hope you will be able to make other arrangements in that time.'

'You're not serious?'

'Indeed I am. And by the terms of the tenancy agreement, you must accept notice.'

'I'm aghast,' said Jim, 'I can't believe you mean it. Is there anything that has particularly upset you?'

'I am not prepared to go into petty details, Mr Cooper, but I will say the general behaviour of your wards leaves a lot to be desired, and I am also unable to come to any kind of agreeable terms with a man who refuses to take his responsibilities seriously and cannot act with reasonable maturity. That is all, Mr Cooper, there is no point in attempting further discussion.'

'Well, I think that's pretty hard,' said Jim, 'and I'm not sure it isn't unfair. Is your mind really made up?'

285

The striking blue eyes were unyielding.

'It is, Mr Cooper.'

'Very well,' said Jim, 'I'm sorry we've been so unsatisfactory. I'll start looking for new lodgings tomorrow. Perhaps, under the circumstances, you should supply us with no more midday meals. I've another week before I start my new hours, I'll see to the kids at midday.'

'Yes, perhaps that would be as well,' said Miss Pilgrim.

CHAPTER SEVENTEEN

Jim said nothing to Orrice and Effel for the moment. He exacted from them a promise of good behaviour, left them a meal prepared, and went off to his work at six-thirty. Walking up to the Walworth Road, he saw Mrs Lockheart on the other side of the street. She was in company with elderly Mrs Hardiman, and the two looked to be having a fair old gossip. Seeing him, Mrs Lockheart waved and smiled.

'How is Rebecca, Mr Cooper?' she called.

'My landlady's still on her feet,' said Jim brusquely, and went on.

Arriving at the club, he encountered Molly, who knew at once from the frown on his face that something was wrong.

'What's up, old lad?'

Jim told her.

'It all means I've got just a week to find three rooms.'

'Well, don't be too down in the mouth,' said Molly, 'that's not like you, old thing. I think I might be able to help. I know a couple who've just seen the last of their children married. I think they're going to find things a bit quiet, and I've a feeling they could do with a bit of rent. Look, I've

287

got to push off now, but if it's possible I'll be back with news one way or the other. So hang on, love, you're my best mate. Don't let your griping landlady get you down.'

She was back at eleven, and with the news that Jim was to call on the couple, with his wards, at seven on Thursday evening. The couple wanted to see what the kids were like.

'I'll be here, working,' said Jim.

'You'll get an hour off, sweetie, trust me,' said Molly, excessively fond of Jim, a valiant old soldier in her eyes. She gave him the name of the couple, and the address, fifteen Webber Street, off Blackfriars Road. That, thought Jim, was a bit far from the kids' school. But he knew Molly wouldn't land him in a dump. The school problem was something he'd have to work out. A tram ride was a start to a solution, and he wanted the kids to stay at St John's.

'Mr Cooper?' Jim, coming from a bedroom to the landing at a few minutes after ten the following morning, put his head over the banisters. Miss Pilgrim stood in her little hall, looking up at him.

'Yes, Miss Pilgrim?'

'Could I speak to you for a moment, please?'

He went down and followed her into her kitchen. She turned and faced him, her mouth set in its firm line.

'It's all right,' he said. 'I think I may have found new lodgings. A friend of mine, Molly Keating, the manager's daughter, has spoken to a couple who have a house in Webber Street, off Blackfriars Road.'

Miss Pilgrim seemed neither pleased nor relieved.

'Blackfriars Road?' she said. 'There are quarters very suspect and dubious off Blackfriars Road, Mr Cooper.'

'So there are off Walworth Road, Miss Pilgrim.'

'But you must think of your wards and their schooling.'

'I'm not in the habit of discounting the needs of my wards,' said Jim. 'You may think I do—'

'Really, Mr Cooper, I am not used to being addressed with aggression.'

'I'm not used to being told I'm irresponsible.'

Miss Pilgrim, wearing her stiff black dress, drew herself up to her full height. Bloody magnificent, thought Jim, but watch yourself, ice maiden, I'm spoiling for a fight.

Stiffly, she said, 'Mr Cooper, I have to apologize.'

'Do you?'

'Yes. I am ashamed of myself. Never before have I lost all sense of humility before God and been so unChristianlike. It was deplorable of me to speak to you as I did last evening. I was quite wrong in all I said. I ask your forgiveness.'

'Miss Pilgrim?'

'I did not even have the grace to thank you for recovering my handbag at great danger to yourself. You were brutally struck.' Miss Pilgrim's firm mouth quivered a little. 'I cannot understand myself. Never, I assure you, have I been so out of temper. I know I am demanding in what I expect of others, I know I am strict and that I abhor a lack of self-discipline in people – in children too – but I am appalled at my own behaviour last evening. You must forgive me.' What she did not mention, and could not, was that it could all be put down to the indecent humiliation she had suffered on that swing, when her legs and underwear were revealed to the gawping eyes of Hampstead Heath. And to his eyes.

'Miss Pilgrim, does this mean you'll withdraw the week's notice?'

'Mr Cooper, I beg you, you simply cannot take Horace and Ethel to Blackfriars Road. There are dens of iniquity close by. St John's is the best primary school in Walworth, and here, in Wansey Street, is an element that will favour the children. We must give them a chance, Mr Cooper, we must put them on the road to a reasonable future.'

'We?' said Jim.

'I will help,' said Miss Pilgrim resolutely. 'It is too much for a man who has his work to go to. If you will give me permission, I will do what I think is necessary with them in the matter of correction and discipline. Children are wild creatures, Mr Cooper, and will run with the devil as much as with God when they grow up, unless they are taught the advantages of good behaviour and of clearly knowing the difference between right and wrong. There, perhaps—' Miss Pilgrim frowned at herself. 'Yes, perhaps I've indicated I'm prepared to interfere in what is none of my business. Please disregard it. I am able to see my faults and admit them.'

'Miss Pilgrim, you're an angel of mercy,' said Jim.

'I would rather you punished me with frank words, Mr Cooper, than with more nonsense.'

'I don't think it's nonsense. I'm very relieved we can continue to lodge with you.' Jim smiled. Miss Pilgrim's lips came firmly together again, as if resolution was her defence against a man's smile. 'Correction and discipline, Miss Pilgrim. What, in your opinion, does that mean?'

'Ethel, I'm afraid, needs the occasional smack. Horace needs to be taught to speak and not gabble. The boy is very bright, Mr Cooper, and I daresay has a great deal of promise. His teachers will attempt some help. I am willing to give further help. With your permission. Regular poetry reading will do it.'

'Poetry reading?'

'Yes. Acceptable poetry to a boy. Not Byron. Tennyson, perhaps, and Robert Browning. There is a fascination for children in such a poem as Browning's "Pied Piper".'

'I was fascinated by it myself. Miss Pilgrim, thank you.'

The ghost of a smile ran its fleeting course over her face.

'I am forgiven?' she said.

'I'm nobody,' said Jim.

'Ridiculous,' she said.

'I mean I'm not Jesus Christ, I'm not saintly

enough to forgive anybody, and there's nothing to forgive. I repeat, you're an angel, Miss Pilgrim.'

'Rubbish, Mr Cooper.'

'And I accept all the help you're willing to give Horace and Ethel.'

'Yes, I am willing. Mr Cooper, would you care to take a cup of Camp coffee with me as a sign that we have come to agreeable terms with each other?'

'Bless you,' said Jim, and made a mental note to inform Molly he no longer needed alternative lodgings.

At the morning break in the playground, Higgs had Alice cornered.

'Yer an 'a'porth of barmy goosepimples, you are,' he said, 'yer been an' picked a couple o' dates, you 'ave. Wivvers wears 'is farver's trousers, and 'is sister's a nicker. Nicked yer skippin'-rope, didn't she?'

'No, she didn't,' said Alice.

Orrice, standing at an open door, was listening.

'Course she did.'

'She didn't,' said Alice. 'Ethel's nice.'

'Yer want yer mince pies tested, then,' said Higgs, 'she's 'orrible. So's Wivvers.'

'So are you,' said Alice.

'Like 'im, do yer? Well, yer won't after I've pushed 'is cake'ole in.'

'Yes, I will,' said Alice.

'What, wiv 'is clock all messed up?'

'Horace could eat you for dinner,' said Alice proudly.

'"Ere, try this for afters,' said Higgs, and with the supervising teacher's back turned, he grabbed her. Pretty young Alice was always tempting to kiss.

A hand tapped his shoulder. He turned. Orrice was behind him.

'Kindly put 'er down,' said Orrice.

'"Oppit, faceache,' said Higgs, and wound a tight arm around Alice. Orrice kicked him in the back of his knees. He let go of Alice and fell down. The teacher turned. Alice surrendered herself gladly to Orrice and walked away hand in hand with him. The teacher arrived beside the fallen Higgs.

'What are you doing, Higgs?'

'Me, Miss Forster?' said Higgs.

'Yes, you.'

'Nuffink,' said Higgs.

'Well, rise up and continue doing nothing on your feet.'

'Horace, you're ever so brave,' said Alice on the other side of the playground.

'Well, Alice, I got to tell you, so are you,' said Orrice. She had stood up to Higgs a treat. 'Good on yer, I like yer, but d'you mind not 'olding me 'and? There's blokes looking.'

'But, Horace, they all know we're sweethearts,' said Alice.

'Oh, me gawd,' said Orrice, 'don't talk like that, Alice, you'll send me to me grave.'

Effel rushed up and glared at Alice.

'What you 'olding me bruvver's 'and for?' she cried.

'Oh, you can hold his other one, Ethel,' said

Alice, 'you're his sister and I'm his sweetheart.'

A whole gang of kids heard that and yelled with laughter. Orrice died.

Life became onerous to him. He couldn't get rid of Alice or her sweetness, and then there was poetry reading every evening in Miss Pilgrim's sitting-room, with Effel made to sit and listen. Their guardian had informed them that their landlady was going to help further their education. While Effel had no idea at all what that meant, Orrice had a ghastly suspicion it meant being turned into a posh cissy. Poetry. Reading it. With Miss Pilgrim's eye fixed severely on him. He might as well die again and this time not get up.

But he accepted his lot in respect of poetry reading because Jim had a good old-fashioned chat with him, man to man, and touched a chord of ambition in the boy. But it took two successive evenings, an hour each time, to get through the first few verses of 'The Pied Piper'. Miss Pilgrim had made him read, re-read and read again. On this, the third evening, he applied himself to an exciting bit, about the rats of Hamelin town.

'*Rats, they fought the dogs an' killed the cats,*
Made nests—'

'And,' corrected Miss Pilgrim.

'Where?' asked Orrice.

'"*And killed the cats*,"' said Miss Pilgrim.

'I said "and", didn't I?' queried Orrice.

'Not quite, young man. But at least you are beginning to read, and not gabble. Start again.'

Effel giggled at the look on her brother's face. Miss Pilgrim laid stern eyes on her.

'Well, it's funny,' gulped Effel.

'It's far from funny, miss, and if you listen it will be as much a help to you, as your brother. Your turn will come, Ethel. You are sadly in need, child.'

'Yes, Miss Pilgrim.' Effel frowned, but secretly found it fascinating to watch and listen, to take in the picture of their awesome landlady making Orrice read poetry. Orrice kept looking as if he was in awful pain.

'Start again, young man,' said Miss Pilgrim, and Orrice started again.

'*Rats, they fought the dogs an' killed the cats*—'

'You are not trying or concentrating,' said Miss Pilgrim.

'Now what ain't I done, Miss Pilgrim?'

Miss Pilgrim sighed.

'You have just massacred the King's English,' she said. 'What haven't I done now is much more acceptable than now what ain't I done. I'm despairing.'

'I'm flabbergasted myself,' said Orrice, and Miss Pilgrim sat up and actually smiled.

'Why, Horace, you said that beautifully. Say it again.'

'I'm flabbergasted myself.'

'Lovely,' said Miss Pilgrim. 'Now, once more with the rats.'

'*Rats, they fought the dogs and killed the cats*—'

'Excelsior,' said Miss Pilgrim.

'*Made nests inside men's Sunday 'ats*—'

'Oh, dear.' Miss Pilgrim was letting Orrice get away with nothing.

'What haven't I done now?' asked Orrice, at which she gave him a look of rare approval.

'You are doing very well,' she said, 'but I thought last night we had overcome the problem of dropped aitches.'

'Yes'm,' said Orrice, 'but can't we get on and see what 'appens—' He checked at Miss Pilgrim's pained look. 'What happens about these rats?'

'You're interested in the tale the poem is telling?'

'I fink—'

'Really, young man, really.'

'Oh, blow,' said Orrice. 'I mean I think I am.'

'Good. Read on.'

Made nests inside men's Sunday hats
And even spoiled the women's chats
By drownding—

'Drowning,' corrected Miss Pilgrim.

'By drowning their speakin' with squealin' and squeakin'
In fifty different sharps and flats.'

'Apart from losing a few g's, very good. Continue, Horace.'

Orrice continued. Effel stopped all fidgeting and listened fascinated to the tale of the Pied Piper of Hamelin. Miss Pilgrim persisted and Orrice persevered, and by his perseverance alone she recognized a boy who might do much better for himself than driving a coal cart or being a railway porter.

The bell for Sunday morning service was still

296

ringing when Miss Pilgrim entered the church. Most people were already in their pews. Mrs Lockheart was again present, seated midway, next to one of Miss Pilgrim's neighbours. Miss Pilgrim proceeded down the aisle in her cool, resolute way. Mrs Lockheart turned her head to look at her. She was ignored. A whispering broke out, and scores of eyes watched Miss Pilgrim all the way to her usual seat in a front pew.

'You can't 'ardly believe it, a missionary's daughter and all.'

'It don't seem 'ardly creditable.'

'Poisoning's wicked, yer know, it's fire an' torture.'

'Imagine 'er doing it an' still comin' to church.'

'I expect a body can get away with it in China, it's full of them foreign Chinese.'

Miss Pilgrim, fully aware of the whispers, discounted them by sitting straight-backed and fearlessly upright.

She was avoided when she came out of the church at the end of the service, except by Jim, Orrice and Effel. Orrice and Effel had resigned themselves to the fact that their guardian meant to take them to church regularly. Jim had not been unaware of the whispers himself, nor of the covert looks directed at Miss Pilgrim. They gave him new food for uneasy thought. However, with Orrice and Effel, he accompanied Miss Pilgrim home without mentioning what was on his mind. In any case, in a crisis he knew he would prefer to stand with Miss Pilgrim. He did not trust the smiling, agreeable, talkative

Mrs Lockheart, who seemed to have set up home in Walworth, hardly the most salubrious neighbourhood for a woman of her kind.

Entering the accounts office at the club at half past eight on Monday morning to begin his new job and his new hours, Jim found Molly there. It was a cosy-looking office, with a radiator, and there were two desks, facing each other. One desk was piled with book-keeping ledgers. A wooden tray contained a host of invoices.

Molly's smile was warm and welcoming.

'Hello, old soldier, lovely morning.'

'It's raining,' said Jim, 'but nice to see you, Molly.'

'Yes, that's what I meant. Lovely. Look, I only work in the afternoons normally, as you know. I can't stand all day in an office when there's life to be lived, but I'm coming in every morning for your first week here. Dad asked what for. I said you were rusty and that I was going to polish you up. Dad asked were you specially rusty, and I said no, just special.'

'Molly, I shan't be able to thank you enough—'

'Don't fuss, old thing, let's get on with the books.'

She introduced him to the ledgers, journals, petty cash book, system of entry and everything else relating to the club's accounts. Jim had a morning of concentrated study and work, with Molly sitting beside him. She left him to it just before noon to do some shopping in the West End.

'I'll be back at two,' she said, putting her hat on, 'when I'll have my own work to do.'

'You're a sweet girl, Molly,' he said, looking up at her. Impulsively, she bent, lightly ruffled his hair and kissed him.

'They don't make too many like you, either,' she said.

Jim had a satisfactory day and a free lunch.

At Scripture lesson on Tuesday morning, Mr Hill had members of his class reading aloud. He believed in that, as did most of the teaching fraternity.

'Fair, young madam, fair,' he said to a girl as she finished her stint. 'You next, Withers,' he said to Orrice.

Orrice came to his feet. Beside him, Alice looked dewy-eyed. Orrice thought of Miss Pilgrim's stern blue eyes and firm, scolding voice. For over a week now she had had him going through Robert Browning's famous poem. He began his reading aloud, from St Luke. He did not gabble.

'"When Jesus heard these things, he marvelled at him and turned him about, and said unto the people that follered him, I say unto you I have not found so great faith, not in Israel."'

Mr Hill looked up.

'"And they that were sent, returnin' to the house, found the servant whole that had been sick. And it came to pass the day after that he went into a city called Nain, and many of 'is – his – disciples went with him, and much people."'

'Dear me,' said Mr Hill, tongue in cheek.

'That all right, sir?' queried Orrice.

'Very good, my lad, very good.'

'Bleedin' cissy,' whispered Higgs to Cattermole.

'You next, Higgs,' said Mr Hill.

'Oh, bleedin' 'ell,' muttered Higgs, and proceeded to make a hash of his reading.

'Headmistress?' said Mr Hill, encountering Mrs Wainwright in the corridor later that morning.

'Trouble?' enquired the headmistress.

'It's wise to fear the worst,' said Mr Hill, 'then ordinary bad news sounds like good news. No news, however, on this occasion, merely a request for Horace Withers to be placed on the list of prospects for West Square next year.' West Square Secondary was the only school in Southwark that offered the equivalent of a grammar-school education. 'He's bright, he pays attention, and he's deserving.'

'Recommendation noted with pleasure, John,' said Mrs Wainwright, 'I've remarked his brightness myself. And I like him.'

'So does young Alice French,' said Mr Hill.

'How very nice for Horace.'

Mr Hill laughed.

'It's purgatory to him. Boys of ten don't inhabit the same world as girls.'

'When I was a girl I was grateful for that,' said Mrs Wainwright.

Miss Pilgrim was continuing to provide a midday

dinner for Orrice and Effel. Jim prepared tea for them at six o'clock, and they had it around the little table in their living-room. Their midday dinner they ate in Miss Pilgrim's kitchen. Effel regularly played up in her dislike of green vegetables. Miss Pilgrim did not say greens were good for her, nor did she force the girl to eat them up. She merely said that if Ethel did not take a sufficiency of such vegetables she would get spots and pimples.

'Don't care,' said Effel.

'Don't you go gettin' no spots, sis,' said Orrice, 'I'll only 'ave to fight everyone that calls you Spotty.'

'Master Horace, you'll do no such thing,' said Miss Pilgrim.

'But, Miss Pilgrim, if you don't fight anyone that calls your sister names, you ain't never goin' to hold yer head up, yer might as well lie down dead.'

'Say that all again,' commanded Miss Pilgrim. Orrice began to say it all again. 'No, not with your mouth full, boy. And more slowly.' Orrice cleared his mouth of food and said it all again in slower time. 'Much better,' said Miss Pilgrim. 'Ethel, sit up.'

'Yes, a' right,' said Effel.

'Miss Pilgrim,' said Orrice, 'you got to understand, a bloke can't let no-one call his sister Spotty.'

'I ain't Spotty,' said Effel.

'No, but Miss Pilgrim says you might be.'

'She's spotty,' said Effel.

'Who's she?' asked Orrice.

301

'Her,' said Effel. She cast a quick glance at Miss Pilgrim. 'She's 'is sweet'eart.'

Orrice growled.

'Your brother has a sweetheart?' said Miss Pilgrim, watching them clear their plates of savoury toad-in-the-hole. 'Do you mean Alice French?'

'She kisses 'im,' said Effel. 'Orrice blushes.'

'Oh, yer bleedin' monkey,' said Orrice.

'Young man, leave the table,' said Miss Pilgrim freezingly.

'Crikey, Miss Pilgrim, don't I get no afters?' asked Orrice in protest.

'None. Leave the table and return to school.'

'Yes, Miss Pilgrim,' said Orrice gloomily. Their landlady always served scrumptious afters, like fruit roly-polies, gooseberry pies and creamy rice puddings. 'Well, I just 'ope Jesus forgives you yer 'ard-heartedness, Miss Pilgrim.'

'You must learn, young man, that my house is not Billingsgate fish market.'

'Yes'm,' muttered Orrice and got up and went out. His head came back as he put it round the door. 'I want you to know, Miss Pilgrim, I forgives you meself.' He disappeared. Effel got down.

'Where are you going, miss?' asked Miss Pilgrim.

'Wiv Orrice,' said Effel.

'You have not received permission to leave the table.'

'Don't care, I'm goin' wiv Orrice, you ain't our mum,' said Effel, and darted out.

Miss Pilgrim sat in frowning contemplation of the

table. She was at the Bermondsey Mission during the afternoon, doing her regular stint there. She was still frowning. The children at the mission were quite unlike Horace and Ethel. None spoke out of turn, they were all polite, all in good grace, all giving thanks for what was being done for them, and all showing humility before God.

It was a shock suddenly to realize they were all regimented.

She searched around. In a cupboard full of odds and ends she found a large rubber ball, the size of a football. She carried it down to the hall, to the congregated boys and girls. She explained the rules of simple handball. She divided them into two teams, each team a mixture of boys and girls.

When the Reverend Pearson put in an appearance, he found the hall in an uproar of girls and boys at rousing play. A large ball was the centre of the activity as it was thrown from one to the other of the joyful participants. The girls shrieked, the boys bawled.

And Miss Pilgrim? Miss Pilgrim was running about, whistle in her hand, following the flight of the ball and blowing her whistle whenever a foul too atrocious to be overlooked was committed. The clergyman, an austere vicar, looked on openmouthed as the whistle blew and Miss Pilgrim raised her voice.

'Elsie! Elsie! Leave go of Mary's hair!'

'But she went an' kicked me, Miss Pilgrim.'

'No touching, no bruising, no handling, kicking or pulling of hair,' commanded Miss Pilgrim. 'The ball alone is to be handled. Play on.' She blew the whistle and the lively, rousing game restarted.

'Miss Pilgrim, what on earth is going on?' Reverend Pearson entered the fray to get to Miss Pilgrim's ear. 'What has happened to the Bible reading?'

'Oh, we've had that, vicar. I've established they all have faith in the Lord. Vicar, do mind out – oh, dear.' The thrown ball struck the vicar on the back of his head.

'Upon my soul, this won't do at all, Miss Pilgrim.'

'I'll speak to you later,' said Miss Pilgrim, and she ran towards a shrieking scrum of boys and girls. She blew her whistle, the scrum unfolded, and there on the floor was a rosy-red, breathless girl with the ball clutched to her tummy, eyes full of delight. 'Foul,' declared Miss Pilgrim. 'Two points to team A. Play on.'

The game went on and on, the repressed energy of the boys and girls in full, exhilarated flow.

Jim went down to answer a knock at the door. He had just returned from his day's work. Mrs Lockheart stood on the doorstep, smiling.

'Hello, Mr Cooper, how nice to see you. Is Rebecca in? Yes, she will be at this time of the day. I'll come in, shall I?'

'Sorry,' said Jim, 'Miss Pilgrim isn't here.'

'Isn't she? My word, she really isn't? And she's such a creature of habit. Well, I'll come in and wait, and perhaps you and I can have another lovely talk. I so enjoyed meeting you.'

304

'So sorry,' said Jim with cutting politeness, 'but I'm busy seeing to tea for my wards, and I've no idea when Miss Pilgrim will be back. Call again another time. Good evening.'

'That isn't very friendly,' said Mrs Lockheart reproachfully.

'One can't be informal all the time,' said Jim, at which point Miss Pilgrim turned in at her gate. Miss Pilgrim froze. Mrs Lockheart smiled.

'Rebecca, there you are,' she said, and Jim, sure that Miss Pilgrim could deal with the woman, made himself scarce. But as he reached the landing, he heard Mrs Lockheart say, 'I called to ask if there was an epidemic of snakes at the time or if your father's menagerie escaped. Was there some talk of an epidemic? Of course, even in China—'

Her voice was cut off by the sound of the front door being closed on her. Miss Pilgrim swept rustling into her kitchen. Jim came down the stairs and knocked.

'Yes?'

Jim entered the kitchen. Miss Pilgrim eyed him coolly.

'I'm not sure I like that woman, or what she's doing,' he said.

'It would be preferable, Mr Cooper, if you did not trouble yourself about her, or put yourself in a position of having to listen to her. Be so good as to forget the unfortunate woman. Now, about your wards. They may be hungrier than usual. Have they told you they had no dessert with their midday meal?'

'They've said nothing to me.'

'Really?'

'Really,' said Jim.

She frowned.

'I should have thought they'd have said something.'

'Not if it meant telling tales,' said Jim. 'Horace is strictly against that sort of thing, and Ethel can keep fiendishly mum.'

Miss Pilgrim explained why she had dismissed Horace from the table, and that Ethel had left of her own accord.

'Fair do's with Horace,' said Jim.

'Fair do's? What kind of English is that, Mr Cooper?'

'No idea,' said Jim. 'Might be Clapham Common or Ilkley Moor for all I know. But it means you were quite right and fair in your treatment of Horace. Actually, I think the boy's got a natural respect for your sex, witness his protective attitude towards his sister, but he's still a Walworth lad and comes out occasionally with a choice piece of the local language irrespective of the company at the time. And Ethel, of course, was bound to follow him out, she seldom allows anything to divorce her from her brother. You aren't worried, are you, about your moment of firmness?'

'One does feel some firmness is necessary with children at times.'

'I'm not going to argue with that,' said Jim, 'I'm with you all the way. Do unto them as you think best whenever I'm not around. By the way, Mrs

Lockheart is a peculiar woman, isn't she?'

'Very. And that is all,' said Miss Pilgrim, rustling dismissively about her kitchen. Jim, going back upstairs, smiled to himself because of the rustle. He could not help remembering the sudden breath-taking display of dazzling white garments, lacily delicate, and the long long legs superb in their grace.

He began to prepare tea for the kids. Orrice helped. Effel read *Rainbow* comic, one that Jim had brought in for her. Orrice was partial to the *Magnet* alone, and to Billy Bunter.

'Everything all right today?' asked Jim casually, slicing a fresh loaf, and using his elbow stump to hold it.

'I 'ad to stand on someone's foot,' said Orrice.

'Higgs again?'

'Don't remember 'is name,' said Orrice. 'I dunno, Uncle Jim, the troubles I got on account of that Alice. Well, yer see, she's supposed to be pretty—'

'She is pretty.'

'Ugh,' said Effel, nose in the *Rainbow*.

'I don't notice things like that meself,' said Orrice. Things, not fings, thought Jim, and smiled. 'Anyways, it don't seem right Alice gettin' teased all the time because she's supposed to be pretty, not when it means I'm always 'avin' to go an' stand on some bloke's foot. Or put me elbow in 'is mince pie.'

'Then she kisses 'im,' said Effel in disgust. 'Kisses me bruvver.'

307

'So you can see the troubles I got, Uncle,' said Orrice.

'No other troubles today?' said Jim.

'She's not our mum,' said Effel with apparent irrelevance.

'Meaning Miss Pilgrim?' said Jim. 'No, she's not, but she's a very fine woman and a very helpful landlady. I'd like both of you to remember that. No sauce, Ethel. Nor you, Horace.'

'Me?' said Orrice. 'I like her, Uncle Jim, she can't 'elp being a woman an' gettin' the rats at times. Effel's always gettin' the rats, but you can't not like 'er.' He paused for thought. 'Dunno why, though,' he said.

Jim gave up any attempt to lead them into disclosing why they hadn't had any afters with their midday dinner. He liked the fact that they'd said nothing, that they hadn't complained. Orrice had accepted his medicine, and Effel had accepted she'd given up her afters in favour of comradeship with her brother. They were good kids, even if Effel did have her mutters, mumbles and little sulks. As for missing their afters, generally speaking they were probably among the best-fed children in Walworth. Miss Pilgrim cooked to perfection and gave them plenty.

That was a peculiar and morbid thing Mrs Lockheart had said.

Was there an epidemic of snakes at the time or did your father's menagerie escape?

Since certain uneasy thoughts wouldn't go away,

Jim telephoned the London office of the *China Times*. He spoke to a young lady, asking her if she could confirm that in 1910 the newspaper had reported an epidemic of snakes in China. Or in the Shanghai area.

'Snakes? In China? Who am I talking to?'

'My name's Cooper.'

'Hello, Mr Cooper. Snakes, you said? In China?'

'Some time in 1910.'

'Crazy,' said the young lady. 'Still, you sound quite sane. That's refreshing in this mad world. Hold on, I'll look up our reference files. Heading of snakes, I suppose. Don't go away, I'm here to serve.'

Jim held on. He had the accounts office to himself at the moment, Molly not being there. He waited a good four minutes. Then he heard a sound or two.

'Hello?'

'You're still there? Good for you. Listen, the only item on snakes I can find refers to a report that a reverend gent called Pilgrim – that's a lovely name for a reverend gent, don't you think? – adored them.'

'He what?'

'Well, he kept a snakehouse behind his mission in Shanghai. That is, he turned a huge conservatory into a home for snakes. He was a serpentologist. Well, a herpetologist, actually.'

'A what?'

'Don't ask me, Mr Cooper, it's news to me too. Our paper gave his hobby – some hobby, don't you

309

think? – a couple of paragraphs. Interested visitors were invited to inspect his collection. A sort of snake zoo, I suppose, very interesting to snake charmers.'

'Did he keep them in cages or were they free to roam around the conservatory?'

'No idea. It doesn't say. But could you keep a snake in a cage?'

'I suppose if you used something like chicken wire with a very small mesh.'

'That wouldn't make me feel very safe,' said the young lady. 'What's your interest, anyway?'

'Could you find out if during the same year your *China Times* reported the death of a man from snake-bite?'

'Great boa constrictors, is that your interest? Look, there's an elderly gent here, that's my boss. There's a beautiful young woman, that's me. And there's Herbert, he's the boy and general dogsbody. Oh, and there's a basement, stacked out with back numbers.'

'It's very kind of you,' said Jim.

'I'm trying to put you off. Oh, all right, I'll consult the reference files again and get Herbert to go down into the depths and ring you back. How's that?'

'Fine,' said Jim. 'My number's Rodney 2917, ask for Jim Cooper.'

She rang back twenty minutes later and informed him that on 27 July 1910, the *China Times* had indeed reported the tragic death of a Mr Clarence Guest at the Christian Mission House of St Luke,

310

where he had had the misfortune to be bitten by a viper, a snake of deadly venom. The Reverend James Pilgrim and his family suffered shock and grief, for the victim was a friend. The missionary destroyed his collection.

'Was there an inquest?' asked Jim.

'I thought you'd ask that, so I delved into it. The answer's yes. The verdict, death by misadventure. How's that, Mr Cooper?'

'Thanks very much, you've been cheerful, helpful and charming. We could do with more young ladies like you.'

'Who's we?' she asked.

'All of us,' said Jim.

CHAPTER EIGHTEEN

The immediate area around St John's Church was bathed in Walworth's hazy summer sunshine. It did little for the sooty greyness of some streets except to make them look a dingier grey. Street kids got dirtier more quickly, for the dust that was grounded by the heavy damp of winter floated in the warm air of summer. Few ragamuffin kids disturbed the relative quiet of Wansey Street, the most respectable-looking residential thoroughfare in the Walworth Road. But what did seem to disturb it were whispers and rumours that travelled as lazily but as perniciously through the summer haze as the myriad specks of golden dust.

The ubiquitous Mrs Lockheart appeared and reappeared, showing malice towards none and friendliness towards all, although she did say strange things about Miss Pilgrim. She stopped Orrice and Effel on their way home from school one day.

'Why, children,' she said, 'you live with Mr Cooper in Miss Pilgrim's house.'

'I'm not children,' said Orrice, 'I'm a growing boy.'

'I've seen you with Mr Cooper in church,' smiled Mrs Lockheart. 'My, aren't you a nice-looking lad?'

'Excuse me, missus,' said Orrice, 'but no, I ain't. Effel, get off my back.'

'Do you both like living in Miss Pilgrim's house?' asked Mrs Lockheart.

'She ain't our mum,' muttered Effel from behind Orrice.

'No, of course not, she's your landlady. Whoever would have thought Rebecca would take in lodgers? Do you look under your beds at night?'

'What would we do that for?' asked Orrice, thinking her nosy.

'Don't you look for snakes?' smiled Mrs Lockheart.

She's barmy, thought Orrice.

'What for?' he asked.

'I don't like snakes,' said Effel.

'Snakes curl up under a bed and wait for it to get warm, you know,' said Mrs Lockheart. 'It gets warm when one is sleeping in it.'

'Ugh,' shivered Effel.

'Now see what you done, missus,' said the forthright Orrice, 'you been and upset me sister. Come on, Effel, let's get home.'

'Goodbye, children, take care,' called Mrs Lockheart after them.

Miss Pilgrim let them in, and at once remarked that Effel had a dirty face.

'I don't mind,' said Effel, and escaped upstairs.

'And your bootlaces are undone, Master Horace.'

'Yes, well, yer see, Miss Pilgrim,' said Orrice, 'I'm goin' to put me plimsolls on.'

'Don't gabble, boy.'

313

'No, Miss Pilgrim, I been trying not to.'

'I concede that. Yes, you have been trying. Your guardian is impressed.' Miss Pilgrim knew it was going to be a hard grind for the boy, since he was in close contact every day with fellow pupils who were never going to try at all. 'Well, we shall do more poetry reading after you've had your tea.'

'Miss Pilgrim, that's not goin' to go on for ever, is it?'

'Indefinitely, boy.'

'Oh, crikey,' said Orrice. Effel appeared on the landing.

'Orrice, can yer come up an' look under me bed for me, and see'f there's any snakes, like that lady said?'

'Oh, yer daft date,' said Orrice. 'Oh, all right, then.' He went up. Miss Pilgrim stood in shock.

Jim came down to see her later. She received him in her kitchen. He mentioned that the kids had been stopped by Mrs Lockheart and been told to look under their beds at night for snakes.

'The woman herself is a serpent,' said Miss Pilgrim icily.

'It's time, I think, that something was done about her tongue.'

'What there is between Mrs Lockheart and myself is my business alone, Mr Cooper.'

'It's mine now that she has frightened Ethel with her stupid talk of snakes under beds,' said Jim. 'Miss Pilgrim, are you in need of a friend's help?'

'I am not, but which friend do you mean?'

'Myself,' said Jim, and she looked a little startled.

'We're on agreeable terms, but I had no idea you considered yourself a friend.'

'I'd be sorry if you thought I wasn't. I'm in great debt to you for all you've done for the kids—'

'The children.' Miss Pilgrim was primly corrective.

'And for me.'

'I've done a little in the name of practical Christianity, that is all, and in turn you and the children have—' She hesitated. 'You have all been very rewarding.'

'Rewarding?'

'I am a domesticated woman, Mr Cooper, I enjoy cooking for Horace and Ethel, and sitting down with them for the midday meal, and providing Sunday dinners for all of you. It is a silly thing, perhaps, peculiar to some women, but I enjoy it.'

'There's nothing at all silly about it, Miss Pilgrim,' said Jim, 'it's a great kindness, and a very happy sign of a warm and generous nature. I've been right all along, you're an angel.'

'I wish you would spare me absurdities, Mr Cooper.'

Jim laughed. Miss Pilgrim drew herself up.

'It surprises me,' he said, 'that a woman of your background and experience should be so shy and modest.'

'Mr Cooper, what utter nonsense.'

'I'll allow modesty,' said Jim in his breezy way, 'that's fitting in any woman, but to find you shy tickles me immensely.'

Her frosty look made its appearance.

'Tickles you?' she said. 'Really, Mr Cooper, for a mature man you sometimes show deplorable immaturity in your spoken word. Shy indeed. I am not a schoolgirl. All I am guilty of is a sense of dignity, which you contrived to destroy on a certain occasion.'

Jim gave her a searching look. Her eyes flickered and a distinct flush tinted her cheeks. So that was it. What a strange, adorable woman.

'Why, Miss Pilgrim,' he said, 'I've never seen anything lovelier.'

'Mr Cooper! How dare you!'

'Well, I've said it, and I'll stand on it,' said Jim with masculine directness.

'You are not to mention the incident, or even think about it!' Miss Pilgrim was actually crimson.

'I thought you were the one who brought it up,' said Jim, who really wanted to laugh about it. A girl on a swing or a woman on a swing, clothes flying high, all such a typical part of the fun of a fair.

'Go away,' said Miss Pilgrim.

'I'm sorry,' he said, 'I didn't mean to upset you. We all think the world of you, even Ethel.'

'I do not like soft soap, Mr Cooper.'

'And I don't like this odd woman, this Mrs Lockheart. Something must be done about her.'

'Nothing can be done about such a woman. Do not interfere, Mr Cooper, or you'll regret it.'

Jim thought for a moment, then said, 'Do you realize, Miss Pilgrim, that Mrs Lockheart's talking to all and sundry, and is probably allowing people

316

to infer you poisoned her brother, a man called Clarence Guest?'

Miss Pilgrim's fine firm mouth tightened, but her eyes looked straight into his.

'How do you know that?'

'Because she spoke at length to me, on the occasion when I let her into the house to wait for you. And I'm damn sure she's repeating everything to everyone she meets. Where's she living?'

'I have no idea, I haven't interested myself in her, and I hope you will not.'

'Aren't you even interested in what she had to say to me?'

Miss Pilgrim, at her frostiest, said, 'Not in the least. She is quite mad. Poison her brother indeed. How ridiculous. Now, if you'll excuse me—'

'There's monkey business going on,' said Jim brusquely, 'and I'm not standing for it. It's putting you in an impossible position.'

'That is my affair.'

'It's mine too, as I said five minutes ago.'

'And I have said it's nothing to do with you,' declared Miss Pilgrim. 'Mr Cooper, I shall regard any interference as grossly impertinent.'

'We'll fall out?' he said.

'We shall indeed.'

'Oh, lord, of all the angels you're the most obstinate.'

'Really, Mr Cooper,' she said in disdain, 'I do wish you would stop addressing me in such an infantile way.'

'I don't see it like that,' said Jim. 'Look here, I'll

compromise, I'll wait until Mrs Lockheart calls again, as I think she will. Then I'll have a few words with her.'

'You'll do no such thing.'

'Just watch me.'

'I need no help with Mrs Lockheart, thank you.'

'Yes, you do. Your friends are avoiding you. I've seen it happen outside the church. By the way, I'm taking the day off tomorrow, with the manager's permission.' Jim had problems of his own to solve. 'I'm going to call on my maternal grandparents again. I should be back by the time Horace and Ethel get home from school, but if I'm delayed—?'

'If you are, I'll prepare tea for them,' said Miss Pilgrim, not allowing her vexations to blur her Christian outlook.

'Thank you. You really are an—'

'Spare me. I am not an angel.'

'Well, I think you are,' said Jim. 'Now I'd better go back upstairs and get tea for the kids.'

He took an early train to Hampshire the next morning, having decided that Arthur Miller, the stumbling block, would be at work and out of the way on a weekday. He knew he should have made an attempt years ago to look up his mother's relatives. What had held him back? The possibility that to open the book on his mother's life might have destroyed his illusions about her? He did have illusions, all based on imaginative pictures and the things Lily had said about her. It was Lily who had been turned away when she visited the family home in Elderfield. That had not encouraged him to make a visit himself. Today, on his second visit, he must at least find out if Arthur had always seen his sister as flighty and feckless enough to have landed herself inevitably in the worst kind of trouble a young woman could, and if Mrs Miller conceded the possibility, or if her daughter had simply been a girl passionately in love.

His train journey was a lonely one. He missed his companions of before, little Effel and talkative Orrice. It seemed ages before he found himself at last in Elderfield again. He walked through the little village and past the tiny shop, and on to the pair of cottages that lay beyond the street. He turned in at the gate of the first cottage, noted again the neat little front garden, and knocked at the door. Mrs Miller, his elderly grandmother, answered his knock. Her face, slightly rosy in the way of a countrywoman, expressed no surprise.

'I thought as you might come again,' she said.

'I thought myself that I'd come when there was a chance of seeing you alone,' said Jim with a smile.

'You thought right.' She opened the door wide. 'I be happy to see you, Jim. My son's at work, my daughter-in-law be up with the sheep and my husband be gone into town. Come in and welcome.'

He stepped in. She looked up at him.

'You're my grandmother,' he said, and kissed her smooth cheek. She took hold of his right arm and of his left arm, above the elbow stump, and she held him firmly for a second or so. Then she kissed him.

'You be my sweet Betsy's son, as I knowed when

I saw you,' she said. 'Where shall we talk?'

'In your kitchen,' he said, 'I like kitchens.'

They seated themselves at the kitchen table, an iron kettle heating up on the range hob.

'You'll take tea?' she said.

'Any time of the day, Grandma.'

'In a minute, then, when that old kettle boils. You be wanting to know about your mother, don't you?'

'I'd like to hear she was something like you.'

Mrs Miller told him about Betsy, a good girl, a lovely girl, who could find no work in the village after she left school, but was offered a job in service later. Up to near London, which worried Mrs Miller a little, seeing so many tales were told about how London put the wrong kind of temptations in the way of a girl far from home. But her father, Mr Miller, said no harm would come to a girl as good and as sensible as their Betsy. Arthur scowled about it, being very fond of his sister and not liking her being away from home at all.

'He really was fond of her?' asked Jim.

'That he were. It turned him bitter and sour when—' Mrs Miller came to a painful stop.

'When he knew she was going to have a child?'

'It were hurtful to all of us, Jim.'

'But Arthur wouldn't let her come back home?'

'He raged about.' Mrs Miller got up and made the tea at this point. She placed the pot on the table, with a cosy over it. She poured milk into two cups. She sat down again. 'Said he'd find the man and kill him. He took a train up to near London to talk to

Betsy. Found out the man – your father – was a soldier, and in Africa. Servin' with Lord Kitchener, that he was.' Mrs Miller poured the tea. 'That to your likin', Jim?' she said, as he took a refreshing sip.

'First-class,' said Jim, and she touched his shoulder and patted him. Affection was present.

'Arthur told Betsy—' Mrs Miller looked sad. 'What he did tell her, all of it, I don't know, but he was in a rage when he took the train and in a rage when he came back. Arthur be a man of strong moods, nor don't hold back with his tongue when he's angered. I only know he told Betsy never to come back home, and had a terrible blazing row with Betsy's father about it. But your mother, my sweet Betsy, were a good girl, Jim, always. She were so pretty, so affectionate, and she give her affection, all of it, to your father. Perhaps she give it in the way she did because he was goin' away to do his duty as a soldier of the Queen, and because it were true love, not because she were a girl who were loose and tarty. She were never that, never. Ah, you should have heard how she could laugh and make everyone else laugh too, but she never flirted or made eyes in her life. She had love for your father, Jim, a girl's once and only love. She came here before you were born, when Arthur weren't here, and she told me and her father of John Cooper, a soldier sergeant, and begged us never to think ill of her or him. After she'd gone and Arthur came home, my husband stood up to him, and there were another terrible row, though my husband be the mildest man and never given to fearsome quarrels. My poor dear Betsy, and you, Jim. There were a home here for you but for Arthur, and it be on my conscience always that my husband and me chose peace and quiet instead of you.'

'My mother had a friend when she was in service, a woman called Lily Downes, who told me many things about her and swore she was a lovely person. I was never sure if she spoke out of loyalty and friendship, if she gilded her memory of my mother. She called here once.'

'Yes. Arthur sent the poor lady packing. Roared at her to take herself off.'

'I feel sorry for Arthur,' said Jim.

'You be like your mother, then. She were sorry for his rages and his senselessness. But you be my grandson, all the same, and you be dear to me and my husband, because of our Betsy. You fought in the war and lost an arm, but you bear no bitterness because of that or because of Arthur. Jim, you be our Betsy's son all right. And you look like your father.'

'How d'you know that?' asked Jim.

'We have things of Betsy's, sent to us after she were killed, poor sweet.'

'I came because I wanted you to talk to me about her,' said Jim. 'I wanted to hear about her from your lips, and I wanted to know if there were things of hers.'

'There are, to be sure,' said Mrs Miller, 'letters to her from your father, her engagement ring, a photograph of your father, a little photograph of you when you were two, and some beads and a brooch. I kept them from Arthur when they were sent to me and my husband, being afraid Arthur would burn the letters and photograph. They be yours if you want, Jim, seeing I think they belong to you more than to us, and seeing they'd be safer with you than with us.'

'I'd very much like to have them,' said Jim, 'but is there a photograph of her? I didn't see one in your parlour when I called before.'

'There be one, Jim. A postcard photo taken when she were seventeen, before she went up London ways to go into service. I kept that hidden too, because of Arthur. You stay sittin' for a minute and I'll get them.' Mrs Miller left the kitchen. Jim heard her climbing the stairs. He looked at the vegetable patch, seen through the window, and at the fields beyond, fields bordered by woods. Here was where his mother had grown up, in the heart of rural Hampshire, a girl of laughter according to her own mother. He could imagine her, a young girl, in a white frock and a large white country sun-bonnet, such as all young girls wore in the late Victorian period, running through those fields and picking primroses and wild flowers in the woods. It was, of course, how he wanted to imagine her, to know her innocent and enchanting in her growing-up years, and without fault.

Mrs Miller returned. She placed a decorated wooden box with a curved lid on the kitchen table.

'Everything's in this box, Grandma?'

'It all be yours, Jim, to take away. The box were

hers too. See?' She lifted the lid. A piece of thin white cardboard had been glued to the curved inside of the lid. Coloured crayons had been used to decorate the margins with flower chains and to make a frame for printed letters in different colours.

'MY TREASURE CHEST BETSY JANE MILLER 1878 AGED 7'

Inside the box were beads, a brooch, a ring, letters and an envelope containing photographs. He picked the envelope out, and extracted the photographs. He looked at the postcard print of his mother as a girl of seventeen. It was a sepia print. The strangest emotions sent his heart tumbling, and made a weakness of his body. There she was, in portrait, with a mass of long, curling hair that even in the inanimate photograph seemed to be lightly dancing on her shoulders.

'Her hair were brown, Jim, her eyes too.'

Jim was looking at a girl quite lovely, a girl whose smile showed the glimmer of healthy white teeth and which was so much in her eyes that one knew she had been close to laughter because some girls always thought that being photographed was a giggle. It was a portrait of a girl in love with life. He saw the brooch, a cameo brooch, pinned to the high neck of her blouse. That brooch was the one in the box.

This was his mother, this girl who loved life and whose laughter came alive for him in the photograph. He knew then that Lily in her loyalty had not gilded the picture. He could be proud of his mother, still a young woman when she had been

324

tragically killed running across a road, and whom he could not remember. He turned the postcard print over, Mrs Miller watching him silently and with great sympathy. On the back of the print, faded but still readable, were pencilled words.

'Watch the birdie, count to three,
Think of sitting in a tree,
Open eyes, what do you see?
Goodness gracious, this is me?'

And there was her name again. *'Betsy Jane Miller 1888 aged 17.'*

He had been born three years later, in 1891, when she was twenty. He felt a great wave of love for her.

'She were a lovely girl, Jim,' said Mrs Miller, 'mischievous when she were young, and a tease, but never unkind, and eager to get out into the world when she were seventeen. She always said her Mr Right were out there waitin' for her, and she'd know him soon as she met him. With your father, love at first sight I think it were. There, that's him, that photograph.'

Another sepia postcard print, another portrait, this time of a man in uniform, smiling beneath his khaki cap, a natural and cheerful smile, and Jim thought he might have been looking at a portrait of himself during his own time in the Army. So this was his father, the man his mother had loved and given herself to. Had she found her Mr Right in him because he looked, perhaps, as if he could match her sense of fun? On the back was written, *'With love to my own Betsy.'*

'I think I'm like him, Grandma.'

'That you are, Jim, he be your father all right, and our Betsy's love.'

The third photograph was of himself as a two-year-old, clad in a little sailor outfit, and standing beside a studio chair. He looked very grave, very puzzled, very small. He turned it over.

'My darling boy James John at two.' They were his father's names in reverse.

How hard it must have been for her, facing the world alone with her illegitimate son. He felt an intense longing to have known her, to have his own true pictures of her, but his memory could not take him back to when he was three, when he had lost her.

'Jim, there be over twenty letters in there, from your father to her.'

'You've read them?'

'All of them. My husband too. Your father had a good man's love for your mother, a fine soldier's love. Betsy were dear to him. Jim, there be no shame in how and why you were born, and it would be a gladness for me and my husband to know you don't hold no shame in yourself or your mother and father, though we be guilty ourselves of the shame of leaving you in an orphanage, my husband and me.'

'There's no shame,' said Jim, 'not in anyone. There's just two people who didn't live as long as they deserved to. Frankly, old lady, I can never make head or tail of our Creator's great design, how it was all arrived at and if there's some profound

326

reason for shortening the lives of the deserving instead of the undeserving.'

'What's a profound reason?' asked Mrs Miller.

'I suppose a reason people like you and me can't understand,' said Jim. He replaced the photographs in the envelope. He fingered his mother's brooch and her engagement ring, then looked at the tied packet of letters in the box.

'Read them somewhere quiet, Jim,' said Mrs Miller. 'I'd ask you to stay for a bite, but Arthur always comes home from his work to his midday dinner, he'll be in a bit after one. I won't say he's not a good son, he works hard, he's a providing man to his wife and all of us, but I'm thinkin' he's likely to go to his grave without ever forgivin' Betsy.'

'How can I keep in touch with you?'

His grandmother lightly pressed his hand.

'Write to my husband, George Miller, your grandfather. Arthur might look hard at a letter with my name on it and in writin' he can't recognize, but he'll leave letters to his father alone. My husband and me will write back, and maybe, sometimes, if you can come again, like you have today, when Arthur be at work—' Mrs Miller's smile was of sensitive affection. 'Well, it would pleasure me, Jim. You take those things of Betsy's now, you keep them for your own, and whenever you think of her you need be in no shame, like I said.'

'I like you, Grandma,' said Jim, 'I like it that you were my mother's mother. I've no wife as yet, but I've two wards, a boy and a girl. I'll bring them to see you during their school holidays. Bless you.'

His father's letters to his mother kept him company and kept him absorbed on the train back to Waterloo. He read all of them, every one, and there were twenty-five of them, written in a good hand and in simple style. They were cheerful and optimistic, unfailingly affectionate and in some places a man's deep love for a woman broke through. The words then were very private, making Jim feel they belonged only to his mother.

He realized he was no longer a solitary man. He had Orrice and Effel, and he had grandparents. He had a grandmother in the mould of a gentle woman, an elderly lady of country grace. And he had things that had been precious to his mother. He had her photograph. He knew at last what she looked like.

He framed the photograph, and that of his father, and placed them on the mantelpiece in his living-room. They enabled him to introduce Orrice and Effel to his parents, and their interest, particularly Effel's, surprised him. They asked questions, and he told them as much as he could of what he knew, and used his imagination to tell them more. From the letters he had discovered his father came from Dorset, and he painted a few pictures of Dorset life for Orrice and Effel. He did not, however, tell them his mother had not been married to his father, but he did say they had died when he was very young.

Orrice said he was awful sorry about that. Effel, gazing again at the photograph of a seventeen-year-old country girl, gulped.

'Well, one thing's for sure,' said Jim with forced cheer, 'we all need each other, don't we?'

The photograph was missing from the mantelpiece the next day. Jim found it in Effel's bedroom, on her mantelpiece. He waited for her to say why she had put it there. He waited in vain. Effel said nothing. He left it in her room. He thought perhaps it represented a memory of her own mother.

Miss Pilgrim, changing the bed linen the following Monday, saw the framed photograph, and asked Jim that evening if it was of the children's mother.

'No, mine.'

'Yours? When she was young, Mr Cooper?'

'Taken when she was seventeen.'

'Such a fresh-faced, lovely girl,' said Miss Pilgrim.

'She was only twenty-three when she died, and my father, killed when serving with Kitchener, wasn't yet thirty.'

Miss Pilgrim's blue eyes darkened.

'I'm sorrier than I can ever say, Mr Cooper. Marriage is an institution blessed by God, especially when there are children, and it was cruel that the marriage of your parents was so brief and fleeting.'

'As I said to my maternal grandmother, I fail sometimes to understand the ways of our Creator.'

'Yes, one does ask questions sometimes, Mr Cooper, but we shouldn't let our faith be weakened.'

'You've never sought the blessing of marriage yourself,' smiled Jim.

'I devoted myself to my parents. There was fulfilment in that. I shan't ask why you have never married.'

'Oh, I'm no catch,' said Jim.

Miss Pilgrim folded a freshly-ironed sheet.

'Your predilection for speaking nonsense is not your most sensible virtue, Mr Cooper.'

'Well, there's hope for both of us still, Miss Pilgrim.'

'Hope for what?' she asked, folding another sheet.

'Your Mr Right may still be out there, waiting for you, and my Miss Right may be just round the corner.'

Miss Pilgrim carefully placed the folded sheets together. Her hands, he noticed, did not have the work-worn look of most Walworth women. Her fingers were long and fine. He supposed she took great care of them because she liked to keep herself immaculate.

'I think your need is greater than mine, Mr Cooper,' she said. 'I am self-sufficient, but you are a man with two wards.'

'My diffidence is against me,' said Jim.

'Diffidence?' Miss Pilgrim sounded a little sarcastic. 'I have never met any man with less diffidence than you.'

'Appearances can be deceptive,' said Jim. 'In any case, I doubt if Molly Keating, the manager's daughter, for whom I've got a soft spot, would take on a man and two wards all at once and at the same time.'

Miss Pilgrim picked up a pillow slip and eyed it critically.

'But you're courting her?' she said.

'Saints alive, no. I really am no catch, Miss Pilgrim.'

'But you care for her?'

'Molly's a charming and warm-hearted young lady, and deserves a man better and more affluent than I am.'

'Utter nonsense,' said Miss Pilgrim crisply.

'We'll leave it at that,' said Jim. 'By the way, I'm taking Ethel and Horace to school tomorrow. I'll be a little late for my work, but can make it up with a short lunch hour. I thought I'd catch Alice and invite her to Sunday tea around our table. It's fair to reciprocate, isn't it?'

Miss Pilgrim turned to face him.

'I'm not sure what Horace will think, but yes, it's fair. Mr Cooper, if the day is fine and warm enough, would you all care to have the tea in the garden with me? My little patch of grass isn't so little that I can't put a folding table on it.'

'There you go again,' said Jim.

'What does that mean?' she asked, regarding him with suspicion.

'Being an angel again.'

'You are becoming quite impossible, and I cannot respond to such absurdities.'

'Nothing absurd about Sunday tea in a garden in Walworth,' said Jim, 'it's close to being a blessing from God.'

'You are ridiculous,' said Miss Pilgrim.

'I accept with great pleasure on behalf of all of us, including Alice,' said Jim.

Left to herself, Miss Pilgrim bustled about her

kitchen in a vexed fashion. Now what had she done? She had invited them into her own little oasis, her own little summer retreat.

Surely she had not needed to do that?

Alice, always early to school, was waiting at the gates. She had taken to doing that, to waiting for Horace and going into classes with him. He arrived with his sister and with his tall guardian, a kind-looking man with one arm.

'Oh, good morning, Mr Cooper,' she said. 'Horace, you're here.'

'I happen to 'ave come,' said Orrice, warily watching out for other boys. A bloke just couldn't trust what Alice might say.

''E's wiv me,' said Effel grimly, but Effel was fighting a losing battle. Every arrow bounced off Alice.

Jim looked down at Alice in her school boater, her curling hair falling to her shoulders, her smile welcoming Orrice, and he thought of his mother at the age of nine.

'Alice,' he said, 'would you like to come to tea on Sunday?'

'Eh?' said Orrice, mouth dropping open in disbelief that his Uncle Jim could play the traitor.

'Oh, could I?' asked Alice in bliss.

'If it's fine, we'll be having it in our landlady's garden,' said Jim.

'I ain't comin',' said Effel.

'But tea in a garden, Ethel, won't that be lovely?' said Alice.

332

'I'm 'earing things, I am,' said Orrice.

'Come at four, Alice,' said Jim.

'Oh, yes, thank you, Mr Cooper.'

'Orrice ain't comin',' said Effel. 'Nor me.'

'Horace will walk you home afterwards,' said Jim to Alice.

'Watcher, Orrice,' said an arriving boy, ''ow yer doing?'

'I'm ill,' said Orrice.

Alice looked up at Jim. Jim winked. Alice laughed. Orrice went into assembly feeling faint.

He spoke to Jim that evening. In his forthright way, he said, 'Uncle Jim, before I go down for me poetry readin', I got to have a talk with you.'

'Man to man?' said Jim.

'Yes, if yer like.'

'About Alice?'

'Ugh,' said Effel, cuddling one of her Ragamuffin Jack books for comfort and consolation.

'Uncle Jim,' said Orrice sorrowfully, 'you done me in proper. Invitin' Alice to Sunday tea 'ere, that done me in a bit to start with, but me walkin' her home, I didn't fink—'

'Think,' said Jim.

'Yes, I didn't think you'd do that to me, get me to walk her all the way 'ome to Crampton Street,' said Orrice, 'and I dunno I can do it except with a sack over me 'ead, so's they won't see me.'

'They?' said Jim gravely.

'Me schoolfriends,' said Orrice. 'It's all over the school already that Alice is me—' Orrice couldn't bring himself to say it. As it was, he had a dozen fights lined up with kids who'd said things.

'Carry on,' said Jim.

'Orrice ain't saying,' muttered Effel, ''cos she ain't 'is sweet'eart. I am.'

'Oh, yer date,' said Orrice, 'you're me sister, you can't be me sweetheart.'

'Never mind, Horace,' said Jim, who agreed with Miss Pilgrim that the boy should acquire some social grace, 'you can talk to Alice about it when you walk her home. Point out to her you can't commit yourself now, not at your age, but you'll think about it when you're older.'

'I'm goin' to work on the railways when I'm older,' said Orrice. 'I thought you was my friend, Uncle Jim, I didn't think you'd 'elp to send me barmy.'

'I am your friend, Horace.'

'Orrice ain't goin' to walk 'er 'ome wivout me,' declared Effel.

'Now see what yer done, Uncle,' said Orrice, 'me life's not me own any more.'

CHAPTER NINETEEN

The vicar appeared at the entrance to the church after the Sunday morning service, to say a few words to each departing parishioner. Mrs Lockheart, who had again been present, was detained for a few moments longer than other people, the vicar regarding her with curiosity while exchanging pleasantries with her. She was smiling when she detached herself to join a group of women who seemed in no hurry to get home. Jim, waiting with Orrice and Effel, saw Miss Pilgrim appear. The vicar spoke to her. Miss Pilgrim eyed him enquiringly, then she nodded and went back into the church with him.

'Horace,' said Jim, 'you walk on home with Ethel.'

Orrice, spotting Alice heading towards him, took Effel away at a fast pace. Jim walked across to the group of women. Mrs Lockheart smiled at him.

'Can you spare a few moments?' he asked.

'With pleasure, Mr Cooper,' she said. She excused herself to the ladies and joined him.

'Let's walk,' said Jim, and took her at a stroll along Larcom Street. 'Mrs Lockheart, it's time you went back to where you came from.'

'Whatever do you mean, Mr Cooper?'

335

'I mean you've done enough damage. If that's what you came for, you've succeeded. You've got the vicar worried now. So give it a rest. Your brother was bitten by a viper, and the inquest confirmed this. I've checked. I suggest that before you leave you write a letter to the vicar clearing Miss Pilgrim of any connection with your brother's unfortunate death.'

'Why, Mr Cooper, I do believe you've been talking to Rebecca. I hope you're not a gullible man. Rebecca has a forked tongue, you know.'

'A forked tongue has been wagging in every street around here,' said Jim, 'but it doesn't belong to Miss Pilgrim.'

'Oh, dear me,' said Mrs Lockheart prettily, 'she has a champion? But how does a viper get from a conservatory into a sleeping man's bed?'

'Snakes its way there. You told me your brother was found dead in his bed. At the mission, I presume.'

'A guest, Mr Cooper.'

'Yet I heard you ask Miss Pilgrim if he said anything during his last moments. That doesn't add up. Nor do you.'

'How clever of that viper to find its way to my brother's bed,' murmured Mrs Lockheart as they approached the Walworth Road.

'Mrs Lockheart, I accept none of your insinuations about Miss Pilgrim.'

'Dear me,' she said, 'I see how true it is that love is blind.'

336

'What's that supposed to mean?' asked Jim, disliking her thoroughly.

'Clarence, poor man, was also in love with Rebecca.'

'So she put a viper in his bed? You're out of your mind, Mrs Lockheart.'

Mrs Lockheart stopped and turned on him, her charming smile vanishing. Her eyes glittered and her expression became waspish. No, thought Jim, not waspish. There was a more appropriate adjective. Viperish.

'You dare say that to me?' She almost hissed the words. 'You will regret that.' And she walked away, back towards the church. Jim walked home. Orrice and Effel were waiting on the doorstep. He used his key to let them in.

'You all right, Uncle?' asked Orrice. 'You don't look very 'appy, does he, Effel?'

'Not my fault,' protested Effel.

'I'm all right now I'm in clean air,' said Jim.

He heard Miss Pilgrim come in ten minutes later. He went down to see her. In her kitchen, she was aproned and busying herself with the dinner preparations. She did not seem as if her interlude with the vicar had disturbed her. She looked her usual composed self.

'Yes, Mr Cooper?'

'The vicar spoke to you,' said Jim.

'That is so.'

'About Mrs Lockheart and what she's been saying to people?'

'The conversation I had with the vicar was a private one, Mr Cooper.'

'I had a conversation myself. With Mrs Lockheart.'

'It's a free country, I'm told,' said Miss Pilgrim, placing prepared potatoes in the pan containing a joint of mutton. 'And I naturally assume your conversation was not about me.'

'It was all about you,' said Jim.

'You had no right,' she said sharply.

'As you pointed out, it's a free country.'

'That doesn't give you the right to discuss my affairs.'

'I'm a friend,' said Jim.

'Then you should do as I ask, and not interfere. It will do no good. That woman appeared out of thin air. When she gets tired of what she's doing, when it begins to bore her, she will disappear as suddenly as she came. I forgive you for discussing my affairs with her, and I wish to hear no more about it. Come down to dinner at two as usual, please – oh, and I have baked a fruit cake for tea. The weather is fine enough for us to have it in the garden, with your guest Alice, and I trust your wards will be on their best behaviour. Perhaps over dinner we can have some interesting talk on Horace's next poem, "How We Brought the Good News from Ghent to Aix".' Miss Pilgrim placed the meat dish back in the oven. 'You know that one, Mr Cooper? *I galloped, Dirck galloped, we galloped all three?*'

'Oh, my sainted aunt,' said Jim, and laughed.

Miss Pilgrim drew herself up and regarded him stonily.

'What is amusing you, Mr Cooper?'

'You, Miss Pilgrim. You're irrepressible.'

'Kindly go away, Mr Cooper, I'm far too serious-minded to appreciate that kind of remark. I'm also busy.'

'Just one question, Miss Pilgrim. Do you know how to handle a snake? That is, how to take hold of it without harm to yourself?'

Her blue eyes took on their familiar frostiness.

'Yes, you have been discussing me with that woman,' she said.

'Can you handle snakes?'

'I refuse to answer. Please go away.'

Jim went. He felt an easing of his worries, however, despite her icy response to his question. She was standing up to everything that Mrs Lockheart was maliciously throwing at her. He had no doubt that the vicar himself had expressed worries to her. She had probably told him in her fearless way not to concern himself. One would have to be lacking in character to doubt the integrity of a woman as admirable as Miss Pilgrim.

The sun of late June made its warm, bright conquest of the haze of Walworth to flood Miss Pilgrim's little garden with golden light. The narrow flower beds bordering the small lawn were a marvel of colour. In the tiny timber shed stood the old hand-mower used by Miss Pilgrim to cut the grass. On the lawn the folding table, covered with an embroidered white cloth, was set for tea, with five placings. Effel and Orrice, inspecting the flowers with Jim, were wide-eyed that there were flowers at all, alive and real.

'Golly,' breathed Effel, itching to pick some.

'Ain't they pretty, Effel?' said Orrice.

'Is it a real garding?' whispered Effel.

'Course it is.'

'It's an oasis, Miss Pilgrim,' said Jim. That was how she saw it herself, but as her own alone. Not even the ladies of the church who sometimes took afternoon tea with her had ever been invited into her retreat. What she was doing by bringing Mr Cooper and his wards into it, she really did not know, except that she did not intend to make a precedent of the invitation.

'Even a small piece of ground can be made to look like a gift from God,' she said. The sound of a knock on the front door penetrated to the garden. 'That will be Alice,' she said, and went to answer the knock. A few moments later she brought Alice through to the garden. Alice stopped and stared.

'Oh, Miss Pilgrim, oh, crumbs, isn't it lovely?' she said. She was carrying a large cardboard box, its top covered by a picturesque illustration. 'Hello, Mr Cooper. Oh, don't you look nice, Ethel?'

'No,' said Effel grumpily.

'Oh, Horace dear, I'm here,' said Alice. Orrice had his back turned to her in the hope that what he couldn't see might not be there.

''E ain't Orrice dear, 'e's me bruvver,' said Effel,

still fighting her battle to keep Orrice exclusive to herself.

'I've brought you something, Horace,' said Alice. Orrice turned.

'Oh, 'ello,' he said.

'Look,' said Alice, and placed the box on one of the kitchen chairs that Jim had helped bring out. He and Miss Pilgrim watched as Orrice advanced cautiously. The boy looked at the colourful illustration. It was of a shining black railway engine thundering along a track. His eyes opened wide. 'My cousin Edward's grown up now,' said Alice, 'he didn't want this any more, so I asked if I could give it to you, Horace. You said you've always wanted a clockwork engine set. Look.' She lifted the lid of the box and disclosed clockwork engine, carriages, a tender, a heap of lines curved and straight, and a signal. 'It's for you, Horace.'

Effel, coming to look, ground her teeth in rage.

'Orrice don't want it,' she said.

'Crikey,' said Orrice, and was breathless. Alice beamed at him. In a Sunday white dress with a pink sash, she was a picture of nine-year-old prettiness. Jim saw more than prettiness, he saw a warm and generous little girl, who spoke well but had no side, and whose fondness for Orrice was founded, perhaps, on some instinctive feeling that he was a fresh, healthy and honest boy who liked fun. So did Alice. Whenever his little grin arrived, Alice waited quivering for fun to break out. 'Alice, you can't give me somefink like this,' he said, 'it's not me birfday or anyfing.' In his excitement he mangled his

341

English and made Miss Pilgrim sigh.

'But my cousin said I could give it to you,' declared Alice, 'I told him we were sweethearts.'

Effel emitted a strangled yell. Orrice coughed.

'Have you two got chest colds?' asked Jim.

'Feel sick,' growled Effel.

'Then go to the kitchen sink, child,' said Miss Pilgrim.

'Ain't that kind of sick,' muttered Effel.

'Oh, you want to suck something, Ethel,' said Alice, 'something like an acid drop or a bit of barley sugar. Horace, d'you want to fix the railway lines together? I can help.'

'Well, I dunno as—' Orrice stopped as he caught Miss Pilgrim's pained look. 'Well, I don't know I ought to take your present, Alice. I don't have nothing to give you, and I betcher this is more than one of them half-a-crown clockwork train sets.'

'Horace, you've got to have it,' protested Alice, 'you don't have to give me anything, honest.'

'I think I'd best let Uncle Jim decide,' said Orrice, who was overwhelmingly tempted, but had a feeling acceptance would put him in chains.

'Well, my lad,' said Jim cheerfully, 'Alice's cousin doesn't want it, and he's let Alice have it to give to you. And you can always ask her the date of her birthday.' Jim was doing what he could, with Miss Pilgrim's co-operation, to help Orrice improve his social graces.

'It's September the eleventh,' said Alice, on to that in a flash, 'and you can come to my birthday party.'

''E don't want no train set, and 'e don't go to no-one's birfday parties 'cept mine,' said Effel, utterly green-eyed.

'Well, Uncle Jim says I best have it, sis,' said Orrice, 'and Alice did bring it all the way. I got to say thank you, Alice, yer a real sport.'

'Oh, that's all right, Horace dear,' said Alice, and lifted her face for a kiss. Orrice took a deep breath, closed his eyes, aimed with his mouth and landed a quick kiss on her cheek. The faintest smile touched Miss Pilgrim's lips. Effel trembled with fury. 'Oh, you are nice, Horace,' said Alice.

Effel let go an old but still telling chestnut.

''Oo's a pretty boy, then?' she said.

'My mum says he's lovely,' declared Alice proudly.

Orrice lifted suffering eyes to Jim. Jim winked.

'I shall put the kettle on for tea now,' said Miss Pilgrim. 'And perhaps—' She paused, then made a further sacrifice. 'Yes, perhaps after tea you and Alice would like to put the train set out on my kitchen table, Horace.'

'Cor, yer rippin', Miss Pilgrim,' said Orrice, 'yer the best sport ever.'

'I doubt it, young man,' she said, and went into the kitchen. The cardboard box containing the train set fell off the chair on which Alice had placed it. Effel had given it a push. Jim took her aside, while Alice and Orrice set the box and its contents to rights.

'What's it all about, miss?' murmured Jim.

'Nuffink,' said Effel.

'Well, listen, lovey,' said Jim, 'you've got Orrice

343

and you've got me, and you'll always have us. But you must let Orrice have his friends.'

'Not 'er,' said Effel, mulish.

Miss Pilgrim provided a perfect Sunday tea in the heart of Walworth, in her own little oasis. Alice and Orrice both thought it as grand as it could be. The sparrows came to look, and hopped about on the grass searching for crumbs. Sparrows thrived in Walworth.

There were cucumber sandwiches, thinly-sliced bread and butter, Kennedy's salmon and shrimp paste, pink and creamy, home-made jam, a marmalade tart and the freshly-baked fruit cake. Alice ate happily and healthily, Orrice ate with the typical relish of a Walworth boy, and Effel with snapping teeth. Miss Pilgrim encouraged conversation as usual. Orrice participated only at intervals, for his mind could concentrate on little else except his exciting ownership of a superior clockwork train set. The one problem about that was his feeling of obligation towards Alice. It could mean he'd never get rid of her.

Tea over, Alice said, 'I heard Horace is going to be put down for West Square. I'm going to try for West Square Girls the year after. Then me and Horace will be able to walk home together, or ride on the tram.'

The folding table lurched. Empty cups and saucers, jam-stained tea plates, the cake-stand and what was left of the cake, and the teapot and the slop basin slithered over the crumpling tablecloth.

Fortunately, most of the things landed in Jim's lap, although the teapot hit the lawn and its handle snapped off. Two cups also lost their handles as they clashed. Everyone looked at Effel, Miss Pilgrim exhibiting utter shock. Effel had given the table a violent shove.

'Effel, wha'dyer do that for?' asked Orrice in dismay.

'Wasn't me,' said Effel. Miss Pilgrim looked at Jim, who was carefully unloading his lap, his trousers wet from tea remnants.

'Ethel,' said Jim, 'go up to your room, and stay there until I come up myself.'

'Ain't goin',' said Effel.

Jim placed the things back on the table, including the teapot and three snapped-off handles.

'I'll glue the handles back on, Miss Pilgrim, until we can get matching replacements,' he said, and rose to his feet. He came round to Effel and lifted her from her chair. With his strong right arm around her waist, he carried her kicking and yelling into the house.

'Oh, blimey,' muttered Orrice.

'She didn't mean it, Miss Pilgrim,' said Alice.

'Master Horace,' said Miss Pilgrim, 'fetch the tray and we'll collect everything up.'

When Jim brought Effel down again fifteen minutes later, Miss Pilgrim was washing up the tea things, and Orrice and Alice were in the garden. Effel was tear-stained. Jim had talked to her at length, and with a great deal of seriousness.

'Please, Miss Pilgrim, I—' Effel gulped, her head hanging. 'I'm sorry.'

Miss Pilgrim dried her hands and did what was surprising to Jim. She went down on one knee in front of Effel. She placed her hands on the girl's shoulders and regarded her in compassion.

'Child,' she said, 'it's easy to upset a folding table, but it's not so easy to bear the consequences. That's an unhappiness, isn't it? We all make mistakes on impulse. Regrets are more lasting. And how silly to think you are going to lose your brother to Alice. I told you that before. You will learn, Effel, we all learn, we have all had our wrong moments as children. There, a few broken handles don't amount to much. It's far more important for you to know you have a very protective brother and a kind guardian. And you are a brave little girl, Ethel. There.' She actually kissed Ethel, then straightened up. Ethel stared, her eyes misty.

'I'm not goin' to be given just bread and water for a week?' she said with a gulp.

'Bread and water?' Miss Pilgrim looked shocked. She cast a glance at Jim. 'Bread and water?'

'Not this time,' said Jim.

'I should hope not,' said Miss Pilgrim. 'Ethel, go and join Horace and Alice in the garden, go and make friends with Alice.'

Effel escaped. Miss Pilgrim regarded Jim severely.

'Really, Mr Cooper, bread and water indeed,' she said.

'The threat was the only thing I could think of,' said Jim, 'she's a little terror.'

'How very perceptive of you,' said Miss Pilgrim scornfully. 'They're all little terrors in Walworth,

346

but most of them grow up to be honest and hard-working. I'm afraid I must blame you as much as Ethel for what she did. You've been too indulgent and not firm enough. I don't mean harshly firm, I mean sensibly firm. You've failed to give her clear lines as to her behaviour, and although I have your permission to be corrective, your lack of firmness has undermined me.'

'Well, I'm damned,' said Jim.

'You will be, Mr Cooper, if you address me like that. You must let Ethel know precisely where she stands in regard to discipline. You should never allow her to be disrespectful to you, to start with. You are a very civilized man, and it's to be hoped you will help to make Ethel and Horace just as civilized. Mr Cooper, why are you looking at me like that?'

'It's the first time I've been dressed down by a young woman,' said Jim.

'Young woman?' Miss Pilgrim seemed affronted.

'Well, of course you're a young woman still.'

'Nonsense. I am a little past thirty. Now, while I dry these tea things, perhaps you would clear the table so that Horace and Alice can put the train set together and enjoy themselves for half an hour before Horace takes her home and I can spend a quiet evening at my embroidery. What is the matter with you now, Mr Cooper, what are you laughing at?'

'God knows,' said Jim. 'Probably at myself.'

Horace was walking Alice home. Jim and Effel were

sitting at the table in the garden, Miss Pilgrim having said they might stay there as the evening was so fine. She had joined them herself, bringing her embroidery out to work on it there. Effel was looking at Jim forgivingly, because he was about to read to her from one of her Ragamuffin Jack books.

'*Ragamuffin Jack was a very happy chap*
Who laughed the whole day through,
He had a fat jolly mother
And a very skinny brother
Whose nose had turned dark blue.'

'I know why, I know,' said Effel excitedly, 'Ragamuffin Jack did it, 'e tells 'is mum 'e couldn't find no pink paint, so 'e used blue.'

'I'd like to find that out for myself,' said Jim, and continued reading, much to Effel's pleasure. It took her mind off Orrice walking Alice home.

Orrice and Alice were midway to Crampton Street. Behind them were Higgs, Cattermole and Stubbs, close cronies.

'Oh, dearie me, ain't they sweet?' said Higgs loudly.

'I dunno who's the sweetest,' said Stubbs.

'I don't even know 'oo's Alice and 'oo's Wivvers,' said Cattermole.

'Yes, yer do,' said Higgs, ''e's the one wearin' 'is farver's trousers.'

'Yer sure 'e ain't the one in a frock?' asked Cattermole.

'Well, I'll tell yer,' said Higgs, 'no, I ain't sure.' He raised his voice in the Sunday evening quiet of

Amelia Street. 'Oi, Wivvers, is that you wearin' a frock?'

'Horace, they're horrid,' said Alice, 'don't let's take any notice.'

'I ain't goin' to, not till I get you home,' said Orrice, 'then I'm goin' to bash 'em.' Higgs, Cattermole and Stubbs had been following them since they turned the corner of Wansey Street.

'You're not to,' said Alice.

'Eh?' said Orrice.

'You're not to fight with them,' said Alice.

Orrice in his wisdom recognized the proprietary note and the necessity of retaining his independence.

'Now don't worry, Alice,' he said, 'you just go indoors when we reach yer house. You been a real sport, givin' me that train set, but me dad wouldn't 'ave wanted me not to put me dukes up. I ain't goin' to fight 'em, I'm just goin' bash 'em one at a time.'

'No, you're not to,' said Alice.

'We can't 'ear yer,' called Higgs, 'can't yer talk louder, we don't want to miss yer lovey-dovey stuff.'

'Ain't it time they started kissin'?' asked Stubbs.

'Wake 'em up, Catters,' whispered Higgs, 'get your catapult workin'.'

Cattermole took a catapult from his pocket, together with a brown paper bag containing lumps of hard raw potato. He slipped a lump into the sling while Stubbs held the bag, drew back the sling and elastic, took aim for Orrice's head and fired. The potato lump struck the back of Alice's head. Alice gasped. The lump had hurt. She stopped. Orrice stopped. They had reached her street.

''Old me cap, Alice,' he said, and gave it to her.

'No, don't,' said Alice, but Orrice was already in action, picking out Cattermole as he saw him slip the catapult back into his pocket. Orrice went straight for him, and at speed. Cattermole squared up. Orrice didn't stop coming. A straight right arm, taught him by his dad, vanguarded by a tightly balled fist, passed through Cattermole's guard. The first landed smack in his right eye, and knocked him down.

Stubbs and Higgs jumped Orrice. Alice stood in shock for a moment. Then she launched herself into the fray, feet delivering furious kicks. Kids appeared by magic in the street.

'Cor, a fight!' A street fight was an event not to be missed. Within seconds, it seemed, there was a crowd of boys and girls ringing the struggle. Orrice was sitting astride Higgs, and Stubbs, behind Orrice, had his arms locked around Orrice's neck. Alice was aiming kicks at Stubbs and Higgs alernately. The three boys rolled over, Orrice in the middle, his Sunday suit collecting the dirt and dust of the pavement. Alice stopped and seized Stubbs by his hair. She yanked. Cattermole, up on his feet, waded in.

''Oo's winnin'?' asked a boy.

'Dunno,' said another, 'except she ain't losin' – lummy, she might be now, though.'

Alice had been pulled down. Orrice gave a ferocious yell of rage, burst free and pulled her to her feet.

'Run 'ome,' he said. Higgs and Stubbs jumped him again. Orrice planted some stiff levellers. Stubbs staggered back, recovered and ran in again. Alice tripped him up, he clutched at her and they went down together. Orrice and Higgs fell on top of them. Cattermole fell on Orrice.

A man came running, from a house across the way in Crampton Street. He broke through the ring of yelling, excited kids. He stooped and hauled the contestants to their feet, one by one, Alice last. She was at the bottom.

She was flushed and grimy, clothes and hair dishevelled, her right knee grazed. Mr French, her father, looked at her in disbelief. Her hair was over her face.

'Is that you behind all that hair, my girl?' he asked.

Alice pushed her hair aside. More exhilarated than found out, she said breathlessly, 'You should've seen, Daddy. Horace bashed them and I kicked them.'

'You what?'

'Cor, your Alice don't 'alf pack a wallop wiv 'er plates of meat, Mr French,' said a boy. 'Betcher she could make Jack Dempsey 'op.'

'I gotter go,' said Higgs.

'Me too,' said Cattermole, hand to his black eye.

''Old on,' said Mr French, 'no-one's goin' yet. You young scruffs, what's the 'orrible idea, turnin' my daughter into a hooligan? And I'm surprised at you, Orrice.'

351

'But it wasn't his fault,' protested Alice, 'they all jumped on him.'

'Bleedin' 'it me when I wasn't lookin',' growled Cattermole.

Mr French gave them all a good look. They were all marked with cuts and bruises. And Orrice also sported a puffy cheek, Higgs a split lip, Stubbs a bleeding nose and Cattermole his black eye.

'I've a good mind to put me boot to your back-sides,' said Mr French. 'You perishers, what d'you mean by fightin' with girls? Who's changed the rules?'

'We ain't, Mr French,' said Stubbs, mopping his nose, 'we didn't ask for Alice to join in. Cor, yer got a bloomin' terror there, she nearly pulled all me 'air out.'

'Orrice,' said Mr French, 'what've you got to say for yourself?'

'We was all mindin' our own business, Mr French,' said Orrice, 'only Cattermole tripped over me arm, and I dunno where Alice come from after Higgs an' Stubbs started kissin' each other.'

''Ere, d'you 'ear that?' asked Higgs of Stubbs. 'D'you 'ear 'im say kissin'?'

'You perishers,' said Mr French again, 'you jumped Orrice and yanked Alice into the middle of it.'

'No, we bashed 'em then, Daddy, me and Horace,' said Alice, her flush that of triumph. Then she added, 'But not on purpose, though.'

'Hoppit,' said Mr French to Higgs, Cattermole and Stubbs, and the three boys gladly departed.

Angry grown-ups could start lashing out. 'Orrice, you'd better get yourself home and cleaned up. And you'd better look out for ructions.'

'Oh, me Uncle Jim knows a bloke 'as got to stand up for girls,' said Orrice. 'You all right, Alice?'

'Yes, thank you, Horace.'

'You can scrap real good, you can,' said Orrice, 'I don't mind yer sittin' next to me in school now.'

'Oh, thanks ever so much,' said Alice, not yet of an age to understand it was better to be more condescending than grateful to boys.

'So long, Mr French,' said Orrice. 'Oh, Alice give me a real superior clockwork train set. She's swell.'

They watched him go on his way, banging his cap against his trousers to knock the dust off. Then Mr French took Alice by the hand and led her home.

'You monkey,' he said, 'your mum'll have a fit about you fightin' with boys.'

'But I couldn't let them bash Horace to death,' protested Alice, 'he's my sweetheart.'

'You're in a hurry, aren't you, at nine years old? Come on, I'll try and get you cleaned up before your mum lays her eyes on you.'

Miss Pilgrim opened the door to Orrice, who hid as much of himself as he could under his cap. But his Sunday cap wasn't quite the friend his weekday one was. Miss Pilgrim did not miss cuts, scratches and bruises, nor the state of his suit.

'Young man?'

'Yes, hello, Miss Pilgrim, I'll just go upstairs for now,' said Orrice.

'Disgraceful,' said Miss Pilgrim.

'Me?' said Orrice, fidgeting on the doorstep.

'Yes, you, sir. You've been fighting again.'

'Me?'

'Don't prevaricate.'

'What's pre – what's that, Miss Pilgrim?'

'Do not attempt to mislead me.'

'Can't I come in?' asked Orrice.

'I do not admit brawling and bruising boys into my house.'

'Oh, crikey,' muttered Orrice.

'Unless they can explain themselves satisfactorily.'

'Well, Miss Pilgrim, me and Alice—'

'Alice and I.'

'Yes, Miss Pilgrim. Well, me and 'er wasn't doing no harm to no-one, just walking, we was.'

'And?'

'And what, Miss Pilgrim?'

'Then what happened?'

'Search me,' said Orrice, who wasn't going to split. 'Oh, yes, well, we fell over, Miss Pilgrim.'

Miss Pilgrim looked down from her tall height into his upturned face, scratched and bruised, and into earnest brown eyes.

'Boy, do you take me for a simpleton?' she said.

'Crikey, no, Miss Pilgrim. Course, I know girls is mostly daft, and you don't meet many women that ain't a bit barmy. I mean—'

'Young man, don't be impertinent, and don't gabble. Slower speech, please.'

'Yes, Miss Pilgrim.' Orrice was acquiring a wholesome respect for her. 'I was only meanin', Miss Pilgrim, that women fuss an' carry on. Effel an' me, and Uncle Jim, we're lucky you're not like that. Uncle Jim says you're an angel with commonsense, he says most angels do a lot of fluttering about, like. I never seen you fluttering about, Miss Pilgrim, like you didn't know what you was doing of.'

Miss Pilgrim's faint smile showed.

'I know what I'm doing now,' she said, 'I'm standing here listening to nonsense. This house is suffering an epidemic of nonsense.'

'Yes, Miss Pilgrim. Can I come in now?'

Miss Pilgrim stood aside.

'Go upstairs,' she said. 'Brush your suit and clean yourself up. Your guardian and sister are about to come in from the garden, and they'll join you. Tell your guardian you're to write out fifty times, "I must not fight or brawl."'

'Eh?' gasped Orrice.

'I think you heard me, young man.'

'What, me, Miss Pilgrim? What for?'

'Fighting and brawling.'

'Miss Pilgrim, that's bloomin' hard on a bloke, that is,' said Orrice gloomily. And he was gloomier still when Uncle Jim backed up Miss Pilgrim's command.

'Well, yer shouldn't go walkin' wiv Alice,' said Effel. Then she thought of what her guardian and Miss Pilgrim had said. 'Well, not all the time you shouldn't, Orrice, not every day. Just sometimes, that's all.'

355

CHAPTER TWENTY

There was a knock on the door at eight o'clock. Miss Pilgrim put her embroidery aside and answered it. An attractive, well-dressed young lady smiled at her.

'Is Mr Cooper in?' she asked.

'I believe so.'

'You must be Miss Pilgrim, his landlady,' said Molly Keating, thinking her handsome but severe at first glance. That blouse. So high-necked, so Victorian. 'I'm Miss Keating. I work with Mr Cooper.'

Miss Pilgrim's cool blue eyes surveyed the caller. This was the young woman Mr Cooper had a soft spot for. She could not fault his taste. There was a perceptible warmth to Miss Keating.

'A moment, please, Miss Keating.' She turned and called in her clear voice. 'Mr Cooper?'

Jim appeared on the landing.

'Miss Pilgrim?'

'You have a visitor. A Miss Keating.'

'Good grief,' said Jim, and came down the stairs to the front door. He smiled at Molly. 'Come up, Molly.'

Miss Pilgrim returned to the quiet of her sitting-room. Molly went up with Jim.

'I was passing,' she said.

'I'm pleased you stopped to look in. You can meet the kids. I've just put Ethel to bed. Horace is writing out lines.'

Molly met Horace first and found him instantly likeable. She looked in on the girl. And the girl was fast asleep, tired out from her long Sunday.

'She looks a pet,' said Molly.

'For pet read pickle,' said Jim, showing her the bedroom he shared with Orrice.

'Troublesome pickle?' said Molly, thinking how well he kept his lodgings, thinking of his handicap and the responsibilities he had taken on.

'Not really,' said Jim. 'Lovable, really, but needs watching. She suffered more than Horace over the loss of her parents. She's still not used to having them missing from her life. It'll take time. Until she's over it, I don't think she'll like me.'

'Understandable,' said Molly. 'You'll have to wait until they're older before they realize just how much they owe you. Then they'll smother you with affection. I like the boy, he's a sweetie. So are you. Well, now I'm here, are you going to take me out? Will your landlady keep an eye on them if we go for a drink? My word, she's a character just to look at, isn't she? What is she, a refugee from the court of Victoria and Albert? I say, sport, have you ever seen a stiffer back or a prouder bosom? Magnificent, but a throwback, isn't she?'

'She's actually a disguised angel,' said Jim.

'She's what?'

'Strictly disposed, but the best kind of Christian,

357

a practical one. She believes the poor should be fed, not given Bible readings. But I don't think she likes men.'

'That accounts for her touch-me-not look,' said Molly, and laughed. 'There are some women like that. Well, will she keep an eye on the children if you insist on taking me out for a port and lemon?'

'I'm sure she will.'

Miss Pilgrim did not disappoint. She readily agreed, much as if she thought it would advantage Jim to spend a sociable hour with the young woman he liked. She raised an eyebrow, however, when Jim said he and Molly would only be down at the Browning Street pub.

'You are taking that charming young lady to a public house, and on a Sunday evening, Mr Cooper?'

'Not to get her drunk,' said Jim.

'Can you not take her for a walk?'

'I'm doing that,' said Jim, 'down to the pub and then to pick up a tram.'

'It is not what I would have responded to when I was young—'

'You're still not an old lady,' said Jim.

'I do not like flippancy, Mr Cooper. But there it is, the war and its consequences have destroyed so much of our pleasanter customs and traditions, all in the name of progress. Go on your way with Miss Keating, I will keep an eye on the children.'

Jim spent a very sociable hour with Molly in the pub. Molly could socialize in any environment, and was always responsive in the company of people she liked. She liked Jim very much. She often wondered exactly how she would respond if he became serious about her. She thought her response might be total. He was such a friendly man, with never an axe to grind, not even about the pitiful pensions the Government handed out to disabled ex-soldiers. It was extraordinary that he should have taken on two orphaned children. It made him an extraordinary man.

He saw her to the tram stop in the Walworth Road.

'Well, I think we've broken the ice,' she said.

'What's that mean, young madam?'

'It's your turn next time to ask me out,' said Molly.

'I've done well enough for myself already,' said Jim.

'In what way?' she asked.

'I happen to have you as a very close friend and colleague,' said Jim.

'Are you crazy?' said Molly. 'Try again.' The tram was coming. 'What am I?'

'Lovely,' said Jim.

'That's better,' said Molly. 'Well, give us a kiss, then.'

Jim kissed her. The tram glided to a stop. Molly, summer dress fluttering, darted. A van, motorized, screeched to a skidding halt, and its driver bawled an obscenity at Molly as she boarded the tram. She turned and waved to him. She waved at Jim, who stood in a state of paralysis. That was how his mother had lost her life. Probably as quick-limbed as Molly, she had darted too, but had not been as lucky as Molly.

He went back to his lodgings feeling a little shaken.

With the kids ready for school the following morning, he said goodbye to them and went down the stairs to begin his journey to work. There was a letter on the mat. He picked it up. It bore no stamp, it was simply addressed to Miss R. Pilgrim. The letters had been cut out of a newspaper and stuck on the envelope. That was the classic way of a writer of anonymous letters. He gave it a moment's thought, came typically quickly to a decision and put the thing in his pocket.

On the tram he opened it. That act would meet with Miss Pilgrim's frostiest disapproval, of course, but when the game was being played in fiendish fashion he had no hesitation in chucking certain principles overboard. He took out a folded paper and opened it. The single word that leapt to his eye had also been made of letters cut from a newspaper. Capitals.

'*MURDERESS*.'

He tore it up and disposed of the remnants when he reached the club.

Higgs came up to Orrice during the mid-morning break.

'A' right, Wivvers,' he said, 'yer copped Catters fair an' square. Yer got spunk, and yer don't split. Yer our mate now, an' we likes yer. 'Ere y'ar.' He put out a hand. Orrice put out his. Higgs slapped a cracked and rotten egg into Orrice's palm. The egg broke and Orrice stared at the mess and smelled the stink. Higgs bawled with laughter. Orrice tripped him up and sat on him, and wiped his hand clean over Higgs's face. Higgs choked on the stink alone. Orrice was up in a flash and away, Alice and Effel flying with him. The teacher on duty rushed at the grounded Higgs. She recoiled at the smell.

'You disgusting boy! Go and wash yourself. And stay in after school for playing with bad eggs. Go on, go on, at once, do you hear?'

In a corner of the playground, Alice and Effel were smothering their shrieks and giggles. Orrice was reading a comic.

'Ethel, isn't Horace a one?' gasped Alice.

''E's still a bit smelly,' said Effel.

'No, he isn't, he wiped it all off,' said Alice. 'Horace, would you like to come and skip with me now?'

'Well, I would, Alice, seeing what I owe yer for me clockwork train set,' said Orrice, 'but would yer mind if I didn't? I got a broken leg from sittin' on Higgs.'

'All right,' said Alice graciously. 'You come and skip with me, Ethel.'

'A' right,' said Effel, still a little in awe of everything Miss Pilgrim had said to her yesterday.

It did no good, Jim's destruction of the first anonymous letter. Others arrived on Miss Pilgrim's mat at intervals. She put each one into the fire. She did not even open them, not after reading the one that had come first to her hand. Eventually she spoke to Jim, in her kitchen. On the table was the latest letter, addressed to her in its usual way but unopened.

'Do you see that, Mr Cooper?'

'What is it, Miss Pilgrim?'

'An anonymous letter.'

'What's in it?' asked Jim.

'I haven't opened it. It is simply one of many.'

'Take it to the police,' said Jim.

'Certainly not.' Miss Pilgrim stiffened at the suggestion. 'Open the letter, Mr Cooper.'

'You want me to? I always think it's best to ignore anonymous letters, to simply tear them up.'

'Really?' said Miss Pilgrim. Clad in a long-skirted dark blue dress, with a collar edged by white lace, she looked to Jim like some aristocrat's most dignified retainer. 'How many anonymous letters have you had to deal with in your lifetime, Mr Cooper?'

'Oh, just one,' he said.

'And what had you done to even suffer one alone?'

'Nothing that I can recall.'

'What did you do with it?' she asked.

'Tore it up.'

'I opened the first one I received,' said Miss Pilgrim. 'It called me a murderess. The others I put in the fire without opening them. Would you like to see what this one says?'

'No,' said Jim.

362

'I thought, as you were interesting yourself in my affairs, that you would be interested in this.'

'I'm interested in you, because I admire you,' said Jim, 'I'm not interested in sick letters. Put that one in the fire too.'

'Very well.' Miss Pilgrim used the bar to lift the lid of her range hob and dropped the letter in. 'Horace is doing remarkably well with his poetry reading, he is beginning to acquire very passable enunciation.'

'I know, but it all goes to pot the moment he leaves the house.'

'He will learn, he's a persevering boy. And Ethel is not having so many grumbles and sulks.'

'And you're evading the issue,' said Jim.

'I beg your pardon?' she said.

'I think it's time you told me about everything that happened at your father's mission in China.'

'That, Mr Cooper, is over and done with.'

'But it isn't, is it? It's come back through the agency of the dead man's sister.'

'A sick woman is an irrelevance, Mr Cooper.'

'It's an irrelevance that won't go away. That old girl, Mrs Hardiman—'

'Do you mean the elderly lady?'

'I mean that old gossip. She stopped me in the street yesterday and enquired after my health. I got the impression she thinks you might be poisoning my food.'

Miss Pilgrim regarded him pityingly.

'And how is your health, Mr Cooper? Are you suffering pains and sickness?'

363

'Like hell I am,' said Jim, and burst into laughter.

'That, Mr Cooper, is definitely not amusing. Nor do I think your charming young lady would approve.'

'Molly?' Jim smiled. 'Oh, I think Molly would consider you remarkable. I don't think the devil himself could make you turn a hair of your head. In a crisis I'd stand with you before I would with anyone else.'

'I really cannot cope with such an extravagance of exaggerations,' said Miss Pilgrim. 'Go and give your wards their tea.'

'Yes, Your Majesty,' said Jim.

'Now what are you saying?'

'That you could have given good Queen Bess a run for her money.'

'Mr Cooper, I shall disgrace myself in a moment by throwing something heavy at you.'

'And I don't think you'd miss, either,' said Jim, 'not after having seen you in action at that coconut shy.' He departed laughing.

A smile touched Miss Pilgrim's lips.

The school was breaking up for the summer holidays. Alice walked to the gates with Orrice and Effel.

'We're going to Margate in August,' she said.

'We're goin' on outings,' said Effel.

'With our Uncle Jim,' said Orrice.

'Oh, I wish I could come,' said Alice.

'No, Margate's best for you,' said Orrice, walking up Larcom Street with her and Effel.

'I mean when we come back, we're only going for a week,' said Alice.

'All right,' said Orrice, 'I'll ask Uncle Jim.'

'Oh, won't that be nice, Ethel, if he takes us all on outings together?' said Alice.

Effel sighed.

Jim called at the Larcom Street vicarage and spoke to the vicar. The vicar was sympathetic and understanding.

'But there's little I can do,' he said.

'D'you think not?' said Jim. 'Well, there's the information I've given you by way of the *China Times*. I think myself that's good enough to justify a short address from the pulpit after your next sermon.'

'Ah,' said the vicar.

'Ah what, vicar?'

'H'm,' said the vicar.

'Are we getting anywhere?' asked Jim.

'I hesitate to use the pulpit. To begin with, Mr Cooper, it will embarrass Miss Pilgrim, and she is not the kind of lady who should be embarrassed.'

'I'll keep her away from church next Sunday.'

'Can I rely on that?'

'Of course,' said Jim.

'These anonymous letters are the last straw, I confess,' said the vicar. 'Yes, very well, I will make a suitable exposition from the pulpit. I am wholly on the side of Miss Pilgrim, a splendid lady.'

'She won't like it, of course,' said Jim, 'she'll regard it as unwarranted interference.'

'I'm aware of that,' said the vicar with a wry smile, 'but it has gone beyond the pale. These whispers have reached every ear, and Miss Pilgrim is being regarded as a pariah.'

'A little worse than that,' said Jim.

'Yes, I must speak out,' said the vicar.

'Would you both like to go to the market instead of church this morning?' asked Jim of the kids.

'Cor, would we, not 'alf,' said Orrice.

'With tuppence each in your pockets?'

'Could I 'ave fourpence?' asked Effel.

'Now, Effel, what you askin' for fourpence for?' demanded Orrice.

''Cos you can buy more wiv fourpence,' said Effel the female.

'Crikey, ain't she crafty, Uncle?' said Orrice.

'Still, fourpence, why not?' said Jim. 'You are on holiday. Fourpence each, then. Off you go. But behave yourselves. No roughhouses, Horace. Keep your eye on him, Ethel.'

'Yes, a' right,' said Effel.

'You're funny, you are, Uncle Jim,' said Orrice.

Miss Pilgrim, dressed for church, was almost ready to depart. She jumped at the sound of a crash. She came at a rush from her bedroom. At the foot of the stairs lay her lodger, Mr Cooper. The back of his head rested on the hall floor, his legs lay sprawled on the lower stairs. His eyes were closed.

'Mr Cooper!' He did not respond, nor did he

366

move. 'Mr Cooper?' She went down on one knee beside him. She touched his shoulder. 'Mr Cooper?' He lay quite still. Concern furrowed her smooth brow. It cleared as he opened his eyes. 'Thank goodness. Are you all right?' He looked up at her. 'Are you all right?'

'What happened?' he asked, blinking.

'You seem to have fallen down the stairs.'

He blinked again.

'Hit the banisters,' he said.

'Yes, I heard you. I think you sometimes forget your disablement. Are you hurt?'

'Not sure.'

Her concern came back.

'Can you move your legs?'

'Give me a few moments.'

'Did you fall on your back?'

Jim frowned. Her hat sat neatly on her head.

'You're going to church,' he said.

'Never mind that,' she said. The bell of St John's was ringing.

'I'll be all right.'

'I hope so, but we can't be sure of that. Can you move your legs now?' She was concerned, but showed no panic. Jim moved his legs and flexed them. 'Good,' she said, 'I thought you might have broken them, or injured your spine.' Jim winced. 'What's wrong?'

'Headache,' he said.

'I think you hit your head on the floor. Can you get up?'

'You'll be late for church.'

'I'm already late. It's not important. Mr Cooper, do please try to get up.'

Jim drew his legs from the stairs and sat up.

'That's something, I'm all in one piece,' he said.

Miss Pilgrim helped to bring him to his feet. He put his arm around her shoulders and she put her left arm around his waist. In that way she got him into her kitchen and sat him down at the table.

'I am very relieved that nothing seems broken,' she said.

'I'm relieved myself.'

'You are shaken up, I expect. Really, Mr Cooper, you should take more care coming down stairs.'

'Just a trip,' said Jim.

'Not on my stairs, I hope,' she said, and went out to inspect the carpeted treads. There was nothing loose. Returning to the kitchen, she said, 'I think you must have lost your balance. A little brandy is called for, perhaps.'

'You have brandy?' said Jim.

'My father always kept some in the house.' Miss Pilgrim searched her larder and found the bottle. She poured a little into a glass. Jim wondered if there was any woman cooler or more efficient than this missionary's daughter. 'Drink this, Mr Cooper. It was my father's medicinal remedy for shock.'

'Many thanks,' said Jim. He drank the brandy in two swallows. Its fire induced a glow. 'You're an angel,' he said, 'and you've missed church on my account.'

'I've already said, it's not important. You may sit

there for a while, and I'll continue with the dinner preparations. Horace and Ethel will be wondering where you are. They went on to church in advance of you?'

'Well, no, they went to the market this morning, they had a few pennies to spend.'

'But they could have gone yesterday. They should attend church regularly. That is your indulgence again, Mr Cooper, allowing them to miss it this morning.'

'I'm a slipshod old devil. By the way, would you like to come with us to Brighton one day next week? It doesn't take long by train from Victoria.'

'Brighton?' Miss Pilgrim looked for a moment as if the invitation related to something sinful. 'Thank you, but no, Mr Cooper. I'm busy all next week.'

'We'll make it the week after.'

'Mr Cooper, you should ask Miss Keating, she will be much more suitable company than I will.'

'Molly's just gone to Devon for a fortnight, and I don't see anything unsuitable about your company, Miss Pilgrim. It's settled, then. Say Tuesday week.'

'It is not settled, Mr Cooper.' Miss Pilgrim rustled about. 'Except that I shan't be going. Please leave it at that. Are you quite all right now?'

'A1,' said Jim. 'Sorry to have messed up your morning.'

'I'm much too thankful you came to no harm to worry about other things.'

'Shall I scrape the potatoes for you?'

'Thank you, but no.' Miss Pilgrim did not ask how he could manage to scrape the new potatoes. 'I prefer to have my kitchen to myself when I'm preparing meals.'

'I'll push off, then,' said Jim.

'It will do you no harm to sit there, Mr Cooper, for a while longer. And you may talk, if you wish. That won't interfere with my tasks.'

He sat and talked. Miss Pilgrim, slightly aloof in her responses, could not think why it was that her kitchen was becoming less and less her own province.

The congregation sat in stunned silence. The vicar, having outlined the known facts concerning events relating to a parishioner whom he did not name, was in chastisement of people who, knowing nothing of the facts themselves, chose to listen to whispers and to pass them on.

'Shall it be said that among you such unhappy people exist? Are there any among you who would condemn any man or woman by whisper alone? I hope and pray there are not. What I would ask of you is to say to those who whisper, "Don't bring me malice and rumour, bring me proof." Few of us are worthy enough to cast stones, and even those who think themselves immaculate should hesitate before—'

'Don't point your finger at me!' Mrs Lockheart was on her feet, her pretty charm wrecked by fury. 'You are a hypocrite to side with a murderess!'

'Madam,' said the vicar, 'be so good as to go to the vestry, and I'll talk to you there.'

'I'll talk to you here!'

The vicar nodded to the organist, and the organ immediately drowned Mrs Lockheart's voice. The vicar came down from the pulpit, and the congregation rose. Mrs Lockheart was a shocking sight in her fury, and people surged to leave the church. The vicar stood on the chancel step, waiting. The church cleared of choir and congregation, leaving Mrs Lockheart in confrontation with the vicar, who then spoke sternly and without compromise to her. She turned and rushed out. There was no-one to listen to her angry complaints, except elderly Mrs Hardiman.

'Well, you can't wonder at it, dearie,' said Mrs Hardiman, when she could get a word in, 'all them things you said don't rightly sound the same as what our vicar said. Now you go 'ome and make yerself a hot cup of tea, and have a good sit down, like.'

'You silly old fool,' said Mrs Lockheart, and went away.

Out shopping the next morning, Miss Pilgrim was stopped by two neighbours. They were friendly far beyond expectation, rejoicing rather than apologetic. Cockneys rarely wore an apologetic air. It did not suit their hearty and challenging approach to life. 'Sorry, ducks,' said it all and did not embarrass either party.

'You must come and 'ave a nice cup of tea, Miss Pilgrim, I don't 'ardly know when the last time was.'

'My old man was saying only yesterday you 'adn't been in lately, Miss Pilgrim. Thinks a lot of you,

371

Alf does. More shame on them as don't 'old you in kind regard.'

'Pity you missed church and all yesterday, Miss Pilgrim. The vicar, well, I never 'eard 'im so downright punishin'. Made everyone sit up, like.'

'Really?' said Miss Pilgrim. 'What about?'

'Well, 'e didn't name no names, but 'e poured 'oly fire on all them whispers that's been goin' on. Been a shame, Miss Pilgrim, a downright shame. When you got a spare moment, come in and 'ave that nice cup of tea with me.'

'Yes, and any time in my 'ouse, Miss Pilgrim.'

'How kind,' said Miss Pilgrim, and went immediately to the vicarage. The vicar was in and received her with a smile. 'Vicar, what was your sermon about yesterday?'

'My word, you do come straight to the point, Miss Pilgrim.'

'I never see any reason not to. I've just listened to some extraordinary comments from Mrs Wills and Mrs Higgs.'

'They were referring, probably, to a few remarks I made after my sermon, when I spoke about people who cast stones because of rumours and whispers.'

'I am appalled you should take a certain person as seriously as that, vicar.'

'The matter had taken on a very serious aspect, Miss Pilgrim. I make no apologies for my determination to protect your good name. I trust I've succeeded in discouraging the misguidedness of that certain person.'

'Such nonsense, vicar. I'm only too glad I wasn't there to listen to you.'

'I'm glad myself. Your presence would have deterred me from speaking out.'

'I should have been there, but my lodger—' Miss Pilgrim came to an abrupt halt, and her lips compressed. 'I cannot fault your motive, vicar, but really. Good morning.'

Jim, who was taking his holiday fortnight, less one day that he owed the club, returned from a visit to the Zoo, Orrice having endured the long day well, Effel a little tiredly in tow. They had never been to the Zoo before. Effel had been dumbstruck and chattering by turn. Orrice had fed the monkeys with the permitted nuts.

Miss Pilgrim requested Jim to see her as soon as he had freshened up. She received him in her kitchen. Her blue eyes fixed him.

'You are an impertinent scoundrel, Mr Cooper,' she said icily.

'A what?' said Jim.

'Wait, I should not want to accuse you on suspicion alone. So first tell me if your fall yesterday morning was genuinely accidental or deviously contrived.'

'Deviously contrived?' Jim played for time to think. 'Have you been reading *Pickwick Papers*, Miss Pilgrim?'

'Not for many years, Mr Cooper. Be so good as to answer the question.'

'Why are you asking it?'

'Because I discovered this morning that the vicar addressed his congregation yesterday on the wearisome matter that has come about through the presence in this neighbourhood of Mrs Lockheart. He decided, apparently, that it was his duty to scotch every rumour. Providing I was not in the church myself.'

'What a splendid chap,' said Jim, at which Miss Pilgrim eyed him witheringly.

'Strangely, Mr Cooper, I was unable to attend church. Why was that? Because I found you unconscious on my hall floor. Or so it seemed. I put aside any thought of leaving you there.'

'You're a natural Samaritan,' said Jim.

'You're a natural humbug. Unconscious indeed. It's my firm conviction that you tricked me, that you conspired with the vicar to keep me here, away from the service. Isn't that so?'

'Well, I'll tell you what is true,' said Jim, 'and that's the fact that I gave myself a nasty bump on the head. It's still tender. But did the vicar actually give his congregation a talking-to? Damn good. He looks a gentle man of God to me, I'm glad to know he can deliver fire and brimstone when necessary. It's my belief that fire and brimstone are a good old-fashioned remedy for people who stray from the path of love-thy-neighbour stuff. Next time I see the vicar I'll shake his hand. I'm very much in favour of him standing up for an admirable woman like you. If that's all, Miss Pilgrim, I'll go and see to the kids' supper. They're both starving.'

374

Miss Pilgrim regarded him in a strangely helpless way. Her mouth quivered. She set it firmly again.

'You deceived me, Mr Cooper.'

'I thought the cause a good one,' said Jim.

'You actually had the audacity to connive with the vicar.'

'Connive? That's a bit much, old thing.'

'I'm not an old thing, nor am I a simpleton.'

'That's the last thing I'd take you for,' said Jim. 'It's true I had a chat with the vicar. We decided—'

'Such impertinence!'

'Oh, lord,' said Jim.

'It was unforgivable. I did not think I'd find both impertinence and deceit in you. What other dubious secrets do you have?'

Jim grinned, then spoke on impulse.

'I'm illegitimate,' he said, and Miss Pilgrim's fearless eyes opened wide. 'My parents weren't married.'

She was silent for a moment before she spoke.

'That is an accident of birth, for which you were not responsible, Mr Cooper. I was speaking of faults and failings, not of something unimportant.'

'Unimportant?' said Jim.

'Uncle Jim? Uncle Jim?' Orrice made himself heard from the top of the stairs. 'I finished makin' the bread and butter, shall I put the sausages on? Effel's slicing the tomatoes. Uncle Jim?'

Jim put his head out of the kitchen door.

'Good on you, laddie,' he called. 'Yes, put the sausages on. All of them. Don't forget to prick them with a fork first.'

'I fried sausages before,' called Orrice, 'I'm not daft, yer know, Uncle.'

'That's a fact, you're not, old chap. All right, leave it to you. I'll be up in a moment.'

'Is that boy handling a hot pan on the gas ring?' asked Miss Pilgrim.

'I've faith in Horace,' said Jim. 'What did you mean, my illegitimacy is unimportant?'

'It's the person who is important, Mr Cooper,' said Miss Pilgrim in matter-of-fact fashion, 'and how he or she face up to the world. You have faced up to it very well. You've overcome the disadvantages of your birth, your orphaned state, and a lost arm fighting for your country. Not many men with those disadvantages would look or behave as you do. You are a man, Mr Cooper, in the best sense of the word, and I hope you never think you have anything to be ashamed of. Except perhaps your deceitfulness. When I think of how concerned I was for you, I'm shocked at my naivety, knowing as I do now that you were lying there laughing at me.'

'Never,' said Jim, astonished that someone so strictly-minded could dismiss his illegitimacy as unimportant. 'You're a magnificent woman.'

'Oh, dear,' said Miss Pilgrim, and sighed. 'I'm so many things, I'm angelic, generous, warm-hearted, remarkable, and now magnificent.'

'Also perfection in a kitchen.'

She shook her head at him.

'I've never known any man whose tongue runs away with him as much as yours,' she said. 'I am no better and no worse, I hope, than my neighbours.

376

Please go and take charge of that hot pan before Horace sets the house alight.'

'Yes, I'd better, I think.'

'And don't speak again of the accident of your birth as if it makes you less than you are.'

Jim smiled.

'Remarkable,' he said, and went upstairs to see how the sausages were doing.

CHAPTER TWENTY-ONE

Miss Pilgrim did not accompany Jim and the children on their outing to Brighton. She had too much embroidery work on hand. Despite the rent she received, she still needed the extra income, for she was no more than solvent. She had very little to call on for a rainy day. She shared with the people of Walworth the strain of being as poor as a church mouse. She could not afford new clothes, and her wardrobe remained a well-preserved one. It was fortunate that in Walworth she could shop economically and well for the necessities of life, and she was a familiar figure to the market stallholders.

She was not turning out as much embroidery as formerly. She did not seem to have as much time. There were thieves about in the shape of her lodgers, who stole hours every week from her. She put her embroidery aside for an hour every evening, except at the weekends, in order to improve Horace's diction. She put it aside frequently for Mr Cooper. She fretted at her slide into self-indulgence. Worse, at the fact that she was yielding so much of her privacy. But the burden she had taken on when accepting lodgers was of her own making, and she must endure it.

Of course, the time would come when her lodgers

would leave. Mr Cooper would realize that if his wards were to have any kind of future, it should not be in Walworth lodgings. He must marry, he must give the children a mother, and give them all room to breathe in a rented house. He had affection for his manager's daughter, Miss Keating. He really must begin to think seriously about her.

Miss Pilgrim's teeth snapped a thread.

Effel turned in her bed, sighed, snuggled beneath the bedclothes and drifted into contented sleep. Orrice lay sound asleep beside Jim, the boy dead to the world. It was the last Friday of Jim's holiday, and he had taken them to Hampshire again. They had met his grandmother, who had heaped apples and sweets on them, and been ever so nice to their guardian. Then they had had a picnic in the country, and a ramble in the afternoon.

While the kids slept the sleep of the contented and weary, Jim slept in fits and starts. Something was happening to his life. Something was not right with his life. Something was missing. He had the kids, he had things of his mother's and new memories of her, he had comfortable lodgings, a steady if modest job, and a landlady whom he could not fault, even if she was a perfectionist in many things. He also had grandparents and the affectionate friendship of Molly. But there was still something missing.

He sat up. His nostrils twitched. There was an acrid element in the air. Silently, and without disturbing Orrice, he slipped from the bed in his flannel pyjamas. He opened the door and moved out on to the landing. The darkness of the hall and stairs was faintly broken by flickers of light. Smoke was rising from the hall. From the top of the stairs his startled eyes saw the cause. Against the front door was a heap of burning rags, the flames feeding on what he could smell, paraffin. By their light he saw a long rag depending from the letter-box, with flickering fire creeping up it. Doorpaint was peeling. Jim ran back into the bedroom, took his old, hard-wearing trenchcoat from its hook, ran down the stairs in his bare feet and into Miss Pilgrim's kitchen. He plunged the coat into her scullery sink and turned on the tap. He flooded the coat, picked up the heavy, sopping garment, ran back into the hall and smothered the burning mass, using his one hand and his body. A tongue of flame, escaping the onslaught, caught his hand and scorched it. He moved, he extinguished the little burst of fire, plunging the hall into darkness, except that the doorpaint was beginning to burn. He lifted the soiled coat and killed the little running flames.

A door opened and Miss Pilgrim appeared, a lighted candle in its holder lifted high in her hand. Her hair was loose and flowing, and she was clad in a long white cotton nightgown. She gasped at the scene.

'Mr Cooper – oh, my heavens, what's happening? What is all that, and that smell, and that foul smoke?'

Jim dropped his coat over the smoking mass.

'Someone tried to burn your house down, Miss Pilgrim.'

'Look at you – wait.' She turned on the gas and lit the hall mantle with the candle. The hall glowed with light. She paid no heed to the scarred front door or the covered heap of blackened rags. 'Come into the kitchen.'

Jim took a look at his soaked trenchcoat lying heavily over the mass. Escaping smoke was lessening. He followed Miss Pilgrim into the kitchen. She lit the mantle there.

'There's a mess to clear up,' he said.

'Never mind that for the moment. Look at your hand. Go to the scullery sink and run cold water over it.'

'It's just a slight burn.'

'Please don't argue. Come.' She went to the scullery sink and turned on the tap. Jim placed his hand under the cold running water. It eased the burning sensation at once. She pushed back the sleeve of his pyjama jacket. 'Let your hand stay there for three minutes. Clear cold water is the best immediate antidote, did you know that?'

'Some people use cold tea. In the field hospitals during the war, the medics used ointment and bandages.'

'Probably as they did during the Crimean war,' said the unflappable Miss Pilgrim. 'Mr Cooper, thank you for what you've just done. The children haven't woken up?'

'No, and I hope they won't. Someone stuffed a

hell of a lot of paraffin-soaked rags through your letter-box on to your mat, and set fire to them with a long rag that was already alight, of course. It could only have been Mrs Lockheart. You'll have to face it, she's off her rocker.'

'Well, you aren't, Mr Cooper, you have a great deal of good sense. Thank goodness the fire woke you up.'

'I happened to be awake at the time. I smelled the stuff.'

'God sometimes takes care of us, and is sometimes indifferent. Who can blame Him, when so many of us are such wretched creatures? But this time, you were His instrument of care.' She turned the tap off and looked at his hand. 'There, we've saved it blistering. Do it again in a couple of minutes, then we'll see if it needs covering up. I do not cover ordinary burns up myself.'

'I'll go and look at that mess, to make sure it's out.'

'I'll do that. You stay here.' Miss Pilgrim went and inspected the charred heap. When she returned she said, 'Your coat is ruined. I shall buy you a new one.' It would cost what she could not really afford, but there could be no question of Mr Cooper paying for it himself.

'But you're insured against fire, aren't you?' he said.

'Yes, of course. All the contents.'

'Then the insurance company will pay. Also for the cost of making good any damage. That'll be for the landlord to settle, through his insurance.'

382

'Dear me,' she said, 'I can't be myself not to have thought of that.'

'About Mrs Lockheart, you'll have to do something,' said Jim.

'That poor woman is a mental case, Mr Cooper. She has been in an asylum for years. She's out now, obviously, but is still not quite sane.'

'Not quite sane? She's a lunatic.'

'Come, Mr Cooper, don't raise your voice, you'll wake the children.' Miss Pilgrim turned the tap on again. 'Let's try some more cold water.'

Jim placed his hand under the stream and smiled at her.

'There aren't many like you, are there?' he said.

'Like me? What do you mean?'

'That my admiration for you is total.'

'I thought it wouldn't be long before your nonsense made its entrance.' She turned the tap off and inspected his hand again. 'There, I'm sure we've nothing to worry about with that. Hold still.' She went into the kitchen, opened a dresser drawer and came back with a large piece of cotton wool, which she used to dab his hand dry. 'Good,' she said, 'I am proud of you, Mr Cooper, and consider myself fortunate to have you as my lodger. Now you may return to your bed.'

'As your lodger, might I point out I'm not a small boy, Miss Pilgrim?'

'I'm glad you're not,' she said. 'Small boys are terrors. Luckily, Horace is an exception. Yes, go up now, Mr Cooper, I'm very grateful that you saved us all, but you have your work to go to in the morning.'

'I'll clear the mess up first, I'll dump it outside.'

'Certainly not,' said Miss Pilgrim, 'I am not going to have it on my doorstep for everyone to look at in the morning. I'll get a bucket and carry it out to the dustbin at my back door.'

'I'll put a glove on,' said Jim, 'and if you'll give me your coal shovel and the bucket, I'll see to it. If anyone's to go to bed, it's you. Off you go.'

Miss Pilgrim, of course, was quite against taking orders from her lodger, and in the end they cleared up the mess together, Jim wearing a protecting glove. Before he went up, he elicited from Miss Pilgrim a promise to speak to the vicar about Mrs Lockheart. She refused to go to the police, but she agreed to ask the vicar for his help. Someone must contact the Asylums Board. The vicar had the right kind of authority to do that.

The next evening, Jim cleaned up the door, rubbed it down and repainted it. Orrice and Effel wanted to know what had happened, and why there was a new doormat, and Jim got away with a reference to an accident involving paraffin.

In her compulsive growing attachment to the children and their welfare, Miss Pilgrim kept a watchful eye on them during the rest of their holidays. The summer went, brief autumn followed, and winter arrived, with its damp and its fogs. The country, struggling to recover from the war, braced itself to fight the hardships of winter. Alice went to and from school wrapped in a warm cosy coat and a woollen hat, and Jim bought warm coats for Orrice and Effel. Alice could not be detached from her growing friendship with Orrice, and Orrice found he could not be detached from his protective role as Effel's brother or Alice's sweetheart. Mr Hill kept an encouraging eye on Orrice's abilities, and Miss Forster did her best with the awkwardness of Effel.

Jim took Molly out on occasions, but did little or nothing, relatively, to advance his cause with her. He knew himself incapable of asking her to take on Orrice and Effel as well as his illegitimacy. Her father, George Keating, was a man of the old school, despite his general geniality.

He arrived home one evening in early December suffering a headache and little bouts of feverishness. He had a bad night, and when he crawled out of bed the next morning he was a sick man.

Miss Pilgrim, in her kitchen and at her breakfast, looked up as knuckles rapped on her door.

'Come in,' she said. She might have sighed at this continuing invasion of her privacy, but her voice was quite welcoming.

Orrice showed his face, a worried face.

'Please, Miss Pilgrim, could you come?' His diction showed definite improvement. 'Could you, please? It's Uncle Jim, me and Effel don't think he's very well.'

'Well, we can't have that, Horace, can we? Is he in bed?'

'No, Miss Pilgrim, 'e's on the floor, 'e just sort of folded up. Could you come and look at him?'

Miss Pilgrim did not reply. She came swiftly to

her feet, picked up her skirts and ran up the stairs. Orrice, following on, saw yards of white lace. Jim was lying beside his bed in his pyjamas. His body was racked with shivering, his eyes closed, his breathing erratic.

Miss Pilgrim pulled the bedclothes far down. Effel stood silently watching, upset and helpless.

'Horace, will you help me, will you take hold of his legs while I lift his shoulders? We must get him into the bed.' Miss Pilgrim spoke urgently. Orrice stooped and took a firm hold of his guardian's legs. Miss Pilgrim, bending, put her hands under his shoulders, to his armpits. 'Ready, Horace? Now lift at one go.'

They lifted him and placed him on the uncovered sheet. Quickly, Miss Pilgrim drew the bedclothes up over him and tucked them in on her side. Orrice tucked them in on the other side.

'Please, ain't he very well?' asked Effel.

'No, Ethel, I'm afraid he isn't,' said Miss Pilgrim. She felt Jim's forehead, and was appalled. He was on fire. 'Horace, who is his doctor?'

'Doctor? He's not been to no doctor since 'e found me and Effel, Miss Pilgrim.'

'Then will you run and get Dr McManus in the Walworth Road?'

'Oh, I know 'im, Miss Pilgrim, I'll run all the way.'

'Yes. Don't worry about school for the moment. Tell him he must come, tell him the message is from me. Go, Horace, be as quick as you can.'

The boy rushed away. Out of the house, he ran fast through the cold, wintry morning.

Effel peeped worriedly at her guardian. Jim was burning but shivering, his mind bursting in his thumping head, his awareness of the presence of Miss Pilgrim a vague, elusive thing of running fire. She hurried downstairs and came up again with two blankets. She laid them over the bedclothes. She felt Jim's hand. That too was alarmingly hot.

''E's only a little bit ill, ain't 'e?' asked Effel anxiously.

'We'll see what the doctor says, child. There, you go off to school. Have you had breakfast?'

'Don't want none. 'Ave I got to go to school?'

'Yes, you must, Ethel,' said Miss Pilgrim. It was better for the girl to be out of the way. 'It will please your guardian if you make no fuss, and please me too. Horace will join you when he comes back. Everything will be all right with the doctor here.'

'We can come 'ome dinnertime?'

'Of course, just as you usually do.'

'A' right,' said Effel, and went to school reluctantly, thinking about what had happened to her mum and dad when they'd been taken ill.

Orrice ran all the way back from the surgery. He found Miss Pilgrim seated beside the bed in which his Uncle Jim lay shivering and restless.

''E's comin', Miss Pilgrim, the doctor. I said I come from you, I told him about Uncle Jim being on the floor all shivery, like, I told him we put 'im in the bed. He's comin', Miss Pilgrim, only I ran back to tell you, like. Is Uncle Jim a bit better?'

Miss Pilgrim saw the boy's worry and concern. Mr Cooper had won himself a place in Horace's

387

affections. She silently prayed for both of them, and for Ethel.

'That's splendid, Horace. I'll let Dr McManus in. You go off to school. Ethel went a little while ago.'

'Yes, Miss Pilgrim.' Orrice hesitated. 'Can't I stay? I can make 'ot lemonade, if yer like. I can do things like that.'

'I'll see to that, Horace. You go to school. I'm sure your guardian will be better when you come home for your dinner.'

'I wouldn't like—' Orrice stopped.

'We'll see, Horace, we'll see. Thank you for going for the doctor. Run off to school now.'

Orrice went even more reluctantly than Effel, but he shut from his mind the thought that having lost their parents they might also lose the man who had saved them from an orphanage.

Dr McManus made no bones about the fact that the patient was already in crisis. Miss Pilgrim put a hand to her throat.

'Crisis?'

'How long has he been sick?'

'I don't know how long he's been as bad as this. He was at work yesterday, and made no comment to me on his return in the evening.' Miss Pilgrim bit her lip. Mr Cooper had made a habit these last two months of putting his head into her kitchen and saying hello to her every evening on his return from work. He had not done so last night. Horace had told her later that his Uncle Jim had a headache and had dosed himself with a Beecham's powder. 'But he did tell Horace he had a headache.'

Dr McManus frowned. Vicious flu was sweeping the country. It had galloped up on this man. It could do that. It could give someone a bad headache and shivering fits one day, and kill him the next. Or take its time to be fatal.

'He's in extraordinary fever, Miss Pilgrim. Perhaps I should arrange to get him to hospital.'

'No.' Miss Pilgrim was swift and emphatic. 'I will nurse him. I have nursed Chinese people in fever, and was doing so when I was sixteen. I will take your instructions, doctor. He'll only be one more patient among the hundreds already in hospital. Let him stay where he is. That is, if you think I'm competent to do as much for him as a hospital can.'

'You know I think you fully competent,' said Dr McManus. 'I've brought tablets and medicine. Give him two tablets every—' He thought. 'Every two hours, and one tablespoon of the medicine in between. Keep him fully covered. Don't worry about food, but you can pour as much liquid into him as he'll take.'

'Fresh hot lemonade?'

'Excellent. Then keep your fingers crossed, Miss Pilgrim.'

'It's as bad as that?'

'You'll know by midnight. I'll look in again this evening. Oh, take two of the tablets yourself, and give one each to his wards. They're a preventive as well as a cure, although as a cure they've been known to fail. I have to tell you that. He's your lodger?'

'He is my friend, Dr McManus.'

'He's a privileged man, then. Oh, one more thing. If you find it difficult to get him to drink the liquids, use a teapot.'

'A teapot?'

'Put the spout into his mouth.'

'That is so practical, doctor.'

'I thought you'd like the idea. Good luck.'

'Thank you for coming so quickly.'

Orrice and Effel ran home from school at dinner-time. Not to see what Miss Pilgrim was giving them for the meal, but to see how their guardian was. Miss Pilgrim came down to let them in and assured them she was doing everything for him that the doctor had advised. She was sorry not to have prepared a hot meal for them, only sandwiches. They were first to swallow a tablet each, they would find them on the table beside their plates, and drink water to wash them down. Then, when they had eaten their sandwiches, they could come up and see their guardian for a moment.

She said nothing about how worried she was. Her lodger seemed worse by the hour, his fever racking him, his shivering unabated. He kept coming to and staring at her out of eyes hotly bright with fever.

She went up to him again, while the children obediently did as she had requested. Effel made no fuss at all about taking the tablet, although she didn't know what it was for. Orrice, sharp of mind, said it was so they didn't catch no flu themselves.

They went up when they'd finished their sand-wiches. Miss Pilgrim was sitting beside the bed, a sponge in her hand, a bowl of cold water resting in her lap. They watched as she applied the sponge to their guardian's forehead. They couldn't think why she was doing that when they could see he was shivering. But his face did look very hot and flushed. He opened his eyes.

'Who's that?' he asked, his voice dry and husky.

'It's us, Uncle Jim,' said Orrice, 'it's Effel and me.'

'I'm wiv Orrice,' whispered Effel uncomfortably.

'Orrice and Effel, Orrice and Effel.' Jim's voice wandered. 'Well, I never, Orrice and Effel. Where's our angel?'

'She's sittin' next to you, Uncle.'

'She's got a sponge,' said Effel.

Jim sang croakingly, 'Angels come to funny places, some of them with dirty faces.' New shivers beset his aching body. 'Not Miss Pilgrim, though, not—' His voice wandered away and his eyes closed. Effel ran out, going into her bedroom. Orrice followed her. Effel was crying.

'Don't cry, sis.'

'Our dad did that,' she sobbed, 'our dad said funny fings when 'e was ill.'

'Our dad won't let Uncle Jim die, Effel. When you're in 'eaven, you can do things for people that's down here.'

'We won't 'ave no-one again, no-one,' sobbed Effel.

They did not want to go back to school for the afternoon classes, but Miss Pilgrim was gently persuasive, and they went in the end. She did what she could for their guardian, she was constantly at his bedside, and she watched him fighting the fever. She gave him the tablets and the medicine at the prescribed times, and she got him to drink the fresh lemonade she made at intervals. He gave no trouble about that. She helped him sit up, she put the glass to his lips and he gulped the warm liquid like a parched man.

She sponged his fiery brow and she kept his restless body covered up. His skin was dry and burning. She knew he was in crisis, that unless she could help him break the fever he would be gone by morning.

The thought distracted her. There was a moment when she found it unbearable and fled downstairs to the kitchen, and to the sink, where she laved her face with handfuls of cold water. She paced the kitchen, her petticoat swishing and rustling, her distraught state made worse by a sense of angry helplessness. She might once have said such anger was a sin, for it was an anger at church and God.

She could not remain long from his bedside. She found herself running up the stairs to resume her watch. And as the time went by she saw him becoming worse. He was in incoherent delirium on occasions. She suffered for him, for what his racked, burning and shivering body was doing to him. But she persevered, she persevered in her watching brief and her ministrations. Sometimes his shivering was distressingly uncontrollable. At other times he tried to throw his coverings off. She kept them tightly around him.

When Orrice and Effel came home from school, she felt there was a pause in the worsening condition. He did not seem so racked. He was quieter. He was still very hot, but not so restless. She asked the children what they would like to eat. They could have supper, not just tea, she said.

'Please, I don't want nuffink,' said Effel.

'I'm not hungry, neither,' said Orrice.

'I don't mind a drink of tea and a biscuit,' said Effel.

'I don't mind that, neither,' said Orrice. 'Miss Pilgrim, would you like a cup of tea? I can make it.'

'Thank you, Horace.' Miss Pilgrim felt exhausted from her day-long watch. 'You'll be careful with the kettle, won't you?'

'Uncle Jim seems a bit better, don't yer think?' said Orrice hopefully. 'D'you think he might like some tea too?'

'Yes, Horace, we'll try that, shall we? It can do no harm. It's more liquid.'

Orrice gladly got on with making the tea. Effel stayed in her guardian's bedroom with Miss Pilgrim. The little girl sat on the edge of the bed, looking at his dry hair, his dry, hot face and his closed eyes.

There was a knock on the front door.

'Will you answer it, Ethel?' asked Miss Pilgrim.

Effel went silently down to open the door. Molly Keating smiled at her.

'Hello, Ethel. Is your Uncle Jim in?'

'Yes,' said Effel.

'Only he hasn't been at work today, and I wondered what had happened to him.'

''E ain't very well,' said Effel, and Molly saw the child's unhappy look.

'Is it the wretched flu, Ethel? Shall I come up?'

Effel led the way up. Moments later, Molly was in shock. Miss Pilgrim kept the children out of the bedroom while she explained the patient's condition and told her of the doctor's visit and prescription.

'Oh, my God,' breathed Molly, 'all he had yesterday was a headache, he said.'

'He's now suffering a particularly vicious type of influenza, Miss Keating, it's put him into a critically feverish condition which I pray will break.'

'It must break,' said Molly, 'he's someone we can't afford to lose. God, he doesn't deserve this. Look, you're exhausted, and it's showing. Go and rest for a while and I'll sit with him for a couple of hours.'

'I would rather continue,' said Miss Pilgrim, 'I'm really more worried than exhausted, and there's the tablets and the medicine. I am in the way of administering them. If you're agreeable, would you care to sit with the children? I think they need a grown-up with them, to keep them occupied. Mr Cooper, I know, would be grateful for that.'

Molly was unhesitating in her response.

CHAPTER TWENTY-TWO

Dr McManus made his promised evening call at a little after eight. Miss Pilgrim's hope that the fever was abating had long since proved false. The doctor's examination was brief, and he advised her that the patient's life was in his own hands.

'It comes down to that in many cases of this kind, Miss Pilgrim. It rests with a patient's resilience or lack of it, with strength or weakness of will, and even with a subconscious desire to live or to give up.'

She was stiff-faced and tight of lip.

'Mr Cooper has much to live for, Dr McManus,' she said. 'As for resilience or strength of will, I could not fault him myself. He's made light of grievous disadvantages, and although he may not know it, he's won the lasting affection of two children he saved from the drabness of an orphanage. He's not a man to give up.'

'Well, that may save him. But continue with the tablets and the liquids. He may be aware that you're fighting for him too. His temperature is sky-high, his condition acute. I know of no other medicine that will help him, except that which I've given you.'

'There is God,' said Miss Pilgrim, 'and his own self.'

'I envy you your faith,' said Dr McManus. 'I'll look in again as early as I can tomorrow morning.'

Miss Pilgrim would not give up her vigil or her ministrations, and Molly would not leave the children, except to dash back to the club and advise her parents she would be at Jim's lodgings all night. She was back in quick time to persuade the children to go to bed. Orrice lay wrapped in a blanket on the floor beside his sister's bed. Neither of them could sleep. Molly comforted them as best she could, but it was close to midnight before they at last dozed off. She went then to see Miss Pilgrim and the patient. There was no change for the better. Jim was a sick man with a restless, aching body and a dry, burning skin. Miss Pilgrim begged Molly to go downstairs.

'Use my bed, Miss Keating. I'll listen for the children, I'm glad they're asleep at last. You go down. I'll call you if there's any real change.'

'But can't I relieve you?' asked Molly in distress.

'I'll see it through until two o'clock, say, and then you can take my place.' Miss Pilgrim was sure that by two o'clock it would all be over.

Molly went down to rest on the bed, and Miss Pilgrim kept her watch on Jim. She was tormented by his obvious inability to get relief. His shivering bouts constantly disturbed him, and the weighty warmth of the bedclothes and extra blankets still did not seem enough. He turned, he tossed and he shivered. She stood up. She drew a deep breath. Her whole being was feverish to save him. She

396

slipped off her shoes. The house was in silence. She drew down the bedclothes and pushed herself in beside him. She pulled the sheet and blankets back into place, and she turned to him. He made a subconscious movement, turning to meet the body of a woman. Impropriety did not enter her mind. She put her arms around him. His own arm came around her. She pressed herself close and held him tightly to her. His body shivered, and to the warmth of the bed coverings she added the healthy warmth of her own body. She lay with him, beneath the weighty bedclothes, and she did not let go of his suffering body. His hot face lay on the pillow close to hers.

She thought about him, she thought of what had concerned him so much, and of his audacious interference. She thought of what she was doing, holding a dying man in her arms, and she thought of another man who had suffered death.

Clarence Guest. Clarence had been a worldly man, with a sophisticated wit and charm. A broker making his fortune in Shanghai, he became a close friend of her parents, and a welcome contributor to the mission house funds. His smile and his worldliness fascinated her, and quite endeared him to her mother, still a very attractive woman at thirty-nine. She herself was just twenty, and Clarence declared her far too delicious to be a missionary's daughter. She was depriving the world of her sweetness by devoting herself to Chinese orphans, he said. She was meant to grace the ballrooms of London and Paris. He called often, and sometimes stayed at weekends. He expressed amazement at her father's interest in snakes, and in the fact that the conservatory was actually used for housing many different specimens, its temperature always kept at tropical level throughout the year. Cho Ling, the family's most trusted servant, looked after the snake-house and its serpentine inmates.

Clarence was going on for thirty, but still engaged himself enthusiastically with her, declaring himself smitten. However, after five months, her father wished her to know he considered Clarence unsuitable for her, and therefore, if she was favourably disposed towards him, to cure herself of her feelings. A devoted daughter, she began to exercise self-restraint in her relationship with Clarence. She did not question her father's advice. But her mother continued to invite Clarence, and to take a special interest in him. He was a man, of course, who was like a breath of fresh air in the cloistered atmosphere of the mission. The snakes fascinated both her mother and Clarence, and they were often in the conservatory together. It was a huge place, and the snakes were restricted by glass surrounds.

The memory of a horrifying moment still caused her pain. Coming back to the mission from a shopping expedition in Shanghai one day, she showered the Chinese orphans with little presents she had bought out of her own hard-won savings, then went up to show her mother a new dress. Cho Ling appeared on the wide landing. Seeing her, his usual placid Oriental countenance took on a look of dismay. She asked him if anything was wrong. He

398

shook his head and hastened away. She walked along a corridor and entered her mother's room. Her mother liked to take a rest at this time of the day. She could not believe what leapt to her eye. Clarence, who had arrived for the weekend that morning, was on her mother's bed, with her mother. What they were doing she had never given name to. Neither of them saw her, neither knew she was at the open door. She wanted to die of shock and shame, and she even wanted to kill Clarence. She retreated in horror, and when she found herself in her own room she could not remember if she had closed the door on the infamous spectacle. Her father was away in Canton.

She did not know how she got through the rest of the day, how it was that she managed to survive the evening meal with her mother and Clarence, or how she got through the table conversation. She escaped as soon as she could. Out on the verandah, the sultry air of the hot evening felt suffocating. Cho Ling, passing by, stopped to look up at her from the ground. He pressed his hands toether, put them to his lips and gave her a little bow to signal devotion.

She hardly slept that night. When morning came a servant found Clarence dead in his bed, body contorted and twisted. And lying in the bed, close to his body, was a venomous viper. She and her mother were brought by the servant to the scene of dreadful death. Cho Ling had also been summoned. He seized the viper by its neck, just below its head, and carried it out. As he passed her, his expression was quite inscrutable. Her mother dropped in a faint.

Clarence's sister and her husband, George Lockheart, were in Shanghai at the time, and they were called to the mission. And the Reverend Pilgrim was summoned by telegraph from Canton.

Mrs Lockheart had hysterics, and her husband voiced suspicions, but the inquest returned a verdict of death by misadventure, especially as a broken glass surround was discovered in the snakehouse.

But Miss Pilgrim had always known who had carried the viper to Clarence's bed. Cho Ling. It was an act of revenge for the dishonouring of the family he served. She knew it, and had said nothing, either then or at any time. After the war, after the death of her husband, Mrs Lockheart suffered a mental breakdown and was eventually admitted to an asylum.

She was back there now, having been quietly apprehended and re-admitted.

Jim shuddered in Miss Pilgrim's arms, and she thought it was the shudder preceding death. She had been there in the bed with him how long? An hour, a full hour, holding him close to her body, trying to give him heat and life. Now he was going. The unfairness of Providence shattered her.

Downstairs was a young woman, a young woman healthy, vigorous and affectionate, and willing, she was sure, to make his life complete for him, to be his wife and to be a mother to Horace and Ethel.

But his body was failing him. He was losing the battle. He shuddered again.

'Oh, my dear,' she whispered in anguish, 'fight, fight.'

Something was wrong, something had drastically changed. Wrong? Wrong? Her blouse was soaking, his pyjamas drenched. His tortured breathing was evening out. She freed her aching right arm and put her hand to his face, and his face was drenched with perspiration.

Dear God, he had not lost, after all. He had won. The raging fever had broken.

But his soaking pyjamas.

She slipped in a rush from the bed. The door opened and by the light of the candle on the little bedside table, she saw Horace.

'I woke up, Miss Pilgrim, I—'

'Horace, oh, my dear boy, you are just the one I want. Bring me clean pyjamas. His. Quickly. Then we shall save him.'

'They're in 'ere,' said Orrice, and pulled open the middle section of the chest of drawers. He snatched up the fresh pyjamas, and watched staring-eyed as Miss Pilgrim pulled every covering down to the foot of the bed. His Uncle Jim lay there, and Orrice saw his perspiration like a shining wetness on his face. And Miss Pilgrim, she showed perspiration too, her blouse was wet and clinging.

'Horace, help me. We must get his pyjamas off. They're soaked. His fever's broken, you see, and he's lying in a pool of perspiration. I must get a mackintosh and a dry blanket.'

'I'll get him undressed, Miss Pilgrim, you get the things.'

'Cover him with these blankets I've pulled off from the top.'

Orrice was already at work. Miss Pilgrim hastened downstairs. Orrice stripped Jim. He saw his left arm, it finished at the elbow, and the elbow was a stump. His body was flooding with sweat. Orrice flung the blankets over him. Miss Pilgrim came back, and Molly was with her. They stripped the bottom sheet from under Jim, working fast. They placed the mackintosh under him, Orrice helping to lift him. They slid in a clean sheet and blanket, the blanket next to the mackintosh.

Orrice said, a little embarrassedly, 'I best put his clean pyjamas on, Miss Pilgrim.'

'Towel him down first,' said Molly, and passed a towel to the boy. She and Miss Pilgrim lifted the coverings, and Orrice applied the towel swiftly and vigorously. Then he put the pyjamas on his guardian, who lay heavily but with no shivers.

'Horace, how very good of you,' said Miss Pilgrim, and she and Molly remade the bed at speed, discarding the wet top sheet and using a fresh one. They stood beside the bed, the three of them, looking down at Jim. He was breathing very evenly, and the sweat was lessening.

'Is he goin' to be all right now?' asked Orrice.

'Yes, Horace, I think so,' said Miss Pilgrim. 'I think he's fought the good fight.'

Orrice looked up at her tall figure. He had never seen her looking so dishevelled, her hair loose, her blouse shapeless, her skirt creased. Her face was pale, her eyes dark.

'Yer an angel, Miss Pilgrim,' he said.

'Yes, she is, Horace,' said Molly. 'Yes, you are, Miss Pilgrim.'

'So much nonsense from everybody,' said Miss Pilgrim, and uttered a long, weary sigh.

'Go to bed,' said Molly, 'I'll sit with him for the rest of the night.'

'I'll stay with yer, Miss Keatin',' said Orrice, 'I'll bring me blanket and sleep on the floor. Then if you want me to do anything or get something, you can just wake me up.'

'Yes, that sounds lovely, old chap,' said Molly.

Miss Pilgrim fell into her bed fifteen minutes later. Exhausted, she slept, her mind full of dreams both sad and triumphant.

Jim opened his eyes. The morning light, bright with the crisp sunshine of a cold December day, flooded the bedroom. He looked at the mantelpiece clock. A quarter past twelve. He heard noises downstairs. He heard the sound of climbing foot-steps. He heard them travelling over the landing. The door slowly opened and Effel put a cautious head around the door.

'Hello, monkey,' said Jim. He felt weak but clear-headed. He also felt he needed a shave. Effel stared at him. 'Come in, Ethel, there's no charge,' he said.

She came in, advancing slowly.

'Are you better, please?' she asked.

'Much. Twice the man I was. Ask Horace if there's any food.'

'Yes, a' right.' Effel hung her head. 'Orrice an' me—' She swallowed. 'I don't mind you're not me dad. Orrice don't mind, neiver. We fink it's nice you're better. We like – we—' Effel rushed to the door. 'We like yer lookin' after us.' She disappeared, scampering down the stairs. Orrice came up.

'I think I've just been approved by Ethel,' said Jim.

'Crikey, yer talkin',' said Orrice, 'yer talkin', Uncle Jim.' Jim sat up, easing his shoulders above the pillow. 'Hold on, though, I don't know Miss Pilgrim wants yer sittin' up yet.'

Jim put his arm around the boy's shoulders and squeezed.

'You'll do, old chap, we'll make a go of things together, you and Effel and me.'

'You betcher,' said Orrice. 'The doctor came early this morning, before we went to school—'

'The doctor?' said Jim.

'Miss Pilgrim sent me to fetch 'im yesterday morning, Uncle, made me run all the way. He told Miss Pilgrim this morning that what you 'ad must've been in a terrible 'urry, 'cos it galloped up on you and then galioped away. He told 'er she was the one who'd sent it packin'. Uncle Jim, Miss Pilgrim, well, we got to buy her a present or something. She sat with yer an' looked after yer all day and all night. Well, nearly all night. Miss Keatin' come too last night, and she sat with yer after you was better.'

404

'Was I as bad as that, Horace?'

'I don't think you was too good, Uncle. Effel and me's just come home for our dinner, and Effel's just told Miss Pilgrim you'd woke up and was askin' for food. I think she's goin' to bring you something up. I best go down and 'ave me dinner, Miss Pilgrim said nobody was to rush up and down and not get on with their dinners. I best go, Uncle.'

'Good luck, laddie.'

Orrice left. A few minutes later Miss Pilgrim came up. She entered looking as composed as always. She was refreshed, and in her dark blue dress with its little touch of white at the neck, she was a tall arresting figure fully in control of herself and the moment. Her hair was smooth and ordered, her blue eyes clear and searching.

'Good morning, Mr Cooper.'

Jim, his eyes dark and a little hollow, said, 'Good morning, Rebecca.'

She frowned at the familiarity.

'You aren't going to be nonsensical, I hope,' she said. 'What a disgraceful man you are, giving the children such a fright. And look at you. Untidy hair, unshaven chin and hollow eyes. You aren't even washed. I'll bring you a bowl of hot water, soap and a towel, and your shaving things. First, though, I've put some soup on for you, and will let you have it in a few minutes with some thick bread and butter. Dr McManus has been and expressed himself satisfied with your recovery—'

'What did he say about you?'

'He was not invited to say anything about me. I

405

hope you never catch such feverish flu again. You must stay in bed for the rest of this week. Your close and affectionate friend, Miss Keating, is going to call each evening to see you, and I hope you'll perceive what is obvious. The children need a mother, Ethel particularly so. You need a wife. It's quite wrong for a man like you, with two wards, not to have a wife who will help you bring them up. I'm positive Miss Keating will look very sympathetically at a proposal—'

'Hold on, not so fast,' said Jim.

'I'm not suggesting you should decide immediately,' said Miss Pilgrim understandingly, 'and if you think I'm interfering in your affairs in a way inconsistent with my objections to your interference in mine, please put it down to my concern for the children and their future. All children should have two parents, or the equivalent of two parents, and a house rather than lodgings. I'll go and get your soup ready now.'

'Thanks,' said Jim, 'that'll give me time to work out how I can get a word in edgeways.'

'I should hope, Mr Cooper, I'm not the kind of person to monopolize a discussion.'

'No, you're not, usually,' said Jim, at which she gave him one of her doubting looks before returning to her kitchen. He lay back and thought about her. She was back after five minutes with a tray containing a bowl of soup, hot and steaming, and two thick slices of bread and butter. He sat up again, and she placed the tray on his lap. 'That smells good,' he said.

'It's lentil soup,' she said, 'and if you do it justice I'll prepare a satisfying supper for you this evening.'

He had a peculiar feeling she was perfectly at home as nurse and provider, that she was enjoying her role.

'I'm not going to be able to thank you enough for everything,' he said.

'One doesn't need thanks for exercising a Christian duty, Mr Cooper. When you've finished the soup and the bread, I'll bring your washing and shaving things. I really don't like a lodger of mine looking like a tramp.'

'You demon,' said Jim.

'I beg your pardon?'

'Don't go for a moment,' said Jim. 'I once told you I was no catch, and I'm still not much of a one. So you'll probably think I've a colossal nerve to ask—' He checked. Miss Pilgrim was viewing him in forbidding fashion. He cleared his throat. He looked at the steaming soup. 'No, never mind,' he said, picking up the soup spoon, 'but I do thank you for everything, for all you did for me. Horace made me aware of how much I owe you.'

She shook her head at him.

'Mr Cooper, if you were going to ask me to carry your proposal of marriage to Miss Keating for you, I shouldn't call it a colossal nerve but an act of cowardice. I can hardly believe that of a man like you, nor would Miss Keating think very much of it herself. You must not be so diffident, you must put the question to the lady herself.'

'That's done it,' said Jim. 'All right, I'll get on

with it, I'll put it direct. To you, Rebecca, which I should, because I love you. Will you do me the considerable pleasure of marrying me? I know I look like an old tramp at the moment—'

'Mr Cooper, what are you saying?' Miss Pilgrim spoke in utter astonishment.

'Molly's a good friend, and always will be, I hope,' said Jim, a little discouraged by his land-lady's reaction. It had taken all his courage to make the proposal. 'But I've never thought about marry-ing her, and I don't think she's ever had that in mind herself. Never mind, I'm sorry if I've shocked you.' He looked up and gave her a smile.

Miss Pilgrim seemed to be having difficulty in drawing breath. It induced her to leave the bed-room without a word and to go down to her kitchen, where Orrice and Effel had just finished their generous helpings of rich lamb stew. She gave them their afters, a creamy rice pudding, but without saying anything. Orrice thought she looked a bit flushed, a bit upset. Effel eyed her hesitantly.

'Please, Miss Pilgrim, ain't 'e very well again?'

'Pardon?' Miss Pilgrim came to. 'Dear child, yes, he's very well. One can hardly believe how well. There, eat your rice pudding while it's hot, and excuse me for a moment.' She went to her bedroom and stared at herself in the mirror. Her face felt hot, and she could not think straight. The words he had spoken, the smile he had given her. For years after the horror of that dreadful day and night at the mission house, the smile of any man brought back to her a memory of the fascinating charm of

Clarence Guest and what lay beneath his winning worldliness. For many months after his death she had been unable to look at her mother without feeling shame and shock. Then one day she heard her father say, 'Maud, no more penitence, I beg you. You are forgiven. We've all sinned, every one of us.' That made things a little better for her, and when her mother developed malaria immediately on their return to England, and became a semi-invalid at times, Rebecca Pilgrim turned into a devoted daughter again, although there were always dark images lodged in the deeper recesses of her mind.

Mr Cooper loved her? He had asked to marry her? Mr Cooper? What had got into him? Dear heaven, had he known, then, that she had been in his bed with him and held his racked, aching body close to hers for an hour and more? Did he think she had compromised herself? No, no, he was far too sensible to think that. Nor could she believe he had been consciously aware of anything outside of his disordered mind.

She put a hand to her throat, her heartbeats erratic.

What could she say to him? That Miss Keating was far more suitable?

She drew a deep breath and went back to the kitchen. The children, with time to spare, were washing up for her. That would have been Horace's idea. The boy was like herself, fundamentally a compulsively busy person, always liking to be doing something, whatever it was. His one objection was to skipping with girls, even with Alice, now his best

409

friend. And Ethel, presently a very relieved little girl, was drying up with care and without grumbles. Once Miss Pilgrim would not have let either of them handle her china.

'Well, thank you both for that help,' she said. 'I'm taking some things up to your guardian so that he can wash and shave. When I come down, you can go up and say goodbye to him before you return to school.'

'Yes, fank you, Miss Pilgrim,' said Effel.

'Honest,' said Orrice, 'I dunno—'

'Now, Horace,' said Miss Pilgrim in reproof.

'I don't know, I mean,' said Orrice. 'I mean I don't know what we'd do without you, Miss Pilgrim.'

She smiled.

'Children,' she said, 'would you like it, then, if I were always with you, to help your guardian take care of you?'

'Crikey, not half we wouldn't, wouldn't we, Effel?' said Orrice.

'I don't mind,' said Effel, typically understating her approval.

'But would you like it, Ethel?'

'I fink so.'

'Truly, child?'

Effel hung her shy head.

'Yes, Miss Pilgrim,' she said, and gulped.

'Well, that's splendid,' said Miss Pilgrim.

Jim looked up as she reappeared carrying a towel and a bar of soap, together with his face flannel and his shaving things. She seemed quite composed. She placed the items on the little bedside table, and took the tray up from his lap. The soup bowl was empty, both slices of bread and butter eaten.

'Good,' she said, 'now you may wash and shave.'

'Yes, I'd like to,' said Jim, 'but I think I'll need the bowl of hot water you promised.'

'Pardon?'

'It's all right, I'll ask Horace. You've done quite enough.'

'Hot water?' Miss Pilgrim suddenly seemed not at all composed. 'Oh, dear, have I forgotten it?' She had. But she was not herself, of course. 'I'll get it, Mr Cooper, I'll take this tray down and be up with the bowl as soon as I can.'

'And that's all?' said Jim wryly.

'All? Oh, are you referring to your proposal? Yes, very well, Mr Cooper.' She made for the door.

'Wait a moment,' said Jim, 'what d'you mean, yes very well?'

'I asked the children if they minded,' she said, her back to him, 'and they were very sweet. They don't mind at all. Naturally, we must adopt them. It really won't be enough just to be their guardians.'

Jim sat straight up.

'Rebecca, d'you mind not talking to the door? D'you mind telling me exactly what you mean?'

Still with her back to him, she said with a slight catch in her voice, 'It means I'm very happy to know you love me.'

'Rebecca, look at me.'

She turned about, and Jim saw that her fearless

blue eyes, which missed nothing, were actually moist.

Incredible. She had been there during all the years he'd spent in Walworth. He had so often tried to convince himself that somewhere out there in the world was a woman willing to share his life, despite his background, a woman who was waiting for him. And here she was, the proudest and most courageous woman he had ever known.

And she had only been just round the corner, more or less.

'Yes, I do love you, Rebecca, probably more than I'll ever be able to tell you.'

'Darling, how much money do we have?'

'Pardon?' said Jim. It was close to Christmas.

'How much money do we have?'

'No, what else was it you said?'

'I'm tragically poor myself—'

'You didn't say that.'

'Well, I'm saying it now,' said Rebecca, 'and I'm happy to have someone I can say it to. One is too proud to admit poverty to others. Perhaps you are tragically poor yourself, in which case we have nothing except what is in my purse and your pocket. Never mind, we shall make do on what you earn.'

'It so happens I have this.' Jim extracted his wallet, flipped it open and showed her five white five-pound notes sitting loose between the covers. 'I've left a few pounds in the account – Post Office savings – and I've drawn this for you. Well, for all of us, but you take charge of it. It's for wedding expenses. You'll make wiser use of it than I will.'

Rebecca took the banknotes and spread them out on the kitchen table, her blue eyes warm and alive. She gazed at the fivers, then looked at Jim.

'Pride in someone is a happy thing,' she said. 'I am very proud of you. Now I can buy myself a handsome costume and blouse for the wedding, which will be very useful afterwards, and a brides-maid's frock for Effel.'

'Effel?' said Jim, keeping his face straight.

'Oh, horrors!' exclaimed Rebecca and clutched her forehead in theatrical despair. 'What is to become of my King's English if Horace doesn't positively mend his ways and call his sister Ethel?'

'You sure you don't mean Orrice?' said Jim.

Rebecca struggled to find a frosty look. Failing, she laughed.

'Jim Cooper, you're as bad as they are,' she said.

'Three of a kind,' said Jim, and Rebecca smiled.

'Four of a kind, darling,' she said.

'What did you say?' asked Jim. Endearments from Rebecca were new.

'Four of a kind,' she said, 'we all care for each other, you see.'

'With all these darlings flying about, I suppose we must do,' said Jim.

'What did you say?'

'Nothing, you darling woman,' said Jim. 'Will you do me a favour?'

'Only if it's serious. You are absurdly ridiculous at times.'

413

'Well, this is very serious. When you wear your new costume for the wedding, will you also wear your very best starched petticoat?'

'Jim Cooper!'

'I want to hear you rustle as you walk up the aisle,' said Jim.

'You absurd man!'

'By the way,' said Jim, 'don't call Horace darling or he'll leave home and join the French Foreign Legion.'

They were married at St John's in the New Year. All Rebecca's friends and neighbours were there, and so were Jim's maternal grandparents, in brave defiance of their son Arthur's sour disapproval. So were Aunt Glad and Uncle Perce. The strains of the Wedding March smothered the delicate rustle and whisper of the bride's petticoat as she approached her waiting bridegroom. Emerging from the church as Mrs James John Cooper, Rebecca looked splendidly handsome in her new costume and a tall close-fitting feather-trimmed hat quite audaciously striking and modern. Effel was a shy, tongue-tied bridesmaid, Alice an excited and proud one. Orrice wore his Sunday suit and a new cap. Higgs and Cattermole turned up outside the church and catcalled Orrice over his dressed-up look. Orrice arranged to fight them both, but couldn't manage the engagement before Monday week, because he and Effel, given dispensation by the school's headmistress, were to accompany their guardian and his bride on a week's holiday in Brighton. Orrice and Effel had never been on a real holiday, so Jim and Rebecca took them along. Jim felt events had enriched him, the more so because the club management had given him a rise of ten bob a week to bring him up to the wage of a married man. Rebecca said a prayer of thanks, for it meant she need no longer slave over embroidery, but could devote herself fully to her husband and the children.

If it was a winter holiday for Orrice and Effel, it was a honeymoon for Jim and Rebecca. It was also a voyage of discovery for Jim. Rebecca, in the intimate finery of her starched and frothy white lace underwear, was worth sailing the seven seas for. And it was impossible for her not to be a pleasure to the man she had admitted into her house with many cautious reservations, but who, with his wards, had gradually thawed out the woman who had frozen eleven long years ago.

After the honeymoon, she took firm control of her newly-won family, and with the help of the vicar arranged for herself and Jim to adopt the children without delay. When it was done, she let the boy and girl know they could call her and Jim their mother and father. Orrice took that in his stride. He addressed Jim as Pa at once, and would have addressed Rebecca as Ma, except that she squashed that immediately. So he called her Mum. She would have preferred Mother or Mama, but let it go. Effel did not call her adoptive parents anything. She liked the situation, it made her feel secure, it made her feel there was affection for her, but she had her shy and sensitive reservations.

Easter approached.

'Would you like to come to tea Easter Sunday, Alice?' asked Orrice of his best friend. You had to make a best friend of someone who'd given you a superior kind of clockwork train set, even if she was a girl.

'Oh, would I, yes,' said Alice, now ten. Orrice was eleven and due to transfer to West Square in September. 'You are a dear, Horace.'

'Alice, you don't 'ave to go off yer chump, yer know,' said Orrice, looking around to see if Higgs was in dangerous proximity.

'But you can call me dear too,' said Alice. 'Are you going anywhere on Easter Bank Holiday?'

'Yes, if it's a nice day,' said Orrice.

'If it is, we're goin' to 'Ampstead 'Eaf,' said Effel, 'they want to try the coconut shy an' go on the swings.'

'Who do?' asked Alice.

Effel looked scornful.

'Why, me mum an' dad, of course,' she said, and did a little dance and a jig as they walked up Larcom Street together, towards the Walworth Road.

Towards home.

Towards Mum and Dad.

THE END